"A truly great storyteller . . . He sets up the story beautifully, with intense suspense, an intriguing investigation that has all the authentic trappings, and a believable cast of police personnel. He gets better and better with each book." —*Library Journal*

"It's fascinating to follow Harstad's hero-narrator, Deputy Sheriff Carl Houseman of Nation County, Iowa, through a crime scene. Houseman proceeds with absolute confidence, making the slightest depression in the carpeting intriguing, treating the reader to insights gleaned from physical evidence that only a firsthand authority can render. . . . Harstad is one of the most reliable and riveting police-procedural writers in the business."
—*Booklist*

KNOWN DEAD

"Instantly propels him into the top ranks of mystery writers." —*Booklist*

"A complicated little conundrum of a plot that keeps Houseman, the Feds, and the reader guessing all the way through . . . An author who knows his territory."
—*The New York Times*

"A series to watch." —*The Plain Dealer*

"Crackles with the electricity of an adrenaline-laced shoot-out." —*The Denver Post*

"Hard-core procedural fans will find Carl's second case authentically . . . realistic." —*Kirkus Reviews*

"Harstad . . . advances the scary (and perversely entertaining) notion that people are just as cuckoo in the heartland as they are in the wicked city."
—*The New York Times Book Review*

ELEVEN DAYS

"A hell of a first novel." —Michael Connelly

"[Harstad's] dry, even droll account of these macabre crimes makes them all the more terrible."
—*The New York Times Book Review*

"With one startling twist after another, this grisly but cunningly sophisticated story is truly frightening. . . . A debut spellbinder."
—*San Francisco Chronicle*

"A major achievement and thriller debut by an ex-cop; a novel that smells and feels right."
—*TimeOut*

"Downright explosive! The descriptions of the police work rival Wambaugh's best."
—*Publishers Weekly*

"The very best procedural novels are those that follow police personnel through the solving of a crime from its discovery to evidence-gathering to the apprehension of the guilty. . . . As a former deputy sheriff from Iowa, Harstad has the procedure down. . . . Deputy Carl Houseman is the epitome of a police officer, and his humanity, intelligence, and ability place him at personal risk as the case races to a heart-stopping climax."
—*Library Journal* (starred review)

Also by Donald Harstad

Eleven Days

Known Dead

The Big Thaw

And coming soon in hardcover from Doubleday

The Heartland Experiment

Code 61

Donald Harstad

BANTAM BOOKS

New York Toronto London Sydney Auckland

This edition contains the complete text
of the original hardcover edition.
NOT ONE WORD HAS BEEN OMITTED.

CODE 61

A Bantam Book

PUBLISHING HISTORY
Doubleday hardcover edition published May 2002
Bantam mass market edition / January 2003

Library of Congress Catalog Card Number: 2001052736

ISBN 0-553-58098-1

Reprinted by arrangement with Doubleday.

Published simultaneously in the United States and Canada

Bantam Books are published by Bantam Books, a division
of Random House, Inc. Its trademark, consisting of the
words "Bantam Books" and the portrayal of a rooster, is
Registered in U.S. Patent and Trademark Office and in
other countries. Marca Registrada. Bantam Books, New
York, New York.

PRINTED IN THE UNITED STATES OF AMERICA
OPM   10 9 8 7 6 5 4 3 2 1

To Erica Harstad, our daughter,
whose excellent mind, quick wit,
and honest appraisals make her
the most reliable of critics.

ACKNOWLEDGMENTS

I would like to express my thanks to those who so generously shared their time and thoughts with me as I worked on this book.

First, to Larry and Maria Brummel of McGregor, Iowa: Their gracious permission to tour their marvelous house set the scene for much of what follows.

To my friends in London: Rachel Coldbreath, who shared many thoughts on the legends and history of vampires in literature, and gave encouragement; Julian Richards, for his friendship and knowledge of the legends and the people who believe them; Grebbsy McLaren, for a fine sense of humor and permission to use a bit of verse; and to Zu, who added insights and a point of view that is uniquely hers. Their warm welcome during an excellent evening in a London pub was much appreciated.

I'd also like to thank a remarkable set of individuals who populate alt.v on the Web. Singling out individuals is very difficult, but B. J., Llewellyn, Catherine B. Krusberg, Julian, Grebbsy, Klattau, Emrys, Jet Girl, Chiller, Tiernan, William R. Thompson, and Elizabeth Miller are but a few. They have been the source of much fascinating discussion regarding vampires in legend and literature. All, of course, are exempted from responsibility for any of the misconceptions on my part.

To a remarkable group of young women from Elkader, Iowa, who were interviewed in order for me to obtain a solid base regarding their possible reactions to a set of circumstances in this book, I especially want to express my thanks. They—Courtney Zaph Bently, Rachel Kuehl Jaster, Carrie Persoon, Barbie Gnagy, Nicole Reimer, Hillary Klingman, and Courtney Burns—provided the background for events in the lives of characters Hester Gorse and Darcy Becker. They were invaluable.

I would like to express my most sincere appreciation to the Valerie Williams Co'Motion Dance Theater, and dancers Valerie Williams and Annie Church, for allowing me to observe a class and hours of rehearsal. Their ability to express and project attitudes through body language was a revelation, and added dimension to the characters of Jessica and Tatiana.

I would like to thank Shannon Bryant for answering my questions regarding potential sources for advice. She started the whole ball rolling for the characters who inhabit the Mansion. I would also like to thank Kate Bryant for her timely advice regarding flute playing and a certain piece of music. Your Uncle Don appreciates you both.

For a fascinating discussion of vampires and related subjects, I would like to thank Julieann Thilmany Theis, who also allowed me to read her master's thesis.

I wish to express my thanks to all those law enforcement personnel who serve in the Midwest. Their professionalism and devotion to duty, and their continuing willingness to share accounts of their work, make these stories possible.

Code 61

PROLOGUE

My name is Carl Houseman, and I'm a deputy sheriff in Nation County, Iowa. I've been doing this for over twenty years now; long enough to graduate from the night shift to become the department's investigator, and senior officer, as well. Long enough to feel senior in every sense of the term. Somehow, when you finally pass fifty and realize a fellow officer was born about the same time you took the oath, you start to wonder if you might not begin to feel old pretty soon. I mean, maybe in another ten years or so.

It's been my experience that cases fall into categories that are a bit different from the examples they cite at the academy. Most of the time, you have more than enough evidence to show how the offense was committed, but really have to work to identify who did it. The rest of the time, you pretty much know who did the dirty deed, but showing how is the problem. In rare instances, a case will develop both ways at the same time. That was what this one did.

ONE

I guess I could say it started for us on Thursday, October 5, 2000. I can say that now. I sure couldn't at the time.

It was exactly 23:33 hours, and I was just leaving the scene of a minor fender bender, and was en route home when the communications center called.

"Comm, Three?" came crackling over the radio, from the familiar voice of my favorite dispatcher, Sally Wells.

I picked up my mike, suspicious already. "This is Three. Go ahead."

"Three, we have a 911 intruder call, 606 Main, Freiberg. Female subject needs immediate assistance. Freiberg officer has been dispatched and is requesting backup."

I sighed audibly. "Ten-four, Comm." I took stock of my current location. "I'll be ten-seventy-six to the scene from about seven miles out on County Four Victor Six."

"Three, ten-seventy-six. Three, not sure if this is completely ten-thirty-three, but you might be aware that the female subject indicated that there was a man trying to come in her window."

I reached down and turned on my red and blue top lights. "Three is en route. Can she ID the suspect?"

"Contact was broken by the caller, Three. Auto call-back rings through, no answer. Female subject was very excited, but described the intruder as a white male with . . ." She paused, and I thought I had detected barely suppressed humor in her voice. "Ah, continuing, Three. Suspect described as white male with teeth."

"Teeth, Comm?"

"Ten-four, Three. Teeth."

"Ah, okay, ten-four. Still en route. Advise when the Freiberg car goes ten-twenty-three at the scene." Teeth?

"Ten-four, Three. Will advise."

Teeth? I distinctly remember thinking that I wasn't going to hear the end of that one for a while. At least it wasn't a gun or a knife. I really hate knives.

Our usual shortage of deputies available for duty had been aggravated by an early appearance of the flu in the last two weeks, so from a total of nine, we were down to five or four effectives, depending on who called in sick next, and when the next officer came back. As senior officer, I still had to pull twelve-hour shifts, but my exalted status meant that I got first choice of which shift I would work. I'd chosen noon to midnight. It was a combination of the shift that was the most fun, and the one where you could get the most actual work done.

About two minutes later, I heard Byng, the Freiberg officer, go 10-23 at the scene.

"I was ten-four direct, Comm," I said, letting Sally know that I had heard him and to keep her from having to tell me. That was because her transmissions from the base station were so much more powerful than ours, she could obliterate a transmission from the Freiberg officer, especially when he was on his walkie-talkie.

She simply clicked her mike button twice in close succession, in acknowledgment.

I passed the last farm before the Freiberg city limits, took the big, downhill curve at about eighty-five, and began braking as I entered the forty-five zone. I was down to forty as I made the next turn, and was on Marquette Street, the two-story frame houses of the residential area changing into the three-story brick storefronts of the nearly deserted four-block business district. I cut my top lights, the red and blue reflections in the store windows being a distraction as I looked for anybody out on the sidewalks. Still slowing, I headed down the gently sloping street that was cut short by the black line that was the Mississippi River.

I heard the static distorted voice of Byng. "Where ya at, Three?"

"Downtown." As I keyed the mike, I saw his car parked off to my right. "Have your car in sight." By telling him that, he could give me better directions.

"Okay . . . I'm on the second floor above Curls & Cuts. Up the stairs on the right, the blue door."

"Ten-four." I swung my car to the right, pulling up near the curb about thirty feet ahead of his car. "Comm, Three's ten-twenty-three," I said into my mike as I unsnapped my seat belt, grabbed my rechargeable flashlight, turned on my own walkie-talkie, and opened my car door. Simultaneously, I heard the voices of both Byng and Sally back at Comm. She, being over twenty-five miles away and using a powerful transmitter, and he, very close but behind a brick wall and using a very weak transmitter, canceled each other out almost perfectly.

Knowing that she was merely acknowledging me, and not being at all sure of what Byng had said, I picked up my car radio mike and said, "Stand by a sec, Comm." The feedback into my now active walkie-talkie let out a screech, and I turned its volume down without thinking. Still with the car radio, I said, "Byng?"

"Yeah, Three. Hey, why don't you come around the back way? I don't know what we got here. Neighbor says the victim has gone and thinks she heard her leave and that she went up onto the roof."

I swung my feet back into my car, started the engine, shut the door, and said, "I'm on my way."

"Uh, Three . . . You might want to check ground level . . . Can't figure why she'd go to the roof."

"Ten-four." I couldn't, either, but people do strange things when they're scared. I sure as hell wouldn't go up, but then I have a thing about heights.

I had to go almost another block before I reached a side street. Freiberg is located between two big bluffs, and is only four streets wide at its widest point. Spaces being at a premium, cross streets are few and far between. The fact that the cross streets all required a bridge to span the open drainage "conduit" contributed to their scarcity. The so-called conduit was about thirty feet wide, ten to twelve feet deep, with limestone banks and a concrete floor. It was dug in the 1890s to accommodate the vast drainage that came down off the bluffs during heavy rains. It ran the length of the town, and emptied into the Mississippi. It was not, as they say, kid-proof, and offered a nearly invisible path for burglars as well. I bumped over the bridge deck, and took a sharp right, doubling back on the other side of the stores and apartments above them. I stopped as close to the bridge as I could, and opened my car door for the second time. "Comm, Three's out'a the car," I said, mostly to let Byng know I was now behind the buildings.

"Ten-four, Three," said Sally. She was monitoring the conversation between Byng and me, and was starting to sound a little concerned.

The conduit was, unfortunately, between the buildings and me. The fire department had fits over that all the time, but there was just no way to put a road in behind the stores on the other side of the big ditch. Not without tearing all the buildings down and moving them into the street on the other side.

Without a road or alley directly behind the buildings, most of them had constructed their own little footbridges across to their loading areas. Easy access, as they say, but easy for burglars as well. For that reason, I had gotten very, very familiar with the area over the years.

The lighting sucked. One yellowish orange light at the road bridge, and one about a block away. Not much room for them, either, because of the hundred-fifty-foot limestone bluff looming up on my left. It was sheer, naked rock for about fifty feet, and then brush and trees began sprouting all the way to the top. The builders had to squeeze the road in, and the whole area was a sandwich of necessity. Bluff, road, conduit, buildings. No room for anything else.

I squeezed the rubberized transmit button of my walkie-talkie. "Which one you in, Byng?" It was really hard to differentiate the various stores from the rear. Looking up, most of them had some light visible in the second floor. Most third floors in this block were empty, mainly because the heating in the winter was so expensive. Even as I spoke, I saw him at one of the windows on the second floor.

"Up here, Three," he said. Very faint. I'd forgotten to turn my walkie-talkie volume back up.

I looked closely at the back of his building. A poorly maintained external wooden stair led up the back, to a very narrow platform at the second floor. From there an iron ladder that was bolted to the brick wall rose up to the roof. Great. If the victim had fled upward, this particular cop was going to have to meet her when she came down. I really do hate heights.

"Byng, you got a location for the suspect?"

"Negative, Three. All I got is what your office said. White male with teeth."

"Okay. I don't see the victim here. You got any better ideas where I might—"

I was interrupted by a female voice. "Help!" It sounded like it was coming from the building, but there was something odd about it.

I played my flashlight along the rows of windows, hoping to see her. Byng stuck his flashlight out the window where he was, and played it down toward the ground. I got a queasy feeling in my stomach. If he was inside and thought it had come from outdoors, and I was outside and thought it had come from up where he was...

The roof. She could be on the roof.

The rear of the store was four windows wide at the second-floor level. Usually, there was a pair to each apartment, with the hall between. The door at the top of the stair very likely marked the division between apartments.

I looked at the reddish brown wooden walkway over the conduit. Nothing special, and absolutely no indication of a foot track on its deck. Its rails were just two-by-fours with peeling paint. I shined my flashlight down into the wide ditch, and checked the damp, accumulated silt as far as I could see. No foot tracks there, either. Too bad. Tracks in the silt had solved at least two burglaries for me in the past. I shined my flashlight up on to the rear of the buildings, left to right. There were all sorts of color variations, pieces of black felt and tar paper dangling from unused windows and old doors. One in particular, a door that just opened up to emptiness because the stair had collapsed years ago, seemed to be packed with a black drop cloth.

I checked the roofline for any ropes or fittings. Just making sure we didn't have somebody who had dropped in, so to speak. There weren't any. Good.

"Where do you want me?" I said into the mike on my shoulder.

"Nobody down there?"

"Nobody I can see."

"Why don't you come on up the back way? I think ... it sounds like she's above me someplace."

"Yeah."

"I'm going up the next flight, see if I can get to the roof from the third floor."

Great. I'm not exactly slight, and I really didn't want to haul my 270 pounds up those chancy wooden steps. Damn.

I took a deep breath. "Be right up," I said.

As I reached the narrow platform at the top, I paused and looked back down, illuminating the area with my flashlight. All the way into the bottom of the drainage ditch. Looking down probably thirty-five or forty feet. Instant vertigo.

I grabbed the railing, and forced myself to look back toward the building. Wow. I hate when that happens. I turned as I let go of the rail, and was at the door in one step, trying to look casual. It's not that I'm ashamed of my little height problem, but it's bad for the image if you're a cop. I took another deep breath, and forced myself to concentrate on the door. Swell. It was about as wide as the damned platform, and opened outward. I had to take a half step back, onto that platform again, before I could get the stupid door open. When I did, the platform creaked. I turned sideways and squeezed around the partially opened door, and found myself in a dim hallway, between two apartments, just as I had assumed. There was an open door on my left, leading into a surprisingly nice, well-lighted kitchen area. The door on my right was closed. Clear at the other end of the hallway was a stair, leading to the third floor. There was an older woman standing near the stair.

"He thinks she's up on the roof," she said loudly. "He's gone upstairs to see if he can get to the roof, but I told him he can't."

"Thanks," I said under my breath.

I heard the voice again, very muted this time, as I was now inside. But there was no mistaking it. Not panicky, but frightened.

Byng apparently heard it as well. Excited, I could hear his voice thundering from upstairs, and on my walkie-talkie at the same time.

"The roof! She's on the roof! Get to the roof!"

Well, I was closest to the goddamned ladder.

I turned, and headed back out onto that creaking platform. I stood for a second, looking at the ladder in the beam of my flashlight. Rusty iron. Bolted to the brick, but I could see the thick rust around the bolts, and some orangeish stuff where the bolts had worked in the brick. Shit.

I could hear Byng's running steps as he came off the stair at the far end of the building, and started down the hall toward my platform. There wasn't room for both of us.

I took a very deep breath, slipped my flashlight in my belt, grabbed the sides of the ladder, and took one step up. "Not too bad. Not too bad"—I kept repeating that as I took the second step.

I let my breath out. Piece of cake. Well, so far. The problem was that this ladder went up a whole 'nother floor, and *then* to the roof. I took another breath, held it, and kept going. Then, about six or seven steps up, I felt the ladder shift. Instant vertigo again. I could feel myself pressing against the ladder rungs, my hands beginning to hurt as they squeezed the flat side rail. "Keep yourself against the ladder, Carl. Press against the ladder, and your weight won't overbalance it and tear it away from the wall," I whispered to myself. Everything in me said to go back down. I honestly think that, if I hadn't been in uniform, I couldn't have done it. But I went up. Over the years, I've learned that, if I can convince myself that I'm pushing the building down into the ground with each step, as opposed to me rising farther and farther above the ground, I can sometimes fool myself all the way to the top. I mean, I know I'm fooling myself, but with sufficient concentration that doesn't matter. I started to do that now. One step at a time, I'd grab the next rung in a death grip, and then gingerly shift the opposite foot up one rung. Pushing the huge building down into the ground. Ridiculous, but it worked. All I needed was concentration. I was moving as fast as I could, and still not getting more than half an inch from the wall. Progress. My thigh muscles were getting shaky, and my forearms hurt from squeezing, but I was going up.

Then I felt the ladder begin to vibrate, and heard Byng's voice below me. "I'm right behind you, Carl."

Well, that shot my concentration all to hell. I tried to move faster, and thought I was doing pretty well, until he said, "Something wrong?" He sounded closer, but I was damned if I was going to look.

"Ladder was moving," I said between gritted teeth. "Not sure about it."

"Hell, they always move. Those bolts go clear through the wall, and they fit loose. Don't worry."

Don't worry, my ass. But I was encouraged. I should have thought about the bolts going through the wall. I stepped it up a bit, and was just fine until I got to the top. The ladder only extended about six inches above the edge of the flat roof. No rail, to speak of, above the edge. I was going to have to shift my center of gravity over the edge without any support. I almost stopped.

"I'm up here!" Her voice was much clearer now.

"Police! We're on the way up!" That was Byng.

"Can you come down here?" I yelled. Christ, why hadn't I thought of that earlier?

"No!" There was a pause. "You let me see you!"

Of course. I gritted my teeth. Just as well. I really wanted to be on that roof. Anywhere but that ladder.

I went up two more steps, my eyes cleared the roof edge. I leaned forward and stepped and found myself on hands and knees on the roof. I crawled about three feet, just to get away from the edge, and then got to my feet. I could see a light-colored figure half crouched behind a skylight.

"Deputy Sheriff," I said.

"Where is he?" came the reply.

I heard Byng on the roof behind me.

"Who?" I asked, moving toward her.

"I don't know," she said in a fairly conversational tone. "But whoever he is, where is he?"

"We don't know, either," I said. "But you'll be okay now." I distinctly remember thinking, *until you have to carry me off this roof.*

Many people don't realize just how dark the rooftops in a business area can be. You rise above the streetlights after about the second floor. I could just barely make her out in the shadows.

She stepped toward us. I shined my light on her. She looked about twenty or so, light brown hair, barefoot, and wearing what appeared to be a pair of faded yellow flannel pajama bottoms covered with pink and blue teddy bears and balloons. She was wearing a black, sequined, short-waisted bolero sort of jacket with big silver buttons.

It was probably the sheer relief of having lived to get to the top of the roof, but I said, "Slumber party?"

"What?"

"Nothing. Sorry. You stay right here, and we'll take a look around."

We did a pretty good search of the roof area. With our lights, we could see most of the way to either end of the block, and look through some of the lower trees on the bluff. Nothing in sight.

"What's your name?" I asked our victim.

"Alicia Meyer."

"Mine's Carl Houseman. Is there a particular reason you came up here? I mean, as opposed to going down the stairs or staying in your apartment until we arrived? Did this guy get in?"

"I think so. Then I thought he was waiting for me down there," she said, pointing toward the edge of the roof.

"Reasonable," I replied. "Any idea who 'he' is?"

"No."

There was sort of a pregnant pause. Obviously, we were going to have to go back down. Look as I might, there was absolutely no sign of any stair leading down into any of the buildings. It was going to have to be the ladder again.

The trip down was easier. For her protection, Alicia traveled between Byng and me. Also for her protection, I went first. I felt it was better to look silly as I crawled backward to the ladder than to fall on her. I kept my eyes fixed on her bare feet as we came down. The rungs of the iron ladder were octagonal, and I kept thinking about how much that must hurt anybody without shoes. I must have distracted myself just enough, because my right foot striking the deck jarred me.

I went into her apartment first, then her, then Byng. We looked the place over very well. Nobody but us folks.

"Now," I said, "what's going on?"

"I saw this guy," said Alicia. "At the window. I know I saw him. Right there," she said, and pointed a trembling finger toward her bedroom window.

I looked at the window, then at Byng. He shrugged. The window she had pointed to was the one adjacent to her kitchen window, and about ten feet from the rail of the platform outside. I knew; I'd just been there.

"That window, Alicia?" I asked. "You sure?"

"Yes, that window." She glared at me, brushing a strand of brown hair aside so she could see me better. "I know what I saw. I know. He couldn't be there, because there's nothing to stand on. I know that. But that's what I saw." Her exasperation was pretty evident. That was normal. She couldn't figure out what she had seen, either, and that was making it damnably difficult to explain it to us.

I was thinking *reflection in the window glass* at that point, and glanced around the room. The TV was off.

"You didn't have the TV on at the time, did you?" I tried to sound friendly and reassuring. Not accusative.

"No."

"Okay. Huh. Well, okay, look. Just tell me exactly what you saw, and show me just exactly where you were when you saw it." I thought that was being reasonable.

She took a deep breath. "All right." With that, she stood, and walked over to the mirror. "I was standing right here," she said. "Like this." She demonstrated by turning her back to the mirror and looking over her shoulder at her reflection. "I turned my head like this," she said, and looked over toward Byng and me. And also right at the window in question. "That's when I saw his face in the window." She gave a very genuine shudder. Whatever else, I was certain that she believed she was telling the truth.

I walked over to her, and asked her to move a little, so I could stand in her place. I bent my knees, as I'm about six-four, and she was about five-eight, and tried to get my eye level on the same plane as hers. I looked toward the window. Clear view. No obstructions. And no reflections.

"These are the lights that were on?"

"No, the ceiling light was out."

I motioned to Byng. "Get the ceiling light?" He did. Still no reflections. I straightened up. "You recognize him?"

"No." She said it hesitantly. Either she was thinking really hard, or she found it difficult to lie.

"Can you describe him?" I asked.

"He was white," she said.

That struck me as a bit odd. Nation County's population, while becoming a bit more diverse, was still about 99 percent white. It was unusual to have a witness describe anybody as "white." It was just assumed.

"White?"

"*Really* white," she said, and her voice trembled a bit. "Like clown white. You know, like paint or makeup."

"Ah."

"But not paint or makeup. I don't think. I don't know. If it was makeup it was really good. And black hair, or really dark brown, I think. Close to his head, kinda like it was wet or oily. It looked black, like his shirt or whatever it was...."

"Good." Always encourage your witness. "Anything else?"

She paused. "Yeah. He had these teeth."

"Teeth?"

"Yeah," she said, and sat down abruptly on the edge of her bed. "God, those teeth."

"Like, what? Big teeth? Crooked teeth? Missing teeth? Anything..."

"Yeah. Long, sharp. Really sharp teeth, you know?" She looked up at me earnestly. "Long, pointy teeth."

I tilted my head. "I'm not sure what you mean."

"Like a snake. Long, pointy teeth like a snake or something." She actually shuddered. "I know what I saw. Just like a snake."

It took me a second. "You mean fangs?"

"Yeah. That's it. Fangs. Two of 'em."

"His front teeth were fangs?" It's rare, after more than twenty years at this, to find yourself asking a question that's never even occurred to you before.

She thought. Visibly. "No, not his front teeth. I could see those because he smiled, like. Not a smile, but like a smile. The ones kind of beside the front ones. You know."

"Sure. Upper teeth?"

"Yes."

"Hmm. Okay, then, why don't you start at the beginning, for me." My legs were still feeling a little unsteady, and I sat down at her vanity.

It turned out that she'd been in front of the mirror examining a new tattoo she'd gotten the day before. She didn't say of what, or exactly where. We didn't ask. She'd been topless, at first, and then with various tops that she'd be wearing. Just trying to get some idea what parts of the tattoo certain items of clothing would reveal. She thought she detected a movement out of the corner of her eye. She looked up, and there he was. Looking in the window, and just grinning or smiling. Revealing fangs.

It would have startled the hell out of anybody. Alicia just froze. No scream or anything. She said he disappeared after a few seconds, and it took her a few more seconds to get up the courage to turn away from the window and call 911 from her bedside phone. She apparently answered the first few questions posed by Sally, and then thought he might come back through the window, so put the phone on the cradle and ran to the bathroom and locked the door. A short time later, she thought she heard him at the front door of her apartment, so she fled to her kitchen door and tried to hear what he was doing. She then thought she heard him enter the living room door, so she fled into the hall. Afraid to go down the hall and past her living room door, she went out the back. She was just starting down the rear stair when she thought she heard something in the shadows at the bottom. Up she went, climbing the ladder so fast she didn't realize her feet were bruising until after she'd reached the top. She hadn't seen him again. She hadn't really looked too hard, either.

As we put the sequence together, it became pretty obvious that it had been Byng at her living room door.

He'd announced himself and knocked, but since she was in the bathroom, she only heard sounds. He hesitated, then tried the door, and it was unlocked. He'd just entered when she got into the hallway. Or so we figured. I think both Alicia and Byng were a little embarrassed.

"He say anything?" asked Byng. "When you saw him at the window?"

"Yeah. He did. He kind of mouthed something, but I'm not sure what. Not for sure." She shuddered. "Jesus, this just creeps me, you know?"

"So you sort of read his lips?" Byng raised his eyebrows. "Kind of?"

"Yeah, sort of. Look, I can't say for sure, and this sounds so dumb. But, well, I thought he said something like 'Can I come in?' or something like that." Alicia looked at each of us. "It just sounds so dumb."

"That's what you think he said?" I asked. "Something along those lines?"

"Well, I guess I was pretty sure then," she replied. "I remember saying 'No!' once or twice. I answered him, you know, so he must have said something. Right?"

"Must have. Hey, did he look like he was dangling from a rope or anything?" I had to ask, because I could think of absolutely no other way for anyone to get up there without a ladder.

"No. I couldn't see his arms or hands. Just his face."

"And you didn't recognize him?"

"No."

"Did he," I suggested, "remind you of anybody?"

She thought. "I don't know. Really. It's one of those things, you know? The more you think about it, the more he might. But I don't think that would be accurate."

I had Byng take most of the rest of the information. After all, it was a Freiberg case, and I was just assisting. While he did, I stepped back out on that godforsaken little platform, and looked at the back for possible handholds. Four big bolts, which were common in these old buildings, protruded from the wall. They were several feet apart, in a straight line across the back, at about eight to ten feet from the ground. They probably ran under the flooring of the second story, and were simply reinforcement. No rings, no hooks, and, anyway, they were well below the windowsill. A couple of hollows where the red brick had decayed and flaked away. A few cracks where the mortar had crumbled out. But nothing else. And my original estimate had been about right. It was a good ten feet from the edge of the platform rail to the window where she'd seen the suspect.

I reentered her apartment. "Do you have somewhere you could go for tonight?"

"Yes. I guess."

"We can either take you there, or follow you. I'd really suggest you go there, just so you can sleep."

"You believe me?"

"Got to. I just can't figure out how he got where you saw him."

"Do you think one of those rock climbers," she asked, "could do it? You know, like the guys on TV who go right up a wall?"

"Possible. I don't do that sort of thing," I said, grinning, "as you can probably tell. Do you know anybody who does?"

She shook her head. "But I'm a cocktail waitress on the boat. I'll ask around."

By "the boat" she meant the gaming boat moored just down the street. It was called the *General Beauregard.* "Good. If you find anybody, tell Officer Byng, here, and we can bring him out back and see what he thinks."

She nodded.

"Just check out his teeth first," I said.

I went with Byng to take Alicia to a girlfriend's house. Not so much because she was an attractive female and he really should have a chaperone, but because it allowed me to leave the apartment by the front stairs. That mission accomplished, Byng took me back to where I'd left my car. We both got out, and looked over the area behind the stores. There was absolutely nothing that we could say was out of the ordinary in any way. Just some trash cans, a little housekeeping debris, bottled gas canisters, and the like. Nothing else at all, and no sign of a ladder.

"You look like you're bleedin' to death," he said.

"What?"

"The rust from the ladder. It's all over you."

I shined my light on my hands. Sure enough, they were orangeish red with rust. So was the front of my uniform shirt.

"Cute," I said. I glanced at Byng, already aware that he'd climbed the same ladder, and I hadn't noticed anything reddish about him. I have a way of soaking up all the dirt and stains for everybody else.

"You must have rubbed your forehead, too. And your nose."

I got a squirt bottle of Windex and a roll of paper toweling from the trunk of my squad car, and did my face and hands. The uniform would have to be washed.

"Think we have much of a case, Carl?"

I shrugged. "Not as it stands right now. You know who she described, don't you?"

"Yeah," he snorted. "Fuckin' Bela Lugosi."

I chuckled. Close enough. "The important part is that she didn't say that. Just described it."

"So?"

"So she didn't have a name for the suspect she described. That's more credible, in a way. You ever know her to do any dope? Something along the lines of acid?"

"Never heard about her," he said, "but I'll check. Think she's seein' things?"

"Don't know. Be kind of quiet about checking up on her. I really think maybe she saw something. I just don't think it was Dracula."

He chuckled. "Me, too. Maybe a blackbird or an owl or something.... We got a few young folks who like to dress all in black, and they're a little pale." He snorted again. "Problem is, they can't fly."

"Yeah."

"That fang business is weird, you know?"

"Just a pair of novelty teeth, I guess. He can put 'em in or take 'em out whenever he wants to. If we develop a suspect, shake him down right away. He'll be carrying his teeth in his pocket."

We had walked along the conduit, and I'd been staying about three steps back from the edge.

"Have a problem with heights?" asked Byng conversationally.

"Sometimes," I said.

He shined his light up the back walls of the buildings, to that door into emptiness I'd observed before. "Bet you'd just hate to open that one," he said.

I looked up, just to oblige. I stared at the peeling white paint of the door.

"What?"

"Byng, I'd swear to God that door was covered with black weatherproofing when I got here. I looked at it...."

We checked. There was no material on the ground anywhere near the door. There was nothing in the nearly dry conduit. There was no wind.

"Guess you're mistaken, Carl."

"Yeah." But I didn't think so. "Think we can get into that building tonight?"

"I suppose. Why?"

"I'd like to see if that door opens."

We drove around the block, parked, I grabbed my camera, and we just walked in the front door, went up two flights of steps, and were on the third floor. Security in a rural Iowa town isn't too tight. The third floor was gutted, totally unused, and covered with birdlime, rat droppings, and accumulated debris. Dusty? Oh, my. Perfect medium for the footprints we could see leading to and from that damned door. I took photos, with Byng holding my little tape measure as a scale. Then we went to the door. I had Byng do it, but it opened easily. There were two ringbolts, brand new, attached to the outer door frame. They'd been painted black, and bright silver shown through where something had rubbed the paint off.

"Rope?"

"I'd bet on it," I said. I didn't know enough about climbing to be able to guess whether the rope would be a safety feature, or would actually be used to help our suspect traverse the flat wall between the victim's window and this door. Or both. "It must have been useful."

"Yeah."

"He must have just about reached this door when I came into the alleyway," I said. "He just froze in the frame. And when I went up the back stairs, I wasn't more than twenty feet from him."

"Me, too," said Byng. "When we went up the ladder."

"Good thing we came fast," I said. "I wonder how close he was to her when she came out the back door. Ten feet or less?"

"Probably."

I got a spooky feeling when I said, "And I'll bet you she didn't hear a noise down below. I'll bet what she heard was him, and she just naturally assumed it was down at ground level."

Byng leaned way out the opened door. "Boy, Carl, there ain't much place to grab hold of on that wall. It'd be a mean climb, even with a rope, I think. Well, though, like she said, those crazy rock climbers can find handholds all over the place." He shone his flashlight out the door, toward Alicia's apartment.

"Hey, Carl?"

"What?"

"I think there's rings in the window frame above Alicia's apartment, too."

"Can I take your word for that?"

"Sure." He chuckled. "He really musta shit his pants when we came up."

"Yeah. Or laughed his ass off watching me go up that ladder."

Examination of the floor revealed that the suspect had paced back and forth between the boarded windows at the front and rear of the building. The boards had been pried, and then replaced, so they could be moved aside fairly easily. He was looking at or for something. Maybe us, as we looked for him.

I shined my flashlight up into the rafters.

"Whatcha lookin' for, Carl?"

"Him."

"Oh."

We were on the way down the stairs when Byng thought of something else.

"This is gonna sound dumb, Carl, but Alicia's boyfriend had his car keyed by somebody last night. Parked on Main Street, pretty near her apartment door. Scratch on the sidewalk side, bumper to bumper, and deep. He's gonna have to have it repainted."

"No shit?"

"Yeah. You think maybe somebody's watchin' her? Doesn't like her boyfriend going up to her apartment..."

Interesting. I couldn't resist. "Maybe he didn't key it. Maybe he fanged it instead?"

We both chuckled. "Any idea who it was?"

Byng shook his head. "He said to me, he said, 'I think I know who it was, but I don't want to say until I'm sure.' That's what he said. I asked him twice, but he wouldn't tell me. Said he'd get back to me."

"Okay. Well, if you see him, you might suggest this

dude with the teeth as a possible suspect. After Alicia tells him about tonight, he might be willing to talk."

As we left, Byng summed it up. "Son of a bitch," he said. "I hate these cases that go nowhere."

I wish he'd been right.

TWO

It was a good day. Bright sunshine in a cloudless blue sky, with the yellow, orange, and red leaves of fall covering the landscape. I was in a very good mood, considering the fact that I was at work.

I was driving up to Freiberg to meet with Byng, and exercising my prerogative of taking the scenic route along the Mississippi. Byng had telephoned the office earlier and said that he'd been back on the roof and could find nothing. That meant that I wouldn't have to go back up that damned ladder. A very good mood.

I picked up my mike, and called Byng on our OPS channel. "Twenty-nine, Three."

"Go ahead, Three."

"Yeah," I replied. "I'm about five out. Want to ten-twenty-five somewhere?" I thought I'd leave where we'd meet up to him.

"Uh, yeah. Why don't you meet me over at the Conception County Sheriff's Department?"

Conception County Sheriff's Department was in Jollietville, Wisconsin, just across the river from Freiberg. A large bridge that crossed the Mississippi in two spans joined the towns, and the two states.

"Ten-four. Be there in a couple of minutes." Well. A nice, if unexpected, change of plan. I hadn't seen Harry and the Conception County boys in a good month.

"Ten-four. Got somethin' over here I think you should see. Talk to ya when ya get here."

For some reason, I didn't like the sound of that.

A second later, Sally's voice crackled on the INFO channel. "Comm, Three?"

I leaned forward, and pressed the second of eight frequency buttons. "Comm, go."

"Three, remember the case you had about, oh, four years ago, when you got your car stuck and had to be towed out?"

Of course I did. It had been at a drowning, where a canoe had turned over, and we were trying to get to the victim in an area without a road.

"Ten-four, Comm, I do."

"They had a similar case in Conception County last night. This might be in reference to that."

"Ah, ten-four, Comm." And I hung up the mike.

"KQQ 9787, 12:29." She gave the call letters as a sign she was through transmitting and ready to receive; and the time was given then so that it appeared on the voice recording, just in case her console clock was different from the electronic clock on the recorder.

I was pretty sure that, if they'd had a drowning in Conception County last night, and Byng wanted me to see it, it was either one of our locals or somebody we had an interest in. You always wonder, and hope it isn't anybody you know personally, and maybe like.

I was pulling up in front of the Conception County Sheriff's Department about eight minutes later.

"Comm, Three's out of the car at Conception County."

"Ten-four, Three. 12:37."

I made a quick note of the time in my log. I had a feeling that it was going to be needed in a report.

I walked in, and got buzzed through the bulletproof area and into the main part of the office. Byng was standing in the hall, and motioned me back to Investigator Harry Ullman's office.

"Hey, Houseman," said Harry, getting up from his desk and extending his hand. "Long time no see!"

"You got that right, Harry. What's up?"

He shook his head. "Another fuckin' floater in the river last night. That's seven this year. Called me out in the middle of the damn night."

"You wear your life jacket this time?" I asked because Harry had fallen in once, on a recovery a few years back, and nearly drowned himself. He couldn't swim.

"Always, Carl. You know me." He picked up an incident report sheet from his desk and handed it to me. "Ring any bells?"

I scanned the sheet, and the driver's license stapled to it. The deceased was a white male, twenty-four years of age, named Randy Baumhagen. His driver's license indicated he was from Freiberg, Iowa, but I didn't know him. His color photo showed a fairly good-looking young man in a frilled white shirt with black trim. The standard uniform worn by employees of the *General Beauregard,* the gaming boat moored in Freiberg.

"Works on the boat," I said.

"Worked. You know him?"

"Nope, just can tell from the shirt." I grinned at Harry. A small "gotcha," but it was all part of the game.

"You must be a detective," said Harry.

"I work at it," I said lightly. "Any reason I really should know him?"

Harry glanced at Byng. "He thinks so."

I looked over at the Freiberg officer, and raised an eyebrow.

"Remember the car that I told you got scratched? The boyfriend of Alicia from last night?"

"You're kidding," I said, without much conviction.

"Nope. Same kid." Byng looked almost sad.

"Well, hell," I said. "That's a shame."

"It gets worse," said Harry, in his garrulous way. "You're gonna love it."

"Oh?" I don't know where Harry got the impression I was as ghoulish as he was. "I don't know, Harry. I'm a sensitive kind of guy."

He motioned to his computer monitor, on a side stand near the window. "Take a look at these."

I walked over, and watched as he pulled up a series of electronic photos that showed young Baumhagen. The first two were of him floating; facedown, in a pretty shallow area, judging from the vegetation. "Pretty close to shore?"

"Just above Frenchman's Landing," said Harry. "Water there's about three-feet deep. Looks like he went right off a floating dock."

"He drown?" I asked as Harry brought up a different set of images.

"Christ," said Harry, "I hope not. Look here."

On the screen was a close-up of the right side of Baumhagen's head. It was just about completely caved in, like he'd fallen from a height and gone into rocks headfirst. That kind of completely. Never happen from a floating dock. He couldn't have fallen more than five feet.

"That ought to have done it," I said. "I didn't see any rocks in the other photos. Murder?"

"You bet," said Harry. "See, I told you you'd love it. Wait, though, it gets better than this, even."

I didn't see how that was going to be possible, but I've learned to trust what Harry says over the years.

The next series loaded. This time Baumhagen was lying on his back. His neck was a mess.

"Whoa," I said. "You don't see that every day. Is that what got him?"

"Not sure," said Harry, "but we don't think so. He's in Milwaukee right now, getting autopsied. Great bunch, some of the same people who worked the Dahmer case. Top of the fuckin' line, Carl. Lemme tell ya."

"Name dropper."

"No, really. Anyway, they tell me that they think the cause of death was the blow to the head, and that the neck was done post mortem."

The hole in the neck was pretty large. "Somebody try to remove the head? Or are the turtles just hungrier this year?"

"The forensics people are just guessing, but they say that it was done with a sharp object, but not a blade. More rounded, like a sharpened pencil, you know? Only probably steel. One of the docs is a farm kid, and he said that it reminded him of the sort of wound you might get from something like a fencing pliers." Harry looked up from the screen. "You know?"

I knew. A fencing pliers was kind of a big gripper or snipper, really, with a long, rounded point on one side of the head, so you could slip it under one of the big staples used to hold wire onto a wooden fence post. Heave on the handle, and you pulled the staple out.

Harry went on. "No damage at all to the cervical vertebrae. Most of the major muscle groups are intact. Just a big fuckin' hole, Carl."

"This is a little way from usual, isn't it?"

"You got that right, Carl."

"Why do the throat bit?"

"I told him about last night," Byng interjected. "About the teeth."

"Whatcha think, Carl?" asked Harry. "Could a guy do this with his fuckin' teeth?"

"No way," I said emphatically. "Never happen. Human can't bite that hard, and fake teeth would be pulled right out of his mouth. Real teeth couldn't do that." I looked at both of them, in the sudden silence. "Well, that's just an opinion," I said.

"I agree," said Harry. "So do the boys in the ME's office in Milwaukee." He reached up and patted me on the shoulder. "Not bad for an Iowa boy."

It was quiet for another few seconds. "You know, though," I said, "if you wanted to make somebody *think* you'd done it with teeth . . ."

Harry chuckled. "And that you'd crushed his fuckin' skull because you got a little eager?"

"Well, no. Although I sure as hell didn't see any rocks in any of the photos that could have dented his head like that. But . . ."

"I know what ya mean, Carl," he said. "From what Byng says, it might tie in." He snorted. "Vampire. Suspect that weird has to be from your side of the river."

"I'll tell you what," I said. "I'll bet the odds are at least fifty-fifty that if we find whatever caused the scratch on that boy's car, we'll find the weapon that did his throat."

"That makes sense," said Harry. He straightened up. "So, Carl, did I lie or what? I said it was gonna be a good one."

"You didn't lie, Harry," I said.

"Great." He seemed quite pleased with himself. "Whatcha say? Let's go get some lunch."

On our way out the door, I asked another question. "Who found him?"

"Couple of old farts on their way to fish." Harry clicked open the remote locks on his car. "Why?"

"Just wondered what they'd be saying."

"They were worried about the deceased scaring off the fish."

"Figures," said Byng.

"I told 'em not to worry," said Harry. "It's Friday. Fish can't eat meat on Friday, either."

The try at humor helped. We had a young man, brutally murdered and thrown into a river, without a real chance to live his life. All we could do to help was to try to get whoever killed him. Not much consolation for his friends and family, and not for us, either.

Harry's one of the best cops around. I knew that when I told him, "You know what? You're such a good cop, I'm glad this is your case. Hell, Harry, I'm glad this is a Wisconsin case."

"Right," he growled, as we got into his car. "And if you poor bastards from Iowa had any talent, you'd have a suspect from your peeping tooth fairy from last night. And if you had a suspect, you could tell me. And if you could tell me who your suspect was, I might have a fucking suspect myself!" He flashed a wolfish grin. "Pedro's sound all right? They have cheese burritos as the Friday Special."

"Great," said Byng.

"We'll work with ya, Harry," I said. "Don't worry. Our main job is to make yours easier. Just as long as you feed us."

"That's what I'm afraid of," he said.

THREE

I was brushing my teeth in our upstairs bathroom when I thought I heard the phone ring. I turned off the water, and listened. Nothing. I turned the water back on, glad there hadn't been a call, because my wife, Sue, was asleep. She was a middle-school teacher, and Saturday was about the only day she could sleep past six-thirty.

I was tapping the toothbrush on the side of the sink, and just reaching to turn off the water, when the bathroom door opened a few inches, and Sue's hand and arm came through, holding out the portable phone. "Okay," she said, her voice throaty with sleep. "He's right here." It would have been better if she'd said that into the phone, but I didn't think it prudent to bring that up. I was going to hear about this. I took the phone, and the hand disappeared.

"Houseman."

"Carl?" It was the voice of Norma, one of the newer dispatchers. Well, sure. Who else? "Yep."

"Uh, we got a call, at, ummm . . . 06:36 . . . and I sent Eight up on it. He got there, and thinks we should, uh, probably have you come up and take a look." Her voice seemed to be about an octave higher than usual. "Eight" referred to Nation County Sheriff's Car Eight, the radio call sign of Tom Borman, a newish deputy with about two years' service. He seemed like a good sort, and pretty serious about his job.

"What's he got?" I asked as I walked down the hall to our bedroom to dress. I was pretty sure he didn't want me to show up in just my boxer shorts.

"The first call said there'd been an accident. That was on 911. Something about a lady in a tub. The caller wasn't really clear, female, just wanted help in a hurry."

"What's he want, help lifting her?" I asked. That wasn't good enough a reason to call me out early, and it was a hell of a long way from being sufficient reason to wake Sue. I guess I sounded a little exasperated.

"No, no. No, we got a second phone call after the Freiberg ambulance got there. I sent them right away. They said"—and she seemed to be reading right off her dispatch log—"this subject is code blue, and we think there should be a cop up here right away, it looks like a suicide."

Well, that explained the call to me. Department policy is to treat suicides as if they were homicides, at least until murder had been ruled out. Who do you call to deal with a possible homicide? I was still the investigator, even though I was supposed to be working the noon-to-midnight shift. I couldn't blame Eight. He was new, and working the ten-at-night to ten-in-the-morning shift. The worst possible shift, as far as I was concerned. Even if he was virtually certain sure it was a suicide, he should ask for an experienced investigator. That would be me. And, since he asked for my assistance, I was now stuck with the report. "Right. I'll get dressed and—"

"It's three and a half miles south of Freiberg, off County Road X8G, then the second gravel to—"

I hate to be rude, but I was trying to pull on my blue jeans and still talk on the phone. Writing the directions down was out of the question.

"Just tell me after I get in the car and I'm headed up to Freiberg. I'll take X8G up, okay?"

"Sure," she said. Her voice got some crispness back into it, and I knew I'd hurt her feelings by implying criticism.

"I'm trying to put on my pants," I said, and grinned as I said it, to lighten my voice. "Only so many hands."

"Oh ... sure ... Just one more thing, maybe, while I have you on the phone. I don't think this should be on the radio."

Having at least managed to get both legs in the jeans, I sat on the end of the bed, and said, "Sure."

"Eight called me on the phone, and said that this is a really bad one, but that it's a confirmed suicide."

"Oh?" I hate pulling on socks with one hand. I also hate junior officers making bald-faced statements like that. I mean, they're probably right most of the time, but all you need in a possible murder case is for some defense attorney to get his hands on a logged statement like that one. *"But doesn't it say, right here, that the first officer on the scene determined this to be a suicide?"* But the log couldn't be changed. Only amended, sort of. "Log it that I say that it's not a suicide until the ME's office says so," I said. "Anything else?"

"Really bad. And to handle it code sixty-one. That's all he said."

We used the signal code sixty-one to indicate that all radio communication regarding a particular incident be circumspect, and terse. It meant we had either a sensitive matter, or a very serious one, or both. At any rate, it was designed to prevent those with police scanners from becoming well informed.

"Okay, kid. You call Lamar yet?" Lamar was our

sheriff, and he liked to be kept apprised of tragic and disastrous happenings in the county. Mainly because he hated to go to breakfast at Phil's Café and have somebody ask him about a case before he knew we *had* a case. Looked bad. I pushed my stocking feet into my tennis shoes.

"Yes, and he said to send you right up."

"Well, let's see if we can't arrange that," I said with a hissing sound as I bent over to tie my shoelaces, the phone pressed tightly between my shoulder and my ear.

"And he said to call him if you needed him to come, too."

"Fine. I'll call you on the radio." I pressed the "off" button on the phone and turned to put it back in the charger.

"You need any help?" came Sue's voice from the other side of the bed. "It sure looks like it from here."

"No."

"I'm going to try to go back to sleep..."

I stood, pulled a dark gray polo shirt over my head, and slid my clip-on holster into my belt, on my right hip. I walked over to Sue, bent down, and gave her a kiss. "Good luck."

"You, too," she said, nearly asleep again already.

I grabbed my gun, my walkie-talkie, and my ID case; billfold and car keys from their drawer downstairs in the dining room, and was in my unmarked patrol car and reporting in to the dispatch center at 07:49.

"What time did you call me, Comm?" I asked. Curious.

"07:40."

"Ten-four." Nine minutes. *Getting old,* I thought.

I left Maitland, the county seat, where I lived and where the sheriff's office was located, and headed up the state highway to the intersection with X8G. It was a really pretty morning again. It was about fifty degrees, and warming. I love October.

The police radio in my car was ominously quiet. That was standard with the imposition of code sixty-one. Only officers can really know the spooky feeling that comes with that particular brand of silence. You know there's something really bad, you're going to the scene, and it's absolutely quiet because most of the communications traffic is either on the phones, or just not happening at all because you're the designated catalyst for the next phase, and you aren't there yet. Sort of undercurrents, I guess. But you learn to hate silence, sometimes.

I was moving about seventy or so, no lights or siren. They weren't really necessary, because there was absolutely no traffic anywhere. I became aware of intermittent sounds, like the faint patter of raindrops on the car. The sun was still shining brightly. Still no clouds. Then it dawned on me. Ladybugs. There were unusually large flights of ladybugs this year, and I was traveling through mini swarms of the little creatures. Well, that was at least one mystery solved today.

I was bothered again about Borman and the "suicide" statement, as I turned off onto X8G and dipped down into a valley along the Mississippi. He really should have known better, even with just a couple of years under his belt.

I traveled along the Mississippi again, past a stretch of maybe thirty small cabins on the right, or river side, of the road. They were across the railroad tracks that ran the length of the county in the valley of the Mississippi. I drove past a large, abandoned silica sand mine carved into the bluffs on the Iowa side, on my left. Then past a small sign near the railroad tracks that proclaimed "Givens' Switch." There was nothing there but the sign, which had recently been placed by the county historical society. Commemorating one of those myriad little places that had just disappeared over the years.

I thought some more about Borman. He was taking a class in "Humanizing the Police," or some such thing, taught by a sociologist via a college extension plan. He was picking up on all these "empathy" techniques, and I strongly suspected that this had somehow influenced him this morning. Or maybe I just was reluctant to acknowledge that he was a younger generation of cop. I chuckled to myself. Maybe, indeed. Fifty-five really isn't that old. Well, not if you're ninety.

About a quarter of a mile later, I turned back west, or inland, onto a gravel road called Willow, slowed to fifty or so, and called in for better directions.

"Comm, Three. Just turned onto the gravel. How 'bout those directions now?"

This sometimes got very interesting, because under code sixty-one rules, it forced a radio transmission that had to be very circumspect. Try that with directions, sometime.

"Ten-four, Three. Take your next right turn to the north. Take the second drive after the curve that sends you back east, toward the river."

I paused, setting the directions in my mind. It was the great big house on the bluff overlooking the Mississippi. It was usually known as "the Mansion," although some of the local kids called it the Dropout Dorm, because of the people who lived there.

"Comm, M Mary?" I hoped she got it, because I didn't want anybody to know precisely where I was headed. I didn't know if the dispatcher, the ambulance crew, or Borman had specifically referred to the Mansion, but I wasn't going to. If somebody with a scanner had missed the initial traffic, I wasn't going to help them out now.

It took her a few seconds. "Oh, sure. Ten-four, that's the one. Confirm with last three: three five four."

The 911 address would be 24354, useless to anyone who didn't have the name of the particular road. She asked for the last three digits to make sure I didn't have the wrong place. Nobody listening would know the first two digits unless they knew where I was all along.

I'd always been fascinated by that house. It was huge, of a kind called Victorian or Queen Anne, or something. It was perched at the end of a long lane on top of the bluff, with what had to be one of the finest views of the Mississippi River that was available from privately owned land. I'd never really been in the place before, although I'd been in the yard once. It was far and away the biggest house in Nation County.

"Ten-four, Comm, I know the location. ETA about five."

If it hadn't been for the 911 address sign 24354, a partially hidden mailbox, and a big, blue plastic refuse bin that was just visible from the road, you wouldn't even have known there was a lane there at all. Located smack in the middle of the Beiderbaum Timber, a wooded area that ran along the west, or Iowa, bank of the Mississippi for about ten miles, the house sat out toward the east end of a long, wide finger of land that pointed right at the Mississippi River. Bordered by two streams, or creeks as they're called locally, the ridge itself was about half a mile wide, with the east end about two miles from the road that ran along its west side. I'd guess that the top of the ridge was about 250 feet above the roadway, covered with trees and low bushes and foliage on the long sides, and ending in a vertical limestone bluff overlooking the river. The gravel drive that extended uphill was nearly a mile and a half long, winding from the valley floor through a heavily wooded area that had littered the road surface with fallen leaves. I crested the rise, onto the top of the finger-shaped ridge, and traveled the last quarter mile on nearly level ground. The trees were just as thick up here, a mixture of brilliant yellow maples and tall, dark green pines. As I drove on to the house, I caught a glimpse of its reddish turreted roof through the trees. I passed through a weathered iron gate set in limestone blocks. They were part of a limestone wall that demarked the area between the woods and the cleared, almost manicured area that displayed the house. My car bumped slightly as I left the gravel and drove onto the wide new blacktop of the circular drive.

The large house was three stories, with two turrets and a vast wraparound porch, all in a dark blue-gray wood frame with maroon trim. Actually, "enormous" was a better word for the house, I thought. It got bigger as I got closer. It stood on a little rise, about ten feet above the level of the drive, and with a wide flight of limestone steps that led up through the little berm to a double door with tall, oval, etched and stained-glass panels. The doors themselves were flanked by very tall, oval windows. Etched and stained glass there, too. It had been built in the 1890s to mark the great wealth of the Givens family, who had amassed a tremendous fortune in grain.

Both the ambulance and car Eight, Borman's fully marked squad, were parked near the front door. No flashing lights or anything. No reason for them. Both vehicles were running, though. There were two other vehicles in the yard, a '90 Buick four-door, and an '87 Ford pickup. Both looked to be well maintained, but showing signs of their age.

"Comm, Three, I'm ten-twenty-three. Be out of the car." I didn't have to say where, as she already knew that. And it concealed my whereabouts from the folks with the scanners. Always a good idea. I swung my legs out of my car.

Comm acknowledged, and then Eight came up on his walkie-talkie. "Three," he said, sounding sort of brittle, "I'm up on the second floor. First room on the left. Come in there and one of the EMTs will show you just where we are."

I headed for the house, and as I came around the side

of the ambulance, saw a young male subject, about twenty years old, sitting on the bottom step. He had ear-length black hair, parted in the middle. A silver stud through the bridge of his nose, right between his eyes, sort of stood out. Dark blue sweatshirt, black jeans, black shoes.

"Hi." Not the best opener, under the circumstances, but you have to start somewhere. "I'm Deputy Houseman."

He just looked at me. He had a lit cigarette in his right hand.

"And you'd be?" I knew I'd seen him before, mainly because of the stud in his nose, but I didn't remember arresting him or anything. The instant database in my head had him filed under "decent kid."

"Oh." Like I'd startled him. Hard to see how. "I'm Toby. Toby Gottschalk. I live here."

Oh, sure. Toby. "What's happened, Toby?"

"Ah, it . . . oh, you know, Edie's done herself." He looked sort of unaffected by the whole thing. Sometimes, that can be one of the effects of an emotional shock in some people. He took a drag from his cigarette.

"Did you see her do it?" The name Edie rang a bell, but, again, no placement.

"No."

"Did you find her?"

"No. No, I just heard Hanna holler, and then she came running down the hall to use the phone. That's how I found out."

You hate to belabor a point, but it can be important. "Hanna found her, then?"

"Well, yeah." A little exasperated. And why not?

"Thanks, Toby. I'll probably have to talk with you a little more, when I'm done in the house."

"I know."

"Okay." Pretty calm and self-possessed. Good, as far as I was concerned. Much easier to interview. I hated to see him smoke, though not for some sort of altruistic reason concerning his health. That was his problem. It was just that I'd quit about five years before, and still had a bit of a difficulty when I was in the presence of a smoker.

I entered the front hall, crossed the foyer, and entered the main hall through another pair of double doors, also with the great oval glazing. This place was really big. And nice, too. There were hardwood parquet floors in every room I could see. I started up the walnut staircase that incorporated an inglenook, got to a landing, and continued up the next flight of stairs to the second floor. I found myself in a long hallway, with another stair at the far end. I saw Eunice Kahrs, an EMT, kneeling beside a youngish female who was seated on an upholstered bench in the hall.

Eunice, the EMT, gestured toward my left. "Just go through that door, Carl, and on into the bathroom. I'd better stay with Hanna, here."

"Sure, Eunice." The young woman she'd called Hanna looked very pale, and was staring off beyond the adjacent wall, to some point known only to her. She was breathing rapidly, and shallowly, as if she'd been crying. "She's the one who found her?" If you don't ask the obvious, things can get by you quicker than you'd think. Besides, it wouldn't be the first time I'd had two people with the same first name in a house.

"Yes. Hanna here found her, and called us." Just like Toby said downstairs. Good. Eunice squeezed Hanna's shoulders. "It'll be all right, honey."

I leaned toward the seated figure. She seemed stunned. "I'm sorry, Hanna, but I'll have to talk to you before I go." She nodded.

I went past her, and turned from the hall into a bedroom that had to be at least twenty-five feet by twenty. I could see Borman's back, and most of Herb Balk, an

EMT, standing in an adjoining room, which appeared to be a bath.

"What've you got?" I asked.

Borman turned, very somber, and said, "A real mess. A real mess. Looks like a suicide, but I've never seen anything like this."

He stepped aside, and Herb backed out of the room, giving me free access. I stepped across the threshold, looked into the room and into the bathtub. I turned back to Borman. "Yeah."

FOUR

When you first enter a crime scene, it's really a good idea to stop, if you can, and just let the, well, the ambience sort of sink in. It's the only chance you get before things get really disturbed, and even with the best scene recording and evidence preservation, it's a chance that will never come again. Just a few minutes to stand still and look around. If you can do it when you're completely undisturbed, it's even better, because there's nobody to hurry you. If not, it sure as hell helps to be the one in charge.

"Give me a few minutes here," I said to Borman. "Why don't you go down to my car and get both cameras. The 35mm and the digital. And call the office, and make sure the ME is on his way." I tossed Borman my keys, and began to try to absorb the room and its contents as well as I could.

The center of attention, of course, was the body in the claw-footed tub.

The white porcelain tub was almost against the far wall, and the drain end was the farthest from the door. What appeared to be a white female, twenty to thirty years old, was in the tub. She was seated, kind of, with her buttocks snug up against the end of the tub. She'd flopped forward and a little to her right, with her back kind of turned away from the door. Naked, like anyone else in a tub. Her head was bowed down toward her chest, with a mass of black hair hanging straight down, hiding her face. She seemed to have spatters of blood on most of her, except her head and her back, although it looked like there was even some blood between her shoulder blades. Both hands were in front of her, almost in her lap, like she had just sort of given up and let them flop down.

There were what appeared to be fresh bruises on her arms and lower legs. The ones on her arms, especially, had a familiar look. They were circumferential, or nearly so, with three lighter-colored, narrow striations. The upper striation on the left side seemed to be a very narrow triangle, while the lower two were more like straight lines. I'd seen very similar marks on women and children a couple of times before. When a person grabs somebody and holds on, there is often a gap between the forefinger and the middle finger, with a much lesser gap between the middle finger and the ring finger, and the ring finger and the little finger. If they grab really hard, when they let go, the gaps appear almost white against the red marks left by the fingers. That's what these looked to be. The ones on her legs weren't that well defined. But they were large, and an angry reddish purple. I thought there might be some elsewhere, but there was too much blood on the skin to be sure.

The tub had been modified into a shower, with an elliptical brass curtain track running around it about five feet above the rim; and a tall brass shower pipe and head rose from above the brass faucets and drain. The cream-colored plastic curtain was about half open and had blood on its lower edge, where it entered the tub.

The tub itself had lots of bloody streaks all around the inside, mostly small spatters and streaks. Some appeared to have been large enough to begin to run toward the tub, before they'd started to thicken. Well, those that I could see, anyway. A little pool of drying blood encircled the brass drain rim. There was little, if any, blood actually filling the tub, and the drain lever seemed to be in the open position. I couldn't tell, at first, where the wounds were. I half suspected the left wrist, which was hidden from my view, and would be until I got closer to the tub. There were signs of a lot of blood, though. More than I'd expect from a wrist. Something related to that caught my attention, but I wasn't able to identify what it was right away. I stared at the blood puddle and the streaks. Then it struck me. Most of the blood didn't appear to have clotted. It was starting to dry, in a normal, evaporative way. But there wasn't much identifiable clotting anywhere, even on the body itself.

What appeared to be a knife handle seemed to be sort of wedged between the top of her right thigh and the side of the tub, but, again, it was difficult to tell from my vantage point. The last thing you want to do is go thundering right up to the body. You can disturb lots of trace evidence that way, not to mention the strong possibility of completely missing something important located away from the body. And as soon as you start to focus hard on the deceased, you begin to set a focal point that's hard to alter later. Later, as in when you're confronted with the evidence you missed in the first place. The salient fact was that she was dead. No need to rush. Keep it broad.

I looked at the dark green and white tiled floor, especially the area between me and the body. It appeared to be clean, with no bloodstains. The pale yellow walls were clean, as well. The porcelain sink on the near wall, at least down as far as I could see into it from my position some ten feet away, was clean, as well. Likewise for the porcelain stool beside it. The brass-framed medicine cabinet with a mirrored front, over the sink, also looked pristine.

There were folded pale green towels on a brass rack with glass shelves, about three feet behind the tub. Nothing there seemed to stand out.

There was a tall, white cabinet with, naturally, brass hinges and handles, all four doors closed.

There was no rug or mat on the floor, and there didn't appear to be any clothing in the room. No slippers. No robe. No unfolded towels. There was blood-spattered soap in the brass soap dish on the right side of the tub. No shampoo bottles, no sponges, no razor, no washcloth anywhere near the tub. Other than the dead woman, that was just about the only remarkable thing in the room.

"Must have been really neat," I said to myself.

"What?" From the EMT Herb, near the door.

"Oh, nothing. Just talking to myself." Oops. Sometimes I concentrate so hard on what I'm doing, I forget other people are anywhere around.

I looked up, just like the other night up on that third floor. I learned to do that long ago. Most cops never look up. Sometimes, they wish they had. I could see a half window above the tub, and a full-sized window at the far end. Both had curtains, and both were opened, with screens.

Box elder bugs and ladybugs were moving inside the window casings. A seasonal thing in Iowa. A couple of ladybugs had flown down into the room. They're such friendly little critters, I didn't bother getting them out of the way. One of the box elders was steadily crawling across the shower curtain, appearing and disappearing in the folds.

No obvious blood marks on the walls. Nothing re-markable about that, either way.

There was a ten-foot ceiling with a four-bulb lamp suspended from a chain. The bulbs were enclosed in white glass globes that hung from the green enameled flowery ends of the brass framework. Nice lamp. Nothing remarkable about it at all. No bloodstains. It'll surprise you, sometimes, just how high they can go if there's a spray or a splash effect. The ceiling itself was either the original molded copper painted white, or one of the newer, plastic versions. Either way, it, too, told me nothing except that it was expensive.

"Well, shit." I failed to catch myself in time.

"What?" Herb, again. The man was a good listener, I had to give him that.

"I said, Herb," raising my voice with a bit of exasperation, " 'Well, shit.' "

"Oh."

"Is Borman back with those cameras, yet?"

"Here I am," said Borman, behind me. "The office says the ME has been notified, and will get here ASAP. And, uh, Lamar says he'll come up, too."

"Good." I stepped back into the bedroom, and started to unpack the 35mm SLR. "How far into the room did you guys go?"

"Which room?"

"The bathroom," I said, snapping the 50mm lens into the camera body. I unzipped the section of the bag that contained the digital camera, but left it in place. I'd duplicate some shots with the digital in order to have them right away. The 35mm stuff was for court, if necessary. I reached into one of the bag's many compartments, and put on a pair of latex gloves.

"I pretty much stopped at the door," said Borman.

"We got to her," said Herb. "Close enough to check vitals. But with that wound in the neck, you could tell there was no point before you even started."

"The neck?" The look I got from him made me add,

"I haven't approached the body yet; just did a long look at the room."

"Big, open slash on the right neck. Deep. Really deep. Got the jugular, at least."

"Oh." I was about as noncommittal as I could be. Neck? Two neck wounds in forty-eight hours, within ten miles of each other, in a basically rural area?

"The knife's down by the right leg," he said. He thought he was rubbing it in. "We didn't touch it."

"Saw it," I said. "Glad you left it alone." Well, at least it wasn't a fencing pliers. I had to take a moment to regain my focus. I wanted very badly to rush in and check that neck wound. But first things had to come first.

I hung both the camera bag and the camera around my neck with their straps, and straightened up, looking around the room. Neat room. As in tidy. Even the bunch of little jars and bottles on the vanity looked organized and orderly. To one side of the vanity top was a large, transparent blue plastic box, with seven rows of four doors. The rows were labeled for the days of the week, and the little doors were labeled for times of day. It was a pillbox, for somebody taking prescriptions. I made a mental note to point that out to the ME, and to get a photo.

Some photos, of mostly youngish people, adorned the vanity mirror. Very neat, in organized rows. One of those large, preconfigured frames with about a half dozen oval cutouts, filled with photos of a little kid, hung above the mirror. Maroon velvet or velour jewelry box. Queen-size bed, with what was now just about an obligatory brass frame. The bed was made, with a paisley bedspread. A nightstand, with a brass lamp. What I guessed to be a door to a closet was closed. Tidy, again. There were a couple of stuffed animals on the top of the bookshelf: a teddy bear, a little stuffed vampire with blue skin and a black cape, and one of those little troll dolls with the vertical red hair, like Don King. Boom box, stack of CDs, about a dozen books on the shelves. There was a small table and a chair against the hallway wall, with an older PC on top. Clunky, with no printer, just a keyboard and mouse pad. On the wall at the head of the bed, between the two windows, was a wood-framed embroidered sign, proclaiming in a homey way that "Absinthe Makes the Heart Grow Fonder." That one made me smile. A nice, normal room, with nothing unusual to catch the eye. Absolutely nothing. The bedroom of a neat, organized person.

The unusual part was what wasn't there. As far as I could see, there was no clothing laid out on the bed, nor on the back of a chair, nor on the chest of drawers. And no sign of the little pile of clothes you might expect to find in the wake of someone on her way to the bath. No underwear, no bra, no shoes or socks. Nothing.

"I'd appreciate it," I said, "if you two would go out into the hall, and not let anybody in unless it's Lamar or the ME."

"You do know who this dead girl is, don't you, Carl?" asked Herb.

"Hadn't got to see her face, Herb, so, no. Just that she's been called 'Edie.' Do you know who she is?"

"Edith Younger." I must have given him a blank look, because he added, "You know. Lamar's sister's kid. She's Lamar's niece."

FIVE

I thought, *Son of a bitch*. I said, "Damn." Sure it was. I'd always known her as Edith. I looked at Borman. "Does Lamar know who it is yet?"

Borman gave me a blank look. "How do I know?"

I sighed. "Go get on the phone, call Dispatch, and see if they know if he knows. If he does, fine, but if he doesn't, when he gets here, tell him I want to talk to him before he gets in here, and then come get me. Got it?"

"Sure," said Borman, heading for the hallway.

"And NO RADIO TRAFFIC, got that?"

"Yes sir." He did a phony pout. "You old guys are so sensitive."

I flipped him off, in a friendly sort of way. "It's not nice to irritate your elders."

"Tell me about it...." was delivered as he left the room. The whole exchange was flat, forced, but you had to try. It was really getting oppressive in there. I wanted to open all the windows, but we didn't need any flies.

I motioned Herb back toward the hallway. "Stop anybody out there from coming in, will you? Until Borman gets back."

Alone again, I took some quick photos of the interior of the bedroom with both cameras, rotating myself clockwise, and making certain I overlapped the photos. Then I stepped back almost into the hall, and took three more shots, to establish the scene. I found I had to reload the camera. The Board of Supervisors had recommended we use twelve-exposure rolls, to "save money." Lamar had bought twenty-four of those rolls, just to give it a try. As it turned out, I had one thirty-six-exposure roll of ISA 400 left in my bag. I loaded it into the camera, and manually forwarded the film to "1." We'd saved money by deleting the auto-wind option, as well. Thus armed, I ventured back into the bathroom.

Between working twelve-hour shifts, and getting very little sleep before getting called out four hours early today, and the semi-stunned feeling that usually accompanies having to absorb a tremendous amount of evidence and data in a very short time, I was beginning to feel a bit overwhelmed. I stood for about ten seconds, taking a couple of deep breaths, and just sort of clearing my head. What I used to accomplish by having a cigarette. Then I started back to work.

I took four shots from the door frame, just to establish the scene. Then I took a bunch of shots of the body, as I moved alongside the tub. Each from a slightly different angle, they'd give about as complete coverage as possible without moving the corpse. I made a very conscious effort to get as much of the bloodstain patterns as I could. About halfway along, I reached into the bag at my chest, and changed from the 50mm to a 70/210mm zoom. I was getting my first good look at the huge cut in the neck, and I wanted close-ups without having to lean over the body. I kept using both cameras, but the zoom on the digital just wasn't in the same league with the single lens reflex.

I've seen lots of cuts, and this was one of the meaner ones. Only about four inches long, but length, as they say, isn't everything. It appeared to be very, very deep, because there seemed to be a bulge of muscle protruding. Muscle will do that sometimes. Especially if there's a lot of tension on it at the time it's cut. But it has to go deep. It was more of a stab wound than I'd expected. Most suicides use a sawing motion. It was not, though, a tearing wound like the one on the Baumhagen boy. For whatever that was worth.

There was a very dark spot, visible through the bloodstain, on the upper portion of the right breast. My first thought was a contact gunshot wound, but as I leaned a little closer I could see it was some sort of tattoo. That was a relief. The neck cut was certainly enough. There was lots of evidence of blood, but it didn't seem like all that much, considering the wound. The spatter marks on the inside walls of the tub made it look like there'd been more blood than there actually had been. I thought about that for a second, and decided that, sitting upright, if she'd lost enough blood to stop all brain functions, maybe that would stop the heart. Right, Dr. Carl. That's why we have medical examiners.

It then occurred to me that the open drain in the tub could explain that, but it just didn't quite fit, somehow. Something wasn't right.

I knelt down, and got some lower level shots of the wound. To get as much of the cut in frame as possible, I took a pen from my pocket, reached out, and pushed some of her hair back out of the way. As I did so, I saw her face fairly clearly. And her eyes. Big, hazel eyes, wide open, and staring right directly at me.

"Holy shit!" I stood straight up, snagging her hair with the pen clip as I drew my hand back. I reached out to retrieve it, fumbled, and watched my pen drop into the tub. Great.

Those eyes had looked so vital; I'd thought she was still alive. That really startled me. I hadn't been expecting them to look so, I don't know, lifelike, I guess. I took a deep breath, and forced myself to squat back down. I took a shot of the pen in the tub, then gingerly fished it out of the little puddle of reddish muck near the drain. Naturally, it had rolled downhill. I took a second shot, depicting the little depression the pen had made in the drying blood.

Only then did I hold it out, push the hair back again, and take the shot. I didn't look at her eyes. I did, though, make a mental note. With her head lolling forward, her eyes must be in a rolled-up position. That might eventually mean nothing, but I sure as hell wasn't ever going to forget it.

I also got some good shots of the knife. It was a new-looking kitchen knife, with a strong, serrated blade. Black polycarbonate handle. Brass rivets. I shook my head. Brass rivets. Hell, even the knife went with the room.

I did a few shots from as nearly directly above her as I could get. I noticed that she seemed to have several colors of nail polish, both on her fingers and on her toes. Black thumb nails, it looked like, with red on the index finger, dark green on the middle finger, dark blue on the ring finger, and white on the little finger. The same sequence was repeated on her toes. I wondered if it meant anything.

I finished photographing the rest of the bathroom, having to reload the camera again. I started to talk to myself, and to her, about that time.

"Sorry, kiddo, but I gotta reload." There was, of course, no answer. "A few more shots to go. I'll be done in a second, and then we can leave you to yourself until the doc gets here."

You do that. Well, I do that. When I'm alone with a freshly dead person. Nerves, I guess. Spooked, or getting that way. That, and it always seems such an intrusion, especially when they're in such a vulnerable position. I always get self-conscious and kind of embarrassed. I have to look at parts of them they'd never let me see if they were alive. And I take photos, to boot. So I try to verbally reassure them.

"I don't know, but I think you maybe might have done this to yourself. No clothes to get into when you get out of the tub, you know? Nothing laid out in the bedroom. Like you had no intention of ever leaving that tub." It was possible. There were absolutely no signs of a struggle, as they say. None but those bruises, and they might not be contemporaneous with her death. The plastic curtain didn't even seem to be much disturbed, hanging properly inside the rim of the tub. It was awfully difficult to imagine someone creeping up behind her, stabbing her in the neck, and having her bleed to death. I'd seen a couple of very determined suicides before, including one woman who'd stabbed herself eleven times in the abdomen with a hunting knife. That had to have taken a while. You could do a lot of damage to yourself if you were in the right frame of mind.

But it still looked... well, wrong. Especially the bruises. But maybe she'd had a fight with her boyfriend earlier in the day. That was possible.

I remembered that Edith had overdosed on pills, at least once for sure. Only once, as far as I knew, because I'd been a night-shift officer then, and had been assigned to that case. That had been a few years back. Not evidence in and of itself, but a prior attempt was at least an indication that she'd achieved a suicidal frame of mind on at least one occasion. But would that even bear on the fact that we had a knife used this time?

Hmm. I could almost hear the endless discussions generated by that, late at night in the dispatch center. That, and the discussion about the position of the knife. Would she have dropped it on that side? Wouldn't it have landed (insert choice) blade forward, rear, up, down, more to the left, more right?... I almost felt I owed it to the night shift to resolve this one quickly.

There was a voice behind me, out in the bedroom.

"Carl, you in there?"

Lamar.

"Yeah, Lamar. You might want to stay out there...."

I was too late, because as I turned to go to the bedroom, Lamar came to the doorway of the bathroom. His limp was more pronounced than usual, like it got when he was really tired. Don't ever let somebody tell you that gunshot wounds go away, even after years have gone by.

He stopped, more from habit of not disturbing the scene than out of any kind of surprise or shock. We'd both been to these things before, many times. For me to try to intercept his gaze, or to usher him back into the bedroom, would have been an insult. So I just stepped aside and let him look. He took about a full minute, and then cleared his throat.

"Suicide, ya think?"

"Not sure yet, Lamar."

"Probably, though?"

"Probably, yes. The ME hasn't gotten here yet. I have some questions about those bruises."

He looked directly at me for the first time since I'd heard his voice. "I know we hear this all the time ... but she just wasn't the type, Carl."

"She did try it before."

"That was before she had the kid," he said. "That little girl of hers means too much to her. She'd never leave her this way."

I didn't say anything.

"The kid's been with my sister most of the time," said Lamar. "Edie, here, hates that, and hates her mom, too." He paused, and corrected himself. "Hated. Anyway, she's been trying to get back on her feet, get the kid back. She'd never give up like this."

Some things are really hard to say, particularly to a friend. But you just have to, sometimes. "That could be, boss," I said. "That could be. But we better wait for the toxicology report, you know."

"Yeah. But I don't think she does dope anymore."

"Okay."

"But you're right."

We both looked at Edie for a few moments.

"The neck, they said?"

"Yeah, and that bothers me a little, too. At least for now."

He made no move to advance, to see the wound himself. "Oh?"

"I can't get a real good look until we move her, but . . ."

He looked at me, eyebrows raised. I didn't want to promote any ideas, but he was also my boss.

"You know how self-inflicted wounds like this tend to look like the subject was trying to saw wood? Back and forth, angle changes, and lots of small cuts and scratches where they're off, and where they hesitate?"

He nodded.

"This looks like a one-shot deal to me. So far, anyway. Sure no hesitation marks." I shrugged. "We don't want to read too much into that, but that's what it looks like."

"Yeah?" Lamar looked at me expectantly.

"And the bruises, like I said. On the other hand," I went on, "there's no sign of a struggle in the vicinity of the tub, or in the next room. You can see that. There's no clothes or anything. Either that she took off or that were laid out for her to put on. Like she was never going to get out of the tub, and knew that." I took a breath. "The clothes bit bothers me, Lamar. I have to admit . . ."

We were both quiet for a while.

"You gonna need help on this? At least for a while?"

"Yeah, I think so," I said. Another officer never hurt. There always seemed something for them to do. "Borman will be okay."

"You sure?" asked Lamar. "He's takin' those social worker classes. . . ."

"Yeah, that's okay," I said. "He needs the experience, and he's already halfway familiar with the case."

"You got him, then. Did I tell you that Doc Zimmer's doing the workup?"

"Okay. That's good." Dr. Henry Zimmer, a local MD. Acting as a Deputy County Medical Examiner, being closest physician to the scene. At this point, we didn't require a forensic pathologist; we needed someone to pronounce Edie dead. We couldn't do that, and it was considered bad manners to just drop an obviously deceased at the nearest ER.

"And DCI, maybe?" Lamar asked.

DCI was the Iowa Division of Criminal Investigation. As a state agency, if we called for one of their agents, if we needed a forensic pathologist, he'd be charged to them. Along with the crime scene processing team, if needed. Tempting. But the state was busy, too, and we always hate to call DCI unless we really need them.

"Probably not yet, Lamar," I said. As I looked at him, though, I began to realize that this had been more of an order than a question. "Although, if this were to be a murder..."

"They really hate to get called in late," finished Lamar.

We looked at each other.

"It's always best to be sure," I said.

"True."

We were both silent in our thoughts for a moment.

"Lamar, tell me the truth. Would you feel better if we called DCI?"

"Yep."

I reached out and patted him on the shoulder. I'd never done that, but it seemed the right thing to do at the time. "Let's go make the call." I certainly didn't want to leave him alone with the body.

As we were about halfway through the bedroom, Lamar said, "Hey, Carl?"

I stopped, and turned toward him. "Yeah?" I thought he'd found something.

"Get Hester. Request her by name, okay?" He paused, embarrassed. "I mean, I know Edie's dead... but I'd just like a female DCI agent on this one."

"Sure."

He reached into his back pocket and pulled out a rolled newspaper. He handed it to me. "You might want to check out the article here, when you get a chance."

"Okay."

"I'm glad you're gonna get Hester."

He meant Hester Gorse, Special Agent, Iowa DCI. Hester and our department went back a long way. She was one of the very best, without a doubt. And what he was trying to say was that he didn't feel too comfortable with male officers examining Edie's body, or going through her personal effects. He'd have to go with me, of course, but Hester would ease his mind just by her presence. The problem was, DCI almost never sent a specific agent on request. They had a rotational assignment procedure, generally based on agent availability, but also designed in part to provide a wide base of experience for their general crim agents. It also served to prevent any hint of collusion between the local requesting department and any specific DCI agent, defense attorneys occasionally being known to grasp at straws. We'd just have to see.

Borman directed me to the phone downstairs. I quietly told him to stick with Lamar. He nodded.

"Oh, and consider yourself assigned to the case until further notice. Authority Lamar."

"Oh! Uh, thanks, Carl."

"Think nothing of it. You need the experience. I need the help."

The first DCI agent I talked with at the Cedar Falls district office wasn't sure, but thought Hester was at home. He gave me the home phone number of his boss,

Alan Hummel. Lamar and I had known Al for nearly twenty years. I explained the situation, in some detail, emphasizing Lamar's relationship with the deceased, and the condition of the body.

"Boy, Carl. That's a shame. But you do need an agent because of the suspicious nature of the thing, right?"

"Yes." Like I'd say differently.

"But you say it's a suicide?"

Well, that was what I'd said, standing in the hall of the huge house, and not being too sure just who was able to hear me. "This isn't a secure line."

"Got it." He paused. "Look, as far as I'm concerned, you've got Hester. I'll have State Radio give her a call. If she's not at home, they'll page her. I'll instruct them to contact your office as soon as they get an ETA."

"Thanks, Al."

"And, Carl, be sure to tell Lamar he has my sympathy."

As I hung up, I saw Toby, the young man from the front steps, standing in the room across the hall. He was staring at me.

"I hope that was a local call," he said.

"Pardon me?"

"I said, I hope that was a local call," he replied.

I've always found that, when dealing with someone who's trying to win the Junior Dickhead award, it's most rewarding to play things irritatingly straight, but vague.

"No, it was long distance," I said, smiling. "Sorry to dash your hopes."

He looked like he wanted to say more, but I held up my hand and dialed the sheriff's office.

"Hey, can you spring some more people for me up here ... maybe two, if you can? Three or four'd be good. I've got folks moving around up here, and I have better things to do than control foot traffic." The dispatcher said she'd try. "And," I said, "Hester should be on her way up pretty soon." Just a way to inform and alert the dispatcher that things might get really busy in a while.

Done with that, I put the phone back on the receiver. Toby resumed our conversation as if I'd never made the second call.

"Who pays for it, then?"

Again, I smiled. He was really trying to get some attention. "Is the phone in your name, Toby?"

"No."

"Whose name is it in, then? Do you know?" The last question surprised him a bit, I saw. Unexpected turn, when he'd thought some sort of confrontation was coming.

"Jessica Hunley." The way he said it, I got the impression that I was supposed to know who Ms. Hunley was. I didn't, but I'd find out. I was also going to find out why Toby was here, if it wasn't his phone. Guest? Resident? Patron? But it could wait.

"Then, can I rely on you to tell Ms. Hunley that I used a credit card?"

"Well, yes. Yes. I'll do that."

"Excellent," I said, heading for the stairs. "Don't go too far, Toby. I'll get to you pretty soon, now." I went up a couple of stairs. "Oh, Toby . . . thanks."

"For what?"

"For getting the message to Ms. Hunley for me."

"Sure." He sounded just a little uncertain, but not ready to concede anything. Good for him. I knew he'd be a witness of some sort, to whatever it was we really had here. Not that I'm cynical, but it's never too soon to start working on a witness.

I stopped on the landing, and looked at the newspaper Lamar had handed me. It was today's copy of the Freiberg Tribune and Dispatch. All six pages of it. On the front page, lower left, was a headline: "Dracula Visiting Freiberg?" The article was about our window-peeking incident from two days ago. No names. But it quoted a "young lady" as describing the window peeker as having "enormous fangs" and "just hanging in space outside my second-floor window." The article was mostly tongue in cheek, naturally, but the damage was done. Shit. Just what I needed to muddle a case. I could almost hear what Harry was going to say about this.

I put the paper in my back pocket, and continued up the stairs. I wanted a cigarette again.

When I got to the top, I motioned Borman over. "Go sit on that Toby kid downstairs, will you? I don't want him wandering off. Get his full name, address, all that shit, and see if he'll do a voluntary statement."

"Sure."

"Don't interrogate him, though. Not yet. No specific questions about what's happening here today. Just background data on Edie, and her," I said, indicating Hanna, who was still on the bench in the hall. For the first time I became aware that she was in pajama pants and a sweatshirt, with incongruous six-eyed work boots on her feet, unlaced. *She did get up in a hurry,* I thought. And hasn't been inclined to go back to her room to dress. I noted that because it made what I'd heard quite believable.

"Okay," he said.

"Be firm, but nice."

"Okay, Dad."

"Do we know for sure what his connection is here? He said he lived here. That true?"

Borman nodded. "He's one of the residents here, as far as I know. Long-term house-sitters, as far as I can tell. I found that out from the lady EMT who's talking to Hanna. There are about six of 'em, I guess."

That was why the locals called it the Dropout Dorm. Not school dropouts. It was sort of a matter of pride in Nation County's four high schools that we'd had precisely two dropouts in the last ten years. The "Dropout" came from dropping out of the mainstream. Something I'd always thought to be a harmless idea.

"Six?" More than I'd expected. "So, where's everybody else?"

"Some of 'em have gone to work already. And there's one girl raking leaves in the backyard."

Well, Jesus Christ. "Uh, you want to get her into the house? Keep an eye on her, too. The damned leaves can wait."

"Okay," he said. "Easy."

"And get her to fill out the same forms Toby does. And find out who the others are, okay?"

He started to go by me, and I stopped him. "Hey," I said, lowering my voice, "you happen to know who this Ms. Hunley is?"

"Owns the house," he said. "Lives over north of Chicago, I think. That's what the lady EMT told me."

"North of Chicago" covered a lot of territory. "See if you can get an address."

As he left, I found myself wondering if I were standing in a hotel lobby. Six? Well, the Mansion was easily big enough to hold that many. I just hoped there weren't any more potential witnesses being overlooked because they were outside doing yard work.

SIX

Dr. Henry Zimmer arrived at exactly the same time that the office called and told us that Special Agent Hester Gorse was en route from her residence, and had an ETA of about forty-five minutes. Things were beginning to move, finally.

Doc Zimmer was a large guy, and altogether an exceptional MD. Doctors just don't like being commandeered for medical examiner duty, because it either means that they have to leave their office, or to show up on their day off, or come out in the middle of the night. But Doc Zimmer never, ever complained. He was always cheerful, friendly, and very good at what he did.

We told him who it was, and where. He instantly expressed his condolences to Lamar.

"Lamar, I'm really sorry."

"Thanks, Doc."

"It seems like just yesterday that I delivered her daughter."

"Yeah," said Lamar. He spoke to both of us. "Look, you don't really need me, so I better get over to my sister's for a while."

"Before anybody else tells her?" I asked.

"Nope," said Lamar. "She's the one who told me who it was, this morning. That's why I told the office to send you."

That was a real compliment, coming from Lamar. He was very reluctant to discuss his sister's side of the family with anybody. I felt kind of flattered.

"How's she taking it?" I asked, just to be polite.

"Her? Hell, she's already talking about suing the lady who owns this place. She's just bein' herself."

When he entered the bathroom, Doc Z. just said, "Oh, boy." He snapped on a pair of latex gloves, and started to examine the body, moving very slowly and carefully, and not moving her about much at all. At one point he gently lifted her head, and studied the gaping wound.

"More a stab than a cut." Then, "Seems to be some rigor present in the neck and jaw."

Rigor mortis is a strange thing. It's the phenomenon that causes the muscles to stiffen after death. It starts when the body gets to about room temperature, half an hour to an hour or so after death. The smaller muscles stiffen completely first, the larger muscles lagging a bit behind. It lasts about twelve hours, and then subsides in another twelve or so. At that point, rigor in the neck told us that she'd likely been dead for more than a half hour. Given that I'd first observed her body about an hour before, it was hardly a revelation. But you have to start somewhere.

Doc Z. reached down and lifted Edie's left hand. "Not pronounced in the left elbow...."

Ah. Now we were getting someplace. The fact that she'd not gone rigid in her larger arm muscles suggested that it was probably not more than four or so hours since she'd died. Roughly, of course. "Suggested." You hang around the courts long enough, you start to think like that. Anyway, call it 05:00, or so.

"Doc, what? About five A.M. or so, you think?"

"Make it four to six." He didn't even look up. "The fingers are stiff, the legs seem flexible... Assuming she died in here, at about this temperature...."

"Okay." Four to six. Assuming a constant, or relatively constant ambient temperature. Close enough. Assume room temperature. We *were* in a room, after all. Assume we had no other way to estimate the time of death, yet. Just ballpark.

I helped him rock the body to either side, and then forward a little, so he could see all of her. Lividity was just barely apparent in her buttocks, her elbows, and on the backs of her legs. The gluteal muscles were important, because they're the largest in the body. They would be the last to go completely rigid.

"Shouldn't there be a little more lividity?" I asked. Lividity is the purplish mottling of the skin that occurs when blood settles to the lower parts of a dead body.

"Not if she'd experienced great blood loss," said Doc Z. "And I'd say she has."

"Right." Well, there went my little theory that she'd just bled until her heart stopped.

Doc Z. stood up. "Do you feel certain about the suicide aspects of this?" he asked, sotto voce. "I have some suspicions about the bruises."

I shrugged. "Me, too, but I don't see any real evidence to the contrary. Not unless the bruises were caused at about the same time she died."

"Those are the sort of pronounced bruises I expect to find in the elderly," he said.

"Abuse?"

"That might be consistent, but what I meant was, in the elderly who are being prescribed blood thinners to reduce the possibility of stroke."

"Oh. Well, there's a pillbox out on the vanity. One of those weekly ones. You could check that."

"Good. I suppose you've already noticed that much of the blood seems to be dried from evaporation, as opposed to being clotted."

"Yeah."

"Attaboy," he said with a grin. "The neck cut bothers me, too." Henry moved her head a bit to see the wound again. "No hesitation marks."

"Right."

"I'd feel a lot more comfortable if we had a good forensics specialist up on this one."

"Okay...."

"I'm not comfortable with this one, Carl. No hesitation marks, no sawing motion, just puncture and pull. That's a deep wound. Very deep. I would expect it not only got the jugular, but the carotid as well."

"Sure. Reasonable."

"But if it did, there are no indications of arterial spurts. None."

No, there weren't. A severed jugular would give you a copious flow, to put it mildly. But a flow, nonetheless. If the carotid was cut, you'd get spurts, all right. High-pressure spurts that could splatter on a wall ten feet away. We didn't know, but the cut did look deep, and if the carotid had been cut, there sure as hell should have been spurts at the location of the event. Forensics expert prior to moving her? . . . You bet. Like they say, err on the side of caution.

"I'll see who we can get for a pathologist. We may have to wait until the DCI agent gets here, to order up the forensics and crime scene analysis people, though."

"Fine," said Doc Z. in a matter-of-fact tone. "I'll be a lot happier. Do you have plenty of photos?"

I told him what I'd taken. He had me take several more as he held her head back, and then as he moved her joints to show the progress of the rigor mortis. I noticed that he had to push a bit harder to move her head up and expose the cut. After he released it, it took several seconds for it to drop back into place. Spooky.

"Unless the lab dictates otherwise," said Doc Z., "she can be removed anytime now."

"Okay." We'd call the local funeral home, and have her taken there. That's where the autopsy would be done.

"Uh, Henry, before we get out among 'em, I think you might want to talk to the local ME over in Conception County."

"Alice? Sure. Why?"

"They had a body yesterday. Young fellow, with a really ugly neck wound. Not cause of death, possibly post mortem. Not quite like this . . . but, enough to make me wonder."

Back in the bedroom, Dr. Z. looked at the contents of the pillbox. He pointed to one, a little green pill with a numeral six impressed in it. "Six-milligram Coumadin," he said. "A warfarin sodium pill. This is a really powerful blood thinner," he said. "It requires a course of treatment, but I see that she has dosages in her noon box on Sunday, Monday, and Tuesday. The rest of the week is already consumed."

"What for? Stroke?"

"That, and some post–heart attack treatment. Not likely here. I'll double-check, but I can't imagine why Edie would have needed these."

"But, since she was taking them, that means, well, the bruises?"

"It doesn't take much pressure to bruise someone who is on Coumadin," he said.

"And? . . . Help me out, Doc." I grinned.

"Well, the bruises tell us less. The autopsy will look into the muscle tissues, to see how deep they are."

Nothing, it seems, is ever black or white.

"Certainly would explain the absence of clotting, though," he said.

After we finished up, I really needed a break. I also could have used a cigarette. Nothing like a dead body to make you want to smoke again. There's just something about hanging around a violent death scene like that that really starts to get to you.

Before I could leave the room unattended, I had to seal it. To preserve the evidence. Pretty simple, really, as all you have to do is put sticky vinyl seals on every entry point.

I did the windows, and sealed the door behind me, and did the same with the bedroom door. Before I left, I opened the door to what I'd assumed to be the bedroom closet, just to make sure it wasn't a staircase. It wasn't. I did notice several dresses that I mentally classified as "formal." Really nice fabric. Two caught my eye in particular; one green velvet, one black with beadwork. The first thing that entered my mind was that she had a job as a hostess at a classy restaurant. Would have been a good guess, too, if there had actually been any classy restaurants within a hundred miles.

The rooms sealed, I decided to relax by seeing how Borman was coming with the interviews. I pulled off my latex gloves, put them in an evidence bag, and went downstairs. I should have stayed in the bedroom.

As I got to the bottom of the stairs, I could hear Borman say, "Just fill out the form there, Jack, and don't give me any shit." He sounded exasperated. Swell.

I stuck my head around the corner, into what was a

really period-looking "parlor," the kind you'd see in an old movie where Clifton Webb would be chatting with Jane Wyman. Except here it was Borman arguing with good old Toby.

"Problem?" I asked.

They both spoke at once, the gist being that Toby didn't think Borman had the right to ask him to identify himself. Borman disagreed. I think the tone was set when Toby said, "You ever hear of the Constitution, Mr. Cop?"

I sighed, and reached into my hip pocket, removing my badge and ID case. I opened it, careful to avoid any sort of flourish. "Toby Gottschalk," I said, showing him my credentials, "I'm Carl Houseman, Deputy Sheriff here in Nation County. Since you've already told me who you are, I can't see the problem with you identifying yourself to this officer."

"He wants my date of birth, my address, and my middle name," said Toby. "I don't have to give that. I know a little something about the Constitution."

The problem was, of course, that they were nearly the same age. From my lofty distance of almost thirty-five years their senior, I thought I'd have a bit more luck.

I smiled at Toby. "Never say you know a 'little' about the Constitution. There's always somebody waiting to show you how right you are." I put my badge case back in my pocket. "What you gotta understand, Toby, is that we have to treat any questioned death as a murder unless and until we can prove it's, oh, like a suicide or an accident. Okay?"

He at least had the sense to just nod.

"Cool. Now, since we're sort of constrained by procedure to assume we're dealing with a murder at this point, we have the right to ask you for a variety of personal identifiers."

"I'm sure that's true," said Toby. "Not to piss you off or anything, but I do have the right to refuse."

"Yep," I said. "You do. But then, we may have to do

things that are not to your liking, to discover that information."

"Such as?" Toby looked completely self-possessed.

I was beginning to like Toby as a potential witness. Guts, fairly smart, and didn't have the sense to concede a point. "Such as," I said, moving a little closer, and smiling, "determining your age by cutting off one of your legs, and counting the rings."

He looked a little startled, but finally started to get the point.

"To tell the truth, Toby," I said, as I went by him toward the window, "we'd just have to arrest you as a material witness. Take you to jail. Keep you until we either cleared the case by determining it wasn't a murder, or until you told us the basic things we have to know in order to positively identify you." I looked back at him over my shoulder. "The food in jail sucks, Toby. And there are only three channels on the TV."

"That sounds avoidable," said Toby, more to get back at Borman than to agree with me.

"And while we're talking," I said, "do you know who that is in the yard?" I looked out the window.

He moved toward the window with me. "The girl raking the leaves?"

There was only one person in the huge, manicured yard.

I nodded. "Yep. That's the one." It was difficult to tell what gender, really, as she was wearing navy blue sweatpants, a long-sleeved dark blue hooded sweatshirt, fawn-yellow work gloves, red tennis shoes, and a purple baseball cap. A riot of color, as they say.

"Melissa Corey," he said. "I call her Doom Girl."

I looked down and to my right, into his unwavering gaze. "You do? Why's that?"

"Oh, she's probably the most depressed of any of us here. One of the really convinced 'life sucks' people. You know? One of those."

I chuckled. I couldn't help it. "Yeah, I think I do." I

turned back to Borman. "You haven't managed to get her in for the basic questions?"

Of course he hadn't. He'd been distracted by his little tiff with Toby. Under other circumstances, the laboring Doom Girl could have made a clean getaway. My tone told him that, and a little more.

"I was just about to—"

I cut him off before he could reward Toby by saying that he'd been successfully distracted. "I'll talk with her for a sec. Why don't you just finish up with Toby, here." Besides, it looked so nice out in that yard.

It was. I went out the front door, and around to the south side of the house, to my left. The majority of the leaves that had fallen onto the bright green lawn were intense yellow, translucent when the bright sunlight was behind them. The largest tree was in the middle of a grassy expanse that had to be at least a hundred feet wide, forming a green rectangle around the house. Melissa's wooden rake was making diligent scraping sounds as she methodically herded the leaves into one of a series of yellow piles that showed her progress around the yard. The sunlight was filtering through the leaves, picking up the faint swirls of dust she was stirring up as she worked.

"You're Melissa?" I asked as I approached.

She looked up at me, continuing to rake. She had a pale face, big dark eyes, with purplish-red hair sticking out from under her ball cap, and a piercing with a small cube in her left eyebrow. "And you'd be?" A soft voice.

"Deputy Houseman, Sheriff's Department." I fished out my badge again. She stopped raking, and examined it and the ID card I was displaying. She looked up. Eyes red-rimmed, I noticed. Whether from crying, or from the dust, I couldn't tell.

"So?" She was trying to be blasé, but there was a little hesitation in her tone. She looked to be about twenty-three or twenty-four, I'd guess. I didn't remember seeing her around before.

"What can you tell me about what's happened to Edie?"

"I hear she's dead." She started to rake again.

"You hear right."

"Well, it happens to all of us, now, doesn't it?" Her voice was soft, and my hearing is a little old. Throw in the sounds of her rake, and the crinkling noise of the leaves . . .

"Pardon? I didn't quite get that?"

"It happens to all of us," she said, louder. "All right?" When she got louder, she enunciated harder, as it were. I could see a little, blue metallic stud in her tongue.

She started raking more rapidly, the only real effect being more dust. The leaves were starting to swirl away from her rake as her speed increased.

"Well," I said, "we all do die, all right. But most of us don't bleed to death."

She slapped the rake into the grass. "Fuck!" She took a deep breath, and looked up at me again. "Fuck."

"You got that right."

"So what do you want me to say?" She looked like she could hit me with the rake at any second.

"You could tell what you know."

"You want me to tell you she was my friend? All right, she was my friend. But it doesn't mean anything. It doesn't mean fuck." Her voice was quite calm. But she started to cry. "It just doesn't mean fuck at all. It just doesn't," and she turned her back, shoulders shaking a little.

I just hate that.

I gave her a few seconds, wishing I had something like a Kleenex to offer her, and then said, "Mind coming into the house for a few minutes? I'm afraid I have some routine questions."

She took a deep breath, wiped her eyes and nose with her sweatshirt sleeve, and straightened up. She must have been all of five-one, and didn't make it to my shoulder level.

We both stood there for a few seconds, and I suspect she didn't know just exactly what to say. I know I sure didn't. Finally, she took a deep breath, and let out "Fine."

We walked back to the house together, and I could see Toby watching us from the parlor window.

"You live here?" I asked, more to avoid a prolonged silence than anything else.

"Yes. If you can call it that."

"Great place," I said. "What's the rent like?"

"It's free," she said, nearly monotone. "We're serfs. We just have to take care of the place."

Serfs? We'd reached the front steps. "Don't hear that term much anymore," I said, trying to lighten things up a little. "Not since the unions came in." Melissa didn't say a word.

SEVEN

By the time Special Agent Hester Gorse arrived at the Mansion, Borman and I had done the preliminary interviews of Toby and Melissa. We'd got the standard personal ID stuff, and statements from both of them that they lived in the house, and that they were asleep when Edie's body had been discovered. And, no, she hadn't seemed more depressed or despondent than usual. Toby, it turned out, worked at the local branch of Maitland State Bank, and Melissa worked at the Freiberg Public Library.

I was a bit surprised that Toby could work at the bank, with the stud in the bridge of his nose, and said so.

"I just take it out," he said. "Like pierced ears."

Hanna Prien, still upset, had also talked to us. Generally, she had the same kind of information for us as

Toby and Melissa, except that she'd been the one who found Edie when she went into her room to get her up for work. They both worked in Freiberg: Hanna at the local convenience store, and Edie had been employed at Wilson's Antique Mall.

Hanna said that she had stuck her head in the bathroom door after calling out a couple of times, stared for a few seconds, trying to put together what she was seeing, and then just freaked. Understandable.

There were two other residents of the house, one Kevin Stemmer, and a girl named Holly Finn. Holly, according to Hanna, had the misfortune of having the nickname of "Huck." That rang a bell, and I pictured her in my mind immediately. I'd never arrested her, but she'd been in the area when I'd popped some others. With that nickname, she was hard to misplace. With Kevin I drew a blank, but was pretty sure I'd remember him when I saw him.

According to Hanna, Kevin and Huck had left for work before she'd discovered the body. They were both dealers on the *General Beauregard;* and worked a 06:00-to-14:00 shift. Toby had notified both of them by phone before I arrived. They wouldn't be home until their shift ended.

"Yeah, I called them right away." Toby was one of those people who seem to have to interrupt. "I talked to Huck, though, not Kevin, really. I thought one was enough, and she'd tell Kevin."

Great.

"Toby said they were real upset, though," Hanna said, almost as if she were trying to excuse their not coming right back.

"Oh, yeah. Huck was, anyway," Toby explained. "I didn't talk to Kevin."

I'd asked if the owner was here, and got kind of a surprised look from all three. Jessica Hunley, according to them, lived in Lake Geneva, Wisconsin. She was ex-

ceedingly wealthy, ran a dance school in Chicago, and
only visited the house three or four times a year.

I'm no expert, but I had a bit of a rough time with
"exceedingly wealthy" and "runs a dance school" being
in the same sentence. That needed to be checked further.

We'd released the EMTs, prompting Toby to ask
why they weren't taking the deceased with them. He got
a straight answer. Melissa then asked just how long we
were going to keep the body in the tub before removing
her. I told her that it would depend on when the scene
had been thoroughly processed, but that it shouldn't be
too very long.

It being Saturday, and an urgent call-out to boot,
Iowa DCI Special Agent Hester Gorse was more infor-
mally dressed than usual, in blue jeans, tennis shoes, and
a gray turtleneck, with a blue microweave rain jacket,
worn to conceal the gun on her right hip. I saw her head
through the window as she started up the steps, and was
in time to greet her at the door.

"Hi, Hester. Thought you'd be here sooner."

"Hard to find this place. I must have missed the drive
the first time." She smiled, in sort of a weary way. None
of us get enough weekends off. She'd probably been
counting on this one. "So, Carl," she said as we paused
in the atrium, "just what do we have here, anyway?"

I told her, in about two minutes. Told her that it
could be a homicide. Told her that it looked like a suicide.

"So, are you leaning either way?"

I shrugged. "It doesn't look right. The clothes, or
lack thereof. The wound, although that could be self-
inflicted, God knows." I'd told her what Doc Z. had
said about the arterial spurts and the bruises. And the
Coumadin.

"But we don't know, yet, if there was any major arterial damage caused by the wound?"

"Right."

She smiled again. "So, do I just sign for the free pathologist and lab team, or am I going to have to work today?"

"I feel so transparent," I said, grinning back at her. "No, I'm afraid you're going to have to work on this one." I told her about the body in Wisconsin.

We went into the parlor, and I introduced her around. We left Borman in charge downstairs, and I took Hester up to meet Edie.

Afterward, we compared notes, Hester seated at Edie's vanity, and me leaning against the bathroom door, where I could keep an eye on the door to the hallway.

"You got an extra pen in that camera bag of yours?"

"Sure." I handed her the bag. "Right-hand front pocket, there."

"I want the lab team here," said Hester, peering into my camera bag. "I don't know just exactly what we have here, but we can't wait for them to come up to process the scene until after the autopsy." The lab team had to come from Des Moines, some four to four and a half hours away.

"I'm for it," I said, as brightly as possible. This third visit to the tub had been difficult. "What do you think? Can we move the body out now? I'd like to get her out as soon as practical."

"No problem. I don't think the victim has any more to tell us until the autopsy."

"Good."

She found the pen, and browsed absently through the bag. "You've got just about everything in here, Houseman. Exam gloves, bags, labels, film, batteries, pens, scissors, tweezers..." She unzipped the side pocket, and looked up. "Girl Scout cookies? Are these Girl Scout cookies?"

"Caught me. Want one?"

Hester ate the chocolate mint cookie in two swift bites, and then looked for a place to put her notepad on the vanity.

"Look at the neat stuff."

"Pardon?"

"Her makeup," she said. "Lipstick colors. Interesting. Like these: Tar, Bordeaux, Garnet, Pulsing Blood..."

"Oh."

"With foundation names like Porcelain. And glitter for the eyelids. Little stick-on holograms. Neat stuff."

"You betcha, Hester."

"No, really. This isn't your mother's kind of makeup, chances are. And not the shades and colors that are usually worn around here." She gave me a smug look. "Sort of a gentle rebel, this Edie. Look more closely. She took very good care of all this stuff. It's orderly. Neat. Her appearance was important."

"I caught the neat part right away," I said. "Always makes me feel out of place. Speaking of makeup, you notice her nails? The multicolored thing. Does that mean something?"

"Probably not. Whimsy, I'd think."

"Whimsy. Like with the frilly clothes?"

"You mean the brocades, the lace, the velvet and satins hanging over there?" She gestured toward the walk-in closet.

"Yeah."

Hester smiled. "I'd think she enjoyed being a girl."

"Oh."

She ate one more cookie, then pulled her walkie-talkie out of her pocket and went on to the mobile repeater channel. That was so neat. She was talking to her car radio via a secure channel, which, in turn, transmitted to State Radio repeater towers down to Cedar Falls State Radio, also via secure link, and enabled her to order up the lab team without the media getting wind of it.

Being from the wrong side of the government procurement tracks, I went into the hall, and down the first half flight, where I could see Borman standing in the doorway to the parlor. I caught his attention, and told him to use the residence phone to call our office and get the hearse coming.

I got back to Edie's room, and couldn't see Hester. I looked around the door frame into the bathroom, and saw her checking the contents of the bathroom cabinet.

"Got something?"

She turned. "No, and that's just the problem," she said slowly. "No open shampoo, no open soap, no razor, just blades."

Oh. "Yeah. Doesn't sit right, does it?"

"Like you said, Carl. Where's the stuff you'd use in a tub or shower?"

We'd talked about that during her first pass through the bathroom area. Although it was barely possible that someone would run out of everything currently in use at the same time, it was unlikely as hell. The problem was, there wasn't a really good explanation as to why it was gone.

"I don't get it," said Hester. "Why isn't it here?"

She came toward the door, and I backed out of the doorway to let her pass. "It isn't like somebody would enter her bath and cut her throat in order to gain possession of a used bar of soap and half a bottle of shampoo..."

"Souvenir?" I just tossed that in.

"Right." She shook her head. "First things first. I want to know where that knife came from."

"The kitchen?"

"I'd bet. We couldn't be so lucky as to have it come from anywhere else."

"Right now," I said, "if this case were on a balance scale, I'd have just about a quarter of the weight in the suicide dish."

She sighed, pulling off her latex exam gloves. "Maybe a bit less. We really need that autopsy."

We moved back into the bedroom.

"So," said Hester, "what can you tell me about the group who lives here?"

I explained that they were local, or very close. Marched to a bit of a different drummer than some, but were known to us as pretty decent people. Those I knew were bright. They caused no trouble, which in cop parlance meant a lot.

"Some, like the one they call Huck, just strike me as people who would really like things to be different. But who know they can't make it happen." I considered. "Like, at a party, when some nice person knows that if they join in the conversation, there's going to be an argument. So they sit on the couch, and are pleasant, and pass the dip, and kind of let the flow go around them."

"Like the hippies used to be?"

"This is going to date me," I said, "but they remind me more of beatniks."

"Angry? Intellectually rebellious? Cynical? Depressed?"

"You got it. All the above. Caused by life in general."

Hester smiled. "You sure this isn't a bunch of retired cops?"

When the hearse arrived, it came complete with two attendants. One of them was about seventy, and the other was a small man in his thirties. This meant that Borman, Hester, and I had to glove up again, and help lift Edie's body from the tub. Messy, if you didn't watch your step. We got the chromed portable stretcher up the stairs, noticing how the bend in the stairway at the first landing was going to make this a tough movement on the way down. Once in the bathroom, we tried to position it near the tub and yet not have it be in our way. Not possible. We were going to have to hold Edie up at about chest height while we slid the stretcher under her. Ugh.

Both attendants were gaping at the body, but neither of them said anything.

Rigor mortis raised its ugly head at that point. Borman had squeezed between the tub and the far wall, and he and I had linked hands under her knees and behind her back near her buttocks. Hester had her feet, and the younger attendant tried to slide his hands under her armpits. No go; a bit too stiff now. So he had to hold her left elbow and her head.

"On three . . ." said Hester. "One, two, three."

We started the lift, and it became obvious that Edie was pretty well stiffened in her sitting position. She also seemed to sort of stick to the bottom of the tub. The cold flesh had flattened at the pressure points, and as she came up, I could see that her right breast and chest bore a large dent from her arm and part of the tub. Some blood, strangely, appeared to have pooled under her buttocks, and that was the cause of the sticking when we started to lift. That should not have been there. Not if the fatal wound had been inflicted when she was in the tub. I caught Hester's eye. She gave an almost imperceptible nod. Evidence like that was not to be discussed in front of noninvestigative personnel, civilian or otherwise.

As we placed Edie on the stretcher, we saw that the knife was stuck to her right thigh by the congealed blood. Congealed, but not yet clotted. We took photos, made another note, and then Hester carefully pulled it free. I got a paper bag out of my camera case, and we placed the knife in that.

"Your camera bag reminds me of my purse," she said.

I snapped three shots of the interior of the tub. The blood under where her buttocks had been was very apparent. It even showed a slight wrinkle pattern from the flattened flesh.

Edie couldn't have weighed more than 125 pounds alive, and having lost all that blood volume, she was down to about a hundred or less. The blanched and flattened areas of her buttocks were very obvious, the result of her weight pressing her into the tub. Her mouth, which had been hanging open as she sat there, now looked as if she were about to cough. Interestingly, her eyes no longer had that "alive" appearance that had startled me before. Must have been the light, that first time. Whatever it was, it was a relief.

Now I was able to get a really good look at the wound in her neck. "Deep" hardly did it justice. But it was a cut, all right. Even, smooth edges.

I took several more photos before she was finally covered.

While Borman and the two attendants maneuvered the gurney to get Edie out of the room, Hester and I had one of those fast chats that, if you hadn't known we were talking about the blood in the wrong place, you'd never have guessed.

"You caught that, too?" I asked.

"Yeah."

"Conclusive?"

"Possibly. Very possibly. But maybe not."

"Really?" It looked pretty conclusive to me.

"Reflex lunge or hip thrust."

"Ah." Well, sure, she could have spasmodically arched her back, for example, and then sat back down in the blood she was leaving. Except... "No fountain, though." I said that because there surely should have been secondary evidence that there had been a forceful gush or spurt, or something to deluge the tub area sufficiently for blood to flow under her when she might have moved. Something that very likely would have squirted past the perimeter of the tub, and onto the floor and maybe even the walls. Especially since the knife had been pulled free.

"True." She grimaced. "Not enough data."

"Think it could have slipped free? I'd say pulled out. You agree?" I was referring to the knife.

"Agree. I think it would tend to stay in."

She finished her sentence as we emerged into the hall to help get Edie down the stairs.

We'd zipped up the white body bag, covered the lump that had been Edie with two blue blankets, and strapped her tightly to the stretcher with all three belts. We had to lift her and the stretcher to about shoulder level to clear the banister at the first landing, but from then on it was a piece of cake. We went by the parlor, and the three residents saw her. They followed us out to the hearse, and watched while we pushed the stretcher into the back.

"Remember," cautioned Hester, "there will be an autopsy done there. Under no circumstance is she to be embalmed until we say so. There will be a forensic pathologist up shortly." There had been an instance several years ago when a funeral home had embalmed a murder victim before the pathologist got there. Ever after that, the officer always made very certain that the funeral home understood the situation.

"Yes, ma'am," said the elder of the attendants. He was lucky. Hester hates that term, and if it had been the younger who'd said it, he would likely have had to ride down the hill in the back with Edie.

As the hearse drove off and we turned back in toward the house, I felt this familiar urge. I really wanted a cigarette, and this was the stage in an investigation where I'd normally have one. I looked up toward the porch. The three looked pretty dejected.

Toby spoke up. I was beginning to think he was compelled. He was smoking again.

"Why do you need an autopsy? Isn't it pretty obvious what killed her?"

Hester took that one, while I tried to smoke his cigarette vicariously. "There's a big difference between 'pretty obvious' and certain," she said.

"Why are you coming back into the house? Aren't you done?" There was no malice in Toby or his questions. Just the same sort of question you always heard from the one kid in class who always had his hand in the air. Questions designed to focus attention on the asker, not the subject.

"Ask us again in five or ten hours," I said. "In the meantime, we can't leave the scene unprotected, and the best way to protect it is to have one or more of us here."

"Oh. But, why—"

Hester cut him off. "Done with your written statement yet?"

"Absolutely."

"Then, would you be kind enough to show me just where everybody's bedroom is?"

Toby, being the compulsively cooperative sort, immediately launched into his task. "And the kitchen," she continued, as they headed up the stairs.

In the meantime, I sat down with Melissa and Hanna to have what turned out to be an interesting but pretty fruitless chat about Edie that lasted nearly an hour. Regrettably, they both smoked, as well.

Melissa and Hanna seemed quite a bit more self-possessed than they had appeared even an hour before. A good sign, and I thought it was due to seeing Edie leave, and the relief that seems to come to the household when the body is finally removed from the premises.

We walked into the parlor. Hanna offered coffee, which I accepted. As I sat on the couch, I felt a jab in my hip. The copy of the *Freiberg Tribune and Dispatch* that I'd put in my back pocket. I pulled it out and laid it on the coffee table in front of me. Melissa reached out for it.

"Do you mind? Is it today's?"

"Yep, it is. Feel free."

She sort of browsed through it as we sat and talked. Interesting.

Neither of them could offer much insight into Edie's character, at least not much that I didn't already know from Lamar. She did have a daughter, about three years old, who lived with Edie's mother. Edie didn't like her mother at all, and according to both Melissa and Hanna, with good reason.

Edie had lived, or had been living, at the Mansion longer than any of the rest of them, and she was the one that the owner would talk with if anything needed to be taken care of. According to Melissa, it wasn't anything particularly special, but Edie was a pretty reliable person, and could be counted on to attend to things.

Edie didn't appear to have been noticeably depressed the last few weeks, and hadn't shown any remarkable signs of mood changes. Both acknowledged they had no idea why Edie would take her own life, although they both thought she had plenty of reason to be depressed. Hanna shared the fact that she, herself, had attempted suicide once before, with what turned out to be something less than a fatal overdose of her sister's phenobarbital.

So, my questions about Edie's emotional state had elicited suicide-oriented thinking among others in the household, with the assumption I was on a suicide track. They seemed very sincere in their efforts to help, and almost apologetic that they hadn't observed any of what they termed "suicide triggers." I did think it a little unusual that both of them were that familiar with the subject of suicide. I said as much.

"We've read about it," said Melissa, "because some of our friends have been really depressed sometimes. We worry about them."

"But Edie didn't fit in that category?" I asked.

"No. I mean, there's depressed, and then there's *de-*

pressed," said Melissa. "Things not going right, that can depress you, but it's something you get over. Lover leaving, grandparent dying, that sort of thing. You know. But, the kind of thing where you just have to end it, that's much deeper, and much more prolonged. Oppressive, always there."

"Okay."

"I'm afraid I'm not saying this very well," she said, and looked toward Hanna.

"It feeds on itself," she said, helping Melissa. "It controls you. The suicide kind."

"But Edie didn't show any sign of that?"

She hadn't, and according to them, Edie really seemed to have her life under control. They were both sorry they hadn't been more help.

What they'd actually done was to inadvertently add another bit of weight to the side of the scales that was labeled "murder."

"So, then," I said, "let's just say for the sake of it that it wasn't a suicide. Do either of you know of anybody who might be, say, an enemy; that would want to kill Edie?"

Absolutely not. They were both in complete and emphatic agreement on that point.

I persevered. "Anybody threaten her? Been bothering her? Harassing her?"

"Just her lame excuse for a mother," said Melissa. "That's been happening for years, I guess. Not new. Why? Do you really think she didn't commit suicide?"

I shrugged. "We have to treat every unattended death as a homicide, until we're sure it isn't."

"Sure," said Melissa.

"Okay," I said, "now, I don't want you to take this in the wrong way at all. But I'd like to know if either of you could tell me if Edie was doing any dope, or alcohol, or anything even prescription, that could affect her moods."

"Is that really your business?" asked Melissa. "Not to be taken in the wrong way, of course."

"Fair question," I said. "The answer is, probably wasn't my business yesterday. Now that she's dead, and my problem for now, yep, it is."

"Aren't you going to do a blood test? I mean, won't you know from that?"

"Sure. But it won't be back for a few days, and when it arrives, it only gives the chemical information, not the substance. You know... it might say acetaminophen, but not a brand name. So if she took Tylenol for a headache, say, it would be a help to know that. That sort of thing." I was also fishing for a known substance, although I didn't say that. A blood scan for everything cost a fortune, and took forever. You had to give them parameters.

"Oh," said Hanna. "Oh, sure. Well, I know she'd drink a beer now and then, maybe some wine. No dope...?" and she looked at Melissa.

It was hard not to grin.

"She smoked clove cigarettes," said Melissa quickly. "That's it."

"Okay," I said, making a note.

"You do know what those are?" Melissa wasn't being insulting, she was just a sincere twenty-something talking to a fifty-something. Usually, the only people my age she'd be likely to know were her parents, aunts, and uncles.

I smiled. "Either of your parents cops?"

"What?"

"I strongly suspect that your folks and I have vastly different, oh... What? Life experiences?"

"My father's a minister and my mother is a music teacher." She paused as it dawned on her. "Oh." A small smile started forming on her lips.

"Right. I think we definitely move in different circles."

The small smile grew larger, into a full-fledged one. "I'd say so."

"And the real point's this: If she did occasional dope here, that's something we have to know. If there's a fair concentration in her fluids, and she did it here, that's one thing. If there's the same concentration and she didn't do it here, that's another thing altogether."

Both the young women looked away from me as soon as I said that. I attributed it to the fact that there was probably at least some dope in the house, even as we spoke.

The phone in the hallway rang, and Hanna answered it. It was for me. As I left the room, I could hear both young women talking to each other in low tones. My best guess was that they were discussing narcotics.

I answered the phone. "Houseman."

"Hey, no kidding?" Sally, at the office.

"Yeah. What's up?"

"There was a man here, came to talk with Lamar. Lamar said for you to talk with him instead, because he was going to have some family things to attend to."

"Sure, okay." Great. Not that I didn't understand, but I really didn't need the distractions, either. Ah, well. I could never say that Lamar didn't delegate.

"Man's name is"—she paused just an instant, so that I knew she was reading from her notes—"William Chester, from Milwaukee."

My first thought was a pathologist that Harry had contacted regarding the death of Randy Baumhagen, late boyfriend of Alicia Meyer. "What does he do? Or want?"

"Beats me. He looks pretty straight arrow, though. About forty, but that's not all bad. Nice eyes. Slender. Still has all his hair. . . ."

"That's not quite what I wanted."

She laughed. "I don't know. Not an attorney, that's for sure. I asked Lamar that, 'cause I knew you'd just shit—pardon the expression—if we sent somebody like an attorney up there."

"You sent him here?"

"Well, to Freiberg. He'll get hold of Byng or somebody, and connect up with you later on. Not at the Mansion, though."

"Okay." That was a relief. "Anything else?"

"Nope. Lamar just said to let you know. He's over at his sister's, I think."

"Yeah."

"Oh, and guess what?"

I was too tired to play. "Tell me."

"I'm assigned to duty as a reserve tonight, up there! Isn't that just so cool?"

I grinned to myself. "It's cool. Just remember to bring cookies."

At that point, Hester and Toby came back. Hester was holding a legal pad, making the final touches to a diagram of the second floor. She handed it to me. According to her diagram, Edie's room was the first one at the top of the stairs, on the right. The northeast corner. The next room on her side of the hall was Toby's; the room after that was Hanna's. Across the hall from Edie was Melissa in the southeast corner, then Holly, known as Huck, and then Kevin.

"They're all about the same," she said. "Basically thirty-six-foot by eighteen-foot rooms, with a dividing wall for the individual bathrooms at about ten feet from the end."

Like I said, it was a big house. Over a hundred feet long, and about forty-five feet wide.

Hester handed me the pink copy of the "Seized Property" form, listing the knife from the tub. "It's from a set in the kitchen," she said. "No doubt at all."

As they sat down, Melissa handed the copy of the *Freiberg Tribune and Dispatch* to Toby. "Seen this?"

Toby looked a bit surprised, said he hadn't, and

opened it up. He looked up at Melissa, rather startled. "That's freaky," he said, mostly to her.

I was curious. "What?"

"The bit about Dracula," he said. "Just floating outside the second-floor window, I mean. Wow."

"I'm sure he had help," I said.

Melissa joined in. "In what way?"

"Oh," I said conversationally, "I'd think a rope, for example." I forced a chuckle. "He wasn't flying."

"Did you, you know, find a rope?" Her large eyes were very steady on mine.

"No, but we found ringbolts." I shrugged. "It's just a matter of the mechanics of the thing."

"I'm sure you'll find an explanation," said Melissa.

Hanna suddenly apologized for being a bad hostess, and asked if anyone else wanted coffee. We all did. We spent the next half hour discussing suicide, death, and how friends should deal with it. To me, it seemed that Hanna was by far the most affected by Edie's death. While she was telling Hester just how she'd found the body, I started to think about the possibilities we had. Somehow, it seemed to me that it just damned well shouldn't be this hard to determine the cause and method of death. What had we missed?

Hester interjected a new item. "Did you know the whole third floor is sealed off?"

"No."

"Yes. It's the owner's private apartment, and nobody can go there unless she's here. According to Toby, here." She shrugged. "The doors to that floor are both locked, anyway. Keyed. New."

"That's right," said Melissa. "We just never go up there unless Jessica's here."

Hester looked up toward the ceiling. "Must be a pretty damned big apartment."

The whole third floor would be about four thousand square feet. I could only agree.

There's a rule of thumb in homicide investigations, whereby you either solve the murder in the first forty-eight hours, or the investigation will drag on for months before an arrest is made, if ever.

It was beginning to look like we'd be lucky to know whether or not this was even a suicide in forty-eight hours.

Then some people arrived who would irrevocably tip the scales.

EIGHT

I could see, through the glazed entrance, three vehicles pulling up to the front of the house. One of our
marked squads, being followed closely by a dark blue
SUV that just had to belong to my favorite forensic
pathologist, Dr. Steven Peters. Third in line was an older,
silver-gray Plymouth Voyager. That one I didn't recognize.

Since it was officially my crime scene, I went to the
door with Hester, while Borman stayed with the three
residents in the parlor. Although they were far from suspects at this point, it was always a good idea to have
somebody about to gauge reactions, and to prevent any
lengthy conversations. Just in case.

Our squad had turned around, and the driver,
Deputy Norm Jones, lowered his window and stuck out

his head. "These guys live here." He indicated the Voyager.

"Right!" I looked at Hester. "Must be our residents who work on the boat."

"Good."

"Thanks, Norm," I said. He waved, and headed back down the lane. That was one thing about this location: It was nice and easy to seal the place off and keep anybody but the invited out.

I turned back toward the SUV, as Dr. Peters emerged. He shook hands with Hester and myself. "Two of my favorite officers," he said, "who always manage to throw a challenge my way."

"This one," I said, "may take the cake."

He glanced around. "Marvelous place here. I never knew it even existed." Dr. Peters was from Iowa City, about a hundred miles south of us.

"Don't feel bad," I said. "There are some people who live in this county who don't know of the place." I saw the two occupants of the older car heading toward the house. " 'Scuse me a sec, Doc," I said.

I quickly introduced myself to the male and female who were headed up the steps into the house.

"Excuse me," I said. They stopped at the foot of the steps. They were both rather pale complected, and wore their gaming boat uniforms: white frilled shirts, black slacks, black bow ties, black suspenders, black shoes. They were carrying their black jackets. They looked like a mime act. "I'm Deputy Houseman, and I have to talk with you for a few seconds, before you go in."

The male was about six feet, slender, with black hair. He had a hole in his earlobe and one in his nostril. Took the jewelry off for work, apparently. The female was about five feet eight, and thin. Dark brown hair pulled back tightly, with ears pierced on the upper curve as well as the lobe. Her jewelry was in place. She, too, had large, dark eyes. Her high cheekbones both had some sort of tattoo, in an exceptionally delicate swirling pattern. I suspected they were temporaries, because they didn't look thick enough to be real.

"Do you have some identification?" the male asked.

For some reason, lots of people seem to think that asking you to produce some form of ID is going to put you on the defensive.

I opened my badge case, and held it wide for them to see, as if the gun on my hip hadn't told them everything they'd wanted to know. "Sure, here. There's an ongoing investigation inside right now. I'm afraid there's one room that's been closed off for the time being."

"Edie's, I assume," he said.

"Yep."

"Well, I wasn't going up there, anyway."

"And," I added, before they could move, "we're going to have some routine questions for you, as well."

"About?" The female. Abrupt. It was time to break the ice.

"You're Holly Finn, aren't you? The one they call 'Huck'?"

That seemed to surprise her. Using nicknames will do that when people haven't told you what they are. It implies you know more about them than you really do.

"Holly's right," she said. "But you might as well call me Huck. Everybody else does."

"Sure," I said. Then I looked at him. "Stemmer, isn't it? Kevin Stemmer?" Just as if I'd actually recognized him.

"Yes," he said.

"You're both aware, I take it, of the, ah, event this morning?" I had to ask, because I certainly didn't want either of them just walking in, maybe thinking Edie was sick or something, and finding out that she was dead. Just to be sure.

"We know," she said. "Terrible, but not unexpected. At least," she added, "not by those of us who knew her best."

Knew her best? Didn't go too far in explaining why

they hadn't just rushed home, but I was willing to bet that she didn't have any idea that Toby and Hanna had been so talkative.

"A bad thing," added Kevin. "But death comes to us all."

Well, sure. But it was the second time I'd heard that kind of sentiment that day, and both times it seemed to be designed to minimize Edie's death, not to deal with it. Not so much of a philosophy, but more like a dodge, really. It irritated me just a bit.

"It's the ones death sneaks up on that I feel for," I said. "I hate surprises, myself."

Hester and Dr. Peters passed by, going on into the house. "Join us as soon as you can?" I saw that Hester had retrieved her laptop from her car. She and Dr. Peters were both carrying black cases as they entered the house.

"You bet." I looked back at the two gaming boat employees. "If you two will just check in with Deputy Borman in the parlor...he'll need some information from you, just as soon as you're ready..."

"I'd really like," said Huck, "to use the bathroom, upstairs. If that's all right." A little sarcasm crept in there. I really couldn't blame her. She did live here, after all.

"Oh, that's just fine," I said, advancing past them up the steps, and holding open the door for them. "Just don't go into Edie's room until we're finished, okay?"

"Of course," said Kevin. Sarcasm again. "Like I said, it's not the first place I'd normally go."

"So," I continued, "just check in with Deputy Borman, and be available in a while."

They turned off into the parlor. I watched the reactions of the other residents. Kevin and Huck got sort of deferential treatment. Toby, especially, seemed not so much glad as relieved to see them back.

I went on upstairs, to Edie's room. I thought we'd just pretty well established the pecking order in the Mansion.

Dr. Peters and Hester were talking in low tones as I got to Edie's room. Dr. Peters gestured toward the bathroom. "My."

"Yeah," I said. I really wasn't looking forward to another complete tour of that place.

"I told him about our little discovery of blood under her butt," said Hester. "And the Conception County incident."

Dr. Peters nodded. "Not conclusive in and of itself. I really think we might need the lab team to give us a thorough workup here," he said. "And I'll talk to my opposite number in Wisconsin as soon as I finish up with the autopsy."

"Agreed," said Hester.

"So Carl," said Dr. Peters, "you have some prelim stuff on a digital camera?"

I did. Hester opened her laptop case. "JPEGs?"

"Yep," I replied. "Standard format. You got a USB port?"

She did, and I produced a USB cable. Plugged one end into the digital camera, the other into her laptop, and in a few seconds, we had photos of Edie in the tub.

The three of us peered at the laptop LCD screen for a few minutes, moving back and forth between the establishing shots and the close-ups of the wound. Not the resolution I'd get either at home or at the office, but good enough for our purposes. Very good, if you considered the fact that we usually had to wait three days to get film developed.

Dr. Peters stepped back from the laptop. "And you have the weapon?"

Hester snapped on a pair of latex gloves, retrieved the knife, and showed it to him by holding it up by the very tip of the blade. He stared at it for several seconds, and she slowly turned it, letting him see all aspects of it.

"Thanks, Hester," he said. She put it back in the paper bag. You always use paper bags on anything that has biological material on it. Allows it to breathe, to dry out, as opposed to decomposing and rotting in the airtight seal of plastic. "Can you enlarge the shots of the cut?"

Hester removed her gloves, and went to her laptop. "You have a bunch of gloves, Carl? I've got maybe one pair left."

I indicated my camera bag. "Oh, yeah."

She smiled, and began fiddling with the laptop. "I can enlarge it a hundred and fifty percent," she said, "but then we start to lose so much detail. . . ."

Dr. Peters bent down, peering at the screen again. "That's fine," he said, straightening up. He took a deep breath, and let it out slowly. Then silence. "And the shots of her backside, please?"

No problem. He looked at them, and the shots of the bottom of the tub. Silence again.

Hester and I exchanged glances. We waited a few more seconds, but Dr. Peters said nothing. Then, just as I was about to ask, he spoke.

"I'm not sure, and I want you to take what I say with a precautionary grain of salt," he said. "But I want to be on the safe side on this." He let his eye roam about the room, and he noticed the "Absinthe Makes the Heart Grow Fonder" embroidery on the wall. A smile flickered over his face.

He got quiet on us again. Then, after what seemed an interminable time, he said, "We want the area gone over very thoroughly." He looked back toward the bathroom. "Very thoroughly. I don't think we have a suicide here. The postmortem will tell me what I really need, but I don't think she died from a self-inflicted wound."

Ah. It was out.

"And," he went on, "judging from the photos of the wound, I don't believe you have the right knife there."

"It was stuck to her leg," I said, speaking just a half second before the real meaning dawned on me.

"I have no doubt of that," said Dr. Peters, smiling, "but I don't think it was the one used on her neck. From the protruding muscle, I would expect it to be shaped more like a gutting knife, with a hooked point. The muscle in her neck was pulled from the wound, I should think, not forced out from the inside."

"Okay," I said.

"And, I should expect to find some arterial damage," he said. "The external carotid, or a branch. Largish artery, at any rate."

I should know by now never to question Dr. Peters, even obliquely. Not that he has ever shown the slightest resentment. On the contrary, he's more often amused than anything else, and always very comfortable with explaining things.

"Ah," I said, sagely, "I wonder, I mean, ah, there's no indication of any arterial spurts in there. Anywhere in there." I even pointed toward the bathroom. Well, like they say, every village needs an idiot.

He grinned. "I noticed that, too. Like I say, let me post her, but at this point I really doubt she died in the bathroom," said Dr. Peters. "I'd like to get a good blood-spatter expert lined up." He addressed Hester. "Who are you people using these days? Still Barnes?"

"Last time I checked," she said.

"Good," he said. "We have a classic hair-swipe pattern on the left tub wall... really shouldn't be there, since her head should never have been down there... unless she was thrashing around a lot, and then we should have more than one...."

It had officially become a homicide investigation.

I drew the autopsy assignment, because I was "just so damned good with a camera," according to Hester, who was at least as good with a camera, but who didn't want to go. She got the interviews with Kevin and Huck, and the reinterviews with Hanna and Melissa and Toby. I'm not sure I got such a bad deal.

NINE

Supper right after an autopsy can be an interesting experience. Not for Dr. Peters, because it was what he did every day, but I was avoiding beef and pork at the buffet. And pasta.

The lab team had arrived, and was processing the scene. Lamar was sending up two reserve officers, relief for Borman and me, although I'd be going back after we ate. Borman was staying at the residence until the other deputies arrived. I hoped he didn't start a war.

Hester, Dr. Peters, and I had decided to dine at Warren's, a halfway decent place that wasn't too expensive. It was also fairly quiet, and we could talk a bit without being overheard by anybody but the waitress.

Hester told us that the interviews hadn't produced much of anything. The suggestion that the death might not have been suicide produced strong denials but nothing more. She also observed that Kevin and Huck were the strong personalities, with Melissa a close second.

"The difference," said Hester, "is that Melissa has no followers, while Kevin and Huck do."

She also thought that Toby was a real easy pick. "That kid," she said, "will do almost anything to get your attention. Talks much more than anybody else up there."

I could only agree.

Hester also said that she'd also been told that Edie had apparently been the "housemother" of the establishment, and seemed to pretty well have been the most stable and solid. "She was the one who talked most with this Jessica Hunley, the owner. Seems to have known her the longest, anyway." She shrugged. "I think she was also sort of counselor-in-residence, so to speak. That's the impression I got. Mostly from Toby, Melissa, and Hanna, though. Not the other two."

The autopsy had been very interesting. First of all, Dr. Peters had established conclusively that the wound in Edie's neck had, indeed, damaged the external carotid artery. Not to mention the jugular vein, numerous muscles, and sliced into the posterior wall of the trachea, and left a cut in the fourth cervical vertebra to boot. The fascinating part was that there were multiple cuts *inside* the neck wound. I'd asked. It meant that the knife had "probably been thrust into the neck, Carl, and then worked back and forth as well as part way in and out, until it was pulled out, carrying some muscle with it."

We'd just shared that with Hester.

"Ah. Then . . . ?"

"Then," said Dr. Peters, "I would expect that a self-inflicted wound of that type would have the sawing motion we all know, but there wasn't conspicuous evidence of the sawing motion; more like short, strong thrusts without actually pulling the blade all the way out. Inside, like that, would require too much strength, because the angle is wrong for a self-inflicted wound. I'd bet strongly on a second party wielding the knife."

"But could it possibly be a suicide?"

"Probably wouldn't have pulled it out after all that," said Dr. Peters. "The self-inflicted neck wounds I've seen, if there is deep penetration, tend to expire without pulling the knife out." He took a bite of his roast beef. "The pain would be excruciating, I should think. Even in a highly agitated mental state."

"Not conclusive," I said, "but narrows the parameters?"

"Exactly. The conclusive part, Carl, is the absolute lack of arterial spurts in the bathroom area. The carotid cut itself would have produced splashes on a wall several feet from the wound. Several pulses, and with obvious trajectories."

"Yeah."

"And, I'm bothered by the nick in the trachea. There should have been aspirated blood. There wasn't. I would say," said Dr. Peters, "at least some of the physical evidence suggests her throat had been cut elsewhere, and she was transported from that location to where she was discovered in her tub."

Well, well.

I took a drink of coffee while he continued to explain the autopsy to Hester.

"When we washed the blood off the exterior," he said, "there was some considerable early bruising around her hips and shoulders, as well as her upper arms and thighs and calves."

"Blows?" asked Hester.

"No, I think not. When we cut into them, some were deep, some were more surface bruises, but there was no obvious tissue damage. I'd expect to find she was, indeed, on a course of Coumadin, and we have the commensurate easy bruising involved. But, of course, with a large blood loss, they may not have presented as well as you'd expect." He thought for a second. "The ones we're interested in, as far as being inflicted near the time of death, though, were broad, with considerable pressure, but no well-defined edges. I'd say some sort of restraint...handgrip marks. But, it occurs to me that, perhaps, something nontraditional was used, too. Something that wouldn't leave striations like cloth or rope. Look for something in that line. Or, maybe not, and it's just that she was in contact with a very uneven and unyielding surface. If so, it was while she was bleeding to death, so there should be significant blood wherever it was." He took a sip of water. "But there was no bruising on the right breast, or on the rib cage adjacent. That pressure was post mortem."

"We're looking for lots of blood evidence, then?" Hester was jotting down notes.

"Somewhere," said Dr. Peters. "All things being equal, and the lab work not being back yet, the evidence suggests she was killed somewhere else, and then placed in her tub, and that her throat was cut in an attempt to make it look self-inflicted." He nodded. "And you're absolutely right. Lots of blood. There was a large blood loss, somewhere. But don't let me mislead you. There are things I have to do yet."

"Homicide?"

"Undoubtedly."

Cool. Now all we had to do was find the location. Well, find a location, place somebody else there, and figure out why. But a location would be a good start.

"That much blood," he said, "even with determined cleanup, there will be trace evidence."

"I'd better call Lamar, and then the county attorney," I said. "They'll both need to know."

I used the phone in the manager's little closet of an office. As I dialed, it occurred to me that, at least this far, we'd managed the media in a pretty cagey way. Anybody listening on a scanner would have heard only the page for the ambulance, Borman simply being told to go there, and him arriving. I never said where I was. Hester had been notified at home, and had called in to State Radio via her cell phone. Dr. Peters had been notified by phone, as had the lab team. Code sixty-one procedure seemed to be working.

Good security, plus the media hardly ever paid attention to suicides, anyway, unless they were either prominent people, or could embarrass prominent people. Edie was pretty much a nobody, bless her. She and her Uncle Lamar didn't even have the same last name.

Homicide had never been mentioned. Well, not till now.

———————————————

I called Lamar first, both because he was my boss, and because I thought he just should know before anybody else.

He answered the phone. "Ridgeway."

I liked that. "Hey, Lamar, it's Houseman."

"It's not a suicide, is it?"

"Jesus, Lamar, are you psychic?"

There was what I can only describe as a moment of satisfied silence at the other end. "Just hoped, I guess," he said. "I didn't want to think I might have let her down. . . ."

Yeah. With suicides, there's always that aspect. "No, not according to Dr. Peters. He wants to wait for the final lab tests, but he says he's sure enough that it wasn't self-inflicted and that we should start treating it as a murder investigation."

"Okay," said Lamar. "You do what you need to."

"Right."

"Want me to keep it quiet with my sister?"

"Maybe for a while, Lamar. Let the lab stuff come back. Or, at least hedge."

"Do what I can." There was a slight pause. "Any suspects?"

"Not really, Lamar. None so far."

"I'll see what I can do, too, but I can't be directly involved. You understand?"

I sure did. A defense attorney would love to have the head of the investigation be the grieving uncle. Absolutely guaranteed a change of venue, too.

"Yep. I'm about to call the county attorney now."

"Good. Keep in touch, Carl, and thanks. OH!"

"What?"

"I almost forgot. There was a guy wanted to talk to me. I told the office to give him to you. Sorry. Not sure what he wants. From Wisconsin."

"Right. Sally already told me. Okay." I could see him tomorrow. "You going to be tied up with family stuff very long?"

"Another day or two."

"How's it going?"

He cleared his throat. "You know my sister...." He hesitated. "You think it'll be all right if I do the interview on her? Just to get the background stuff?"

I sure didn't know anybody else who would. "That's fine," I said.

The county attorney was a decent lawyer named Mike Dittman. As with most county attorneys in Iowa, it was a part-time job, with the vast majority of his income coming from private practice. As I dialed his number, it occurred to me that this was October, and that he would be preparing for income tax time. Lots of his clients retained him to do their taxes and their estates. This was approaching his busiest time of year in his private practice.

"Dittmans'," said a pleasant, woman's voice. His wife, Karen.

"Hi, Karen, it's Houseman." I called there often enough that she knew just who it was as soon as I spoke.

"Oh, hello, Carl. Just a sec." I could hear a muffled "Mike! Mike, it's for you," as she covered the phone.

After a second or two, Mike answered. "Hello?" I could hear the click as she hung up the other phone.

"Mike, it's Houseman."

"Oh, shit," he said, only half kidding. "What's up?"

"We had a suicide call this morning. Lamar's niece, Edie Younger, remember her?"

"Oh, sure. Oh, that's too bad. She was getting her act together pretty well, wasn't she?"

"I think so. There's a complication, and we're probably going to need some legal advice."

Silence.

"Dr. Peters is here. His preliminary finding is that it looks like murder."

"Oh, crap. Oh, boy. Uh, Carl, it's my sister-in-law's birthday today, and we're just heading to Dubuque...."

"Okay," I said. "Just wanted you to know, and let you know we're going to need to search the whole house. I think we have enough to justify a warranted search."

"Which 'whole house' are you talking about, Carl?"

I told him about the location, and the other residents. I also told him that the owner wasn't there.

"Look, why don't you just go with a consent search, for now, if you can. I mean, I trust your work, but I'd be happier if you could go that route for now."

I was positive I could get a search warrant application done well enough to stand any challenge, but I also knew that he was going to have to defend it if anything went wrong.

"Okay, Mike. But I just hate to do the consent searches, you know. I mean, if they deny permission, then we have to sit on everything and do a rush application. And in this one, any of the five can say 'no' to a request."

"No," he said, "go for a consent search. Any of them can consent to the common areas of the home. Individuals can only deny access to their own rooms."

I knew him well enough to stop arguing. But I was

disgusted. There are a multitude of ways to get the results of a consent search tossed out of court, and the resulting evidence right along with them. In a really serious case, there is absolutely no substitute for a warranted search issued from the district court. Besides, consent was the lazy way. The way you'd proceed if you wanted to go to your sister-in-law's party in Dubuque.

Hester could sense something amiss as I sat down. "What?"

"Mike wants us to go with a half-assed consent search," I said.

"That's no good, unless we're really lucky."

"Tell me." I shrugged. "I'm thinking in terms of a search warrant application, anyway."

"Will the county attorney be up?"

"No, he's going to a party in Dubuque." We both smiled at the same time. This was going to be a really fast case of "Do you mind if we search this property that is under your control?" I figured we could have an application in two or three hours, max, and be back in the house within four. If . . .

"Dr. Peters?"

"Yes?" He knew what was coming.

"We might need some preliminary notes, before you leave . . ."

Just then, this strange dude walked up to our table. He was dressed plainly, in olive slacks and a flannel shirt. I didn't know him from Adam, and it didn't appear that either Hester or Dr. Peters did, either.

"Excuse me," he said politely. "Would any of you be Deputy Houseman?"

"I would. And you are . . . ?"

"William Chester. I spoke with your sheriff earlier today, very briefly. May I have a minute of your time?" He handed me a business card, which proclaimed him to be William Francis Chester, MA, of Milwaukee, Wisconsin. Along with his post office box, phone number,

and e-mail address was the title Anthropologist &
Bioarchaeologist.

Well, at least he wasn't either press or an attorney. I
fished out one of my cards, and handed it back. "Yeah.
The office said you'd be up this way." And I had totally
forgotten he was coming.

As I spoke, he pulled up a chair and sat. "I'll just
take a moment of your time, for now," he said. "I understand you've had a possible vampire sighting here."

I looked at Hester, and she avoided my gaze, obviously enjoying my plight. There's something about being
public servants that makes us relish coworkers having to
deal with loonies.

"No, we haven't," I said firmly.

"According to the local paper . . ."

I cut him off. "It's a window peeker. That's all there
is to it. Nothing more."

"I see." He looked at Hester and Dr. Peters for any
sign of support. Two more deadpan expressions were
never seen. "Your sheriff said that . . ."

Right. Lamar. "That's okay, he might have been a little unclear. He, oh, lost a relative today." I didn't want
to be rude; I just wanted to be rid of him. "Sorry I
couldn't be more help."

"I hunt them, you know," he said, looking at me.
"I've been hunting one in particular for a very long time.
I think this could be that one."

"Hold it right there," I said. "I'll say this one time.
Just one. Do not hunt anything in this county that does
not require a hunting license. Am I clear? If you interfere
in any way with any investigation you'll be wearing orange and eating shitty food for several months." I stared
at him. "I promise."

"Oh, I believe you," he said with a slight smile.
"Completely. But being so sensitive sort of gives the
game away, doesn't it? Now I'm even more inclined to
believe that you do have a vampire incident here."

People can be pretty exasperating sometimes. It did

occur to me, rather belatedly, that he might have something that Harry could use regarding the death of Randy Baumhagen. Might. It was connected to our case, after all, and that was what had brought our vampire hunter to us in the first place. All the way from Milwaukee, for God's sake.

"Well, just a second," I said. "I know vampires don't exist, but we might have somebody who dresses up like one. Thing is, he might be involved in a case back on the Wisconsin side. Do you have a name to go with whoever you're hunting?"

"No. No, I don't. Just methods, habits. No name. Not yet."

"What methods?"

"Well, he appears at a door or window. Asks to come in. If he's invited, he enters, and begins the seduction of his victim."

"And, then, if he's not invited in? What, does he just stay out?"

"Oh, yes. Vampires can't come in unless they're invited." He was serious.

Hester just couldn't resist. "What does he do to them?"

"He eventually consumes some of their blood."

"Well, of course." I kept a straight face. It was a vampire, after all. What did I expect?

"He experiences what they experience, when he does that. He shares with them. They tell me it's very intimate." William Chester looked at us each in turn. "It's the pheromones. He ingests their pheromones and experiences what they feel."

Dr. Peters snorted. "No. No, I'm afraid that doesn't work."

"You laymen must understand..." began William Chester.

"I'm a forensic pathologist," said Dr. Peters.

Silence. Then the vampire hunter fished in his breast

pocket and handed Dr. Peters his card. "Then you may well need this," he said, with remarkable aplomb.

Dr. Peters, to his credit, accepted it with good grace, and put it in his pocket.

"Look," I said, "they have a case back across the river in Conception County. You might be able to give them a hand with that. Not that it's a vampire," I said quickly. "But check in with Investigator Harry Ullman. Tell him Deputy Houseman sent you. Tell him I think you might have something he could be interested in." I didn't tell him to have Harry call me. Harry was going to do that, without a doubt.

"Excellent. I do have quite a depth of knowledge on the subject, by the way. I know how to... well, track them. Follow, if that's a better word."

"Stalking is a crime," I said. "People are pretty sensitive about that."

"Thank you." He stood. "If I develop anything, I'll be in touch."

"Anytime."

I watched him leave. Hester kicked me under the table. "Way to go, Houseman."

"What?"

"Harry's gonna kill you."

"Not if I can point him at Lamar first," I said.

"Aren't you going to call him?"

I chuckled and shook my head. "Nope. Some packages are best left unannounced." I looked over at Dr. Peters. "You sure shut him up when you told him you were a forensic pathologist," I said.

"It stops lots of conversations," said my favorite ME. "Trust me."

It was totally dark when we got back to the Mansion. I grabbed a bunch of "Permission to Search" forms from the briefcase in my trunk before walking back up the steps to the huge house. Hester had preceded me, and was on her way to talk with the three lab techs up in Edie's room.

I found the group in the kitchen, with my favorite dispatcher, Sally, doing guard duty. She had joined the Sheriff's Reserve about six months back, and was in full sheriff's department uniform, including handgun and cuffs.

"Hey, Sally! Lookin' good, there."

"Houseman," she said, with her mouth full, "you missed a great meal!" She swallowed. "I didn't know you guys got to eat like this."

The long table in the kitchen was set with rustic sorts of dishes, with the remains of a big tossed salad, the remaining third of a big bread loaf, a large glass dish with some sort of casserole, and a big glass pitcher of tea.

"You're catching on really fast, there, kid," I said. Sally, being about five feet tall, and weighing in at all of a hundred pounds with her red hair wet, could afford to eat. "Everybody behave while we were gone?"

Sally nodded, and Holly Finn said, "We wouldn't want to argue with Annie Oakley, here." She said it pleasantly enough, but there was a mocking tone about the statement, as well.

"You got that right, Huckleberry," said Sally. Touché.

I got the impression they didn't like each other.

Hanna was standing at the cupboards, removing coffee cups, and Toby was just setting a pie down on the table. Everybody else was seated. Everybody together. The timing seemed good to me.

"Well, as long as you're all here," I said, "I'm going to officially request your permission to search this house."

Verbal pandemonium. Something like, "No way," from Huck, "Not likely," from Kevin, "Sure," from

Toby, "Well," from Hanna, and all at the same time. Melissa, having been drinking tea at the very moment I asked, got in her reply in the pause that followed the initial outburst.

She swallowed. "Why?" The only sensible response in the lot.

"Be glad to tell you," I said. "Is there any coffee still in the pot?"

Hanna got busy, pouring me a cup. Genuinely nice, I thought. She did seem to be the one hardest hit by Edie's death, as well.

I made them wait a few seconds, as I took the proffered cup from Hanna, and laid my "Permission to Search" forms on the counter. This was one of those little semi-crucial moments in an investigation that just won't happen twice.

Toby stood perfectly still, halfway between the table and the counter, the pie in his hands, staring. I certainly had his attention.

"We have strong indications that Edie didn't commit suicide," I said. "Several." I paused, and nobody seemed to breathe. "We're now in the preliminary stages of a murder investigation."

I was really expecting surprise, at least on the part of most of them, and probably an argument that a murder was impossible, or at least way out of the question. I expected that.

What I didn't expect was Toby tossing the whole pie on the kitchen counter, saying something about "I gotta go," and disappearing out through the screen door into the dark night. To be fair, I don't think anybody else expected that, either.

TEN

We had to get him, and we'd be one hell of a lot better off if we got him soon. I headed out the door and just hollered "Stay here" to Sally as I passed. I didn't want any more people splitting on us. By the time I got out the door, there was nothing to see but the blackness surrounding the small area lit by the light from the Mansion's windows. Black ground, black grass, black trees, and a black sky speckled with stars. I thought I heard some movement off to my left, but since I didn't have a flashlight with me, I'd never know what it was. Then silence. Shit.

I could hear Hester's voice, Sally's voice, and then the screen door opened behind me, and Hester said, "Where'd he go?"

I didn't even look back. "I don't know. See if one of the reserves can get some flashlights out of their car." I was trying to get my eyes adjusted to the dark as soon as

I could. It wouldn't help much, but at least I would be able to see if I was going to collide with something within a couple of feet. I couldn't imagine Toby making very good time, wherever he was headed. Not without breaking his neck.

Sally came around the side of the house a few minutes later, with her flashlight on, and said, "Here's a light for you, too."

So much for my night vision.

It was so damned dark up there in the woods, we brought two squad cars around the side of the house, on the lawn, and tried to light the area with spotlights and headlights. Not much help, but we extended our sight line to the surrounding woods. No sign of Toby. Since Sally and I had the only flashlights, we began to move toward the nearest trees.

"I think I might have heard a noise over that way," I said, shining my flashlight to my left.

"Okay."

Hester and Reserve Officer Knockle, who was nearly seventy, and had been on the reserve since 1966, stayed at the residence. We'd called for assistance, but it would be a good twenty minutes before one of the regular deputies on the night shift could get up to us.

"We're never gonna find him, Houseman," said Sally. "Not in a million years."

"Probably," I said. "So we better spread out."

"No way," said Sally. "I'll come along, but I draw the line at wandering around out here by myself."

I raised my voice. "Toby! Come on, now, Toby!"

"Like that'll help," came a soft mutter from my partner.

"Hey, Houseman!" I heard the screen door slam, and Hester hurried over to us. "Better be careful. Knockle says there are lots of foundations scattered through this area."

"Really?"

"Says they're from the old German commune? I don't know . . ."

"Oh, hell," I said. "That's right." I pointed my flash-light beam to my left again. "About a quarter of a mile, I'll bet. It was the start of a small town, called Kommune, in the 1820s or so, up here on the hill above the river. Sure . . . failed by 1860 or '70, I think. Abandoned."

Sally'd heard of Kommune, as well. "My grandpa used to tell us about that." She looked over to our left. "Shit, I thought that was miles from here."

"There's probably a path along the bluff or the hill, to the river, then," said Hester. "They would have had an access of some sort, and it sure wasn't the current road."

Well, that made sense. "If there is, we'll try to find it. We were going to start over that way, anyway," I said. "I thought I might have heard him over there when I first got out the door. See if you can contact whatever car's responding, and have them take the road as close to the base of the cliff as they can. Shine lights up toward the top, and see if they can find a path. Might be enough to keep him up here."

"Got it," she said. "You sure you'll be all right in a few hundred feet of uncharted wilderness?" I knew she was grinning.

"I'll be just fine," said Sally. "Carl's going first."

"Watch him," said Hester. "He's a little out of shape. Wouldn't want you to have to carry him back."

"I'll just call for a wrecker," said Sally.

We traversed the lawn in seconds, now that the headlights let us see where we were going. The wooded area was going to be a different matter altogether. It didn't look like the headlights penetrated the trees beyond a few feet.

There was something of a path. It was dusty, and big bunches of dry leaves and twigs were clumped along it.

"Might as well assume he took the path," I said, and headed forward.

I stepped on some twigs just about as soon as I got to the path, causing a brittle snapping sound, and eliciting a pithy "Shhhh," from Sally. "Don't step on every twig you can."

I assured her I wouldn't. We called out Toby's name three or four times, but got no response. We were on a gentle downslope that was taking us out of the splinters of light thrown by the cars. The house, I noticed as I looked back through the trees, had all but disappeared from view.

I told Sally to turn off her light. There was no reason to deplete both sets of batteries. After a few more yards, I told her that I was going to turn mine off, too, and to stand very still.

"If Toby's near here," I whispered, "if we're quiet, I'll bet he spooks first."

"Don't be too sure," came the whispered reply.

We stood on the path for about a minute, in darkness and dead silence. I was about to turn on my light and start moving again, when we heard a rustling off the path, to our left. I heard Sally's intake of breath, but she didn't make another sound.

We stood stock-still. We waited at least another minute. Damn. It was still way too soon for my eyes to adapt. That would take another twenty minutes. Come on, Toby. Jump.

Suddenly, I heard a twig crack and snap. To my left, but kind of behind me. My first thought was that it was Sally, trying to get past me for some reason.

"Did you hear that?" Her whispered question came from directly behind me, right where she should have been.

When you're in the dark, and your partner asks a question, you really have to give some sign that you've heard, or they just keep asking.

"Yeah," I whispered back, not turning. I reached

down, and unsnapped my service weapon, leaving my right hand on the butt.

"It's just me," she said, as I felt a hand on my back. There's always a need for reassurance, and to tell the truth, I was glad she'd reached out her hand. Reassurance goes both ways. "A deer?"

Possibly. I said as much. Then I said, "Shhh."

We waited a few more seconds, and there was another sound, a little farther ahead and still left of the trail.

I decided it was time to turn on the lights.

I snapped my flashlight on, and could see nothing but trees.

"Shit," said Sally, caught by surprise. Her light came on immediately.

We did both sides of the path. Nothing.

"What the hell is it?"

"Not sure," I said, pointing the beam of my light down. I couldn't tell which, if any, of the twigs I was looking at had been the one that had cracked. Roots, some limestone showing through the surface of the path, and the twigs pretty much ruled out a footprint.

"Let's go toward it, anyway," I said, starting forward along the path.

All of a sudden, there was a loud rustling in the dried leaves off to the right, of somebody or something moving fast. Then a yell and a thump.

Silence. Both our flashlights shined toward the sound. "Toby?" I hollered. "That you, Toby?"

"Help! Help! I broke my fuckin' leg!"

Sally and I both went crashing through the small branches and leaves, toward the sound of Toby's voice. We had to glide our feet, making whooshing sounds in the leaves that blocked out everything else. We stopped again, and he was so loud and clear, we had to be within yards. But we couldn't see him.

"Toby, where are you?"

"Down here! My leg's all broken!"

Sure enough, about ten yards out, off a bit to the left, if you looked really close between two trees, you could see sort of a lumpy area when the flashlight beams moved over that way.

We reached him in just a few seconds. He was lying on his side, in a limestone foundation, on a bed of about a half billion leaves and twigs. He was holding his right leg, bent at the knee, with both hands. Both Sally and I clambered in with him.

"Which leg?" asked Sally. It's training: You're taught not to assume anything if possible, but sometimes it just sounds dumb. I'm sure she thought so, too.

"This one. Aw shit!" He indicated his right leg. It looked fine to me.

"Let me see," said Sally. She had just finished her EMT training, and sounded suspiciously happy. She began to feel his leg.

"Ouch!"

"Hurt?" Sally has a way.

"Oh, shit, yeah, it hurts! Jesus Christ, lady!"

"Toby," I said, as much to distract him as anything else. "What the hell'd you run for?"

" 'Cause you're gonna find out, that's why!" He was pretty near tears.

"Find out what?"

"Just find out," he said. "Ouch!"

"Your leg looks just fine to me," said Sally. "It's not broken."

"Fuck of a lot you know!"

"You might have a sprained knee," she said. "Don't be such a baby."

"Toby!" I barked out. His head jerked around to face me. "Toby," I said, very slowly, "tell me what we're going to find out." I lowered my voice deliberately, to give it the contrast that would make him listen. "I mean it, Toby."

"He did it," said Toby. "He killed her. He finally fuckin' killed her."

"Who killed her? Kevin?" He hadn't been at the top of my list of suspects.

"No." He was very quiet. "Oh, fuck, you'll find out anyway. And he'll know all about it...."

"Who?"

I waited. Finally, he said, "Daniel. It was Daniel. He did it. And now he'll get us, too."

"No, he won't," I said, just about automatically. Always reassure the victim.

"Don't fuckin' count on it," said Toby, his voice shaking from both pain and fear. "He ain't just anybody, you know...."

"Well," I said, "I'm not, either." I smiled reassuringly.

He reached up, almost as if he was going to try to grab my collar. I was at least a foot too far away.

"You're a nice guy," he said, "but you just don't know who you're dealing with."

"Try me."

"Daniel's ... Daniel's ..."

"Come on," I said encouragingly, and trying not to sound exasperated.

"He's a vampire." He looked about as startled as I suspect Sally and I did. "Oh, fuck, I can't believe I said that."

"Vampire? Who's Daniel? What do you mean, he's a vampire?"

"Daniel Peel," he said. "And I *call* him a vampire because he fuckin' *is* one. A real fuckin' vampire, man, who drinks blood, and never ever dies." He moaned. "Fuck, Toby's dead. Toby's dead and fuckin' gone now. Just plonk, plonk, plonk." He started to shake.

"Oh, come on, Toby, cut the bullshit. Who in the hell ever heard of a vampire called Dan?" I snorted.

Toby said, in a startlingly cold voice, "I have. And you will, too. Don't you fuckin' laugh, he's probably coming for me right now."

The memory of whatever had made those sounds a few moments ago, on the opposite side of the trail from Toby, suddenly gave me a spooky feeling in the middle of my back.

I heard Sally rustle around, and then heard her working the slide on her department-issue .40-caliber Smith & Wesson. Snick, clack. Bothered her, too, I guess.

"You sure he's out here?"

He paused, then said, "No."

"Do you know where this Daniel is right now?"

"No."

"Where is he usually?" He was clamming up on me.

"Could be anywhere," he muttered. "Anywhere."

Well, vampire or not, whoever this Daniel Peel was, Toby was certainly convinced that he'd killed Edie. We had our first suspect. We also had our first murder witness.

"Can you get to your feet?" I asked.

"What for?"

"For we don't have to carry your ass all the way back," I said, in a friendly way. "Try to put some weight on that knee."

I reached my hand down, and helped him up. He stood on his good leg.

"Go ahead, put the other one down, Toby."

He gave me a dirty look, but did. Gingerly. Then with more weight. "Ow." Sort of an obligatory complaint. Now that it appeared it really wasn't broken, I think he was beginning to realize that he'd scared himself into calling for help when he really hadn't needed it. Excellent. He was in good enough shape to go to the office, and be thoroughly interviewed. Very thoroughly.

"Sally, you go up first." I leaned toward her, and whispered, "Safe and holster your weapon." She did, with a snap as she lowered the hammer drop. But she did it reluctantly. If you're spooked, though, the place for your gun isn't in your hand. "When you get to the top, tell everybody that we've got him and he's okay." She had a walkie-talkie, but with the combination of limestone foundation and beaucoup trees, there was little chance of her contacting anybody from where we were.

Toby said, "Be careful, lady."

Sally climbed up a pile of soft dirt that had washed out of one of the limestone block walls, stuck one foot into a large horizontal crack, and simply stepped out of the foundation and back onto firm ground. I could see her removing her walkie-talkie from her utility belt, and heard her calling "81." That was the number assigned to Knockle.

"Hokay, Toby. Look, we'll have Sally grab your hand, and I'll give you an assist from down here. See how she got to the top using that dirt pile?"

"Yeah," he sighed. "Sure." His head was moving around like he was going to see something. Fat chance of that in the dark.

"Just don't step in her tracks, or you'll sink down too far." I shined my flashlight on Sally's path out of the foundation, just to let him know exactly what I meant. I looked up, and Sally indicated she was ready. She held out a hand, and helped Toby up as I pushed.

I went up the same way that Sally had, but sank appreciably farther into the dirt. I had to put my flashlight down, and use both hands to get to the top of the wall, and as I pushed myself upright, one of the blocks I was kneeling on came loose and went thudding back into the foundation.

"You okay?" asked Sally.

"Yeah, just fine."

"You sure make a racket," she said.

I assumed the lead, with Toby close behind me, and Sally bringing up the rear. "Just where can I find this Dan the vampire?" I asked.

"I don't know. Hell, anywhere. He could be down in

the woods back there," said Toby, his voice tense. "I don't know."

Almost as if by magic, Sally was in the lead.

"What's he do?" I asked. "Drink blood?"

"Sometimes." He sounded out of breath.

"You want to stop for a few seconds?" Even though Sally had said he was all right, I didn't want him fainting from the pain of a possible sprained knee or ankle. It was still too far to carry him.

"No!" he whispered, but with considerable emphasis.

As we got closer to the house, and the trees thinned, the headlights of the cars we'd positioned to help began to interfere with our vision.

"Tell Eighty-one to turn off the car lights, just parking lights will do," I said. Sally complied.

They went out about five seconds later. Much better. I realized that Toby hadn't really complained about any pain since we got out of the foundation. "You okay, Toby?"

"Oh, yeah," he said. "Just fine. Dead man walkin', that's me." I thought the sarcasm was appropriate this time.

It was a strange situation, really. I was in possession of a name, purportedly that of a suspect. That was good. The fact that I didn't have the foggiest idea who this Daniel Peel was didn't bother me much, seeing as it was fairly easy to find people in the information age. I was about to set Toby down and have a nice, heart-to-heart chat. Whether or not this Peel was actually a suspect didn't really bother me. Just the additional name would enable us to open more avenues of inquiry, as it were. Sure didn't hurt to have Peel's name, though. Not a bit. The problem, in a nutshell, was Toby's announcement that Peel was a vampire. I mean, it's always better to have your only witness not be delusional. Sanity really does enhance credibility, no matter what they say.

We kept Toby outside in the back of a squad, with Sally standing right by his door, while Hester and I talked.

"Vampire? You're kidding. Carl? You are, aren't you?"

"No. 'Fraid not. That's what he says, anyway."

"Named Daniel?"

I found myself getting a little defensive. "Well, nobody's really called 'Count' much anymore."

"And," Hester asked, struggling, "is there, maybe, a werewolf named Bob?" She lost the battle, and kind of giggled. "Jesus, Houseman. Where do you *find* these people?"

"Okay, okay." I sighed. "But, we do have Toby saying that this Daniel Peel dude killed Edie. And he did run out of the house...."

"He probably couldn't keep a straight face anymore," she said. Then a deep breath. "Okay, right. Look, it's just late, and we've all had a long day, and it looks like it's just getting a good start, so, what do we need?"

It was good to get back to business. "We need an interview with Toby, a good one, and real soon. First of all"—I thought for a second—"I don't think we want Toby back in the house with the rest of them, especially not with the vampire business. If we do have something to that, I don't want them to know that we know."

"Can we keep him isolated?" Hester asked the question even as she came up with the answer. "Of course we can. He's a runner."

"You got it. A material witness, who's demonstrated his desire to flee."

According to the Iowa Code, any officer may arrest any person as a material witness, provided that the person is a material witness to a felony, and if the person might be unavailable for subpoena. Toby claimed knowledge of a felony, all right. He'd already run once.

And we were, via the bridge across the Mississippi at Freiberg, less than five miles from Wisconsin. We can't subpoena from another state, and we sure can't subpoena somebody we can't find, even if they stay in Iowa.

I went to the squad car.

"Hey, Toby?"

"What?"

"You know that I'm a deputy sheriff, don't you?"

"Now what?" He had a right to be suspicious, and he certainly appeared to be.

"Well, Toby, since you've run once, and since you're a material witness in a felony case, I'm placing you under arrest as a material witness."

"You can't do that!" They always say that. Hell, even their attorneys say that.

"It's done, Toby," I said. "Don't be too bothered about it. I told you about that earlier today, didn't I? We'll take good care of you." I gestured to Sally. "Go ahead and take him in. Stop and have him checked at the Maitland Hospital before you book him. Just in case of some lawsuit over his leg." I moved a bit closer to him. "Okay, now, you've got the right to remain silent, anything you say can be used against you in a court or courts of law. You have the right to an attorney, and to have him present during questioning." I smiled. "Got that?"

"I don't believe this," said Toby. "I just don't believe this."

"But, do you understand what I've just said? You gotta understand it, Toby."

"Yeah, yeah, I understand all that shit. But it just isn't gonna help, is all."

"Don't worry," I said. "It should be a lot easier than running through the woods in the dark."

"Yeah. Right."

"Hey, Toby, just consider it revenge for scaring the hell out of me." I smiled.

"What?"

"When you ran right by us in the woods. Just before you fell in the foundation."

He shook his head. "I never ran by you. I was lying down until I got up when you turned your lights on. When I ran into the hole." He gave kind of a satisfied smile. "Like I said, dude. Like I said."

Sally and I exchanged what I would call meaningful looks and then she glanced back toward the woods. "I think we'll be leaving now," she said quickly. She turned to Toby, in the backseat behind the thick Plexiglas screen. "Now you behave, Toby, and just be quiet back there, and put on your seat belt." She got into the squad, and left the door open while she buckled herself in.

"Don't pick up any hitchhikers," I said. That earned me a look from Sally. "Don't forget, cite under Code Chapter 804.11. Make certain you include that."

"Okay, boss."

"And no questions to him until one of us gets down there."

I went back to Hester. "We can talk to him when we get back to Maitland. Ought to be good enough."

"You know what bothers me?"

"Tonight? Hard to tell," I said. "What?"

"The man who joined us at the restaurant. That Chester dude."

"Yeah."

"So, somebody shows up who hunts vampires, then we have a suspect say that our victim is killed by a vampire. What're the odds?"

"Tonight? Pretty good."

"Yeah," she said. "I'm afraid we better talk to this Chester guy again. Not right away. Damn. Not tonight, anyway." She brushed a wayward strand of hair from her forehead. "But this stinks. It almost feels like some sort of setup."

"Maybe..."

"Do you want your office, then, to get hold of this vampire hunter and set up an appointment?"

"Oh, Harry will keep us in touch," I said, half kidding. "Right now, the two of us are the only people who know all the connections. I'd like to keep it that way."

"There's a third one, Carl." She was beginning to smile, broadly.

"Who?"

"Dangerous Dan the Vampire Man," she said, and snickered. "Honest to God, I'm never coming to Nation County again."

"We're entertaining, you gotta admit," I said.

"Right. So, anyway, regardless, then we need a search warrant application for the house and related property, real quick." She looked tired. "And then we need to do the damned search, and in a house this big, that could take a day or more." She regarded the Mansion, looming in the dark. "Easily. Can your department stand the cost of putting the residents up for the night?"

Well, we sure as hell couldn't leave them in the house.

"Let me call Lamar," I said, "but I think we should talk to the group inside, first."

"Sure."

We explained to Hanna, Huck, Kevin, and Melissa that we were going to make out an application for a search warrant, and submit it to a judge.

"Then what?" asked Huck.

"Then," I explained, "the judge either issues the warrant or he doesn't. If he does, we begin the search."

"If he doesn't?"

"Then," I said, "we go home to bed."

"What about us?" asked Melissa.

"Well, that's the tough part," I said. "We can't let you just go about your business, because we have the right to secure the premises while we make application to search it."

"You mean we can't go to our rooms?" This from Hanna.

"Not without an escort," I said.

"I don't think you can do that," said Kevin. "I don't think that's legal."

I sighed. "Okay, let me explain it this way. If I tell you it's legal, and it isn't, then I can't use anything in court that I find here at the house. See?"

He just looked at me.

"Neither can I use anything that I'm led to by any evidence in the house that I've discovered under the search warrant." He was still quiet. I sure had their attention, though. "Judges call that the fruits of a poisoned tree. Means it's all tainted and unusable. Okay so far?"

"Yes."

"Good. So, then, you understand that when I say we sure as hell *can* do that, that only an idiot would tell you that if it wasn't true, because then it would totally screw up his investigation. Right?"

"Yeah."

"So you don't have to worry, even if I *am* an idiot." I grinned. "And what are the odds?"

He didn't return the grin, but Melissa and Huck did.

"The bad news," Hester said, "is that, if we do get the warrant, you all won't be able to remain here tonight, and can't be let back in until we're done."

That didn't go over well.

Once we got that all straightened out, and the group had started to settle down, I dropped the bomb.

"Oh, yeah. Before we do anything else, any of you know the whereabouts of a Dan or Daniel Peel?"

You could almost hear their mouths clamp shut. They tried as hard as they could to communicate with one another without speaking, and I think they were remarkably successful. Even I could read the looks that selected Holly Finn, or Huck, as their spokesperson. Not bad at all.

"Certainly," she said. Her mind was racing, I could tell by the clipped tones and her eyes darting upward, left, then right, then back to me. All in a split second, she appeared to have considered what she wanted me to know, what Toby might have said, Toby's precipitate flight, and the death of Edie. I know by what she said next.

"Dan comes here once in a while, just like other people do. I don't know where he lives, and I'm not even sure what he does for a living." She glanced around, having given her instructions to the crew. She continued, "He's okay, he seems to be harmless." She looked me straight in the eye. "I assume Toby told you he thinks he's a vampire?" She grinned, and it looked genuine.

"Peel thinks he's a vampire, or Toby thinks Peel's a vampire?" I wasn't quite clear.

"Oh," she said, "Toby thinks he's one, all right."

"Why's that?"

"In case you hadn't noticed," she said, with mock confidentiality, "Toby is a little bit dorky."

"So, you're saying that Dan Peel doesn't think he's a vampire?"

"He might," she said. "It's hard to tell what somebody thinks."

"Sometimes it's easier than you think." I stared at her for a second. "You know where this Dan Peel is now?"

"I wouldn't even guess," she said.

Huck had just established herself as leader, and written Toby off as an idiot. And, incidentally, dodged the Dan Peel question for the moment. I filed it away, and got on with the search warrant application.

I called Lamar, and he came through with the authorization for housing the displaced residents of the

Mansion. Hester and I went directly to our office in Maitland. I did the search warrant application, while Hester interviewed Toby, and various reserve and off-duty officers were called out to get ready to transport the house residents to the two motels that would take the county's payment vouchers. Two of them would stay at the house, to secure it from any interference. They went north, waiting for word from us.

Hester and I went to the judge, search warrant application in hand, arriving at 01:44 on the eighth. Judge Winterman was the chief judge of the district, and was an exceptionally thorough man, with very high standards. If you got a search warrant from Winterman, you'd done a good application. Hester and I'd been absolutely accurate, naturally, and even Judge Winterman had to smile when he got to the "vampire" part. Didn't say anything, though. Didn't even guffaw. Bless him.

He did say, "Good luck to you."

As soon as we got back in the car, we radioed the others, and set things in motion. We headed back, as well.

At 02:28, Hester and I took the lab crew into the sitting room of the now deserted house. The plan was this: They were to complete photography, and then reseal Edie's bedroom and closet for tonight, then go to a motel and get some well-deserved sleep. This would establish the true beginning of the search, for the record. Two sheriff's deputies would guard the premises, and at the same time search the music room and the main dining room, photographing thoroughly everything of interest, and recording anything of evidentiary value they discovered. Which meant nothing, we hoped, and why we'd picked two areas where we least expected to discover anything interesting.

The search warrant generally permitted us to search for "materials relevant to a criminal investigation," but the more specific section delineated "blood, in any form, or any substance appearing to be blood, on any implement, interior or exterior surface of the house, upon any object or item within the house, or in any device that may have been used to transport blood away from the residence; or any device or instrument that may have been used to remove, or eradicate, or conceal any blood or bloodstains, whether within the principal structure or at any point in the contiguous yard," as well as "any knife, or other cutting instrument that may have been used to inflict the wound to the person of the deceased." Not too likely they'd find that in the music room or dining room.

We also had the office make every effort to contact Jessica Hunley, the owner of the house, and try to have her present as soon as we could. We didn't want to break the locks on the doors to the third floor if we didn't have to, for one thing.

Hester and I had a fast conference in my office, way in the back of the building. Privacy was pretty well assured. Toby had told Hester that this Dan Peel subject had visited Edie several times in the past, and that they'd sometimes gone up to the "private" third floor. Private, because it was the area of the house especially reserved for Jessica Hunley when she was visiting. Toby thought Edie had been in possession of a key to one of the two doors to Jessica Hunley's private apartment.

"No shit?" I said. I was very glad we hadn't let Toby back into the house.

Hester had also asked Toby if he knew if Edie and this Peel had been upstairs on the third floor the night before. He said he didn't know, that the Mansion was really a quiet place, and it was hard to tell where anybody was at any given time, unless you saw them.

Hester and I had both noticed how quiet it was in the Mansion, and I suspected it was the fact that many of the older homes in our area had insulated interior walls, as well as exterior ones. Especially places built before

1900. Frequently sawdust-filled, the walls were usually left intact unless there was extensive remodeling. So, Toby was probably telling the truth.

Well, at least about the quiet.

When asked if he had a key for the third floor, Toby had said "no." When asked if he'd ever been to the third floor, he'd replied, emphatically, "No way." Hester had asked him what he thought Edie and this Peel did up there. "Really private stuff," he'd answered, but said he couldn't elaborate. She'd pressed, and all she'd been able to elicit was "Well, you know, intimate stuff, sex stuff and things." Hester asked if Edie and Peel had done that sort of thing elsewhere in the house, and Toby had said that they hadn't.

That made sense, at least to me. Edie was, or had been, the building super, more or less. There was every reason to believe she'd had access to the third floor. That would mean she had her own key. With the prohibition on visiting the third floor, it would guarantee privacy for her and her lover. We had to get to the third floor, where I fully expected we'd find the murder scene. But we had to do it methodically, so unlocking it could wait until the full lab crew was ready some time tomorrow.

What Toby failed to do, or refused to do, was give Hester anything on the subject of vampires. Hester said she asked him, and he just wouldn't say anything. He just looked away and wouldn't say anything about it.

"Why?" I wondered aloud. "I mean, the little shit brought it up in the first place...."

"The fact he seems to wish he hadn't brought that up makes me think he gave something up he shouldn't have. And that's big," she grinned, "because Toby tends to run on just about everything."

"You don't actually think..." I said.

"Oh, hell no, Houseman. Not for a second. But I think we might have some blood games in the bedroom going on. That's my take, for what it's worth. So don't be surprised if we find something like that, that's all."

"Close enough to a vampire for my tastes," I said. "Don't they read about blood-borne pathogens?"

Hester grinned. "When you smoked, Houseman, did you read any of the literature about lung cancer and heart disease?"

"None of your business," I said. I smiled. "Yeah. I didn't read much of it, anyway."

"Can't run, can't hide, Houseman."

We got to the nitty-gritty. "Speaking of running," I asked her, "why do you think he was really running out in the woods tonight?"

Hester smiled. " 'Sa matter, you don't believe that he was running to warn a vampire that there were cops on his trail?"

"Nope. I don't, you don't, and he doesn't."

"I can't tell, yet," said Hester slowly. "He wasn't just running to get away. To avoid the entire event, I mean."

"Yeah. You're right." I looked at her. "Distraction? Are these people *that* good?"

She tilted her chair back on its rear legs and stared at the ceiling. "What would you say Toby's main character trait was?"

I thought for a second. "Know-it-all?"

She chuckled. "No, deeper than that, though you're right, that's a big chunk of it. I'd say 'eager to please' summed him up. Wouldn't you?"

"Well, sure," I said. "Now that you mention it. The know-it-all comes from him just sort of falling all over himself to let you know he'd like another dog biscuit."

"Exactly," said Hester. "Exactly. So, he was running to please somebody. To do what somebody wanted him to do ... or what he thought they'd want him to do." Her chair came back level, and she pursed her lips. "Who would benefit from his running like that? Huck? I don't think so. We gotta find out who, Houseman. 'Who' would make the 'why' a lot easier."

"Easy in theory," I said. "It's in the finding out that we get to the hard part, here."

"I'll keep at him," she smiled. "I'll find out."

There was no doubt in my mind.

"I hate to get all legal," I said, "but can you think of any reason not to let Toby take off? I mean, he's talked, and there's no pending action."

"No, not really. I think he'll stick now, and he's probably over being so scared. Especially when he can stay away from that house tonight."

We called Magistrate Benson, who sleepily agreed to release Toby on his own recognizance. The night shift could let him out, and give him a ride to Freiberg. I walked back to the cells, and told Toby. He did seem pleased.

Before I left, Sally was given the assignment of coming up with everything possible concerning both Peel and Hunley. She was scheduled to start her dispatch shift at 04:00. She'd assured us that the vampire-induced adrenaline rush was guaranteed to keep her alert through the rest of the night.

I got home at 03:36. Sue had left a note telling me that there was some chow mein in the refrigerator. I put it in the microwave, and discovered while eating it that I should have left it in at least a minute longer. The edges were cold, the center a bit cooler. Too tired to wait any longer, I ate it anyway, with a slice of bread.

ELEVEN

I walked in the office door with a full four hours' sleep, and went directly to Dispatch. Borman was already there, looking fresh and ready to go. Ah, youth.

"Morning," he said.

"You look fresh. Get enough sleep?"

"You betcha. More than enough." He looked awfully happy, and well he should have. This was an opportunity for him to be one up on just about the whole department, on a big case. The pecking order in most cop shops depends a lot on who's been deemed to have a "need to know" and who hasn't. Ours was no different.

"Get anything for us?" I asked Sally.

"Some, but not a lot," she said. She got up from her seat at the main console, and Elaine Boyce slid into her chair. Sally scooped up a bunch of papers and notes, and the three of us went to the kitchen, Borman in the lead.

The jail kitchen is right next to our dispatch center. It's our home away from home. We contract with a nursing home to provide meals for our prisoners, so the kitchen is pretty much ours to use as we need. It's just about ten yards of countertop and cabinets, with a stove, sink, refrigerator, coffeepot, and a long church basement–type table, with collapsible chrome legs, and a worn linoleum top, straight from 1950. Surrounded by steel folding chairs, with "NCSD" in black stencil on their backs. Nation County Sheriff's Department.

Sally sat and began spreading out her papers. "Get me a cup of coffee?"

"Sure." I glanced inquiringly at Borman, and he nodded. I went to the full pot, and poured three cups.

"Make that four?" Hester's voice.

"You bet. Still take milk?"

"No, just black," she said. "Morning, Sally."

"Hi, Hester. I don't have much."

"Right," said Hester, referring to all the paper.

I sat three cups around the table, and pulled up a chair. "So..."

"First off," said Sally, "don't forget to call Harry over in Conception County, Carl. He called at 07:12, and says he really wants to talk to you." She handed me that note. "Now, how about a fast background on the younger set at the Mansion? They were easy, since we know all of 'em."

"Go for it," I said, raising my coffee cup.

"First one is Toby Gottschalk. Son of Robert and Gwen, raised on a farm about five miles out of Freiberg. We have one beer ticket on him at age sixteen. Two moving violations, both for failure to have control at property damage accidents. Nothing major at all."

"Go on," said Hester.

"The next one," said Sally, "is Melissa Corcy. A bit different. She has a juvenile record I can't access, but I seem to remember that it was over simple possession, wasn't it, Carl?"

It rang a bell. "Oh, shit, sure I remember," I said, kind of embarrassed. "She and her older sister had some weed up in their room and their mother called us, didn't she?"

"You got it," said Sally. "Her mom is divorced, two times, maybe three, with a last name of Warrington, and Melissa's sister has a last name of Burgess, after the mom's first husband."

"Anything else on her?" asked Hester.

"Not much. Went to school at the U of Iowa, according to Betty." Betty was another dispatcher. "Betty also says that Melissa's a whole lot brighter than her mom."

"Okay. Good," I said.

"Kevin Stemmer has nothing but two moving violations, both for speeding, both under ten mph over the limit." Sally smiled. "Mike gave him both tickets, and says that he tried to talk his way out of both of them. Took one to court, and lost his ass. Otherwise, nada. No sense of adventure."

"Or smart enough not to get caught," said Hester.

"True," said Sally. "Now for Holly Finn, or Huck. I was in on an arrest involving her; they had me for a matron. I think you were on vacation, Carl. Back in '97?"

"I dunno," I said. "I know I took vacation that year . . . I think."

Sally laughed. "Trust me. Anyway, it was for assault."

"No shit?" I was truly surprised.

"Yeah. Remember Quentin Pascoe, the guy who sexually abused that four-year-old here in Maitland?"

"Yeah," I said. There was no way I'd ever forget Quentin Pascoe.

"Well, when he was out on bond, he must have said some lowlife thing in the Fast & Easy one night. Our girl Huck was in there, heard him, went over to the bar, and knocked him on his ass."

"I never heard that," I said. "Good for her. You guys busted her, huh?"

"We sort of had to," said Sally. "She got him with a chair."

"Even better," I said. "Intelligent people tend to use tools." My estimation of Huck went up several notches.

"Other than that, she went to school at U of Wisconsin, Madison. Was a music teacher for a year, I'm told. Then quit, and went on the boat."

"Probably more money," said Hester.

"Hanna Prien," said Sally, "has absolutely no record whatsoever. Born, raised, and remains in Freiberg. Betty says that she was a bright kid, but no gumption at all. She went to school with Betty's daughter for a while."

"Anything more?" asked Hester, gesturing at the stack of paper in front of Sally.

"Oh, sure. First, we contacted Jessica Hunley at her residence in Lake Geneva, Wisconsin. She left about 6:45, and expects to be at her house here at about ten." Sally looked at us, with a grin. "She was 'absolutely horrified.' I like that."

"Okay . . ." I took a sip of coffee. "Did she already know?"

"Yep. Still 'absolutely horrified,' though."

"Nice to know," said Hester.

"So, while I was at it, I got her DL," said our favorite dispatcher. She pulled a sheet from the pile, with perfs on the sides, right off the teletype. "She's forty-three, five feet nine, green eyes, a hundred twenty-nine pounds, gives an address in Lake Geneva, Wisconsin, and owns two cars."

"Okay." I reached out and took the DL sheet.

"Wanna know what kinds of cars? Please say yes. Please?"

How could I refuse? "Sure," I said.

"One: a silver 2000 Mercedes Benz ML55 AM6 SUV." She looked up. "Those run over fifty grand."

"Wow." I guessed there really was such a thing as a wealthy dance instructor.

"Two," continued Sally, savoring the moment, "a silver 2000 BMW Z8. Convertible, no less."

"How much?" I had to ask.

"Well," she said, "my sister looked it up on the net, and she says that they go for about a hundred twenty-five thousand."

Impressive.

"This is a dance instructor?" asked Hester.

"Yep. That's what everybody says," said Borman.

"I quit dance lessons when I was thirteen," said Hester. "Mother always said it was a mistake." She reached over and took the vehicle sheets from Sally. "There's got to be more to this woman than teaching dancing."

I agreed.

"Whatever else she does," said Sally, "she's got a clean record. TRACIS, NCIC, Wisconsin, and Iowa indicate no criminal history. Not even a traffic ticket."

"Wow," said Hester. "Not bad."

I looked up.

"I mean, no traffic tickets. Wisconsin drivers are terrible."

Sally and I smiled. "I'd be careful, too," I said, "if I drove cars like that." I looked across the table. "Anything else on her?"

"Nope," said Sally, "which brings us to our Daniel Peel."

I perked up right away.

"You told us last night," said Sally, addressing Hester, "that Toby said he was about thirty or so, white, male, and in pretty good shape?"

"Yep."

"Well," said Sally, "I ran an Iowa check. Nobody, and Iowa files go three years either side of a possible date of birth. So I did an alphabetical. There was a . . . umm . . . let's see. Oh, here," she said. "We have a Dabney, a DaMar, two Darwins, four Davids, a Dawane, a

DaVere, and a DaBurl under Peel." She sat back. "Everything but Daffy. None of these even close to thirty. Youngest is forty-three."

"Yeah...." There was bound to be more.

"So," she smirked, "just on the off chance you didn't spell it right, I did a sound-alike pass, and got it spelled Peel, Pele, Peal, Pfeil, Pale...lots, let me tell you." She shrugged. "So I did a fifty-state check, with a date of birth of 06/30/1970, and got nobody that matched." She looked disgusted. "NCIC will check one year either side of a DOB, but you need the month and the day right. That means that we'd have to run the name three hundred and sixty-five times, and we'd only get a two year spread even if we did."

Great.

"So, I called Gray Eyes, and explained part of this to her. Murder suspect." She held up her hand, to forestall complaints. "I certainly didn't mention the 'V' word. Don't worry."

"Gray Eyes" was a dispatcher buddy of Sally's who once worked for the California Highway Patrol. The two of them had met at an APCO meeting, and Gray Eyes happened to be, in Sally's estimation, just about the greatest dispatcher ever. She'd been hired away from the CHP, and was now working for NCIC in Washington. They'd kept in touch. Obviously.

She looked up. "She expanded the search, because she's allowed to actually *program* a search. By making him between twenty-five and fifty. DOB between 1950 and 1975. We got one dude in North Dakota, who was forty-seven, and two in Montana, for shit's sake, one twenty-five and one fifty exactly."

"That's it?"

"Oh, no, not really. In California, there were two hundred eighty-seven, actually, and four hundred sixty-two in New York." She indicated the papers. "Total of nearly nineteen hundred in the U.S., so far, and the Illinois, Texas, Louisiana, Florida, and Arizona computers are down for routine maintenance, and can't be accessed for an expanded search at this time, and we haven't done all the ages yet." She took a breath.

Oh.

"So," said Hester, "what did their criminal histories say?"

Sally didn't even look up. She did raise her wrist and put up one finger, though.

"Then," she continued, "I sort of exceeded my authority a little, and used our Deputy Houseman's name and ID, and started looking for vampires."

"You did?" I was aghast. Not that she'd actually done it, but that she'd said so in front of Borman and Hester.

"Yep. Well, not vampires, really. But cases where there was a conspicuous blood involvement." She looked up. "Relax. Hester and I talked about it last night," she grinned. "After you'd gone night-night. I don't get all the credit."

"We used your LEIN ID," said Hester, "because mine would attract too much attention."

"So, who am I, Carl the Obscure?"

No response.

A conspiracy. Well, so what? I know when I'm outclassed. LEIN, by the way, stands for Law Enforcement Intelligence Network. Certain officers in Iowa have been certified to operate within that system, and we all have an alphanumeric ID. The programmer in Des Moines wouldn't think much of my ID, but Hester's would signal a DCI interest.

Sally pushed a LEIN Records Search Request form over to me. "Sign here," she said. "Just to cover my ass."

I did. "And..." I was really curious.

"Well," Sally said, "I guess there really *are* people out there who believe they're vampires. And they get caught, when the victims either die or complain, or the neighbors do."

She pushed over a list. "These are crimes in Iowa and

Wisconsin and Minnesota involving the 'ingestion of blood from unwilling victims.' Or so they say."

I thought the "unwilling" qualifier was interesting.

There were eighteen incidents listed, along with the investigating agency, and date of filing. The oldest was 1993. The most recent was July 2000. I pushed the list over to Hester. Sally had underlined the '93 case in red. The investigating agency was listed as Walworth County, Wisconsin. Sally had also made the notation "is co. where lk. gen. located."

"The county where Lake Geneva is located?" said Hester. "Really?" She passed the sheet to Borman, politely.

Sally was very pleased. "You betcha."

"Then I guess we better talk with 'em...."

Sally pushed another sheet of paper toward me. The phone number of the Walworth County Sheriff's Department was on it, along with the headquarters number of the Wisconsin Bureau of Criminal Apprehension.

"Then..." she said, not missing a beat, "you'd better return the call of the county attorney. He called about thirty minutes ago, wanting to know how it went last night."

I winced. I'd forgotten about him.

"And call Lamar before you go up."

"Any word," asked Hester, "from the guys up there?"

"About every thirty minutes all night long," said Sally. "They finished the search of their assigned rooms in less than an hour. Bored out of their minds the rest of the night."

I called Harry over in Wisconsin first. I knew what was coming.

"Houseman, you rotten son of a bitch," said Harry, laughing. "Where did you find this fuckin' Chester dude, and thanks for sending him to me, you bastard."

"Anytime, Harry. What are friends for?"

"Right. Anyway, you turn up anything new for me, other than a dickhead vampire hunter?"

I took a breath. "Well, yeah, we did."

"Really?" Suddenly, he was all business.

"Yep." I told him about Toby, and the vampire business from last night.

"You gotta be shittin' me, Carl...."

"Nope."

There was a silence. Then, "Care to meet with me and Mr. Chester today?"

"I'll make the time, for sure," I said. "When?"

"Dunno yet. Let me shake the motels for the little bugger, and I'll get back to ya."

Hester was doing the call to the Walworth County Sheriff's Department and the Wisconsin BCA, so I did the county attorney and Lamar. Sally went home to get some well-earned rest. Borman washed up the coffee cups and pot. I honestly think he expected Sally to do it, until it seemed to dawn on him that he who contributed least got the crap job. That was okay. He'd contribute soon enough, I was certain. He still wouldn't be able to get Sally to do the cleanup, of course.

"Are you really serious about this vampire stuff, Carl?" Borman seemed so sincere sometimes it was almost painful.

"Yes. And your lips are sealed. Right?"

"Oh, sure. Right."

"One slip on this can cost a job. I'm serious."

He seemed to listen well. I hoped so. I got on the phone again.

Mike Dittman, the county attorney, was a little surprised that we'd bothered a district court judge in the wee hours of the morning, but was even more startled that we'd started the search and then gone to bed. I reassured him that we had people doing stuff on the property all night.

"Are you sure we can do that?" He was asking me.

"Yep. Judge agreed we could, said you'd probably be able to find the applicable citations before the suppression hearing." Judge Winterman had a fine sense of humor. Well, I thought so, anyway.

Lamar just wanted me to know that he'd told his sister that it was not a suicide.

"That's fine, Lamar."

"You know what she said?"

That had to be rhetorical, but I answered anyway. "No..."

"She said, 'I bet it was that Finn bitch.' Just like that."

"No shit?" Our girl Huck? Hard to believe.

"That's what she said. Anything to it?"

"Not as far as I know, Lamar, but I'll sure as hell check."

"Oh, Carl... you just might want to think about a statement for the press. We can't expect them to stay dumb forever."

Not even on a Sunday.

My plate, as they say, was filling up. And we hadn't even gotten back to the Mansion yet.

Hester had disappointing news. Anything regarding the incident in Walworth County was in their confidential records section, and wouldn't be available until tomorrow. Wisconsin BCA's weekend answering service was a State Radio dispatcher, who had no access to records, either. He offered to contact an agent, and have one go into their records section, but he wasn't sure he'd be able to find one with the proper credentials to get to their records on a Sunday.

"For 'credentials,' substitute keys," said Hester. "We wouldn't be able to get them, either, unless it was really urgent. I told him to try, but not to call out the director, or anything."

We met the lab crew as they pulled in the department's parking lot. Specialist Christopher Barnes, of blood-spatter fame, would meet us at the scene.

We arrived at the Mansion at 09:38, let the two officers who had spent the night go home, and logged ourselves in. It was to be a daunting task, as there were six rooms on the second floor, seven on the main floor, and an unknown number on the third. Not to mention the basement.

Chris Barnes was waiting for us. He was the best blood-spatter pattern analyzer in the Midwest, at least as far as we were concerned. He was also easy to work with, and eager to explain any aspect of his art.

We started in the basement. It was enormous, with vaulted ceilings and seven separate and distinct chambers. The pillars were brick, with a concrete floor, concrete walls, and plastered ceilings. It was just about the cleanest basement I'd ever seen, with just a little debris in the fruit cellar, and some empty bags of salts near the water conditioner. But even those bags were neatly folded and stacked.

The oil furnace was quite large, converted from a coal burner, complete with a big boiler and very complex piping. One of the techs started there, checking for any traces of burned materials. Borman stayed with him, to assist in recording, preserving, or photographing any evidence that was discovered.

A lab tech named Grothler and I drew the main floor by default, as Hester, Chris Barnes, and the chief lab technician were going to do the second floor. Hester had started out as a laboratory technician years ago, and since we felt the most likely area where we'd locate trace (as in blood) evidence was the second floor, the most experienced people got that job.

I hadn't been there more than a minute, it seemed, when the phone rang. It was Harry.

"You can run, Houseman, but you can't hide. How about meeting with us right now?"

"Sure, Harry. Where?"

"My office. Quieter."

I told Hester, and she decided to remain with the search team. I got in my car, and headed over to Conception County. It was clouding up, I noticed, as I crossed the mile long bridge spans to the Wisconsin side. Cooler, too. Rain wasn't too far off. *And there,* I thought to myself, *go the beautiful leaves.*

It really was quiet in Harry's office. I mentioned it as I sat down.

"I told everybody to get the fuck out onto the streets," said Harry.

I looked at William Chester. "Harry has great administrative skills," I said.

He nodded, but didn't answer.

"Carl," rumbled Harry, "you wanna tell Mr. Chester here what you told me?"

"Might as well. But, first, Mr. Chester, you have to understand something. I'm going to ask you to sign a form, promising not to reveal anything that's discussed here. Under severe penalty." With that, I opened my attaché case and withdrew one of our standard forms. I passed it over to him. "Please read that carefully."

He took it from me, and glanced at it. "I've signed these before," he said. He pulled a pen from his shirt pocket, and signed it with a flourish. "I'll just need a copy...."

"No problem," said Harry. "Machine's in the next room. I'll be right back."

I looked at our vampire hunter. Or, rather, tracker. "Okay, this is what's happened since we last talked...."

Five minutes later, I was through.

"I see," said Chester. "So, then. Are you willing to concede that you're dealing with a vampire, now?"

"Not even for a second." I wanted him to be very clear about that. "What I'm dealing with is quite possibly some poor deluded bastard who believes he's a vampire. Nothing more. Because I know vampires really don't exist."

"As you say," he said.

I hate it when people do that. "So, what I want from you is this. I want to know how somebody who might think he's a vampire thinks a 'real' vampire behaves. How he's going to act. To convince himself and maybe some others that he's for real."

"In exchange for which?" asked Chester.

"In exchange for access to some, but not all, of our information. Access to all I can think of that might deal with the vampire stuff, but not with the core case data."

"Unless I need it?"

"Let me put it this way ... If I think we need you to testify as an expert, you get what we got. Fair enough? That way, if you make a significant contribution to the whole investigation, you get the material you want. But you can't talk to the press, and you're locked in as a prosecution witness first."

He thought for a moment. "Agreed, but I can publish my data afterward? I need to do that."

I glanced at Harry. "Okay with you?"

"Yep."

The way he said it, I knew that Harry would renege at the drop of a hat. That was going to have to be between him and Chester.

I told him some of what I knew. He was impressed, in a satisfying sort of way.

"My God, do you realize what you have here? You have a nest. You have a vampire's nest, with a house full of Renfields and blood donors. My God." He appeared stunned.

"Renfields?" asked Harry.

"Renfield was the slave of Dracula," said Chester.

"Oh sure," said Harry, with great aplomb. "And there are more of these than you expected?" I think he did it just to needle Chester, but the tracker didn't appear to notice.

"I've been looking for years," he said. "Years. Never anything like this. Never."

"Well," I said, wanting to get back down to business, "I'm really pleased for you. Now, then, we need a little information...." I'd been fairly careful, and didn't think it ever occurred to him that he was a suspect. I had to keep it that way, at least until he'd been ruled out. Although it was unstated between us, I knew that Harry felt the same way.

It was also sinking in that this man really, truly believed in vampires. Since he did, just how reliable could his information be? As it turned out, pretty good, if what you wanted was mostly folklore. And that was just what we wanted.

"What is this guy trying to say?" I asked, for openers. "Assuming that he has actually killed...."

"Oh, he has, he has," said Chester.

"Right," said Harry. "So, what's with the throat injury bit? Post mortem and all."

"Ah," said Chester. "Are you so certain they've been inflicted after the victim has died?"

Harry and I said, in unison, "Absolutely," and "Bet your ass."

"Oh." Our expert cleared his throat. "Then, possibly, to disguise the true nature of the wound? To obliterate, say, a bite mark?"

He sounded so hopeful.

"Not a chance," I said. "No bite mark."

"I think he's doin' it to make people talk about neck or throat injuries," said Harry. "How about that?"

"He could. I'm not saying that as fact, but, yes, he could."

Chester warmed to his subject, and I spent about an hour with him and Harry. The upshot was that blood, while significant to a "vampire wannabee" as Harry called him, wasn't in any way a source of nutrition.

"Unlike true vampires, poseurs will consume, maybe, an ounce or less at a time, for the most part," said Chester. "Daily would be too often. You'd end up with diarrhea and other things if you did more than that. Like a bleeding ulcer will do to you. Sometimes, they might overindulge. But not often."

That was good to know, but it left me wondering what had happened to much of Edie's blood.

He also said that, at least the more sophisticated of the "poseurs" would dress the part, in a costume reminiscent of the movies.

"Just to convince their following, you know. They'd expect a Dracula, at least now and then."

"Sure."

"He'll try to tailor his lifestyle according to that preconception, too. Sometimes for himself, sometimes for his followers or victims."

Renfields apparently came in two flavors. The first was just, in his own terminology, somebody who was enthralled by a vampire. The second, according to him, was somebody who was more into the taste of blood itself. More of a participant.

"Those are the 'clinical' Renfields," he said. "It's a disorder."

"So," I asked, "what are these people likely to be like? You know, how will they respond to an investigation?"

Chester laughed for the first time. "They'll not be cooperative, in any real way. They'll protect him from you. They'll tell him everything you say. They'll deny his very existence, for the most part. They'll mislead you at every turn."

"Hostile, then," said Harry.

"Yes."

"What do they see in this guy?" I thought that might help.

"He protects them, for one thing. He's powerful. He avenges them, if necessary. He is deliciously evil. He's immortal. He's sometimes the source of some very intense sexual interactions. Just as often, the modern vampire's the source of some chemical substances. He's completely amoral. He has to be. After all," he said, confidentially, "he isn't human."

"Everything your mother warned you about," said Harry. "Right?"

"Absolutely," said Chester. "But you have to understand, these Renfields are quite often victims of a previous...person. Their experiences have made them depressed, or at least unhappy. Dependent, but not in an obvious way. Often happens when they're adolescents. Nothing to do with vampires, at that time. Nothing at all, until they meet him. Then he addresses, well, psychological needs."

Just what I wanted to hear.

"So, like, why do you hunt these people?" asked Harry.

William Chester hesitated for a second or two, then said, "My sister. One of them got to her, years back. She didn't survive."

"Ya know who it was?" asked Harry. "The one who

got her?" Harry wasn't known for his delicacy, but nobody ever seemed to really mind. I could never figure that out.

"No. No, I don't." Chester leaned forward. "But this one is closer than any I've encountered before."

It seemed to me that he denied that a little too quickly.

_____

Before I went back across the Mississippi to Iowa, I reiterated the "no interference" provisions to Chester. He was to confine himself to contact with either Harry or me. Period. No approaching our potential witnesses or suspects, or it was curtains.

I left secure in the knowledge that Harry was going to check out every freckle on William Chester's body before he was through. He did strike me as being sincere, but cops learn not to take people at face value. How much actual use he was going to be was another thing altogether.

_____

I got back to the Mansion and found that it had only taken the basement team two hours to finish up. They'd found two suspicious areas that might have been places where blood had been wiped up, but obtained no positive results with leucomalachite green. Leucomalachite green is neat stuff. They mix it with water, sodium perborate, and glacial acetic acid. A drop or two on the test swab, then a couple of drops of hydrogen peroxide, and bingo. If there's blood there, it turns sort of an aqua color instantly. It's used to see if there is any reason to use other testing substances to cover an area. Neat stuff. It also saves you a lot of time if it turns out there's not any blood in your sample.

What we were looking for was, essentially, wipe marks, where somebody had mopped up, or sponged up, or any way removed traces of blood. There just about had to be some trace evidence, because, although Edie apparently hadn't been killed in the tub, she sure as hell had been killed somewhere. The murder site should have been pretty well doused. Then, to move a bloody body from some location to her second-floor bathtub was a process that would very likely leave a trail of at least some blood.

The immediate problem was, the main floor had three types of surface where blood was likely to have been deposited. First, there were large areas of rug or carpet. Second, equally large if not larger areas of polished hardwood flooring. Third, the tiled floor in the kitchen and pantry. Not to mention the wooden mop boards and the painted walls themselves. And furniture, of course, all either polished wood or fabric. Looking for possible wipe marks on surfaces where there are countless swirls and traces from constant wiping and cleaning is less than rewarding. We couldn't even eliminate the wipe marks that had left tiny trails of bubbles. Someone could have used detergent to clean up the mess. You'd have to test just about everything. We would, if necessary, or so we said, hoping that the team on the second floor would turn up something. If it did, we could follow a trail back from the tub to the point of the murder. Right.

TWELVE

"Hello? Is anybody here?" came from the front doorway. A woman's voice.

I was on my hands and knees, with a small Mini-Mag flashlight, side-lighting possible wipe marks on the dining room floor. I scrambled to my feet, and headed for the door.

Borman, who'd been in the music room, beat me to the door by seconds.

"Yes?" I heard him say, in a deferential tone.

Her voice got closer as she said, "I own this house. Could you direct me to whomever is in charge?"

"Uh, sure," said Borman. In two sentences, she'd let him know she was important, and he wasn't. Not bad.

I came around the corner from the dining room, and saw two women in the atrium, beginning to advance past Borman. I could see how Borman had been intimidated. One of the women seemed to be about twenty-five or so, the other I would have guessed at thirty-five, max, if her driver's license data hadn't said she was forty-three. Both were quite fit, slim, with Jessica Hunley about three inches taller than her completely leather-clad young companion. But the remarkable thing was the younger one's hair. It was absolutely metallic-looking, starting with a lemon yellow at her forehead, and sweeping back through lime green, blue, red, and ending in purple. It shimmered iridescently. Arresting, so to speak.

I resolved to be just a bit harder to intimidate than Borman. "Hi. Name's Houseman." I stuck out my hand. She didn't have much choice, and we shook. Strong. "You must be Jessica Hunley."

"Yes."

There was a momentary silence, so I took what advantage I could, and thrust my hand toward the other woman. "Deputy Houseman..."

"Tatiana Ostransky," she said. "I'm with Jessica." Her handshake was cool and firm.

Jessica started the game with me. "Deputy? I would have hoped the sheriff would be here."

"Two reasons," I said. "First, I'm the department investigator. Second, Edie was his niece. He has other things to do today."

That surprised her.

"So, you're the one in charge here?" Nice, wide, absolutely insincere smile.

"You betcha."

She fixed me with a gaze that told me she knew just exactly what I was up to, and that she thought she could beat me at that game any time she chose. Cool.

I gestured toward the parlor. "If we go in there, I can give you some information."

I was curious as to why anybody coming to the house wouldn't have been at least announced, if not delayed, by the two reserve officers outside. As we headed in toward the parlor, I saw them coming around the side of the house. Bored, they'd apparently decided to check the perimeter.

In the parlor, nobody sat.

"What," asked Hunley, "is he doing in the kitchen?" She pointed to the lab tech, who was staring back at her.

As part of my answer, I opened my old leather briefcase, and fished out her copy of the search warrant. I handed it to her, and said, "We're executing a warranted search of this premises. He's one of the lab technicians."

A search warrant lists the premises with the greatest specificity, and explains very tersely why the place is being tossed. In this instance, the exact wording was "evidence material to a homicide investigation." Knives were also listed, along with bloodstains.

Jessica Hunley took out a pair of reading glasses from a case at her belt, and read the search warrant over very carefully. She was dressed in loose-fitting olive slacks, made with a microweave fabric, a white jersey turtleneck with the sleeves pushed up, and black leather shoes that appeared to be almost as soft as gloves, that zipped rather than tied. Her brown hair was tied with a white band in a short ponytail. She seemed to be a perfect match for the house. Refined. The glasses made her appear more interesting, if such a thing were possible.

She abruptly removed the glasses, and handed the paper to her companion. "I wasn't told this was a homicide case," she said. Her tone was completely noncommittal.

"Don't feel bad," I said. "We weren't, either."

"Is there a suspect?"

"Yes," I said. Silence. I wasn't going to tell her who, of course, and apparently she wasn't going to give me the satisfaction of asking.

"So," she said, changing the unspoken subject, "where is everyone?"

"Well, most of them have been put up in area motels

for last night, but they should be allowed back in here sometime this evening, I think."

"Most of them?"

"Well," I said, "all but Toby. Toby's in jail." I do love my job.

Jessica's mouth opened slightly, but before she could say anything, Borman picked that moment to glance out the window and announce that the reserve deputies were now outside. Not his fault, but any immediate reaction I was hoping to get from Jessica was forever lost. I sure would have liked to hear what she was going to say.

Judging from the way Borman was looking at Tatiana of the shimmering hair, I'd say he probably wouldn't have heard Jessica at all.

The main result of Borman's announcement was that all four of us glanced out the window. I checked automatically for Jessica's car. I couldn't see quite all of it, because both reserves were standing around it, but it was the BMW Z8. I'd never seen one before. It struck me that, although completely modern, the car went with Jessica Hunley just as the old Mansion did.

"I'm glad you got here when you did," I said to Jessica. "We're going to need somebody to unlock the third floor for us."

"Why? It's only unlocked when I'm here. There couldn't have been anything to do with this...this killing. Not up there."

"Well, like they say, a lock only keeps an honest man out," I said. "Let's just agree it's *supposed* to be locked while you're away."

"Let's say it's supposed to stay locked when I say it is," she said, and reached into her slacks pocket, and produced a remarkably small cell phone. She dialed, while saying, "I'm calling my attorney.... This is Jessica Hunley. Is he in?" There was a brief pause. "Yes, it's me. I'm at my house above the river," she said. "There are some local cops here with a search warrant. Get up here now." She spoke in a near monotone, and if I hadn't been party to what was actually going on, I would have thought her completely unconcerned. She terminated the call and put the phone back in her pocket. She looked at her watch. "He'll be here in ten minutes," she said. It was a statement of fact, not an estimate.

Well, he either had to be a local or a damned good swimmer. I was anxious to see which of our local attorneys she had so thoroughly wrapped around her finger. "We can wait," I said. "We have lots to do yet, before we go up to the third."

She moved to hand the copy of the search warrant back. "No," I said, "that's yours. We're required by law to either leave it with the owner, or post it on the premises where the owner can easily find it." As she folded it, I asked, "Do you have the only key to the third floor?"

To my surprise, she said, "I think I'll wait for my attorney to be present before answering more."

"That's fine," I said conversationally, "but you really don't need to do that. You're not a suspect here."

"Anyone," she said, "can be sued."

Ah. Right. Absolutely right. I had a feeling that Jessica would qualify as a very deep pocket.

I asked her and Tatiana to please remain in the parlor, and told Borman to stay with them. No complaint from him.

I went to the kitchen, told the lab tech to keep going, and then went up to the second to give them the news.

As I walked down the hall, I saw there were two yellow chalk marks in the blue and red and gold Oriental carpeting. I couldn't see anything particularly different between the areas inside or outside the circles, but I knew they'd found something. All three of them were in the bedroom across the hall from Edie's. By the clothes scattered about, I assumed it was the room of one of the males.

"Hester, got a second?"

"Sure."

I told her what was happening downstairs.

"Crap."

"Right," I said. "You should see Jessica Hunley and her buddy Tatiana."

"Why?"

"A tad more ... oh, sophisticated than we're used to. She drove the Z8." I grinned. "I think Borman's wondering if he can take Tatiana home as a war bride."

"Like you're not susceptible, Houseman," she said, raising one eyebrow.

"Well, Jessica's more my age, but I don't think she bakes."

"A cookie factory would make a fine dowry," she said. "Watch yourself."

Hester was right, of course. " 'An attractive member of the opposite sex can influence you, without your being aware,' " I quoted from my Academy days. "Although it never seems to work for me."

She laughed. "You're hopeless."

"What did you find here?" I asked.

"Possible stains in the hall, a possible wipe-up stain on the floor beside Edie's tub, and lots of SPF fifty sunscreen, and makeup in the guys' rooms, as well as the gals'," she said with a chuckle. "Really light shades. Some really nice Victorian clothes, and lovely old-fashioned jewelry. Appliqué tattoos. Nice CD players. Not much else. No weapons—not yet, anyway. Nothing to indicate anything sinister at all." She glanced around. "We have three more rooms to go. There are tons of nooks and crannies...."

I told her about my conversation with Chester. She asked if he'd be any real help, and I told her that we'd just have to wait and see.

She'd apparently been in the main kitchen downstairs just before I'd returned.

"You know how many knives there are in a kitchen like that? Knives that could be a murder weapon?"

"Lots, huh?"

"We've seized sixteen or seventeen, so far, to send to the lab. We may never know which knife was used."

When I got back to the parlor, Tatiana was sitting on a davenport, with her legs pulled up onto the seat, so that her chin was almost resting on her knees. Her arms encircled her leather-clad knees, with the wrists crossed about halfway between her knees and ankles. Everything she owned was pointing at him. The light through the window was doing great things to that hair. She was saying, ". . . and you've *really been* in high speed chases?"

I'm not certain what Borman was about to say, but when he saw me, he caught himself and said, "Well, a couple of times." Between her posture, her shimmering hair, and her feigned interest, he was totally wasted. I honestly think that, if she'd asked to see his service weapon, he would have handed it over. He might have unloaded it first, but he would have done it. I made a mental note to keep those two as far apart as I could.

"We don't encourage chases," I said. "Of any kind. Too dangerous." He caught my meaning, I think, but without a bucket of ice water, I was not going to get his undivided attention.

"My attorney will be here in a moment," said Jessica. She smiled sweetly.

Borman's walkie-talkie crackled and hissed to life. "Eight, there's an attorney out here, says he's supposed to talk to the lady with the great car." Knockle, the older reserve. I nodded to Borman, who keyed his mike and said, "Let him in."

A few seconds later, the front door opened and I was surprised to see both Junkel and Koch, of Junkel & Koch, Attorneys at Law, enter as a group. Or, more correctly, as a firm. Both were definitely not dressed in their court clothes, Junkel in jeans and a sweater, and Koch in shorts, sandals, and a polo shirt.

"Gentlemen," I said, "come on in."

They looked past me.

"Over here," said Jessica Hunley. "This man has told us we can't leave this room."

Not quite true, but both Junkel and Koch hurried over to her, and gave me obligatory dirty looks as they passed. I looked over at Borman.

"Gonna be a long day," I said.

As things progressed, and they did so fairly rapidly at first, the true clout of Junkel and Koch became apparent. First, because I knew Junkel was rumored to be under consideration for a seat on the Iowa Appellate Court, and because Koch had been a state senator and was rumored to be being groomed as a possible gubernatorial candidate for 2002. Second, they were both known to be extremely wealthy. And third, after they'd talked with Jessica for a few seconds, they asked me for the phone number of the county attorney. As Koch called him, Junkel scanned the search warrant copy I'd given Jessica. While I was busy thanking God that Winterman was the issuing judge, I could hear Koch begin to have the county attorney jump through hoops. After a few seconds, he handed me the cell phone. "The county attorney would like to speak with you," he said.

"Carl?" My prosecutor sounded a little worried.

"Yep?"

"Carl, we might have a problem. I mean, if that third floor is locked, and she has the key, and there isn't really any way the door has been pried or anything, I think that it might be a good way to defuse the situation if you people just didn't go up there today."

All in one breath.

"I don't think that Judge Winterman will agree with that, Mike," I said.

He sighed. "Let me be the judge of that. Do you realize who those attorneys are?"

"Yep." I tried to keep things to one-word responses, since Junkel and Koch were listening.

"I don't think that if we piss them off, Carl, that they will let the search go unchallenged. We don't want to lose the case by having the search declared invalid."

"Won't happen," I said.

"You sure?"

"Yep."

There was a pregnant pause. "I'm hoping, here, that you know something I don't."

What were the odds? "I do." I knew that Edie was supposed to have a key of her own.

"Boy, Carl, I hope you're right."

I couldn't resist. "Me, too. Catch you later." I broke the connection.

Attorney Junkel looked at me. "You're in charge?"

"Deputy Houseman, at your service," I said.

Attorney Koch, who had been conferring with Jessica Hunley in a muted voice, turned and looked at me very closely. "Aren't you . . . ?"

"Yep," I said. "It was me." I gave him my best smile. About ten years ago, I'd arrested his nephew for third-degree sexual abuse, a felony, after he'd allegedly gotten a girl drunk and had sex with her after she'd passed out. After a little bargaining between the county attorney and Attorney Koch, the kid had pled to a charge of serious misdemeanor assault. Got a $250 fine. Not my idea, and I'd been told at the time that Attorney Koch thought I was being "obstructionist" and "vindictive" by arguing against the plea bargain. All I'd said was "He screwed her after she passed out; he didn't beat her up." I'd lost the argument, of course, but I'd had the satisfaction of scaring the little shit. Scared his nephew, too, by the way.

There was absolutely no doubt in my mind that we had to go to the third floor, and no doubt in my mind that we'd get up there. Just how we were going to get that done, on the other hand, was something else again.

I excused myself, saying I was going upstairs to check on the progress of the team on the second floor.

"Team?" said Junkel.

"Yeah. There are officers and lab techs on the second, conducting the search."

"I think I'd like to go up there," he said, "and see just what they're doing."

"Not a chance," I said. "Borman?" He obliged by tearing his eyes from the two women for a second. "If anyone who isn't a member of the search team tries to go to the second floor, arrest them for interference, and call me right away."

"You bet."

I looked at the four other people in the parlor. "Nobody to the kitchen, either. Just the restroom on this floor. If they need a cup of coffee or anything from the kitchen, you'll have to get it for them. Within reason." I smiled at Jessica pointedly. "We wouldn't want him fixing supper."

Jessica glanced at her watch. "He may have to, if this takes much longer."

THIRTEEN

Sunday, October 8, 2000
14:26

___

I went right back upstairs to Hester, and we had a conference.

"It'd help if you were to find a blood trail leading to
the third floor," I said.

"Well, give me your wrist."

"Not yet, but let's keep that option open." I looked
back down the stair. "I'm staying up here a minute or
two. I want them to think I'm in conference." I just hate
it when attorneys get involved so soon. They belong in a
courtroom, not at a crime scene.

___

Finally, as Hester and company continued on the second floor, I returned to the parlor, carefully stepping over
the chalk marks in the second-floor hall. Looking back at
them, they seemed to be just about perfectly located in
front of Edie's bedroom door. Damn. That could be a

problem. They didn't lead anywhere. Just the way they would if she'd been brought here, and then they sat her down while they opened the door. No indication of direction.

Downstairs, Borman was just standing in the parlor doorway. "I think," I said to him, certain that I would be overheard, "we're just about done up there on the second floor. Or, should be within an hour or so."

Borman said, "Good, and then up to the third floor?"

"Oh, yeah," I said. "No problem at all."

"So, what," asked Junkel, "have you heard from the county attorney?"

"I'll be talking to him again shortly. We really are trying to be accommodating with this, but we also have a duty, and a higher obligation to the court." I shrugged. "You know how that goes."

By pulling both Borman and myself off search duties, we had probably lost two or three hours by now. We'd done it to be accommodating to Jessica Hunley in the first place. I'd hoped Ms. Hunley would have arrived, smiled, handed over the keys to the third floor, and left. Not to be. We'd tried to be accommodating when we simply should have taken the lock off one of the doors to the third, and reimbursed the owner.

There's always an upside, though. Although it had been in the back of my mind, I was quite aware that we had also kept Jessica Hunley from talking to the other residents of the house. I knew they'd talked on the phone, but so far they hadn't been able to sit down and exchange information as a group.

FOURTEEN

By 17:00, we decided we were ready to proceed to the third floor. Hester and I approached Jessica Hunley with two questions.

"First," I said, still in my friendly mode, "now that your attorneys are present, I'm going to ask again if you have a key to the third floor."

Junkel answered. "Yes, she does, but that doesn't imply that she either gives permission for its use, nor if she does allow its use, that she willingly acquiesces to this search." He looked at Hester. "Who's this?"

Hester said, "Hester Gorse. Special Agent, Iowa Division of Criminal Investigation." She produced her badge, and showed it to Jessica first.

"With the mobil crime lab, then," said Koch.

"No. I'm a general crim agent." She replaced her badge in her pocket.

"He," said Junkel, meaning me, "told us he was in charge."

"He is," said Hester. "We assist departments with primary jurisdiction."

"So," I said, "may we use the key for the third floor? To limit damage."

"Yes," said Koch.

"Now, then," I said, again directly to Jessica Hunley, "what sort of things are up there? I'm asking to see, I guess, if it's a fully furnished floor, or partially, with empty rooms."

"Don't answer that," said Junkel.

"Then we have to assume the worst, as far as the length of time it will take to search it. Okay." I turned to Hester. "Then we better feed the crew before we go up."

"Right," she said, with a twinkle in her eye. "There's no other choice. We have to assume it'll be a long one."

"Want me to go get the food?" offered Borman.

"Nope. We'll order out." I looked at Hester. "It can be delivered to the reserves outside, since nobody else is allowed in. They can bring it in to us."

"It's already after five," said Jessica.

"We'll go for supper," said Junkel, in that special, accommodating way attorneys have with wealthy clients. "We'll be back in about an hour and a half or so." He, Jessica, Tatiana, and Koch, in that order, headed for the door.

Payback time.

"Stop right there," I said. With authority, the way we were taught to do verbal crowd control at the Academy. It almost always works, and it certainly did this time.

I had their full attention. "If you choose to leave, you will not be allowed back in. You will leave the key to the third floor when you go."

"*I don't think so*," said Junkel.

"And," I said, "you will undergo a personal search

before you leave. As expressly permitted under case law." I stared at him. "You should know that."

Both attorneys knew I was absolutely correct regarding the search. Although it was originally an outgrowth of drug cases, where individuals were present when the door was broken down and would try to leave with the contraband on their persons, it also had application here. We were looking for trace evidence, including such things as rags or sponges that could have been used to wipe up bloodstains. They could also be concealed about the person, and removed from the scene. Well, maybe not under Tatiana's leather outfit. But the four of them would have to be searched when they left.

Playing the good cop/bad cop at the same time, I said, "But if you like, we will have our officers transport food in for you."

Jessica Hunley had had just about enough. "Thank you. We accept your offer. Now, can we just hurry all this up?" Junkel started to say something, but she just glanced at him and he closed his mouth.

We all ate in the parlor, with introductions all around for the lab crew and Chris Barnes. Chris introduced himself as a crime scene reconstruction specialist. That got the two attorneys talking between themselves. Good.

It was a strange sort of meal. We had four large pizzas, and cans of Coke and Diet Coke. They had full dinners, including salads and desserts, with bottled water.

I sat beside Hester and we started dividing up a pizza.

"Hey, Houseman, isn't this bad for your cholesterol?"

"Mumpbfh." That was sort of a "so what?," but with my mouth full of hot pizza it came out a little garbled.

"I thought so," said Hester.

I swallowed, took a swig of pop, motioned her to lean closer to me, and whispered, "There's something bothering me...."

"Mushrooms?"

"Nope. No, I have this feeling that we've forgotten to do something." She looked at me. "Well... that I've forgotten to do something, I guess."

"You've got your inventory sheet?"

"Yep." I took another bite of pizza.

"Just cross-check yours with the application, and see what doesn't fit. That might do it." She picked up a slice, and started it toward her mouth.

"Wonder where I put that?" I said absently.

She stopped in mid-bite, and put her hand over her mouth. "What?"

I grinned. "Just kidding."

By the time we got to head up to the third floor, it was completely dark outside. I checked my watch, and logged us at the locked main door at 18:51. As often as she looked at her watch, I could probably have just asked Jessica.

There were two ways up to the third floor. Simply following the main stairs up from the second floor, and unlocking the door at the third-floor landing reached the primary entrance. The second path was from the main floor, at the back of the house, via what was originally the servants' stair. Jessica, intending the servants' stair to be used as a private entrance to her apartment on the third, had hired carpenters to seal the door on the second floor. There were, according to her, locks both on the entry door on the main floor, and on the third-floor stair door as well.

Hester, Chris, and I conferred for a moment. We all felt that the main entrance to the third would be the place to start, as it was the most likely for Edie to have used. After all, like I said, "If you want to sneak off to be alone, why traipse all the way down to the first, and then back up to the third, when you just have to walk out of your door and go up one flight?"

We three agreed, as well, that if she had been killed on the third, it would have made much more sense to transport her body down one flight than take the old servants' stair. Unfortunately, the trace bloodstains indicated in the hall outside Edie's door didn't provide a clue to direction.

"Hey, Hester, you guys ever find Edie's keys?"

"Not yet," she said.

Just before we went up, I made a decision that I never would have considered if there hadn't been two very picky attorneys still in the house. I stationed Borman at the main-floor servants' door that opened on the back stairs leading up to the third. I just didn't trust those two as far as I could throw them, and lacking that delightful opportunity, I didn't know how far that was.

So I just stuck Borman there.

"Nobody gets up, right?" he confirmed.

"Right," I said. "Nobody but us even gets to open the door. They can't even have a chance to claim some sort of irregularity." I looked around, to make certain we weren't overheard. "And no way they can open the door and listen to what we say upstairs, either." I grinned.

He and I both checked the lock. Tight.

"You can verify that it's locked?" I asked, wiping the fingerprint dust from my hands. The knob had already been processed for latent prints.

He tested the door. "Yep." He looked disappointed. "Can't a reserve do this?" He had kind of a point.

"Nope. In court, we don't want anybody making an issue out of reserve versus deputy sheriff." I shrugged. "Just best that way, and one less thing to worry about."

"Okay. Yeah, I agree, I can see that."

"Look," I said, "when the next shift of reserves gets up here, we'll open the door from the top, and start down it. Then, we can have a reserve here, and you can come on up."

He brightened. "Okay."

As the rest of us approached the third-floor stair via the more conventional front way, we passed down the long second-floor hall. The leucomalachite green that was sprinkled on the suspicious stains on the carpet in front of Edie's room had been covered by two transparent plastic covers that looked as though they had been liberated from the kitchen. The stuff under them gave off a ghostly green luminescence. It was completely dark outside by now, and the hall was lit by converted gas lamps by the door of each of the six rooms. They looked to be about twenty-five-watt bulbs. Dark enough for the bioluminescent chemical to glow. We stepped carefully over the stains, and continued toward the stair.

The door had a dead-bolt lock, similar to the one on the servants' stair down on the first floor. It certainly looked solid. The lab crew had dusted the whole door and frame for latent prints. Nothing. That didn't surprise me. There hardly ever were any prints on surfaces that required hand movement. Like doorknobs. And if you were to place your hand on a door frame for any reason, chances were you'd move the hand as you removed it. Smears, or less. Latent prints, at least good ones, are very rare.

I inserted Jessica Hunley's precious key, and opened the door. There was a light switch just inside, and I turned it on. I stepped back, and let Chris Barnes go first. If there was any trace evidence on those stairs, we didn't want to disturb it, we wanted to keep it. As he shined his light on the polished wood steps, looking for stains or traces thereof, Grothler ran a drop cord from a wall socket in the nearest bedroom, and connected it to a little hand vac. New bag attached, and he was ready to go. After Barnes got up about five steps, but hadn't actually stepped on the stair yet, he backed off and Grothler vacuumed carefully up to the last step Chris had been able to see well. Then they went through the entire process again, with the next set of four or five steps. If you're one of the people who aren't directly involved, it seems to take forever.

It happened as Grothler was vacuuming the second set. With the whine of the vacuum in the staircase, it was pretty difficult to hear much of anything, but Hester grabbed his arm and said, loudly and distinctly, "Quiet!"

As he looked up at her from the depths of concentration, and obviously without quite comprehending, she reached out and snapped off the switch of his vacuum.

"I heard something..." said Hester, and she reached back and put her hand on her gun.

We all heard what came next. There was the slamming sound of wood on wood, loud, and then the muted thunder of somebody running down stairs. A muffled thud followed, felt as much as heard. Simultaneously, there was a yell from Borman that sounded as if it was coming from the floor above us. Up the back stairwell, I thought. It was funneling his voice, and we were hearing noises that originated below coming from above....

Borman hollered, "Stop!"

Then we heard two shots.

FIFTEEN

Hester flew up the stairs, right over Grothler, and I spun around and went charging down the main staircase to the ground floor. I had my gun drawn by the time I blew by Jessica Hunley and company, who were lying on the floor of the parlor.

"You okay?" I hollered, as I headed for the back door.

I think it was Hunley herself who said, "yes." I'm not sure. By the time she got it out, I was through the kitchen, and heard the back screen door slam.

I went by the broken frame of the servants' stair door to the third floor as I, too, flew out the back door. I just about stepped on Borman, who was kneeling at the corner of the building, gun drawn.

"You okay?"

He seemed a bit confused. "Huh?"

"You hurt?"

"No." He shook his head, as if to clear it. "No, not really."

"Where's Hester?"

"I think she's after him...."

I was aware of some blood on his right cheek. "After who, where...where did she go?"

He just pointed toward the dark area behind the house.

"Get some people and some lights up here," I yelled, as I went thundering into the dark yard. "Hey, Hester!"

My eyes hadn't quite adjusted to the dark, and I heard her voice off to my left, well before I saw her.

"Over here. Slow down. He's gone."

I slowed to a fast walk, and almost stepped on her before I saw her, crouched down, looking farther into the darkness. I could see well enough to catch the movement of her head as she spoke to me.

"You might want to get down a bit, you're silhouetted against the house lights...."

I dropped to one knee, breathing hard. "Who is it?"

"Beats the shit out of me," she said. "You're slowing down."

"Yeah." I took another deep breath. "Hard"—another breath—"to stop me, though."

"I saw him heading this way," she said. "Lost him in the dark."

"What's going on?" Old Knockle. The reserve was coming around the far side of the house, shining his flashlight into the backyard. Right on us.

"Turn off your light!" It snapped off. "Stay there, and make sure nobody circles around to the front of the house," I yelled to him. "Play your light out toward the trees."

He did. Nothing, of course. No movement. No sound.

"Borman might be hurt," said Hester.

She was right. And he had a walkie-talkie. We were going to need reinforcements before we started to go after anybody in those woods. This was definitely not Toby or his ilk.

She and I both went cautiously back toward Borman, keeping in shadow as much as possible.

"It's us," I said. "Don't shoot." You can't be too careful.

"Right," he said. "Right."

When we got back to him, I could see he had a scrape on his cheekbone, his shirt was torn near the right shoulder, and there was an enormous slash right across his chest, through his shirt, and slitting the underlying Kevlar bullet-proof vest.

"Holy shit," I said. "He had a knife?"

Borman looked down at his chest. "Yeah, he did, I think. It was so fast."

"You sure you're all right?" I asked.

He nodded. "I looked. No cut or anything." He patted his ruined vest. "Close, though."

"No shit," I said, impressed by the damage.

"What happened?" asked Hester as I gently reached over and pulled Borman's walkie-talkie from his belt.

"Hell," said Borman, "I was just standing at that door, and I heard a commotion that sounded like it came from upstairs, and then the door busted open and hit me in the face and knocked me against the back door, and then this asshole came through and"—he gasped for breath—"I thought he just shoved me in the chest, you know, and then"—another breath—"I could see it was a fuckin' knife, and he was heading past me and to the yard."

"That's when you shot?" asked Hester.

"Yeah," said Borman. "Yeah."

As I made sure the walkie-talkie was on the right channel, I asked, "Think you might have hit him?"

He just shook his head.

I pressed the transmit button on the walkie. "Comm, Three. Ten-thirty-three."

You announce an emergency, right out of the blue, you get some pretty good attention.

"Three?"

"Ten-thirty-three, Comm. Up at the search location. Armed suspect, officer slightly injured, suspect fled the scene on foot. Get us as much backup as you can find."

"Ten-four, Three. Comm, all Nation County cars, we have—" I turned the volume down so I could talk to Borman for a second.

"So, you don't think you hit him?"

"I'm positive," he said.

"Got a description?" asked Hester.

"Dark gray shirt," he said. "Dark pants. I think. Yeah, maybe black or dark blue. Kinda tall, maybe dark hair."

"Happens really fast, doesn't it?" said Hester.

"Damn," I said, mostly to myself. "Sure you might not have hit him? Make findin' him a lot easier."

"I couldn't have," said Borman. "I shot up in the air."

Well, you could have knocked me over with a feather. "Up in the air? Like, you . . . you fired *warning shots?*"

"Yeah."

"He slashed your chest with a knife, and you shot up in the air?" Hester gave me a "shut up he's got enough trouble right now" look. I ignored it. "He tried to do you, and you fired warning shots?"

Borman looked like he could crawl in a hole, but defended himself. "He didn't kill me. . . ."

"Of course not, you idiot," I said evenly. "If he'd killed you, I wouldn't expect you to fucking shoot at all!"

"Carl," said Hester. "Cool it for a minute."

"Yeah. Jesus H. Christ." I looked at Borman. "He was running away from you, then?"

"I dunno," said Borman, embarrassed. "No, I guess

174/ D o n a l d H a r s t a d

not. Not right then. He was kind of in front of me, but
he was starting to move, I think. I think he might have
been surprised to find me at the bottom of the stair. And
I think he thought he got me, you know? I just . . . I got
my gun out real fast. I, well, I'm not comfortable with
taking human life without good reason."

I just didn't understand. "Well, somebody around
here sure as hell isn't worried about it! He may have
tried to get you with the same fuckin' knife he used on
her! You listening to me?"

"Houseman," said Hester, "just lay off for a minute."

"Yeah." Thoroughly disgusted, I put the walkie-
talkie in front of my face, and called Dispatch again.

"Three, go ahead."

"Yeah, Comm, have a couple of cars search the base
of this bluff, down by the highway. We're looking for a
white male, tall, gray shirt, black or blue pants, dark
hair. Armed with a knife. Use caution."

"Ten-four, Three."

"And get hold of One, and tell him we need at least
four or five more officers up here on the top of the hill,
to search going down. Then get Freiberg PD stopped before he gets here, and have him go back and look up
Kevin Stemmer." I paused. "Just check location for now,
and if he can't find him, let us know right away."

"Ten-four, Three. Ten-fifty-two has been dispatched." An ambulance. A good idea, as I thought Borman should be checked out. Mostly, I thought, for a
suspected injury to his common sense. But it was really a
very good idea.

"Ten-four." I put the walkie-talkie down, and talked
directly to Hester. "I want that Stemmer dude located,
mainly to make sure it isn't him."

"I don't think it is," said Borman.

I took a deep breath. "Okay. That'll help. Look,
we'll go over our deadly force procedures later. You did
okay." I don't think I was too convincing. "You get
checked out, make sure you're all right. Then, if you

can, I want you to sit down and describe every detail of this guy you can remember. Everything. Take your time, and don't rush. You got all night."

"Right."

"Let's get you back inside," said Hester, and sort of gently pushed Borman back up the stairs and into the kitchen. "Where you can sit down."

As Borman entered the house, Hester turned to me. "Our man Peel?"

I nodded. "I think it sure as hell could be. Alive and well, unfortunately. Well, we're just gonna have to work a little harder to find out, I guess."

She smiled. "See? You can adjust, after all."

"Hmmm."

Lamar pulled out all the stops with the assistance. He'd contacted state patrol, as well as the boys across the river in Conception County, Wisconsin. Adjoining counties in Iowa, too, judging from the sudden surge in radio traffic. It began to appear very unlikely that Peel, or whoever it was, was going to be able to get off the bluff. Within minutes, we had two squad cars sitting at the base of the bluff face, right at the only possible path down from the house. We had officers in the woods shortly after that, accompanied by the Conception County K-9 unit. Their black Labrador appeared to pick up a trail right at the back door of the Mansion, and pulled his trainer toward the woods in hot pursuit, then seemed to pause about ten yards from the back door, and started "casting about," as they say. Looked like he was earning his keep to me.

The radio informed me that Lamar was on his way, as well, and that he had two DNR Fish and Game officers putting their boats in up at Freiberg. They'd be on the river in our area within a few minutes.

All in all, it looked like whoever had come thundering

out of the third floor was going to be in our custody fairly soon.

Unfortunately, Jessica Hunley and company had fled the house when the shots were fired. Reasonable, I suppose, and certainly justifiable in court, but we'd lost the threat of a search to hold them in the house.

Hester and I decided to let them take off, with the promise that they'd be available in the morning for "a few more questions." We offered to put up Jessica and Tatiana in a local motel for the night.

"I won't hear of it," said Junkel. "They're more than welcome to stay with us."

I expressed the gratitude of the taxpayers.

As they left, they met Lamar at the Mansion end of the long drive. He pulled halfway into the trees to let them by, and then came to where Hester and I were standing near the front steps.

"That's a nice car, there," he said, as he got out of his four-wheel-drive pickup. "Who belongs to that?"

"That'd be Jessica Hunley," I said. "Owns the house, too."

"How's Borman?"

Well, I told him. And, since warning shots had been fired, and since I was the supervising officer at the scene, I told him about that, too.

"You talk to him about that?" he asked.

"Yeah. You could say that."

"Okay, Carl. No need for me to say anything, then."

That, it seemed, was to be the end of that.

Lamar decided that, since the small army of officers that were in the woods could handle the search, Hester and I should join the rest of the search team, and get the business in the Mansion conducted and behind us.

"Before hell freezes over," he said. "Be really nice if you could do that."

SIXTEEN

The longest warranted search of my career resumed on the third floor of the Mansion, duly logged in at 20:12. Participants were recorded as me, Hester, Grothler, and Barnes. Hester, by virtue of already having been there, however briefly, went first.

The third floor was divided into two equal segments. One half was a well-furnished apartment, in a loft style, and furnished with very modern furniture, in complete contrast to the rest of the Victorian-style house.

The only separate area in the apartment half was the bath. The rest, kitchen, living area, and bed were separated by kind of artfully arranged furniture. Hester stood just inside the main door.

"Didn't get much of a look as I came through," she said. "Nice." She had her gun in her hand, as did I. We were taking no chances that there was a second suspect who'd decided not to run with the first. "This stuff is just about all IKEA," she said. "Wow."

"Oh." I assumed that was either a brand name or a designer's name. Or, maybe a style? I didn't want to embarrass myself by asking.

Outside, we could hear some officer calling over his PA system. "Peel, we know you're out there! You might as well give up."

I looked at Hester. "Who gave out the Peel name?"

"Not me."

"Had to be Borman or Lamar," I said. It was too late to hold it back now, regardless of who had released it. Considering how Borman's night was going, I hoped for his sake it hadn't been him.

The lighting, which we'd accessed via the main switch panel by the entrance, was muted but very thorough. Track lights, free-standing lamps, lights built in to the kitchen cabinets, all came on with the master switch. Made it really easy to check it all out.

The bed was what I'd describe as "king-size plus," and was in the far corner. Solid all the way to the floor, with cabinets underneath. Nice, indeed. The most interesting thing about the bed was the tripod with video camera positioned to cover about a three-quarter view of the bed and its sometime occupants. Two halogen lights, on their independent stands, were set to light the area covered by the camera.

There was a huge black and white photo, framed and lit with two special ceiling lights, on the wall above the bed. Being a WWII buff, I thought at first it was a photo of an anti-aircraft emplacement in Normandy. A closer look showed it was a series of sunken concrete entrances, very much like church doors. They were arranged in a circular shape, with a large hub in the center that also had doors, with names chiseled on the lintels. What had made me think of WWII was the abundance of undergrowth. There was a small label in the lower right corner. "Circle of Lebanon." Interesting.

The kitchen was all built-in stuff, including a dish-washer and a really nice combination microwave and gas stove setup. Nice hood. My dream kitchen.

I looked at Hester. "This is the kind of place I'd kind of hoped to get to when I died."

"Yeah."

I noticed the computer, of course. I do that. Nice Dell outfit, with one of the new two-inch-thick monitors ... flat panel displays like that ran about $2,500. Nice. An ergonomic keyboard. The whole unit had its own IKEA desk, with matching executive chair. The thing that struck me most about it, though, was that the thing was so uncluttered.

There were some extra boxes attached to the computer. I looked more closely at them, and saw a note entitled "Suggested Replacement for SOHO Server." I knew just enough to know that SOHO stood for "Small Office/Home Office." I knew what a server was; it connected several computers, and also connected them to the Internet. The list included things like Emulator, 300 W power supply, motherboard, 2 PIII CPU, 256 MB SDRAM DIMM minimum, floppy drive, DVD-ROM drive, PCI adapter, Ethernet adapter, networking card, keyboard and mouse, two 60 GB HD, and the like. Hmmm.

"Hey, Hester, when you get a minute ..."

She took one look at the note and said, "Apparently they're thinking of upgrading the SOHO server."

"Yep," I said. I kept my eyes moving about the place, just in case our Mr. Peel had had a guest.

"And," she added, "they may not have decided yet, because there are no brand names attached to the descriptors."

Ah.

"And I hope they're running ME." She said that mostly to herself, her eyes, too, constantly moving about the vast room.

"Mmm." Noncommittally, I hoped. I didn't have the

faintest idea why she hoped that, and didn't want to seem uninformed enough to have to ask.

"Every bedroom we searched," she said as she passed me, moving toward the center of the third-floor apartment, "had a computer. None of them even close to this beast. I think the residents bring their own, and then link to the net through this stuff. Nice system." As she spoke, she darted her hand inside the doorway of the bathroom, and flicked on the light. She stepped in as I covered her. "Nothing," she said, reappearing a moment later. We continued to move about.

There was a very strange structure dividing the third floor neatly in half. It looked like a small, peaked-roof house, about eight feet high, with sash windows on all four sides. The windows on the long sides were offset, on the near side to accommodate a glazed door, and on the far side to accommodate the corner of the huge main chimney. Inside the structure was a large, flat-topped skylight leading via wooden ducting to the six bedrooms below. Above the structure was the peak of the main roof, with glazed skylights that corresponded to glazed areas in the peaked roof of the little house. There was little, if any, room inside the little place for anything but a narrow foot purchase for somebody who might clean the glass.

"What the hell do you call this?" I asked Hester.

She looked at it for a few seconds. "Thingy, I think," she said.

"Nobody inside," I said, looking through the window on my side of the structure. I could see Hester through the glass, on the other side.

"Right."

On the opposite side of the newly identified "thingy" was a room that ran uninterrupted the full length of the house, about a hundred feet, and was some eighteen feet wide. We entered swiftly, me first this time, and Hester right behind, going left and hitting the light switch. After a moment's flickering, the fluorescent lights came to life.

It was a dance studio with a polished wooden floor, and a multiple-mirrored interior wall. A wooden rail in front of the mirrors, attached with large brass fittings, and large stereo outfit at the near end, with some folding chairs, a bench, and a clock on the wall at the far end. Suspended fluorescent lights in standard gray shades. Austere. I took it in in about two seconds. Nobody there, nor could there be without being seen immediately.

"She takes her dancing seriously," said Hester.

The security sweep completed, we holstered our weapons and got to work looking for evidence.

"She's got to pay for those cars somehow," I said.

Hester shook her head. "Not by dancing."

We took our time, and did a very thorough search, beginning with photographing both rooms. Then the place was divided up among us, working in teams of two. Grothler and I got the "living area," which was fine with us. It was all so neat and organized, and so modern in contrast to the rest of the house, there wasn't much of a place to conceal anything. Nooks and crannies were at a premium, thank God. That's why, I guess, I found myself photographing the bookshelf, and then looking behind the books. Well, you could hide things back there.

There were some interesting books, so interesting that I got my zoom lens out of my camera bag, and used it to photograph readable sections of the shelves.

Gray's Anatomy, Chaos by Gleick, and Hawking's *A Brief History of Time* were books I had at home, and lent a familiar aspect to the shelf. Then, though, there were several volumes that I'd never heard of. First, *Treatise on Vampires and Revenants: The Phantom World*, apparently translated by one Harry Christmas. I sure didn't have that one at home. Neither did I have *Death, Burial, and the Individual in Early Modern England* by Clare Gittings, although I have to admit it did look interesting. *The Vampire: His Kith and Kin* by Montague Summers, struck me as sounding like good reading for a stormy night. *Reflections on Dracula* and *Shade and Shadow* by Dr. Elizabeth Miller looked to be the sort of thing I'd pick up for myself. I was beginning to think I'd found the source for Toby's vampire tale.

There was a very nice photo volume entitled *Highgate Cemetery, Victorian Valhalla,* photographed by John Gay and introduced by Felix Barker. I opened it up, and thumbed through the black and white photos of the famous cemetery in London. As I did, a slip of notepaper fell out. On it was written "Beware David R. Farrant, British Occult Society," with "Egyptian Avenue & the Circle of Lebanon," written at a slant, and the whole thing had a smiley face under it with the word "Isadora." On the open page was a smaller version of the huge photo on the wall. I checked in the list of photos in the back of the book, and discovered that the Circle of Lebanon was a wheel of crypts in Highgate Cemetery in London. Strange. I copied the note onto my log sheet, along with the name of the book, and Isadora. Just for future reference.

Beside the cemetery book was one entitled *The London Nobody Knows* by Geoffrey Fletcher. Next to it was *London Under London, A Subterranean Guide* by Trench and Hillman. Two books I thought I'd like to read.

The *Oxford Dictionary of the English Language* dominated a shelf all by itself. I'd heard of it, but never actually seen one. It was the really cool edition, the one that came with the magnifying glass. I thought it looked out of place in such a modern room, and should have been in the library downstairs, with the mahogany table and the five-foot wainscoting.

The last shelf contained a series of almanacs, woodworking guides, a carpenter's handbook, and *The Joy of Sex*. I smiled to myself, because their shelf order made me think of splinters in unusual places.

There was nothing behind the books or behind the shelf. I went back toward the center of the room, and cleared my throat. Hester turned her head toward me. "I know what that's a photo of," I said, pointing to the wall.

"Really?"

"Highgate Cemetery, London. It's crypts. In a circle, pretty old."

"Ah." Not as much reaction as I'd hoped.

"Check this," she said. She drew my attention to the built-in wardrobe closet. Lots of stuff, much of it women's clothes. Some Victorian-looking stuff, brocaded and velvety, in deep reds, blues, and greens, with lots of lace at the neck and cuff. Pretty. Some men's clothing, as well. Looked to be for somebody about six feet, slender build. Big-sleeved shirts, laced-at-the-v-neck kind of stuff. Mostly white and off white. Black trousers, and one formal set of tails. Really nice. With them on the hangers were blue jeans, sweaters, sweatshirts, and sweatpants.

On the floor of the wardrobe were several kinds of footwear, including Wellington boots, laced Victorian women's high-topped shoes, and men's and women's tennis shoes.

On a series of little pegs on the inside of the door were hanging several pairs of black velvet restraints, black velvet blindfolds, and a brown leather switch with a tasseled end.

"Little something for everybody," said Hester.

"Not quite," I said. "No cookies."

Between both teams we eventually found only three groups of items of particular interest, which were photographed in place, and then taken as evidence.

The first interesting little group was discovered by Hester, in the wastebasket in the kitchen area. A fairly large pile of stripped casings from a variety of rechargeable lithium batteries, the kind that are used in cameras, video cameras, flashlights, that sort of thing. The metallic cases were split, and folded back. A bunch of packaging material, that had obviously contained the shrink-wrapped batteries. Also in the white garbage sack inside the wastebasket were about ten empty packages of Sudafed cold medications. Nothing more.

"Look at this stuff," said Hester. "I believe we have a tweaker."

Both Grothler and Chris Barnes were on the battery casings like a pair of hounds.

"Yep," said Grothler. "Took the lithium strips out. You bet."

"Nazi formula," said Barnes. "Watch for anything that looks like ether. Needs anhydrous ammonia, too, but it's probably stored remotely."

What they were referring to was the formula for methamphetamine developed by the Germans in WWII. Speed. The allies developed their own methods, too, but needed central manufacture. Used as a way to keep soldiers awake and alert for extended periods, the so-called Nazi method involved ephedrine, lithium, and assorted other elements, cooked using ether and anhydrous ammonia. It was quick, effective, and made small amounts that were ready for use. The Germans apparently needed their troops to be rather more self-sufficient in the face of Allied interdiction of supply lines, I guess. The mixtures were both chemically dangerous and quite explosive. No particular problem for soldiers in the field. In your house, though, you could easily blow yourself up, or burn your house down.

At any rate, you sure didn't have to be a soldier to use the stuff.

Hester, who'd continued to search that area while the discussion was taking place, held up a small glass bottle. A brownish crystalline substance was inside.

"Bingo." She held it up to the light. "I'd say meth, all right. Crystal meth."

The question quickly came down to just who the tweaker was. This elusive Peel dude? Jessica? Or maybe Edie, who had, after all, possessed a key to the third floor?

The second item discovered was a black steel filing box containing nine VHS videotapes. They weren't labeled, but were numbered one through nine, neatly, with numerical stickers in the left corner. A glance showed that tape number ten, identically marked, was in the camera.

The tapes and camera were seized, due to the high probability that we might just have tapes depicting either the real Daniel Peel, or the man who had fled down the stairs and sliced Borman's vest, or...well, both, if they were either the same man or two different people. Along with others, presumably Edie chief among them. Because Edie was likely to be on them, I truly was not looking forward to viewing those tapes.

The third item was what we used to call "pay dirt." It was in the center, lower drawer under the huge bed. A knife, and an unusual one at that, wrapped in a cloth with dark, reddish stains that appeared to be blood.

The knife was really strange-looking. I suppose it was nearly sixteen inches overall, with a blade some eight to nine inches long. The handle was slightly curved downward, ebony, and with a silver metal butt cap that was shaped like an eagle's head. The beak on that bird looked very sharp. The blade itself was the really weird part. It was about three inches wide, tapering sharply to a very fine, slightly up-curved point. It was a double-bladed knife, so the blade looked as if it had had about a quarter-inch slot just ground out all along its length, making two blades, effectively. The inside edges of both halves had been sharpened, too. Four cutting surfaces for the price of two, so to speak. The thing that really struck me about the knife, though, was that slot between the blades. I vividly remembered the lump of muscle protruding from Edie's neck wound. With this knife, it would have been easy to snag muscle in the slot, and if there was any twisting, to effectively pull muscle and other tissues right back out of the wound.

"This could be it," I said.

"Sure is big enough," said Grothler.

"You mean the split in the blade?" said Hester, to me. "Snagging tissue?"

"Yes." I nodded. "It looks like that'd do it." It would explain the number of cuts inside the wound as well. Not so many thrusts, but twice the cutting surface.

"Could well be," said Hester, reaching for an evidence bag.

We also found some fairly benign sorts of things that might have a bearing on the case. One was an antique crystal candy dish, with a silver lid, containing a number of small white pills. They seemed to have cartoon characters pressed into them. I saw Woody Woodpecker, for sure.

Hester looked carefully at the container, and chuckled. "Ecstasy. Possibly from Holland." She pointed to the elaborate initial etched into the silver lid. It was an "E," very much embellished. It, too, was seized as evidence.

There was another bottle, green glass with a brass top, and mounted in a brass tube with legs. Antique, too, I thought. It contained a number of dark green pills, smallish, with a horizontal break line and the numeral 6. Curving across the top was a word, which I could only make out with the help of my reading glasses. "Coumadin." We all knew that was a blood thinner, but weren't sure just how many different conditions would require its prescription. It was also an anticoagulant. Hester and I exchanged glances over that one, and she nodded.

"Yeah."

"I think so, too," I said. "I wouldn't be at all surprised if the lab found a quantity of Coumadin in Edie's tissue samples."

Another container, this time an old 250ml Erlenmeyer flask, graduated, held a large number of coated, pink pills with the inscription "Mellaril 200." No idea on that one.

The last pill jar was a deep red, also appeared to be antique, with silver scrollwork and a silver stopper. Eighteen blue, diamond-shaped pills, with a brand name on one side and the inscription "VGR50."

"Anybody know what this is?" I held one out in my hand.

"Hang on to it, Houseman," said Hester, with a grin. "You may need it sooner than you think."

I bit, I admit it. From her comment, I sort of assumed it might have something to do with Alzheimer's, or something like that. "Memory stimulant?"

"Probably, in your case, that would be all it is," she said, laughing. "It's Viagra, Houseman."

"Oh." I put it back. "Hey, I'm sorta proud I didn't know what it was."

"That's the memory part," she said.

We were all aware of the fact that most of the seized pills appeared to be prescription drugs. We were also aware that we'd not found any prescription bottles of any sort.

Pending the results of the toxicology exam, all meds were photographed in place, and seized.

Chris did the back stair, the one Borman had been guarding, with great diligence. Hester followed him down, after I took photos. The steps were pretty clean. Not only in the evidentiary sense; they gave every indication that they were cleaned and vacuumed regularly. No cobwebs. No dust. Just shiny hardwood and clean pastel green plaster. Nothing, until the second step from the bottom. Chris went on point, came back up for his stuff, and after a few minutes, we shut off the lights.

Green luminescence shone on the bottom two steps. In wide swaths, with a discernible swirling pattern.

Chris looked up the stairs at our three faces peering down at him. "Looks to me like it's a blood response, not detergent. We'll see, and I wouldn't be surprised if there was a mixture of both. But for now, I'd be inclined to say somebody wiped up some blood here. And not too long ago."

The rest of the steps were clean. Period. According to Chris, that was far from typical.

"I'd be inclined to think there should be more blood-staining around here. Drips. Spills. Seepage. Something."

But there wasn't.

We photographed the stairs by using a time exposure, darkening the entire third floor, and using a slow pass with a flashlight across the walls of the stairwell, first one side, then the other. That way, the luminescence would show up, and we'd also be able to show the scene. Without the dim light of the flashlight, we'd only get the green on film, without any clue as to where it was located. That was the theory, anyway. Just to be safe, we also outlined the areas where the wipe marks were, and took shots of them in good light.

We all sat around for a few minutes, completing our inventory of seized items, finishing up the sketched diagram of the third floor, and making sure we had everything.

"We done?" asked Hester.

Well, as far as we were concerned, we were. Others, it seemed, had different ideas.

SEVENTEEN

Monday, October 9, 2000
01:47

I guess I hadn't fully comprehended the extent of the isolation of the third floor from the rest of the Mansion. As we descended the stairs, we gradually became aware that there was quite a bit of activity around the place. The closer we got to the ground floor, the more my suspicions were confirmed.

We got to the bottom of the stairs, and saw the press people gathered outside the front door. The scene was brilliantly lit. Shit. They had TV cameras and everything. I identified Iowa TV units from Cedar Rapids and Dubuque and one from La Crosse, Wisconsin.

Our call for reinforcements had gotten a little more attention than I'd hoped.

Lamar was, well, eager to see us.

"Somebody told these assholes we were hunting for a vampire up here," he said, the tense being past accusative. "Who did that?"

I started to say that I didn't know, when he continued.

"They want to know who and how many he's killed, where the vampire is, who the vampire is...." He looked me square in the eye. "Any suggestions?"

"I suppose," said Hester, "that means he hasn't been caught yet?"

"Hell, no, he hasn't been caught," said Lamar, with considerable disgust. "They can't even find a good track, and the useless dog got away from his trainer." He shook his head. "Goddamned animal started to track Borman at first. You know that? Worthless...."

There had just been too many people around, I guess.

"I got the plane up from Cedar Rapids PD, with their FLIR, and all they can see is cops, deer, and that useless fuckin' dog wanderin' around." Lamar gestured toward the woods. "We used spotlights from the Conception County helicopter. All the way to the river. Then the FLIR, when it got here. Nothin', nothin' at all." I thought he was going to spit. "Then this goddamned rain on top of it...."

It was raining, not hard, but one of those drizzly, persistent rains that can go on for days. A cold, damp night, peculiar to October and November.

"The rain affect the FLIR much?" I asked.

"I guess," he said. "It tends to even out the temperatures, if somebody's gonna hide in the woods, so they tell me." He shrugged. "Just makes it harder, is all."

FLIR is a Forward Looking Infra Red device. It can see a heat differential of less than half a degree Fahrenheit. Any mammal would show up, and clearly enough that you could spot the antlers on a buck deer from about five hundred feet up. The beauty is, the target has no idea you're looking at it. You can hide under things, of course. Behind things, inside things. But if even your legs were uncovered, it would have you. But the rain, like Lamar said, would make it less effective.

"Where could he go?" I was thinking out loud, more or less.

"I hope," said Lamar, "that you didn't come all the way downstairs just to ask that."

Lamar hates the press. It isn't always so obvious, but he really does. He's also very nervous around them, and will do almost anything to avoid having to talk with them. The fact that the so-called vampire's victim was his niece just compounded the problem past all reason.

"You give a statement yet?" asked Hester.

"Nope. Nothin' to say, I guess."

"Let's give a joint statement," she said. "You and I can write it up real quick, and I'll go with you and both our offices can issue it."

He nodded, and the two of them went into the main dining room, and sat at the long, beautiful table. The setting was quite a contrast to the turmoil both inside and outside the Mansion.

There was a familiar voice at the door.

"Hey, Houseman, kin we have your picture, or you gonna feed all of us?" Harry.

As it turned out, Harry had been in Milwaukee most of the day, talking with the pathology team that had done the autopsy on Randy Baumhagen. The death had been the result of the blow to the head with one of those ubiquitous "blunt instruments." Probably about three to four inches wide, probably fairly heavy. The throat injury was, as we had been told in the preliminary report, the result of the use of a sharp object, but not a blade.

All well and good. But Harry had been busier than that. He'd talked with people about William Chester.

"He ain't got a sister, Carl, and he never fuckin' had one. Dead or not."

"Really?"

"He was livin' with some gal, over around Walworth, who died in a car wreck. That's it. He lied."

"What do you think? We dump him?"

"I dunno. Everything else checks out so far. I dunno." Harry looked around the interior of the Mansion, taking it in for the first time. "Nice fuckin' place."

"We like it," I said.

"So, the press people tell me that you found our boy?"

I explained that he'd more or less found us. I gave Harry all the details.

"Warning shots?"

"Yeah." I sighed.

"Kids these days," said Harry. "They just think too much." He looked around some more. "So, you think he was up there all the time, then?"

"Yeah. Zonked, maybe. Enough pills up there to keep you out for a while." I motioned him over to the stair, near the inglenook. "Hear anything?"

He tried. "Nope."

"Quiet, isn't it?" I gestured around me. "I mean, even with all the commotion outside."

"Well, yeah, now that you mention it."

"I'll tell you, Harry, this is the quietest house I've ever been in in my life. You could make a lot of noise one or two rooms away, and never be heard. Not to mention up a floor or two."

"It's all the insulation in the interior walls, I betcha," he offered. "These old places are like that."

"I think so, too," I said.

"So, where ya think he's got to?"

"Beats me. Lots of area to hide in out in those woods. Lots." I raised an eyebrow. "Maybe we got lucky, though."

"How's that?"

"Maybe he's a good swimmer, and made it to the Wisconsin side."

While Harry paid his respects to Lamar and Hester, I called the office to find out whether or not the Freiberg cops had been able to find Kevin Stemmer. Turned out they had, in a local bar called The River Bank. Strike one suspect.

The news conference was remarkable. Hester and Lamar stood together on the front steps, starkly lit by the TV reporters and their lights, and with their breath visible against the shadows of the house, gave a prepared statement. Actually, Lamar introduced them both, and then let Hester do the statement, but it was obviously and effectively a joint release. The rest of us watched intently from the corner of the porch. We were safely off camera, and had a view from the left rear quarter, where we could just see their brightly lit faces.

"This is an ongoing investigation into a possible homicide," said Hester. "I emphasize 'possible.' Since it is ongoing, there is very little we're able to release to you at this time. The deceased is one Edith Younger, of Rural Route, Freiberg. An autopsy has been performed by the medical examiner's office, and the results are expected to be formally submitted at the conclusion of all the routine laboratory testing."

It was a nice release. They'd done a nice job. Predictably, as soon as she'd finished the last sentence, the assembled reporters all started asking the vampire question. Hester held up her hand. "There has been a rumor started that there is somehow an involvement of a so-called vampire in this case." She drew a deep breath. "Vampires are mythical creatures. Period." She produced a great, open, honest smile. "Any suspect or suspects in this case would be human beings," she said, in a calm, clear voice, "and would be treated as such. You can count on that."

"So, who are you looking for with all these people?" the Dubuque TV reporter asked.

I found myself just as curious about her answer as the media.

"We have a possible suspect, who may be in this vicinity. We are checking to see if our information is correct."

Cool. I almost clapped.

"Is it true that this suspect has been shot?" I peered into the group, but with the TV lights and the light rain, I couldn't see who was talking.

"Nobody has been shot," said Hester. Too true.

"We were told that a person had been shot, and had fled into the woods." I moved a step or two to my right, and looked hard into the assembled media people. It appeared as if the La Crosse TV reporter was the one doing the talking. As my eyes moved over the group of media people, I recognized William Chester standing near the La Crosse SUV. I suspected I'd identified their source, although where he had gotten his information was beyond me.

"No one was shot and then fled into the woods," she said.

She tried to forestall further questions by saying, "The law expressly does not allow the release of more information at this time. The sole reason we chose to respond to the first question was to put an unfounded and kind of silly rumor to rest. We are allowed to do that under departmental procedure." The smile again. "We're encouraged to do that, in fact."

There was a barrage of questions, many containing the "V" word. One actually asked if the vampire had drained the blood from the victim.

"I'm really sorry, but I can't say more at this time. We'll keep you posted on the critical steps in the case. Thank you." She and Lamar turned, and began to walk back into the house.

Hester should have gotten some flowers for her performance.

"Is the dead girl any relation to you, Sheriff?"

Lamar stopped, and stood for a second, with his

back to the cameras. We had a good view of his face, and it was absolutely stony. He turned.

"Edith Younger was my niece," he said. "That's why I'm not personally involved in this investigation."

He turned, and ignored the hubbub behind him. Then, he did something I'd never seen him do before. As they headed into the Mansion, he held the door for Hester.

About fifteen minutes later, we had all the arrangements made to secure the house pending the return of the owner, and the search warrant team was going to head in for the night. The area searchers were still out there, but it was beginning to look like our quarry had given us the slip.

"We'll keep at it all night," said Lamar. "And do a daylight search, too. He's gotta be somewhere."

"Hey, Lamar," said Hester. "You puttin' everybody on double time and a half?"

"No," he said gruffly. "They're all just workin' a shift."

"Not since midnight," said Hester. "Happy Columbus Day!"

Lamar looked at her. "Well, shit."

Columbus Day be damned, Lamar decided to leave three officers in the woods, with orders to search until 9 A.M. They'd be relieved, and the next trio would search until four o'clock.

"I'm not sure he's gone far," said Lamar. "Somethin's not right."

It was hard to fault that reasoning. Besides, we'd had a little bit of luck come our way. When you do an application for a search warrant, you have to describe the property to be searched with exceptional accuracy. According to the Platt maps, the area surrounding the Mansion was owned by the State of Iowa, as part of the adjacent wildlife refuge along the Mississippi. The demarcation between the Hunley property and the state land was the woods, naturally enough. That meant that we were searching on state land. There was no permission required from the Hunley people in order for us to tramp through the woods all day and night.

Before we left, Hester and I decided that we'd better get an interview in with Hunley and Ostransky fairly early tomorrow, and see just what they could tell us about Peel, vampires, and the kinky stuff on the third floor.

We pulled right past the reporters, who were caught, as usual, completely flat-footed. We were headed down the drive before any of them had a good chance to get a photo.

Just as we reached the end of the lane, and were stopping before entering the main road, I saw some blue out of the corner of my eye. I slammed on the brakes, just about causing the lab van to rear-end me. I opened my door, took off my seat belt, and started into the overgrown area on the right.

"You see him? Have you found him?" came from Chris.

"What? Oh, no, no, but you better come, too. We forgot something." What I'd forgotten, and what had bothered me while we were still up on the third floor, was sitting just off the driveway. The garbage. In the big, blue container. Of course.

We made an executive decision, seeing as how all the contents of the big steel box were in several black garbage bags. Just take the bags, list them on an amendment to the inventory sheet before we left the property, take a copy back to the house, and just haul the bags down to the sheriff's department, and lock them in the evidence room, and go through them tomorrow. Anything we didn't seize, we could just haul back. And, since it was my bright idea, I got to cram all five bags into the backseat of my car.

The ride home was uneventful, but a little smelly.

———————————

I was less than popular at the office when I put five bags of garbage in the evidence room, and locked the door.

"That shit's gonna stink up the whole office," said Deputy Kline, who'd been with the department long enough to know what he was talking about. "I'm gonna have to go out and drive around, for Christ's sake."

"Imagine that." I dropped my notes on my desk, and fumbled for the key.

"You find the guy you're lookin' for?" he asked. He'd been assigned as the general duty deputy for the night, and was the only one not up at the Mansion. He was actually in the office because it was centrally located, and it made more sense for the only one on duty to be there than anywhere else.

"Nope," I said, inserting the key and opening my drawer. I shoved my notes in, took my undeveloped film from my pocket, and put that in there, too. "I'm beginning to think he got away," I said. "Although it must have taken some talent."

"For sure," said Kline. "You got an army up there."

"Yeah," I said, very tired. "That we do."

I walked out to Dispatch, and left a hurried note for Borman that we were going to start about 09:00, maybe as late as 10:00, and that he could meet me at the office when I got there.

When I handed the note to Winifred Bollman, the duty dispatcher, she looked up and said, "Jeez, Carl, you look wiped out."

On that note, I called it a night.

EIGHTEEN

I woke up about 08:02, to a ringing phone. I answered it, sleepily.

"Yeah?"

There was about a one second pause, then, "Hello, my name is General Norman Schwartzkopf, and I'm calling you on behalf of ..."

I hung up. Iowa was predicted to be a close contest in the upcoming presidential elections, and we were getting a lot of automated phone calls. I turned over, thinking I could get another thirty minutes of sleep. I lay there thinking about that extra sleep for thirteen minutes.

I rolled out at 08:15, and drank my first cup of coffee in relative peace. Always a good way to begin a day. I'd just missed Sue. Education did not wait for Columbus and his day. I called the office as I poured my second cup.

"Houseman? We thought you'd be up here by now." Sally.

"Mmm? Who's 'we'?"

"Hester and me." She giggled. "Really, we thought you older folks needed less rest."

"Thanks, brat. So, anything happening?"

"I'd better let Hester take that one," she said, and I found myself on hold. We'd installed hold music about a year earlier. The only good, reliable station we got was a country & western FM outfit that played music all day long. Unfortunately, they had an amateur portion during their broadcast day that began at 08:00 and lasted until 10:45.

"Carl?" Hester's voice interrupted some unfortunate young man's rendition of "Sixteen Tons." It was sort of too bad, because I'd never really heard somebody so close to being a tenor sing it before.

"What's up?"

"You can forget our interview this morning."

"What?"

"Yeah," she said. "Ms. Hunley was called away on urgent business."

"You're kidding?" Damn.

"Nope. Her 'awnt,'" she said in a pretty good imitation of a downstairs maid, "with whom she resides, was suddenly taken ill."

"I'll bet. And she of the iridescent hair went, too?"

"Oh, yeah. Tatiana had to go with. It's a two- or three-hour drive, you know." She sounded a little aggravated. "At least, that's what Attorney Junkel said when I called. He said they left really early this morning."

"Right." Well, shit. "Gone to Lake Geneva, then?"

"You bet. Located on the other side of America's Dairy Land."

Eastern Wisconsin put them out of our reach, at least for a while. "Well," I said, trying to make the best of it, "we can always let you beat up Toby."

She laughed at that.

It occurred to me that, while she might be out of our reach, Jessica Hunley was now within the grasp of one

Investigator Harry Ullman, Conception County's best. A silver lining, maybe.

_____

I'd pretty much decided to spend Columbus Day playing catch-up with the case, anyway. That originally had meant interviewing Jessica Hunley and Tatiana Ostransky, the five remaining residents of the Mansion, and then sorting through all the garbage I'd dumped into the evidence room last night. Since Jessica and Tatiana were gone, I thought I might as well go straight to the garbage, to see just what we had, and then get to the five sometime in the early afternoon. Very early if the garbage search didn't pan out.

The phone rang again. "Hello?"

The familiar pause, and then "My name is Senator Tom Harkin, and..."

Click.

I always stayed on just long enough to hear who the recording was. It was becoming a big thing at the post office, kidding each other about what important recording had called. It had kind of a baseball trading-card aspect. "Hey, I got two Colin Powells, but no Jimmy Carters." "Really? I got a Jimmy _and_ a call from Tipper. Beat that!"

_____

I got to the office at 09:09, where I met Borman, who was standing at the counter and talking with Sally in Dispatch.

"Ready to get going?" I asked him.

"Not really." He was acting kind of funny, not looking right at me, and obviously pretending to fiddle with some papers on a clipboard.

"There a problem?" I really hated to ask.

He didn't say a word. Sally broke the awkward little silence with "He's been suspended for a day."

Well, damn. It had to be the warning shots from last

night. "With or without pay?" was the first thing I asked. It was important, but not for the money. Without, and he only had one more screwup and Lamar would fire him. With, and he'd be able to erase it with good performance over the next three months.

"With." He was honest-to-God petulant. Twenty-five years old, and pouting.

"Well, that's good," I said. "Why don't you just go home, and come back in tomorrow like you had a day off?" He'd gotten off pretty easy, I thought, because warning shots were prohibited by department policy.

"He wants to ask you something first," said Sally.

I looked at her. Her tone of voice told me she was at least half on his side, for some reason.

"Well, go ahead," I said, remembering in the nick of time not to say "Shoot."

"You had to tell Lamar, I suppose," he said. "Didn't you?"

Honest. That's what he said.

"You shouldn't even have to ask that," I replied. "Of course I did. I was present, I was senior officer, and it was my responsibility and duty to do so. You know that."

Silence for a few seconds. Then he asked what I considered the second dumb question in a row. "I don't suppose you could have waited for me to tell him first, then, could you?"

It wasn't only a dumb question, there was resentment creeping into his voice. If I hadn't liked him I just would have told him to grow up. Instead, he got a bit more than he bargained for.

I looked at my watch. "Okay. Sit down." He looked blank. "I said to sit down."

He did.

"Deadly force is justified only to protect your life or that of another, right?"

"Sure." He couldn't really say anything else. That was the fact of the matter.

"And only if there's no other way to accomplish that protection. Right again, no?"

"Yeah," he said, "sure. Of course."

I looked at Sally. "Since you're carrying a gun as a reserve, you knew that, too, didn't you?" She nodded. She damned well better have.

"This is for you, too. Sort of a refresher. The most dangerous shot you can fire is a warning shot." I was warming to my task. "Let me tell you why. Number one: You have *absolutely* no business discharging your weapon if deadly force is not justified. It can't be justified, because you are making a deliberate effort *not* to hit the individual. You with me?"

He nodded, but was beginning to look bored.

"I'm doing this because I think you have potential, so listen up. Number two: You have no goddamned clue as to where those bullets went, do you?"

"I shot into the air," he said.

"Exactly. Unless they defied gravity, they came down. Do you know where they came down?"

"No."

"Damn right, you don't. In some departments, where they have more people and could afford to have you off for a while, you wouldn't get back off suspension until you produced both rounds for the sheriff's inspection. Did you know that?"

No, as a matter of fact, he hadn't.

"Number three: When the bullets stop, if they should because they hit somebody, it damned well isn't anybody who you'd be justified in shooting, is it? We had two reserves in the yard around the other side of the Mansion. What in hell would you have done if one of 'em had come down and hit Old Knockle in the head?" I waited a second. "How about an answer?"

"I don't think they went in that direction."

"You don't think? Well, that's swell. Do you know?"

"No," he said, "I don't know, but I know I didn't hit Knockle."

"That's really lame," I said. "But don't let's stop there. Number four: The suspect who got you to pop two warning shots may very well have killed Edie in the preceding twenty-four hours." I saw he was going to say something, and held up my hand. "No, we're not sure. Just a good bet. At the same damn time, the son of a bitch had just slashed you across the chest with a very sharp object, and would have severely injured you if you didn't wear your vest. Right?"

"Yes, but that's why we wear 'em."

He was starting to piss me off. "Did it ever occur to you," I said, very slowly and distinctly, "that he was trying to cut your throat, just like he did to Edie? That he just missed because he was in a fucking hurry?"

He got pretty pale, pretty fast. Obviously, it hadn't occurred to him at all.

"So, he was still facing you, he cut at you, and you shot in the air. Assume for a second that you *had* hit Old Knockle." I let him think about that for a second. "Can you imagine me telling Lamar that you'd killed Knockle because the man who probably murdered his own niece, and tried to kill you...." I stopped, and let it sink in. "Now imagine this. Imagine that I'd said to myself, 'Carl, why don't you wait and see if Borman can tell Lamar on his own?' You with me?"

"Yeah."

"And Lamar hears about this from somebody else. Before you tell him. Now, wouldn't that look like we were both trying to cover it up?"

"It might." He looked up. "Yeah, it would. I'm sorry. You're right, Carl, you had to do it."

I turned back to Sally. "You understand this, too?"

"Oh, yeah. You betcha." She smiled. "Got it."

"Okay, then." I looked over at Borman. "Go home. Come in tomorrow fresh and ready to go."

"You still want me with this investigation?" He sounded genuinely surprised.

"Of course I do. So does Lamar." But I made a mental reservation. The sulking, plus the arguing, followed up by the sudden agreement and phony ". . . you had to do it . . ." apology really pissed me off. Insincerity? Maybe. Whatever it was, he'd showed me a side of himself that I hadn't seen before. He'd also had Sally half convinced that he'd been wronged by both me and Lamar. That was a new talent he'd revealed, and one that I didn't want to see again. I still thought he should be on the case, because he knew quite a bit about the thing, and because I still had a good impression of him from before it began. Stress might be a factor, but I was going to be watching him.

My little stint as wise and fearless leader over for the morning, I collected Hester from the main office, where she was typing a report, and we went right to the evidence locker. Ugh. It did smell, but not as much as I'd feared. My nose told me that the residents at the Mansion had recently thrown out onions, garlic, and some meat.

My nose was only two thirds right. They'd thrown out onions and garlic, all right. But the third one wasn't meat. It was a bloody body bag. I stopped as soon as I saw it, and called for a little help.

Chris Barnes and the rest of the lab crew were at breakfast, just about to leave for Des Moines. He got to the office in five minutes.

We all stood looking at the bag. It was a white nylon bag, with black nylon handles, and a black zipper. A small label proclaimed it to be a "500 VSA." A good bag, it was one of the expensive double-thick ones, with reinforcements at the ends and on the bottom. There was quite a bit of blood in it, and a darkish smear on the outside of the bag. Chris looked very closely at that, and said it looked like a wood stain, possibly from where it had been stored.

"Well," said Chris, "this goes a long way toward explaining the lack of a blood trail."

"Except for the spots, next to her tub, on the carpet outside her room, and at the bottom of the back stair," I said.

"Right. Where somebody rested the body, and it was bent forward or to a side, and put pressure on the bag, and forced a bit of blood out of the zipper." Chris shook his head. "I'd just guess that she hadn't bled out all the way when they bagged her," he said. "Don't quote me on that, not yet. We gotta test the blood first. See if it's human, and then see if it's hers." Using a gloved finger, he stirred a little pool of blood that had accumulated in one of the folds of the bag. "It sure as hell should have clotted by now."

"Right." That was from Hester. "How long till we can have the results?"

"For human, maybe today, depending on when I get to DM." He paused when she cleared her throat. "Okay, today, then, for sure. As for the DNA match . . . hard to say, but as fast as we can get it done."

"You know," I said, "having a killer with his own body bag sure makes a case for premeditation. You just can't plan much farther ahead than that."

We filled out the evidence sheet for the bag. It consisted of a copy of my logging, where I had entered the time I pulled the bags from the big blue box; the time I placed them in the evidence locker, the time I took them out, and the time I signed the body bag over to Chris. My signature by every entry, and his and mine on the last set. Maintaining the chain of evidence is crucial, but a pain in the butt, regardless. Like they say, the only time it's going to be important is the time you forget to do it.

We all pitched in and did the contents of the rest of the garbage bags. We found one bloody bath towel, a bloody washcloth, a bloody bottle of shampoo and one of conditioner, a bloodstained bar of soap and a hanging soap dish, a bottle of bath oil with a blood-encrusted rim, a brass rack with a curved section to enable it to be hung over the edge of an old-fashioned tub, and a bloodstained pink lady's razor. All in a white plastic sack, in a brass wastebasket. Even the wastebasket had matched, apparently.

"I'll bet they knocked the stuff into the tub when they put her in," said Hester, her voice distant with thought. "Maybe snagged it with the bag, then grabbed for some of it before they thought, and then pitched it to make sure they hadn't left prints. Wiped some of the mess up with the towel."

"No wipe marks on the tub," I said.

"They could have wiped their hands on it," said Barnes, not looking up from his itemization of the evidence. "Hard to say just how it got there."

"They had the presence of mind to put the knife in the tub, to keep us from looking for the real weapon." I shook my head. "Pretty cool, whoever it is."

"Yeah," said Hester, disgusted.

"Well," I said, "I guess we could start with who sells 500 VSA body bags, and see if there's any chance they might have a limited sales area...." It was pretty weak, but we had to begin somewhere.

Another thing we found was a bunch of old e-mails that had been tossed out. They appeared to be from several people, and addressed to the following: OnceLost @gottadance.arts, WailingSoul@gottadance.arts, MagikBoi @gottadance.arts, DealerofDarkness@gottadance.arts, Clutch @gottadance.arts, EtherialWaifGurrl@gottadance.arts, Choreographer@gottadance.arts.

They were addressed to a wide variety of people and places, from bookstores to eBay, from names similar to their own, to simple ones like *DarcyB2@UIU.grp.edu*. Some were long, some very brief, and they appeared to be pretty innocuous. Nonetheless, I saved them all, to read for content, and to check names and addresses.

"I wish," I said to Hester, "that that search warrant had included computers and information thereon."

"Well, we didn't have any evidence pointing to computer involvement then. We still don't," she said.

"Give me a little time."

We went through the rest of the bags, snagging about a half dozen more e-mails, and about a thousand items of generic debris that could have come from just about anywhere. We relooked, hoping for anything else. Nothing. Not one more item that even appeared to have bloodstains or marks on it. No phone bills, no notes other than common, everyday grocery receipts. Lots of political pamphlets from a bumper crop of politicians, from Bush and Gore to Nader and Buchanan. Not to mention the local and state candidates. It looked like the residents of the Mansion had been deluged just like the rest of us. The political pamphlets probably accounted for half the paper in the bags. I did notice, though, that all the political mail was addressed to "Occupant."

"Doesn't look like anybody living at the Mansion was registered to vote," I said.

"Huh?" That had taken Hester by surprise.

I explained.

She went back to sifting through garbage. "The things some people consider important...."

"Hey! I'm a trained observer, that's all."

"Focus, Houseman," she muttered. "You just got to focus."

Finishing the garbage survey didn't take as long as I'd expected. I looked over at Hester as we were both taking off our latex gloves. "Not much, was there?"

"Good Lord, Houseman. You got a body bag out of this! What more do you want?"

"Well, yeah." What more, indeed? "Something identifying the suspect, though, would sure have been good."

Chris and the rest of the lab team headed for the Iowa Criminalistics Laboratory in Des Moines, body bag in hand, so to speak. That left Hester and me to begin our scheduled business.

Hester phoned the Mansion while I sorted the e-mails into some coherent order. I just sorted by recipient name. There were two double entries, as I termed them, that were from a "gottadance" to a "gottadance."

The first was from Choreographer to OnceLost. It was dated September 16, 2000, and timed at 21:56. The text was brief and to the point.

> "Hi.
> We should be there either next weekend, or the one following. Checking to see that you have a good supply of fresh vegetables and that wine we like.
> Hope all is well. Got your August report and approved the payments.
> Oh, and try to get George Hollis for the furnace. He's more reliable than Norman Brecht, and charges the same."

No doubt who Choreographer was. Apparently "gottadance" was a wide area network, and seemed to include Jessica Hunley's terminal in Lake Geneva, as well. Judging from the content, I assumed OnceLost was Edie. Had to check, to be sure.

The other double entry was from Choreographer to Clutch. It was dated October 2, 2000, and timed at 22:40. The text read:

> "Hi.
> I think it did go well. Thought about it all the way back. I agree with you.
> Many thanks."

Like that told me a lot. Unfortunately, people just don't annotate e-mails for the cops.

In the rest of the e-mails, content identified Clutch as Huck since she talked about her job on the gaming boat. DealerofDarkness had to be Kevin. Kind of left MagikBoi for Toby, which I thought was a bit of a hoot. WailingSoul and EtherialWaifGurrl were up for grabs, but I was willing to bet the former to be Hanna and the latter Melissa.

Hester got off the phone, and said the group was expecting us after lunch. She sat down on the other side of my desk, and started going through e-mails with me. I told her that I had pretty well identified Choreographer as Jessica, and OnceLost as Edie. We started in from there.

After the first complete sorting, there were five e-mails in the OnceLost pile. One was a receipt from Amazon.com for a vegetarian cookbook; two were eBay-related messages indicating an initial bid and an outbid notice on a Raggedy Ann doll. She'd lost the bid at $12.50. The other two were both from *DarcyB2@UIU.grp.edu*. The first was dated July 12, 2000, and timed at 23:15. It included a received e-mail, and like so many, contained the original message that DarcyB2 was replying to.

> *"Dear E,*
>   *I'll sure try to get there for the event! It's been a long time since we have been able to get together for a good talk. Looking forward to seeing you.*
>   *Yes I remember the D&E. We sure had big plans then! I remember Lindzy, too.*
>   *Hugs,*
>   *D"*
>   ——*Original Message*——
> *From: "OnceLost" <OnceLost@gottadance.arts>*
> *To: <DarcyB2@UIU.grp.edu>*
> *Sent: Wednesday, July 12, 2000 4:19 PM*
> *Subject: Birthday and stuff*
>
> >*"D,*
> >*Justa thot. The 19th of August is my Shanna's*

>*birthday. I think I can get a Raggedy Ann for her*
>*like Lindzy, our first customer at the D&E*
>*Salon. Remember? She would love to see her*
>*Godmother I know. I would love to see you too*
>*and have some things I really need to talk about.*
>*Really hope you can make it. Mom won't be*
>*with us if that helps.*
>*Sorry its been so long since I wrote.*
>*We miss ya.*
> *E & S"*

The second was dated July 24, 2000, and timed at
16:44.

> *"Dear E,*
> *I am so very sorry to have to tell you this, but*
> *I won't be able to make it after all. I have to be a*
> *bridesmaid for my roommate's sister Ellen, who*
> *is getting married on that date in Santa Fe, New*
> *Mexico. It's a really big wedding.*
> *We really have to get together, really. I'll call*
> *when I get back for sure.*
> *Love and hugs to Shanna and to you.*
> *D"*

Interesting. I showed it to Hester. She read through
them, and then said, "I had a Raggedy Ann when I was
a kid, too."

"I hope she wasn't counting on the one she bid for
on eBay," I said. "There's an e-mail here telling her that
she got outbid."

"Oh." She sounded a little distracted. "She had a
child. . . . I didn't know she had a child."

"Yep. Kid lives with Edie's mother. Not sure just
why, but Edie and her mother didn't seem to get along."
I thought for a second. "I seem to remember some sort
of custody thing. You know, not a battle, just voluntary.
Edie didn't fight it, anyway."

"Any idea how old?"

"Not sure, but I'd guess about three or four, maybe?"

"Ah. That's quite an age," said Hester. "Quite an age."

"Just so you know," I confided, "with Edie being Lamar's niece and all, she attempted suicide about, oh, a year or so after her mom got the kid. I got stuck with that one, and if I remember correctly, it was the second or third time. None of 'em really serious. Pills, either the wrong kind or not enough. You know."

"Might work for us," she said, "but it could play hell with a jury at some point."

"Well," I said, "in Edie's case, I'm afraid that knowing she'd tried to do herself in before just gave her killer an idea. He just screwed up faking it, that's all. That'd make the jury think."

The mere existence of the body bag spoke volumes about the malice aforethought in the mind of the killer or killers.

"Hey, Hester," I said, "how many people you suppose have a body bag at home? Just lying around out in the garage, for example?"

"Not a lot. How many you know would know where to even get one?"

Not average citizens, anyway. "Well," I said, "let's start with funeral homes. Then hospitals. Then ambulance services. Police departments. Maybe even a few fire departments." I shrugged. "It's not a military bag. That leaves civilian agencies who would have them, plus manufacturers and sales outlets. That's about the only ones who would even have access."

"Wonder if a sales or manufacturing place would question a request for one?"

"Well, I'd hope. But you never know."

"I think," she said, thoughtfully, "that it had to come from somebody who wouldn't ask, and who wouldn't have to mess with accounting for it."

"Okay."

"So, like, if you had a relative or a good friend who *owned* a small funeral home, for instance. They would order often, I suspect. The owner wouldn't have to account to anybody else for the items." She smiled.

I didn't even answer her as I reached for the phone, and dialed Dispatch.

Sally answered. "Jiffy Dispatch, at your service."

"I hope you never get inside and outside lines mixed up," I said.

She giggled. "You'll never know. Whatcha need?"

"Well..." I gave her the gist of what we'd been talking about, and asked her to check for any funeral homes with the same name as any of the five surviving residents of the Mansion, or Hunley or Ostransky, or Peel.

"Sorry I asked," she said. "Give me a while on this one, okay? And how far away do you want me to look?"

That was a good question. It's always tempting to say, like, the whole world. To make it reasonable, and to increase my chances of ever getting another favor like this, I said, "Two hundred miles..." Before she could object, I added, "... because Hunley lives about that far away, for one thing."

"This," she said, "will cost. Big time."

"Anything you want," I said. "Just say what and when."

"Well, Houseman," said Hester, "how about you and me go get some lunch, and then lean on some witnesses?" That was more like Hester's normal good spirits. She'd seemed just a bit down since the bit about Edie's daughter came up.

I smiled. "Might as well. Can't dance."

Before we could get out the door, Sally called the back room and reminded us that there was a wake for Edie from 4:30 to 6:00 P.M., at the funeral home at Freiberg. Swell. I just hate to go to wakes where we're involved in a case. They're usually pretty sad, and they can really skew a cop's perspective. You just don't want to get emotionally involved. Makes you rush things, because you want to do something for the grieving survivors. Rush, and the case can get away from you.

We decided we had to go, though. Lamar would want us to. And we'd be near Freiberg anyway, while we were at the Mansion.

There was a consensus that I'd better stop at home and get rid of the blue jeans and tennis shoes, and put on something a little more presentable. Considering that I'd also have to be working, and maybe doing grungy things, when I got there I settled for a pair of wash pants, olive, and dark hiking shoes. A shirt, and cardigan sweater-vest to hide the gun at my hip, rather than take a chance and leave it in the car when we went to the wake. I didn't think it was too startling a contrast to my normal attire. Apparently I was wrong. As I walked back out to the car, Hester looked up from her notes.

"Well, the new Houseman. Hardly recognize you."

I got in the driver's seat, and started to buckle my seat belt.

"My," she said, "I hope we don't get you dirty." As I threw her a look of disdain, she continued with, "Maybe you should have eaten first."

"Now, come on. They're just wash pants."

"You're too modest, Houseman," she said. "You're creepin' up on presentable on me."

"You know," I said, as we headed out for lunch, "I'd think the group up at the Mansion would want to go to the wake, too."

"It could be tough for 'em," said Hester. "Hard to fit in, I'd think."

I grinned. "Then I'll be in good company. Really, though, it's not going to give us much time to do interviews."

"Give me a little while on this," she said, "but we may just have enough to get selective."

We were barely in the car when lunch was canceled.

"Three, Comm?" came crackling over the radio.

"Three..."

"Ten-twenty-five with the search party up north. Eighty-one says they have something for you."

Fantastic! "Ten-four, Comm. We'll be ten-seventy-six," I said, turning left instead of right at the bridge, and heading north. "ETA about fifteen."

"Ten-four. They advise at the bottom of the bluff, on the highway end. They'll be in plain sight."

"Ten-four." I was really, really tempted to ask if they had somebody in custody, but I was aware that the media were probably monitoring our radio traffic even then.

"You think they got him?" asked Hester.

"I'd think so," I said. "But maybe not."

"Hard to think why else they'd call us up," she said.

"If I'm gonna miss lunch," I replied, turning onto the main northbound highway, "they damned well better have a warm body for us."

They did, as it turned out.

"Eighty-one, Three," I said into my mike, as I got within a mile of the bluff.

"Three, go."

"I'm a bit less than a mile from you."

"Ten-four, got you in sight. Pull in here," he said, and I saw a figure in blue jeans and a dark green jacket step onto the highway on the bluff side. There was a sheriff's car parked in a level area just off the roadway, where the county kept a gravel pile for use on the roads. The figure waved, and I recognized Old Knockle. As I got closer, I saw there was a blue Chevy parked ahead of the squad car, and as I pulled in, I saw that it had Wisconsin plates.

As we got out of the car, I said, "Don't you ever sleep?"

"Only got an hour to go. Hello, Hester."

"Right," I said. "What you got?"

"Well, we were up the road there, me and Tillman, and we were comin' in to relieve the other guys, and I noticed this car, here. Ran the plates, and they're expired. To a woman named Gunderson, over by Madison."

"Okay?" I was awfully eager to see what else he had, but I didn't want to rush him.

"Well, while Tillman was checkin' under the seats," he said, provoking a wince from me, "I looked up there." He pointed to the bluff. "There was a fellah up there lookin' back at me."

"Recognize him?"

He pointed to his glasses. "Surprised I even saw him, Carl."

"What'd he look like?"

"He's just a man in a gray sweatshirt with a hood, I think. Not much more. Anyway, I yell at him, and he just stares at me. I holler 'Who're you?' and he just motions like he wants me to go away."

I hate to admit it, but my heart rate was elevating.

"Where'd he go?"

"Well, he sort of disappeared, Carl. But I think he went back toward the top of the bluff."

"And where's Tillman?" My heart sank. Tillman was about twenty-five or so, and had been a reserve for about three months. A great kid, but I was pretty sure he didn't fully appreciate some aspects of the job. Like risks, for example.

"He took up the hill after him," said Knockle. "Told me to stay here, and call for help."

I looked up the bluff. There was a ravine that was full of big rocks and old, fallen trees. But it looked passable, at least up into the tree line.

"How'd Tillman get up there?"

"He went up the ravine, Carl. Didn't look too easy. You better watch your step."

"No shit." It was no time for pride. "Did he have a walkie-talkie?"

"No, we only got one, and he told me to keep it 'cause he'd need both hands."

I looked as Hester went by me, toward the ravine. "Coming?"

My good slacks. My better shoes. Damn. "Yeah, I'm coming." I reached into the car, and pulled out the walkie-talkie, and slipped it into my back pocket. "The team you were going to relieve still up in the woods?" I asked Knockle.

"I ain't heard from 'em, Carl, and I called three or four times."

"Did you use your walkie or the car radio?"

"Oops. Sorry, I used the walkie."

As I headed toward the ravine, I said, "Use your car radio, get some more people up here, and get your shotgun out and keep your eyes open. I don't want you getting hurt on me. You're too old to bury."

He grinned. "You bet."

The damned ravine was really wet, to start things off. The rain had soaked the rotting timber that was crammed into the rocky waterway, and there was still a thin trickle of runoff flowing down from the hill. On top of that, everything was covered with soggy, moldering leaves. And I could catch the occasional whine of a mosquito as I took my first steps onto the big rocks. Great. My good slacks.

Hester was ahead of me, and I wasn't able to gain on her at all. It took both hands just to stay upright, and the handholds I found among the decaying branches were treacherous because the sodden bark just peeled off in my hands. Underneath, the smooth wood was slippery as the rocks under my feet. But, up I went. I was pretty certain that, as we passed the limestone bluff and went up into the wooded area, the footing would get better, and the slope would be less steep. I was half right.

After about three or four difficult minutes, I saw that Hester was stepping spryly from a boulder and into the tree line. About a minute later, I went for the trees at the same place. The footing was a little better. The slope, unfortunately, was steeper.

I kept losing sight of Hester as she moved about among the big maple and walnut and pine trees. I stopped to catch my breath, and heard her call out.

"What?" It was difficult to get much volume, I was breathing so hard.

"Here...," she said.

Well, swell. Two more gulps of air, and I headed up-slope again. Then I heard another voice, and realized she was talking to Tillman. They seemed to be stationary. Good. I slowed a bit, as the tone of their voices didn't seem especially urgent. By the time I got to them, I was only breathing sort of hard.

They were on either side of a rock outcropping that jutted out from the hillside about twenty feet. It was a good ten feet high, and seemed to be split about down the middle by a fissure that was about four feet wide.

I've been around long enough to realize that, when there's an officer acting really alert on either side of an opening, with a gun in his or her hand, that there's a very good chance there's somebody inside that opening. Somebody who's being difficult, at best.

"What's up?" I said as I moved to the right, or Tillman side, of the split.

"I think he's in there," he said. "I saw him go in. I don't think anybody could climb up the inside of that to the top up there, do you?"

I thought of the wall outside Alicia's apartment. "Don't be too sure," I said. "You heard anything since you saw him go in?"

"Nope."

"Hey, you in the rocks!" I shouted. "Out, now!"

Nothing.

"Police! Come out now, and keep your hands where we can see 'em!"

Still no response. I remembered when I was a kid, and we would think there was something fierce or ferocious in a hole. We'd grab a stick, and poke it in the hole to see what might come out. Nothing ever had. Buoyed by memories, I nevertheless realized that poking a stick into the crack between the halves of the outcropping wasn't quite the solution we needed. I looked around, and saw several small rocks that had flaked off the limestone over the years. I picked up three nicely shaped ones, hefted them, and decided they'd do admirably. I whistled softly through my teeth. When Hester and Tillman glanced toward me, I held up the rocks and made a tossing gesture. They both nodded, and returned their gaze to the target area. I holstered my gun, and lobbed the first one at the fissure. It bounced off to the side. Close, though. I tossed the second one about seven or eight feet higher, and saw it enter the crack. It clattered off the sides twice, and then I heard a muffled thump.

"Hey! Stop throwing the damned rocks!" came from the split.

I was grinning from ear to ear at that point. "Come out slowly and with your hands where we can see them!"

"Okay, okay." With that, there was a shuffling and a grunting, and a man emerged, hands up, head down, wearing a gray hooded sweatshirt and blue jeans. His head was down more to avoid thrown rocks, I thought, than for any other reason.

While Hester and Tillman covered me, I approached slowly, gun back in my hand, but pointed down. "Stop right there."

He did. I still couldn't see his face.

"Who are you?"

He looked up at me. "Bill Chester. You know me."

Honest to God. Our intrepid vampire hunter. "What the hell are you doing up here?"

"Can I put my hands down?"

"Yeah, go ahead. So, what the hell are you doing up here?"

"Can't a man just take a walk in the woods?"

Tillman spoke up. "I told you to stop. I got a uniform on. You saw us down at that car, with a marked cop car. Why'd you rabbit on me?"

I thought that was a pretty good question.

"I'm not sure I have to tell you that."

I was getting a little tired of Mr. Chester. "That your car?"

"No, it belongs to a friend of mine."

"Your friend here, too?" I asked.

"No. I'm alone."

"You drove over here just to take a walk up a bluff?"

"There's nothing wrong with that. Absolutely nothing. I can drive and walk just about anywhere I want to. I don't see any 'No Trespassing' signs."

"That car's got an expired registration," I said. "You just admitted to driving it here. We're going to have to charge you, and impound the vehicle."

"What?"

"And your fleeing obvious officers will suggest to a court that you were fully aware that the registration was expired, and were trying to avoid capture." It was a moment.

"That would be chickenshit. I am appalled!"

I just smiled. It would at least make up for my good wash pants.

"Care to tell me why you're really here?" asked Hester sweetly. "I do have some influence with these two officers."

"You might have him start with that," I said, indicating

the edge of a dark green backpack protruding from the fissure.

Chester stepped back, and moved as if he was going to reach for the pack. He glanced at us, to see what the reaction would be, and found himself staring down the muzzles of three handguns.

"Freeze," said Hester. "Don't move a muscle."

He stopped. "I was just going to hand it to you."

"I'll get it," said Tillman. He moved slowly past Chester, reached down, and retrieved the backpack.

A long time ago, the Supreme Court ruled that we could make searches "incidental to arrest." In this case, that meant that we had every right to examine the contents of the backpack before we handed it back to him. Just in case there was a "weapon contained therein," as we say.

"Look through it," I said to Tillman, as Hester and I lowered our guns again. I stepped closer to Chester.

"I told you to steer clear of this case," I said, "and I meant it."

"I haven't interfered. Not once."

I decided not to mention my suspicion that it was him who had leaked the vampire stuff to the press. Instead, I said, "You're less than half a mile from the Mansion right now, and there's nothing else on this bluff but the scene of a possible crime."

"He's less than a quarter mile from there, Carl," said Tillman, who probably hunted in these woods.

"I had no idea...." said Chester, just as Tillman held up a small gray case with an LCD screen in its face and a keypad. It looked like a hand calculator.

"This is a GPS receiver, Carl," said Tillman, "and it works." Tillman was young, and his father owned a large, modern farm, so I took his word for it. They used them a lot these days, to place herbicides and other things with amazing accuracy.

I gave Chester a disgusted look. "Wanna try that again?"

"Is this guy a priest?" asked Tillman, holding up a crucifix that looked to be about a foot long.

"Nope," I said. "He's a vampire hunter."

"No shit?" said Tillman. "Way cool."

On the way back down to the cars, with Tillman toting the pack, I asked Chester why he had tried to defy my order to stay away from the scene.

"In the first place, I was lost," he said, without much conviction. "In the second place, I hardly think it's fair that you have patrols out just to keep me from my job."

Aside from the fact that only a dedicated egocentric would think our patrols were meant for him, it was the first time I had heard him refer to a job.

"Just what would your job be?" I asked between mossy limestone stepping blocks.

"To bring the vampire to justice," he replied.

"That's our job," said Hester. "Just ours."

"God's justice," he said. "Not the laws. The justice of the righteous."

"Oh," I said, "that's just fuckin' swell." I stumbled, and made my usual graceful recovery. "In the first place, he's probably not anywhere around here."

"Who? The one you were all chasing?"

"Whoever it is you're looking for, Chester," I said.

When we got to the cars, I told Tillman and Knockle to get a wrecker for Chester's car, and then escort it and him to the jail. I reiterated the traffic charge.

"Aren't you going to charge me with interference?" asked Chester.

"No. But don't push it. I'm willing to cut you some slack, because you weren't actually in contact with anybody but us. But, like I said, don't push it."

"Of course." He was smiling.

"Knockle," I said, "do not give this gentleman a ride back to this area. Keep his car in Maitland as evidence, and take him directly back to his motel over in Wisconsin, as soon as he posts bail." I paused. "And tell Harry that he's over there, and what happened."

"You bet, Carl. Hey, too bad about those pants. You looked pretty good before you went up the hill."

NINETEEN

When we finally got headed up to the Mansion again, Hester and I tried to come up with a game plan. To begin with, we wanted to know what Edie's five housemates knew about who had been upstairs when we went to the third floor. We were virtually certain that it was this Peel, but we needed to be sure. It was apparent that he'd been up there a while, possibly since Edie's murder. Had they known? I was willing to bet that at least some of them had. So was Hester.

We were pretty sure that the unknown called Peel had killed Edie, probably killed Baumhagen, and had been the window peeker at Alicia Meyer's. It looked like we were going to have to find out about Peel from the group at the house, though, since Jessica Hunley had split too soon to be interviewed. It was a case where, the more we knew about Peel, the more we'd probably know about the why and where of the killings.

We also wanted to determine two things about the movement of Edie's body. First, we needed to make sense out of the bloodstains. Both the stains on the carpet and those on the servants' stair had been explained by the action of setting down Edie's body in the body bag. Whoever was moving it needed either a rest, or a way to open the doors. Either way, the problem was determining why the stains were at the bottom of the servants' stair, which only went to the third floor; and on the second floor in front of Edie's door. If she'd been killed on the third, and we certainly had no real evidence that she had, it might explain the movement. Except to get her down to the second, the logical way was to go via the main stair, which we had gone up. To go down from three all the way to one via the back stairs, then right back up to two via the main staircase.... Illogical. Not to say not possible, but not logical.

As Hester said, "Especially since it doesn't look like she was killed up on the third, anyway."

"Since it didn't appear she was killed in the basement, on the first floor, on the second floor, or on the third floor...." I said. "Unless she was killed on the roof, she wasn't killed at the Mansion at all." Not a brilliant deduction, by a long shot, but at least logical.

"Sounds that way," said Hester. "You really think that's likely? Not the roof," she added quickly. "But, I mean, if you kill her away from the house, why drag her back at all? Why not leave her there?"

"Oh, maybe because you'd rather have the cops looking at suicide, instead of a missing person. If it was a suicide, we sure wouldn't pry as much as a missing person case."

"I don't think so," said Hester. "To deliberately cast suspicion, you should kill her there. Otherwise, even a dumb cop is going to figure out that she was done elsewhere, and there goes your plan."

"I'll try not to take that personally."

"Sorry. Didn't mean it that way." She chuckled. "So

all we have to do is prove who killed her, and why, and then we can explain the evidence."

I glanced toward her and smiled. "Simple, no?"

We drove in silence. Hester had her attaché case opened, and as I drove, she was leafing through our preliminary reports, as well as the reports of everybody else at the scene who'd had to write one. As I turned into the Mansion drive, she stacked the papers neatly, closed her case, and said, "I've got another question, that just might at least have an answer attached."

"That'll be a relief."

"Okay, now you're going to have to go with the flow here." She leaned her head back against the headrest, and shut her eyes. "We've had a total of two runners: Toby and the Unknown who is probably Peel. Right?"

"So far."

"We have no idea what Toby was up to, do we? I mean, he *said* he was running to get away from Peel, who was a vampire. Isn't that it?"

"Yep. That's what he said." I slowed, to give us time to finish the conversation.

"But you don't believe him, do you?"

"Toby," I said, matter-of-factly as we crept up the drive, "is a lying sack of shit."

"Oh, yes," said Hester, sounding happy. "He sure is. Now, then, hang on. We have the elusive Mr. Peel trucking out the very same door, and also into the woods, right?"

"Yep."

"Now think back," she said. "Don't we assume that Toby was just trying to get away, for whatever reason?"

"Yeah. I think we can do that."

"And don't we think Toby's a general screwup, when it comes right down to it?"

I chuckled. "Oh, we do, we really do."

"Now, and jump with me here, we also think that our Peel dude was fleeing, as well, and basically just trying to get away. Right?"

"Okay . . ."

"But what if they were not running so much *away* from something, as running *to something*?"

I didn't answer for a second. Then, "And Toby is so much of a fuck-up he couldn't find it in the dark?"

"You got it."

"Damn," I said. "Damn. I think you might be right."

She sat up straight, eyes wide, and said, all perky, "Oh, I am. I know I am."

"So now, we just have to find where?"

"That's it," she said. "If we find that, I'll just bet we find out a lot more at the same time."

Time being short before the wake, we knew we were going to have to target one particular individual first. Did we do one of the innocuous ones first, or go for one who would produce a useful effect that we could use later? We decided to go for the latter.

"So, who first?"

She thought a second. "You think that Holly, a/k/a Huck, is the strongest personality up there?"

"Well, her or Kevin. She strikes me as the more stable one."

"I'll go with Huck," said Hester. "I think Kevin might be her most enthusiastic follower, though. And he might be her 'muscle' with the rest. Strong ally, you know."

That seemed possible.

"So," I said, "we concentrate on Holly slash Huck for our break?"

"Don't you think?" said Hester.

"Well, sure," I said with some spirit. "Unless it turns out we have to concentrate on somebody else."

It's nice to have a plan.

We relieved the two reserves that were stationed just outside the gate. They were curious about why we'd been summoned to the base of the bluff, and we told them that there had just been some weirdo up on the hillside. It had the advantage of being the truth.

They showed us two little plastic vampires, a small plastic gravestone, and a large paper bat.

"Where in hell did you get those?" I asked.

They'd found them hanging from the mailbox, and from the gate pillars. One of the women in the Mansion had pointed them out. Probably placed there by local high school kids. Halloween was close enough that the things were probably on sale all over. It was to be expected because of the coverage, I guess. I was glad it wasn't more than that.

"There are pictures of them in place," said one of the reserves, a man named Vinton.

I was impressed that they'd thought to take photos, and said as much.

"Oh, it wasn't us," he said. "One of the TV stations from Cedar Rapids had a crew up when we got here. They got 'em on tape."

Great.

We radioed in when we got out of our car at the Mansion. It was 14:00 on the button. By 14:02 our plan was already in trouble.

Huck greeted us at the door, dressed in a black turtleneck and black slacks and shoes. Appropriate for the day. I noticed the tattoos on her face were gone. She ushered us into the parlor, with an explanation ready.

"I'm really sorry, but Hanna can't join us. She's not feeling very well, migraine I think, and she's lying down upstairs."

No problem. Although I made a mental note that Hanna might just be the weakest link, and being kept out of reach. Sometimes it bothers me, that I think that way all the time. She could just as easily be having a real migraine.

"And, I'm sorry, but Toby's still taking a shower; he got up late."

Two down. The two I'd have picked as the greatest liabilities. Interesting.

"That's just fine," said Hester. "No problem."

As we seated ourselves, me on the couch, and Hester in one of the overstuffed leather chairs, we were already down from five to Huck, Kevin and Melissa. So much for approaching the group as a whole.

"We would really like to get to the wake as soon as we can," said Huck. "We feel we should be there for as long as possible." She smiled, almost apologetically and, I thought, quite sincerely. "Edie's been our friend for quite a while."

They'd arranged to limit the interview by controlling both the number of individuals present and the time spent. Not bad. I remembered what William Chester had said about them not going to cooperate, and gave him some points.

"We'd like to go, too," said Hester. "Since Edie was Lamar's niece."

"Of course," said Huck. "So, then, what can we do to help?"

"Well, for starters," I said, "why didn't you let us know that Peel was up on the third floor?" I was really eager to see who was going to field that one.

"We didn't know he was there," said Kevin, "and I don't think it's fair you should assume that we did."

"But you knew he and Edie were meeting up there sometimes, didn't you?" asked Hester.

"Sometimes, maybe," he said, and made his first mistake. He was looking squarely at Hester, in order to appear sincere, and missed the look he got from Huck, which would have told him to let her speak. As it was, all Huck had gotten out was "Wuh—" before being cut off.

I spoke very quickly. "Sometimes in her room, sometimes the third floor, then?"

"Usually her room," he said. "That's why we had no reason to suspect him to be on the third."

I smiled at Huck. Just to let her know that I knew, too.

"But sometimes on the third floor?"

"Sure," he said, just as Huck interjected, "We really don't know."

"Anywhere else?" I asked.

This time it was only Huck, who said, "Now, wait. We don't really know those things. We're guessing," and she shot Kevin a glance.

"Is there a reason," I asked, "why you aren't letting Kevin speak for himself?"

"I am speaking for myself," said Kevin. A little too quickly. And, again nearly simultaneously, Huck said, "I *am* letting him speak."

I held up my hand. "Just a second. Whoa. One at a time."

They exchanged irritated looks.

"Let's start again. Why don't you guys just listen up for a second, here, and I'll tell you some of what we know, and then ask some questions."

They were quiet; I'll give them that.

"We've already established your knowledge of Peel." That had been pure luck. There had always been the chance that Toby had tried to cover by giving us a wrong name. "We've already established your knowledge of a relationship between Peel and Edic." I looked at the three of them. "We've already established that you knew that he was sometimes on the third floor." I gave them a second to digest that. "I want to remind you that this is a murder investigation, and if you start to try to backpedal now, you may give the impression of complicity."

Kevin proceeded, smoothly, to make his second mistake. "Let *me* remind *you*," he said, "that you have neglected to advise us of our Constitutional rights."

I looked at Hester. It had to be her. She nodded, and looked coldly at Kevin.

"A *Miranda* advisory," she said, evenly, "is triggered

by a custodial interrogation." She didn't blink. "That's two complete and separate elements. Custody. Interrogation. This, right now," she explained, "is a noncustodial interview. So, I'd suggest you lose the smart-ass attitude and pay close attention."

I watched Huck and Melissa's reaction very carefully. They were why Hester had to be the one to put Kevin in his place. So far, it looked like they were getting the hint.

Kevin took the bait.

"Don't condescend to me," he said. "I'm no fool."

Hester made a little tent of her fingers, resting her elbows on the arms of her chair. "Want a second to consider the fact you're the only one in the room who had to say that?" she asked.

Huck jumped in and rescued him. That was fine. The fact that she had to do so wasn't lost on anybody.

"Wait," she said. "Like you said a second ago, let's just sort of start over, okay?"

"Sure," I said. I was becoming fascinated, watching Kevin try to stare Hester down. I reached across the coffee table, and tapped him on the knee. He flinched, and looked at me.

"In all sincerity, I think you're not quite understanding what's going on here. Someone has been killed, and we're trying to get to the bottom of it. Someone you knew pretty well. Possibly while you were here. That's pretty weighty stuff." I leaned back. "This isn't a game."

"I'm not playing games," said Kevin.

"Then it strikes me, Kevin," said Hester, "that you're being very nonchalant about the death of someone who lived in the same house with you."

"I'm sorry to have upset you," said Kevin blandly.

"We're not upset," I said, making some notes on my pad, "so much as we're curious about a lack of reaction."

"I," he announced, "happen to be a Nihilist." Although his facial expression didn't change, he sneered with his voice. "That's N-I-H-I-L-I-S-T, Deputy," he said, watching me write. "It means that I believe that there's no purpose in existence."

"I know," I said, not looking up. "We used to say it was a predictable result of an egocentric confronting reality." I looked up, with the most pleasant expression I could muster. "Sittin' round the doughnut shop, we talk about that sorta thing a lot."

Before he could answer, I said, "Look, you guys are the ones we have to talk to, because you're the ones who might have some information. There really isn't anybody else. We can keep this on a fairly friendly basis, if we work at it. But you do have information we need. You may not know what you have," I said, "but there could well be things you've noticed and don't realize they're significant." That was pretty standard, and I wasn't so sure that they didn't know what they had, but it did serve the purpose of giving them an out, if they suddenly wanted to "remember" something. Or, in the particular case of Kevin, gracefully retract a lie.

"Edie," said Kevin, "is the one who knew, if anybody did. Too bad she's not available."

He said it straight, but he meant it sarcastically.

"Edie's been talking quite a bit to the pathologist," I said.

Just as I said it, Toby came through the dining room door, his jaw dropped, and he said, "What?"

"Hi, Toby," said Hester. "Have a seat."

"Oh, yeah. Right, right."

He looked really fresh, and it looked like they'd been telling the truth about his being in the shower when we'd arrived.

"We're just discussing what we all know about Mr. Peel," said Hester.

"Oh," said Toby. "Not much," and he looked meaningfully around the room, "do we?" It was hard to tell if it was a question, or a really broad hint.

"Well," I said, "we know what he looks like. We know his name." I figured it was time to jump in with both feet. "You told us he was a vampire.... So, where does that leave you?"

For a few seconds it got so quiet you not only could have heard a pin drop, I swear you could have heard it whistle as it fell.

Melissa broke the silence by speaking for the first time. "He is," she said. Straight up, matter-of-fact, with no inflection. "We all know that, too."

She'd said, "He is," without hesitation. Nobody else qualified it by saying "He thinks he is." Just the silence of agreement and acceptance.

"Why do you think," she said, still with no emotion, "we call this Renfield House?"

"Wasn't that the vampire's slave in *Dracula*?" asked Hester. "Renfield?"

Melissa nodded. "Of course."

I still didn't quite realize what I was dealing with. "You're saying that he is a vampire. You don't really believe that, do you? Don't you mean that he *believes* that he's a vampire?"

"No," said Melissa. "He is a vampire. That's all there is to it."

I glanced around the room. There sure didn't seem to be any visible dissent.

"Now, really," I said. "Come on. This isn't Transylvania. Hell, it's not even Los Angeles. There's no such thing as vampires."

She shrugged. "You're entitled to your beliefs. So are we." She gave me a secretive little smile. "We know. That's enough for us."

I don't know that I was exactly surprised that somebody other than Toby would be capable of being conned into seriously believing in vampires, so much as I was just beginning to appreciate the ramifications for our case.

"Okay," I said, slowly. I pretended to write some

notes, then looked up. "Okay, so, then, if he is, why stick around?"

I half expected Toby to be the first to speak up, but it turned out to be Melissa.

"We aren't afraid of him," she said. "We learn from him. You have to try to imagine the knowledge of a man who has been here so long." As she spoke, she became flushed. "The strength. The power. The confidence."

"And the wealth," added Toby again. "Do you have any idea what compounded interest can amount to in three hundred years? But, like Melissa says, it's the power. Nobody fucks with him, believe me."

"But he possibly killed Edie," I said. "Remember that."

"There's a downside to everything," said Kevin, cynically. "Of course we don't agree with you, but if you say he killed her, then we have no choice but to believe you."

"Mind sharing how you think she died?" I asked.

"I have no opinion."

"Do any of you happen to know one"—I pronounced it slowly, as though this might be the first time I'd heard the name—"Alicia Meyer?"

"I do," said Huck. "She works on the boat."

"Yeah, so do I," said Melissa.

"And, how long has this Peel been interested in her?" I was out on a limb, but it was just a short one.

"What?" I'd evidently caught at least Melissa by surprise.

"You know," I said conversationally, "interested enough to show up outside her second-floor window, all duded up with the teeth and all, and asking if he could come in?"

"I have no idea," said Melissa, making a damned fine recovery. "That's his business. Like they say, 'All I know is what I read in the papers.' So, you want to hang that Peeping Tom incident on Dan, too?"

"I believe it was him that night, behind her apartment.

But, if you know how serious he is about her, I'd really like to know."

"Why?" asked Huck. Perfect.

"Because Alicia's boyfriend is dead," I said. "One Randy Baumhagen. I assume you read about him in the papers, too."

"That was in Wisconsin, wasn't it?" asked Melissa. "But, yes. In the *Conception County Sentinel,* in fact. Why does that have anything to do with us? He just drowned."

"Well, let's say that's up for grabs. Did any of you know him?"

"I did," said Huck. "I talked to him in a bar once or twice."

"Was he with Alicia when you talked to him?" I asked.

"Yes."

"And did Peel ever meet Alicia or Randy?"

"I asked her up here last month. He met her then," she said.

"Why," asked Hester, "did you bring her up here?"

"To see the place," said Huck. There was something about her voice. Confusion?

"Not specifically to meet him, then?"

"Not specifically to meet anybody. To see the house."

"But you knew he was here at the time?" Hester didn't sound at all like she was pressing Huck, but she was. By now she'd elicited the fact that Peel had been here "last month," and at the same time as Alicia.

"Oh, well . . . sure. I guess."

Hester has a sense of just where to find the jugular, so to speak. "Now, be kind of careful, here," she said, "because you aren't the only person we've talked with." She let that sink in for about a beat. "Now, are you sure you didn't bring her here because of him? Maybe even because he"—and she paused, again—"requested it?"

Huck shot a glance at Melissa. It was quite a tell, for a professional dealer.

The honor of capping the screwup belonged to Melissa. "I never said anything," she said, her voice up about an octave. "Not even before you came home. Just ask Toby!"

Good old Toby, the only one who had been in a real position to spill his guts, let her dangle. "Hey, I wasn't with you and Deputy Houseman when you two were out in the yard. Who knows what you told him then?" He was a little smarter than I'd given him credit for.

"Well, you little prick," said Melissa, with commendable accuracy.

"I really hate to change the subject," said Huck, "but we all do have to be at Edie's wake, and if we don't get going now..."

We'd gotten our wedge driven into the group. Not exactly where, nor in the manner, we'd expected, but it was in place. Good enough for government work, as they say. Hester and I excused ourselves after making an appointment to talk with Huck after the wake. We weren't really expecting to get much from her, but we wanted to deprive the group of who we considered its strength right after the wake. Emotions would be high, and without the moderating efforts of Huck, the cracks could become much wider. We had high hopes, even though they would have a chance to regroup on the way to the wake. I thought they were rattled enough to stay that way.

TWENTY

When we got to the funeral home, there wasn't much of a crowd, except for five or six media folks hanging about outside. They at least had enough good sense not to go in. I brushed the spatters of mud off my pants as best I could, and made sure I'd scraped all the leaf particles from my shoes. I did notice that Hester didn't seem to have suffered any negative effects on her clothes from the climb up the ravine. I was, as usual, amazed by that. Inside we found Lamar and his wife, along with Edie's mother and a couple of Lamar's relatives I'd never met before. Embarrassingly, I couldn't remember Edie's mother's name. I had just about decided on directly asking her, no matter how stupid it might make me sound, when Lamar came over. He thanked us for coming, and led us immediately over to his sister.

"June, this is Carl Houseman, I think you know him? And Agent Hester Gorse, of the DCI."

"Hello, June," I said.

"Hello," said June.

I recognized her, but barely. She seemed to have aged a lot more than I would have anticipated in the five or six years since I'd met her the first time.

"I'm sorry about Edie," I said.

"Don't feel sorry for her," she said. "Feel sorry for Shanna, her kid she left in the lurch. But thanks for comin'." She gestured to a small table with a lace cloth, where somebody had placed four photos of Edie. One was a framed graduation picture, color, taken with her in a maroon cap and gown. The other three were taped to a piece of black construction paper. One of Edie with her mother in a swing when she was about six, I'd guess. Another one of Edie in her graduation robes, and one with Edie and her daughter, Shanna. Cute little kid. It was kind of a pathetic photo memorial, though.

While Hester said the obligatory things, Lamar and I approached the coffin, hardly making any sound at all on the soft carpet. Edie's body looked just like what it was, a dead woman in her mid-twenties. She was clad in a nice knit beige dress, with a white scarf concealing the wound in her neck. Her hair was a lot lighter than it had seemed when she was in the tub, and for a second I thought she might have a wig. Nope. Washed, dried, and nicely combed. *Too young to be there,* I thought. I took a breath and spoke to Lamar.

"They did a nice job," I said softly. Having been at her autopsy, I could hardly believe they'd managed to put her back together as well as they had.

"Yep."

Cops tend to be connoisseurs of that sort of thing. Especially when we've viewed the deceased at a crime scene, and know what the mortician has accomplished. Lamar knew; he'd been there often enough.

When I turned around, I saw several more people had entered the main room. Three young women, well dressed in dark colors. They were all in slacks and sweaters, and obviously together for mutual assistance. They looked to be about the same age as Edie, and seemed pretty sophisticated.

"Who are they?" I muttered to Lamar. One thing cops will do is check out who comes to the funerals of murder victims. Sometimes it can be very instructive.

"Classmates, I think," he said. "High school."

"Ah." I had purposely "forgotten" to sign the sympathy book at the entrance. This would allow me to go back to sign it later, and check out the names. Cop thing. I made a mental note to check for three women's names in a group.

Lamar and I sort of wandered over to the leather chairs that lined one wall, and stood there, looking somber and wishing we were somewhere else. Hester joined us, and that was a real highlight. Ought to give you some idea.

A few moments later, accompanied by a flash as some intrepid reporter took a photo through the open door, the crew from the Mansion came in. All were in black or a combination of black and dark colors, gray or maroon. Kevin, Huck, and Melissa wore black leather knee-length coats. Toby just had a black leather vest over his maroon turtleneck, and Hanna was carrying a dark green suede jacket. Very presentable, I thought, and the dark colors were certainly appropriate. Granted, they looked rather pale, and the women wore very dark lipstick. So what.

Well, apparently Edie's mother felt otherwise. Even in the muted space of the funeral home, I heard her say something about "the freaks." Several heads turned toward the five, who were signing the sympathy book. They'd obviously heard, but were choosing not to notice.

Lamar left Hester and me, and went to his sister, to make sure there wasn't a scene. When the five got to them, Lamar set the example, shaking their hands and thanking them for coming. This left his sister with little real choice, although she certainly didn't shake hands.

The five proceeded toward the casket, and stood in a group, and held hands for what seemed a long minute. As they turned, Hanna's hands went to her eyes, and she started to weave. Huck and Melissa escorted her to a chair, while Kevin and Toby came over to Hester and me.

"She all right?" I asked as they passed.

"Fine," said Toby. "She's fine. So, we're 'freaks,' I hear."

"Let it ride," I said.

They continued toward the three girls who had come in together, and who Lamar had identified as Edie's former classmates. Kevin and Toby seemed to be introducing themselves, and making small talk. Good.

Huck approached Hester, and quietly asked if she knew where they might get some aspirin or Tylenol for Hanna. Hester took her to find the funeral director.

So far, not too unusual a wake.

Old Knockle came in, looking distinguished in his uniform. I was impressed. He'd had to take Chester to Maitland, get the bond, and get back here in pretty short time. Since I was now by myself, and he was, too, I waited for him to do the obligatory stop at Lamar, the mother, and then the casket. When his counterclockwise tour brought him to me, I suggested we go to one of the adjoining rooms, where they had coffee and cookies set out.

"Second reason I came, Carl."

He and I secured two chairs within easy striking distance of the cookies, and started what I assumed would be a fairly bland, time-killing conversation. It did start that way, and I found myself telling him how impressed I was with the Mansion.

As it turned out, he'd helped restore it years ago, and his late uncle had been caretaker for the last members of the original family who had lived there.

"When did they move out?" Bland. Just curious.

"In the late fifties."

"What did the original owner do, do you know?"

"He was into grain shipping, and mining, and lumber," he said. "They were into just about anything in this area that could make 'em rich."

"Worked," I said.

"Indeed it did," said Knockle.

"You know, I always wondered why they put it there in the first place."

Knockle settled in, and I began to suspect I'd bitten off more than I'd intended. "The original owner, a man named Givens, wanted privacy. That old German Kommune had drilled way down, and got a well going before they went belly up. So he had a well ready made. It was close to the mine he owned, just south of there. That silica outfit."

I nodded. "Didn't they use that to cast fine gears or something?"

"For fine glass, originally," he said. "Sand's got the consistency of grainy flour, produced a fine glass."

"Ah."

"The gear casting came later. Fine grain again, didn't have to machine them much after they were cast."

"Oh."

"Old man Givens was really a penny-pincher in some ways, though. Used to visit that mine every day, to check things. Then right across to the old steamboat dock, where they loaded his grain. That ain't there no more, 'course. Took that out about 1930. Mine's closed, went out back in the late sixties."

"Yeah."

He kept on. It was my fault. I knew Old Knockle talked a lot.

"Old man Givens got so tired of making that trip down to the valley and then over to the river, he had 'em put in some sort of cable car when they was fixin' up the railroad about 1890 or so. So he could just go straight on down. His wife used to use it, too, to go to Chicago. For culture. Yep, the train stopped right there, if the flag at the stop was up. Had their very own car on the siding. Named the stop Givens' Switch, just for them. Really rich." He chuckled. "Called the cable car Givens' Railroad, up here in Freiberg."

That got my attention. I leaned well forward. "What happened to the cable car?"

"I don't truly know," he said. "I seem to remember hearin' that they'd replaced it with something, but if I ever heard what, I forgot it by now. There's nothin' there now, I can tell you that. We were all over that hillside yesterday." He smiled, and got up to get another cookie. "Don't get yourself all excited, Carl. Want another cookie?"

"Sure." While he got them, I was thinking that, while the cable car might not be there, there surely had to have been a path down the bluff at that point. Had to be. Maybe trees had grown over it, but leveled ground could enable a faster passage. . . .

He sat back down and handed me my cookie. "You know, did you see those big bolts in the wall, upstairs on the second floor?"

"What? Uh, no, no I didn't."

"You know," he said, "that big old house was built in two parts. Halves. The north side was built first. They added a matching south side some ten years after the north side was finished. Secured the two halves together with big railroad shafts and bolts. Just like the courthouse in Maitland."

I'd seen the bolts in the courthouse. "Oh, yeah, the big bolts."

"The ones in the house are covered by big lizards." He thought a second. "No, dragons."

"Gargoyles?"

"Yeah. That's it."

Now he had me going. "How did you know they were bolts, then? Was that common?"

"Coulda been, but I seen some of the blueprints for the house, at the historical society."

"Oh." Blueprints. "Here in Freiberg?"

"Oh, no, nope. Not here. Over in Lake Geneva, in Wisconsin, where the family moved. When they had too much money to spend here," he said with a grin. "It's all donated to their historical society over there."

"In Wisconsin . . . that makes sense," I said. It did. It also made sense that it was out of my jurisdiction and I wanted to see it. "When did you see that?"

"The blueprints? Oh," he said, "maybe ten, fifteen years back, I think. When Emma and I went in to Madison for her mother's funeral. Maybe twelve?" He nodded vigorously. "Twelve. Yep, twelve. We took a swing down to the lake afterward, you know. Might as well get some use out of the mileage, see."

"Absolutely." Luck smiles sometimes.

"I see that the crew from the Mansion came," he said.

"Yep."

"You think they're weird, Carl?"

"No weirder than anybody else."

"Some of 'em seem nice. But I don't know why they dress like that. Just to make people look?"

"Making a statement. Nothing else."

"I think they do it just to aggravate people." He stared across the room to where Toby and Kevin were still talking to the girls. "The darkhaired kid with the thing through his nose, see him? That's what I mean."

"Pretty harmless, I think. Really. Remember, not too long ago, burning the campus down? The sixties and seventies?"

"Yeah."

"Which you rather have? That, or these kids?" I suppressed a smile. "Or, back in your day, the agitators who wanted to go against the King?"

He looked at me squarely. "You ain't too big for me to whip."

I almost missed what he said, because my eye had

settled on the figure of William Chester, standing near the coffin. I drew Knockle's attention to him.

"What's he doing here?"

Old Knockle stared for a second. "Oh. Uh, well, I know what you said, but he had the bond money right with him, and since I had to bring him back up this way, and I was comin' right here anyway, I thought it'd be okay if I left him in the car." He cleared his throat. "Looks like he got out."

"That it does."

"I'm really sorry, Carl. He said he'd stay in the car."

"I just bet he did." I didn't want to draw too much attention to Chester, but for two cents I would have just walked up and knocked the idiot over the head.

After taking some of the sting out for Knockle by getting him another cookie, I went looking for Hester. I saw her two rooms away, but before I could get to her, I felt a tap on my shoulder. Byng, in uniform. He looked very concerned.

"Carl, you got a second?" he asked in a low voice.

"Sure."

He motioned me toward the hall, and I followed.

"I got a call from Harry," he said. "They got a missing persons report on Alicia Meyer. She's been having a real rough time over her boyfriend and all, a'course. She was at a friend's house over in Conception County last night. They went out to eat at Gourmet Georges'. She went to the john, never came back. Guess her friends spent most of the night lookin' for her. Can't find her. She's just disappeared."

"What time, any idea?"

"Not sure, but it had to be before one A.M. That's when Gourmet Georges' closes for the night."

"So, like what? Somebody snatched her right out of the women's room?" That was spooky.

"Oh, no. No, I forgot. Her car was gone, too. Like she just drove off."

That put a completely different complexion on the

case. I was relieved. "Ah. So, maybe she just wants to get away for a while?"

"It's not like her, they say."

"They always say that, don't they? I mean, if it was like her, they wouldn't have reported it."

He let that sink in. "Well, sure."

"I'll bet Harry finds her before supper," I said.

"Hope so," he said. He looked around. "Lamar's here? I really ought to express myself to him before I leave."

"Good idea." I pointed out the receiving line. "Don't forget to sign the register."

I found Hester in another anteroom, talking with the funeral director and two older gentlemen I recognized as teachers from Freiberg High. I motioned, and she got away fairly quickly. I told her, quickly and quietly, about the cable car, and about the blueprints. I also mentioned William Chester. She'd already seen him.

"I hope he's not here for the reason I think he is," she said very quietly.

"Pardon?"

"I hope he's not here hunting," she said, a little louder.

"Yeah."

Just as I was about to mention Alicia Meyer taking off, we were interrupted by one of Edie's three classmates.

"Excuse me, are you Deputy Houseman?" She was about five-ten, slender, brown hair and eyes, maybe twenty-five or so.

"Yes."

"Hello, I'm sorry to bother you, but my name is Darcy Becker, and I knew Edie, and the sheriff just said that I should be talking with you." She seemed very confident, self-assured, and sophisticated. Polished. As Old

Knockle would have said, you could tell she'd been away.

Since Lamar had handed her off, I was fairly certain that she'd approached him with something important about the case. Something he thought we should hear, and something he figured he shouldn't.

"Nice to meet you. This," I said, gesturing toward Hester, "is Special Agent Gorse of the Iowa DCI."

"Hello," said Hester.

"Oh. Are you, well, working together? About this?"

"I'd suggest," said Hester, "that we might step outside."

The media were out there. We ended up moving out through the kitchen, past the preparation and, if necessary, autopsy room; and ended up in the garage between two parked hearses. It was a little gloomy, but it was private as hell.

"So, Lamar said you should talk to me?"

"Yes," she said. "He said that this . . . well, I thought that since Edie had, well, taken her own life . . . I thought I might know why. The sheriff said I should talk to you right away."

"Why did you think she might have killed herself?" asked Hester.

"Well, I know she's been kind of down. Lately. Well, for a while, really. But lately, things had taken a turn, I think. . . ." She looked at us beseechingly. "I don't really know, but she had gotten mixed up with some older man. I think."

Hester and I exchanged looks.

"It's possible," I said. "Why do you think that?"

"Well, we tried to get together, and we talked on e-mail, and I couldn't make it, and she called me, because it was going to be her daughter's birthday, and she was worried, it seemed to me. No. Well. No, no, she was frightened. Scared. Worried and scared, I guess."

"About . . ." I prompted.

She sighed. "Well, I called her, I mean when I couldn't make it. And we talked on the phone."

You have to be so careful not to spook somebody, but at the same time, you sometimes just about have to drag the simplest stuff out of them.

"About some older man?" Hester, this time. Gently, not wanting to stress her.

"Yes. I think she was, well, involved. Pretty far, I think. And I think he was either married, from what she said, or at least there was another woman in the picture, and she was afraid to let him go, and afraid to stay." She looked at Hester. "You know?"

"I think so," said Hester.

It struck me then. "You wouldn't be 'DarcyB2' would you? Your e-mail address?"

"I...Yes, I am." She looked at me and thrust her head forward slightly. "How on earth do you know that?"

"Let's back up a bit," I said. "There are a couple of things you apparently haven't heard about this."

As it turned out, on Sunday she and her two friends had heard Edie was dead, that it was suicide, and they had scurried around and gotten away from Iowa City and Marengo, where they worked, and headed up after lunch. Darcy's only solid news was from her mother, who was the one who originally called on Sunday.

"In the first place," I said, "Edie didn't commit suicide."

"You mean it was an accident?" She looked surprised.

"No, I'm afraid not. Edie was murdered." Boy, if I thought she'd looked surprised before...

There was a sort of gasp, her chin quivered a little, and then instant tears. No real crying. Just tears.

"Like to sit down?" I offered.

"No, no, that's fine." Darcy had come equipped with

a pocket full of tissues. She blew her nose. "Oh, God. The poor kid. The poor, poor kid."

We couldn't have agreed more.

In the next few minutes, we got an encapsulated life story of Edith Younger. It was kind of interesting, because it was as close to being from Edie's perspective as we were likely to ever get, and was something we probably wouldn't have gotten otherwise. It was very helpful.

Darcy had moved to Freiberg with her parents when she was in third grade. She first met Edie on the first day of school that year, and by the end of the semester, they were fast friends. They remained so all the way through high school, going so far as to want to own a beauty salon together, in about fifth grade, and planning to jointly operate a horse ranch by the time they were juniors.

Darcy said that Edie was quite intelligent, and had absolutely excelled in high school. Got fine SAT scores. Was ready to go to college with Darcy and the rest, when she found herself just a little bit pregnant early in the summer of graduation.

"He was a real loser, and we told her that he was," said Darcy. "The problem was, her mother told her the same thing. You know how that is?"

We said we did. The young man was a bit of a jerk and a rebel. Only not particularly good at it. Edie was apparently on the outs with her mother, who had been "just mean to her, all her life."

When I asked what, exactly, she meant by that, Darcy told a little story.

"Oh, an example would be best. Well. One night, my date and I came to her house to pick her and her date up. He was already there, we were going to double. And Edie made kind of an entrance, you know, from upstairs? Came down, looked really pretty, and her mother said 'Oh, you look so pretty. I just wish you'd picked that other dress.' That sort of thing, see? All the time. Just always had to down her a little."

"Okay." I mean, it wouldn't have bothered me a whole lot, but I could see how it could sting. I could also see how it could get a little old after a while.

So Edie got pregnant. Nothing deliberate. Just what happened because she got involved with the young man to spite her mother. Edie had pretty strong principles, and decided to keep the baby. She also decided not to keep the young man. Her mother had, ostensibly, supported her all the way. That was until the baby was born, and it turned out that Edie couldn't support the kid. Her mother had become absolutely relentless about putting her down, for her small income and for getting pregnant.

Edie moved out, and took the kid with her. That lasted for about three months, according to Darcy. Then Edie decided that it wasn't healthy for her little daughter to live the way they had to live. Edie absolutely refused to move home. Her mother offered to take the child for a while, to help.

"She didn't see it coming?" asked Hester.

Darcy shook her head. "It was her mother. Well. It was, and she just always loved her mother, regardless. She just couldn't stand her, you know?"

Hester nodded.

"And then the lawsuit started, for custody of Shanna," said Darcy. "It's still going on, as far as I know." She thought for a second. "I suppose it's not, is it? Not now. It's finally over."

Darcy then told us what she knew about the "older man."

"She met him after she moved into the Mansion," she said. "Edie thought that was such a nice place, and there was no rent, so she could save and get Shanna back in a year or so."

She said that Edie met him at a party thrown by the owner.

"You sure it was the owner?" I asked.

"Yes, that's what she told me. The Hunley woman, the dancer, from over by Chicago. She needed house-sitters."

That would have been Jessica, all right.

"Edie told me that he was an unusual man." Darcy looked at Hester. "He was a very strong personality. Very sophisticated. Well educated. She thought he was very upper class. You must understand that. She was just enthralled with that. She was in love with him, I think. But she was afraid of him, too. Well. He was into some strange things. Very personal, but spooky, strange things."

"Like what?" I was hoping, I guess.

Darcy pursed her lips, and then said, "Well, I suppose it doesn't matter. Not now. Well. She said that he liked to tie her up sometimes, and liked to, uhm, well, drink her blood. Just a little." By the time she'd finished, a blush had crept up from her neck to the lower part of her face.

Son of a bitch. I said it, in fact. "Sonofabitch" sort of all came out as one word. I startled Darcy, so I apologized. I didn't explain.

"What was his name?" asked Hester.

"Dan," said Darcy.

"Dan who?" I asked.

"Peale," she said.

"How do you spell that?" Hester asked what turned out to be the best question of the day.

"D-a-n," she said, "P-e-a-l-e." She paused. "Daniel, actually, I think."

"You're sure?" I asked.

"Yes. I have it in a letter, somewhere. Wait...No, I don't, it was on my old computer, and I got rid of that when I got my laptop." Darcy shrugged apologetically. "But she did write it. And that's the way it was spelled. He's from England, somewhere around London, I think."

I looked at Hester. London?

"London? England?" I asked.

"Oh, yes. Didn't I say that earlier?"

"Uh, no. No, you didn't. You said something about 'upper class,' but not English."

"Oh, I'm sorry, Mr. Houseman. Yes, English. Edie thought he might be sort of incognito. Yes. She thought he might be a nobleman or something."

"Any idea why?" Hester asked. "Any evidence to suggest that?"

"Just the way he behaved," she said.

"Ah," said Hester. "Did Edie have any experience that would help her tell that?"

"No," said Darcy. "Well. Just movies, I guess."

"Oh," I said.

"Oh, God," said Darcy.

It turned out that she was feeling especially guilty since she and Edie had grown apart. She felt that she let herself be romanced, as she put it, away from her old friend by college and then her job.

"It was just circumstance," said Hester. "Different paths, and her child and everything. And you just grew apart." She sounded so wistful, I began to think that she was speaking from experience.

We gave Darcy our cards, and told her to call us if she either discovered or remembered anything we might want to know.

The upshot was that if my conversation with Knockle had been good luck, our talk with Darcy had been serendipity.

Hester and I decided to leave as soon as we could gracefully get out. I was really eager to get to the office and run Daniel Peale through the system in both the U.S. and U.K.

As we worked our way to the main entrance, I noticed that Melissa and Hanna were still occupied in their small room, and that Toby and Kevin were still talking to the two friends who had come in with Darcy.

Huck was standing by herself, looking intently at a nondescript oil painting of some idyllic countryside, with horses and birds. The visual equivalent of elevator music. I think she'd turned her back to avoid the hostility emanating from most of the other mourners. I stopped beside her.

"Ugliest painting I ever saw in my life," I said.

She turned, and actually smiled. "You got it."

"You be coming right down to the office?"

She looked over her shoulder toward Toby and Kevin. "We're all in the same car. When the boys"—and she inflected the word disparagingly—"get done trying to score with typically quiet grace, we'll have to take Hanna back, and then maybe we can come on down."

That could take a while, and I really wanted to keep going with Huck, and not give her much opportunity to reflect and withdraw, or to support the others.

"You could ride down with us, so we can get started," I said. "They could pick you up at our office."

"That sounds all right, actually," she said. "If you can give me a few minutes to say good-bye to some people."

I found Hester again, passing by Toby and Kevin, who were still hitting on Darcy's friends. I idly wondered how their efforts would be rewarded after Darcy talked with her buddies.

I told Hester about the plan to take Huck with us, and she thought it was a pretty good idea. We wanted to catch the reaction of Toby, Kevin, Melissa, and Hanna when Huck told them she was going with us, so we used the old cop trick of facing one another and making small talk. That way, each of us could see about half the room, and yet appear to be looking at each other.

"At about your five o'clock position," said Hester. "William Chester just approached Huck."

"Really..."

"Don't look. They seem to be talking."

"Does it look like he knows her?" That would be interesting.

"I don't know. He seems to be doing most of the talking." Hester paused. "Whoa, she just took a really fast step back. He's moving closer...."

I couldn't wait. I turned, just as Huck backed up one more step, quickly, abruptly, almost into the wall behind her. Her eyes were wide, and she looked startled and frightened.

I was beside Chester in three or four fast steps. "Mr. Chester," I said softly, "why do I see you everywhere I go?"

He'd been speaking pretty intensely to Huck, and it took him a second to change directions. "What? Oh, Deputy... uh, Heightman?"

"Houseman. Remember what I told you? About licenses? Hunting?"

"Yes. Yes, I do. But I think you should know some things."

"Then I suggest you look me up back at the sheriff's department in about three hours."

"Fine," he said. He started to turn back to Huck.

"I'll arrange for a ride. Until then," I said, "I'm afraid this young lady is committed to talking to me right now." I glanced at Huck. "Are you ready to go?"

She sure was. I extended my right arm between her and Chester, and gestured toward Hester with my left. "Why don't you go over there?"

As she brushed by me, I turned back to Chester. "Look," I said, as pleasantly as I could, "she's a potential witness. I can't have you bothering her. What on earth did you say to her, anyway?"

He shrugged. "It's of no consequence to you."

"Don't get cute."

"Right. Look, Deputy, I don't mean to interfere with the secular authorities on this. Really I don't."

When someone who's not ordained starts calling me "secular," I get nervous. "I'd really suggest you not bother anyone else here. There are several cops present, out of uniform. I'll pass the word to keep an eye on you."

"I can talk to whom I wish."

I figured I might as well be a complete hypocrite. "This is a funeral home, for God's sake."

I snagged Knockle as we were headed out the door, and gestured toward Chester. "Get that son of a bitch," I whispered, "back to the office in about three hours. If he can, let him rent a car. If not, you bring him."

"Sure, Carl," he whispered back.

"In the meantime, get his sorry ass out of here before he causes trouble. He resists, bust him, but do it very quietly. Got it?"

"Sure."

"And try to steal me a cookie, before you go."

As we got to the door, I half whispered to Hester, "You know? This has got to be the most interesting wake I've ever been to."

"Glad you had a good time, Houseman, you ghoul."

The media were still outside, of course. I spoke to Huck, who was right with us. "Engage us in conversation as we go by the news people. Don't laugh or anything, but make it look as if you ride with us every day." I was glad I'd switched to my old unmarked car. No cage for prisoners.

She nodded. "Think they'll notice anything wrong?"

I looked at her black hair, black lips, and black nails.

"Nah. We'll get by 'em with the least fuss." I thought she looked a little green around the gills. "You okay?"

"Fine," she said. "I'm fine."

When we got to the car, the first thing Huck said

when she got in back was, "You always have this much crap in your car?"

Hester turned around and said, "I think he cleaned it last month. You should see it when it's really cluttered."

I picked up my mike. "Comm, Three."

"Three, go." It was Sally.

"Three and I-486 ten-eight, ten-seventy-six S.O., ten-sixty-one one female subject."

"Ten-four, Three ten-eight, ten-seventy-six. 17:42."

Just to reassure Huck, I turned to the backseat, and said, "That meant that Hester and I are back in the car, that we're en route to the sheriff's office, and that we have one noncop female person with us."

"Oh."

"And she said okay, and repeated that we were headed in that direction in case any other officer needs to know that, and then said the time, to let anybody else know that she was done talking to me and that the channel was clear." I always do that, when I have a passenger. They like to know.

As I pulled away from the curb, Hester asked Huck to hand her my camera bag, which was sitting among the other debris in the backseat. When she got it, she rooted around for a minute, and produced my bag of Oreo cookies.

"Cookie?" she asked Huck.

We all had one.

"You guys," said Huck, with her mouth half full of Oreo, "travel in style."

The ice broken, Hester turned to the backseat. "What did William Chester have to say?"

"Was that the last dude I talked to?"

"Yes."

"That man is weird. Really. Scary weird. He said that I was going to have to atone for all the evil, and that he would see that I went back to my grave."

"No shit?" Hester sounded angry.

"Yeah." She paused. "You happen to know what he does for a living?"

"He hunts vampires, as far as I can tell," I said.

I could see Huck in the rearview mirror as she hugged herself, as if she were very cold. "Yeah. That's kinda what he said he did."

TWENTY-ONE

We got Huck to the office and interviewed her at length. She seemed to be in that semi-euphoric state you reach after some heavy emotions, and was pretty frank and cooperative.

I'd given the new spelling of Daniel Peale to Sally as soon as we got in the door. She produced the basics in a few seconds. I put on my reading glasses, and read the descriptors to Huck.

"Okay, closest one we get, from the national computers, is this." I held up the torn-off perforated sheet. "It says here that Daniel Gordon Peale is a white male, thirty-five, six feet one, one eighty-three pounds, black and brown." I glanced up. "That would be black hair and brown eyes." I purposely left out the address information and put the paper down. "That sound like him?"

"Yes it does." She mused, "Gordon? Gordon. Never knew that."

"And ... we have a black '96 Lexus, and a green '81 Dodge four-door. Ever seen either of these cars?"

"He doesn't own cars here," she said. "He either gets a rental car when he gets into O'Hare, or we go pick him up in Dubuque when he gets a commuter connection." In answer to the question of who transported him, she said that it was often Toby, and sometimes Kevin. This last time it had been Toby.

"Why does he fly?" I asked.

"Well," she said, "it's a really long swim from London."

"London?" asked Hester.

"Well, yeah. He's an Englishman, after all." Huck looked perplexed.

"How about this," I said. "He lives in Moline, Illinois."

"Oh, no," said Huck. "No, that's not the right man. Dan lives in London. England."

"Well," I said, trying to sound immensely competent, "we'll check that." I picked up the phone and got Sally. "I need a really fast check, U.K., London. For the same dude. Dan Peale."

"This one is gonna cost you big," said Sally. "How soon is really fast?"

"Five or ten minutes or less."

"Shit, Houseman. . . . I can't be any quicker than the machines. Okay. Lemme see what I can get. . . ." And her voice trailed off as she began concentrating. I hung up.

"So," I said, "while we check that out, what can you tell us about Dan Peale?"

Even now, Huck was a little reluctant. I honestly think that it was William Chester who had disturbed her the most. Well, with a boost from seeing Edie in her coffin, and the death of Randy Baumhagen. But Chester had dropped in a dollop of fear from an unknown and unexpected source. I decided it was time to push her over the top.

"Oh," I said, almost as an afterthought. "Before you

start, did you know that Alicia Meyer was reported missing last night, over in Conception County?"

"What?" said Hester. "When did we get that?"

"That's what Byng was telling me up at the funeral home," I said, watching Huck. "I was interrupted just as I was going to tell you."

Huck took a deep breath, and said, "I can't go with this. Not anymore. This is just so over. So damn over."

We both looked at her expectantly.

"What is it you want? All the sordid little details, I suppose. Right?"

"Yeah," I said. "I'm afraid so. Start wherever you need to."

At that point, Sally knocked at the door, stuck in her head and one arm, and held out a computer printout. "For you."

I was impressed.

I read it to Hester and Huck.

"This is from a computer search, done at our request, by the Metropolitan Police, London. City Directory. There is no such person as Daniel Peale, Dan Peale, or D. Peale in all of North London." I handed the sheet to Hester. "Not one single one, Huck," I said.

After a second, Hester handed the printout to Huck.

She looked at the sheet for some time, then handed it to me and said, "He has an English accent. He may not live in London itself. . . ."

"We're checking with Scotland Yard on that," I said. "I'm afraid it looks like he's an American, though." I put the sheet down on my desk. "Anyway, while we wait, what else do you know about him?"

"Well, he's from England . . ." and she gave a forced smile. "At least, that's what I was told, anyway. He visits us along with Jessica about three or four times a year. He's Jessica's guest, not ours." She dropped her voice. "Lately, he's been showing up maybe every other month, when she's not along. She doesn't know about that, I think. Well, didn't."

As she talked, any reticence disappeared, and she began divulging some of the more sordid details about the Mansion.

For example, Huck thought Daniel Peale had been sexually active with all the young women in the house, and she thought maybe he'd had sex with Toby as well. No real surprises there, but I was rather startled that she was starting off with these details.

"Everybody up there's poly, you know? But he's the full-time lover of Jessica Hunley," she said. "She owns him, like."

Blow me down. So to speak. I had to nail down just one term.

"Poly? Poly what? Sexual?"

That elicited a smile. "Polyamorous. You can love more than one person at a time."

"Okay." You have to be sure. "But he's mostly Jessica's full-time lover?"

"He is as far as she's concerned. She was really pissed off that he was there without her this time," she said, "because he's not supposed to do that." She tossed her hair. "They've been down that road before. I've never heard a screaming match like that one."

"Anybody get hurt?" asked Hester.

"Well," she said, "they both had a little blood on them after . . . but they're into that anyway."

"Violence?" I picked the one that was easiest for me to handle.

"Nope. Blood."

Blood games were something I'd heard about, but had never encountered in more than twenty years of police work. One of the things I'd enjoyed about working in the rural areas. As it turned out, everybody that Dan Peale had relations with ended up donating a little blood to his fetish.

"How about Jessica?" asked Hester. "Does she sleep with everybody up there?"

"Well, I don't know about Toby, maybe some heavy

snogging, but he told Kevin that she only screwed him once, and I think she was a little higher then than she usually lets herself get, you know? A little carried away. Anyway, it made Toby's whole year, but she never did him again. I know that Kevin did her a few times, about a year ago. Then she dumped him, and she just never came back for more." She smiled wickedly. "I like to bring that up once in a while, when he gets obnoxious in bed." She found her thread again. "But to answer your question, yes, she drew a bit of blood from him." She shrugged. "Jessica and I got into a smoochy phase for a while, too. It happens."

She was so open about it, I was a little disconcerted, somehow. I wasn't positive she was telling the truth, and if she was, I wasn't too sure I wanted details. "Much blood, ah, exchanged in these encounters?"

"You aren't into that, are you?" she said, with a little laugh.

"No, 'fraid not."

She scooched down in her chair, and regarded me in earnest. "Okay, look, this is how it goes. . . ."

She explained that, most of the time, there wasn't much blood involved at all. It was frequently produced by nicking the skin between the fingers or toes, for instance. Just a few drops. Sometimes, if things were truly intimate, blood could be taken from a tiny cut on the lip, or the earlobe, and exchanged with kisses. Sometimes, if things really heated up, little cuts on the buttocks, or an area near the genitals or breasts.

"Depends," she said.

"On?" I figured that if I was going to get an education, it might as well be thorough.

"Well, on whether or not you're in love at the time, for one thing. Or on just how fucked up you are, for another."

She went on, describing how more severe cuts could be inflicted, depending on the mood of the donor. She was pretty circumspect, and I could tell she was trying not to go somewhere, but that the questions were leading her there anyway.

She stopped talking, and looked at the door to my office. "Could you close the door?"

Hester reached over and pushed it shut.

Huck looked at the windows. The curtains were pulled.

"Well it's been a day," she said, with a sigh. "What the fuck. Look, I was an abused kid," she said. "My mother had a boyfriend when I was about thirteen or so. Okay? And he used to get at me in a sexual way, and he'd smack me around once in a while, just to keep me in my place. And, like, Mom knew, 'cause I told her. And she, well, she ignored me, okay? So it went on. All through high school." She shrugged. "Until I was a senior, and he left her for some skanky twenty-year-old." She looked at Hester. "So I could handle it, you know? No problems. It was over, right? Well, I didn't socialize much, I mean, he didn't want me out of the house all that often. And I could, well, remember when home had been a safe place once, and I thought that now it could be again." She shrugged. "We all make mistakes, now and then. But I really liked music. I was happy in music, and I was good with my music." She stopped, and it didn't look like she was going to restart.

"What instrument?" I asked.

"Flute." A wistful smile. "I was good, too. Went to the University of Wisconsin at Madison on a music scholarship." She'd been slumped while she was talking, but when she started about her music, she almost imperceptibly straightened. "Once I got to play the 'Jolivet Concerto for Flute and Orchestra,' with the whole symphony. Well, it was at a rehearsal, not at a concert, but the conductor said it was 'flawless.'" She brightened. "Leiberman's, too. I was pretty good," and her voice trailed off.

Her hands came up, and she spread her fingers wide, and looked at them for a moment. "Now I deal cards for a living. Dexterity is very important for a blackjack dealer, too. I'm pretty good at that, and the breath control is a snap," she said, lightly.

Then back to the here and now. "So, about halfway through my first year as a middle school music teacher at a little town in northern Wisconsin, I discovered I couldn't handle the past as well as I thought." She chuckled ruefully. "Christmas vacation, and I decided to spend it by myself in my apartment. Ever drink absinthe? That is some fine shit, let me tell ya. Just never get drunk on hard liquor when you're secretly all fucked up in the head, and all alone by yourself. Boy."

Hester and I were both very quiet.

"So, back to our problem," she said briskly. "Things got to me. Really, really got to me. They don't want you teaching their kids after you've had an 'episode,' you know? So when I got out of the treatment facility I resigned. It was the easiest thing to do, for all concerned, really. I went home, and there was mother dear who was in a state of mourning over her lost love, and just couldn't get real concerned about me, except that I was broke. And I hated that, and when I was 'discovered' by Edie, who talked me into living at the Mansion, I just moved in. Rent-free. I figured I'd just take some time, then maybe go back to teaching or something. No more, I guess."

She shrugged. "Anyway, I suppose I got into the blood stuff because I was accepted, and felt somebody actually cared, you know?" She looked at us both for a second. "And Jessica takes us places, too. Chicago several times. New York once. We get to go to things like concerts with her, and galleries. Shows. More than just tickets. She, like, knows some of the artists, and we get to meet 'em, and go to social things with really cool people."

I nodded.

"And I get to be around music, and music people...." She sort of drifted off. Then, "But it still hurt a lot, inside. A lot, and it never went all the way away. But

Dan, he showed me a way to make the pain go for quite a while."

She stood.

"Now, don't go all embarrassed on me, I wear exceptionally nice underwear," she said, and abruptly pulled down her slacks.

On the inside of her left thigh were six or eight long, pale but pronounced scars running from about two inches below the groin to about an inch above the knee. She looked at both of us. "Both thighs, underneath both breasts, and the inside of the upper left arm, but this way I can still wear nice clothes, you know?" she said, pulling her slacks back up. "I do it to myself. It looks weird, I know it. But it actually makes you feel better about some things, to do that. It's the endorphins, I guess. The body releases them to cope with the pain caused by the knife, and they make you feel good all over, inside and out, for a while."

She sat. "Those were for Danny boy. Sometimes I just hate myself for that." Her face kind of twitched for a second. "But, anyway, when I used to do that, there was a lot more blood than you get from your earlobes. For everybody. But I haven't cut for over a year now."

We were silent, and I was feeling very, very awkward.

She flashed a smile. "I'm sorry if I embarrassed you two. Really." She looked past me, at the wall. "But then I started to catch on. I mean, I was really into Danny boy, let me tell you. I'd do anything he wanted, because he cared, didn't he. Oh, yeah. He said he was trying to help me. Get me over the pain. Past it. To replace the hurt with love. But I wasn't quite so fucked up one time, not as much as usual, anyway, and I really *listened* to the son of a bitch talk to me. And I caught on. I mean, there we are up there on the third, and we're in that great bed, and he's touched all the right places, and we've done our thing, and now he's a little thirsty, and he's making me feel like he really gives a damn. And he's talking to me.

And I actually listened to what the bastard was saying. You know what? He was bringing up all the old pain, everything I'd told him. And while he was doing that, he was saying that 'one last cut, and then you'll never do it again. One more and it'll all be out, all the pain, let it out.... The last one.' That prick was depressing me on purpose! *So I'd cut myself.* Encouraging me to do it again! Can you believe that?"

She'd been leaning farther and farther forward, as she spoke. She became aware of it, and sat back, very carefully, and composing herself almost instantly.

"Pardon me. I really don't like to rant." She shrugged. "But, I mean, all he wanted was my blood." She forced a weak laugh. "I mean, it didn't have to be my personality, but why not just my body? So, anyway, that's why I stopped." She forced a smile. "It didn't make me feel *that* good, not anymore. You know?"

TWENTY-TWO

Monday, October 9, 2000
19:18

More to just take some of the tension out of the air, I simply said, "So, that's why Toby thinks that this Peale is a vampire. He has a blood fetish."

"Noo, I don't think 'thinks' is the right word," said Huck. "No, Toby *believes* that Dan is really a vampire, is immortal and will never die, can't stand exposure to sunlight, is supernaturally strong, and has to consume blood to exist." She looked at Hester and me in turn. "Really, I'm serious. Toby believes Dan is a vampire, because Dan himself really believes Dan's a vampire, and Toby really needs to believe in Dan." She smiled, apologetically. "That's pretty complex."

"But don't vampires have little quirky things that give them away, that you could use to prove it, sort of stuff?" I was curious.

"Such as?"

"Well," I said, drawing on my vast movie experiences, "like, not reflecting in mirrors? Having to be invited in? You know. That stuff."

She smiled. "Movies, huh?"

"Well, yeah."

"Let me tell you what Dan tells people when they come up with some things that he just can't do, or can't bring off. He says that those are false aspects of the vampire. He says that they're purposefully invented and promulgated by vampires, to mislead normals into looking for false signs. To lull humans into a feeling that, like with your mirror trick, they can test for vampires. When the test fails, they feel safe."

"So, anything he can't do, he just says that it's a false expectation?"

"Yep. But falsehoods planted by very smart vampires. Just so they have an easier time of hiding."

"That," I said, "strikes me as being awfully fucking convenient."

She smiled at that, too. "Well, yes." She giggled. "Awfully. But he exhibits enough of the familiar traits, like stamina, strength, being nocturnal, being very convincing in everything."

"Did he ever say how you get to be a vampire?" asked Hester.

"Well, he says he was 'turned' a long time ago, by a female vampire. He says you can't be born a vampire, or anything like that. You have to choose, like he did." She shrugged. "I suppose if I'd actually expressed an interest in becoming one, he might have said more. You should ask Toby about that."

"Toby," I asked, "wants to be a vampire?"

"In the worst way," said Huck, with a little smirk. "You know what I mean. He's really a wannabe, for all the wannabe reasons."

"Does anybody else think Dan Peale is really a vampire?" asked Hester.

"Oh, yes. Hanna does. I think Melissa does, at least

I think she probably does now. Kevin doesn't really say, but I'm sure he leans that way, too." She shrugged. "There are times I'm not too sure, myself. Honest."

"What is it that makes you think that he's a real vampire?" I was really curious.

"You saw that photo on the wall, up on the third. The one taken at Highgate Cemetery?"

"Yeah. Circle of Lebanon. . . ."

"Well," she said, in a very low voice, "one of the crypts there is Dan's."

"Pardon me," interjected Hester. "His?"

"That's what he says. His. He told me." She looked at the curtains again. "Maybe that's why you can't find him in the London Directory?"

"Serious?" I asked.

Huck giggled nervously. "Shit, I don't know. Sitting here with you two, oh, maybe not. But I don't want to take any fuckin' chances." She looked me square in the eye. "Would you?"

"Well," I said, truthfully, "I'd really need a lot of evidence. One whole hell of a lot of evidence."

"Me, too," said Huck. "But let me tell you. . . . Look, he is really strong, all right? And he is an absolute sex machine. Really, he can keep it up for seven, eight hours easily. He refuses to go out in the sunlight without max-SPF lotion. He's got . . . well, a really dominant personality. Really." She twiddled her fingers for a second, considering something. "It's a lot more than that. Things he says. Things he does. Really, like, supersophisticated, well educated, and he . . ." She laughed. "Shit, I can't believe I'm telling you this, but he, well, talks about things that happened in the 1700s and 1800s. Like he was *there,* you know?"

"You okay?" She was getting brittle again, and close to the edge, I thought.

"Yeah. Yeah, I'm fine. But, and I'll tell you straight up, you watch him drink some blood, watch him drink *your* blood, and the greedy, slurping sounds, and he . . ."

She shuddered, and then just stopped. None of us spoke for a few moments. I figured it was time to change our tack just a bit. "So, why would Dan kill Edie? Any idea?"

Huck shook her head. "Are you so sure that he's the one who did?"

"He's our chief suspect," I replied. "Unless you know different."

"Well, if he's your best suspect, then you're probably right. If it's any help, it sounds like you might be right."

"But you don't know why he did it?"

"Edie was getting so controlled, you know? It's not like she'd ever walk away. So, so she'd do what he wanted, I know that."

"What exactly did he want?" asked Hester.

"Oh, you know. Sex, of course. Blood sharing, not like me, Edie didn't go for cutting on my scale. But a little. He could at least get a taste. With me," she said, ruefully, "he could drink the stuff." She shuddered again. "Compliance. Service, and I mean that in a business sort of way." She struggled for a word. "Hausfrau? Geisha? She provided all the creature comforts when he came up without Jessica. Especially access to the third floor, where all the privacy was. Edie had the only access key except for Jessica, as far as I know."

"Third is a big plus, then?"

"Privacy. I mean, if there was a chance somebody else was going to drop in, you wouldn't be so comfortable with . . . well, with debasing yourself, actually." She shrugged. "All I know is that when he took me upstairs, he'd have to get the key from Edie. She didn't like that, not a bit." She looked at Hester. "I mean, she was worried for me, too, you know, but jealous at the same time? Especially later, when we were doing him on about a fifty-fifty basis." She sniffed. "No secrets up at Renfield House."

"Is that the only connection you all have with him?"

asked Hester. "Nothing more...oh, I don't know, social? For want of a better term."

"Oh, yeah," said Huck, with enthusiasm. "That's just about the best part, really. I mean, we really dine, you know? Full, formal dining, with seven course meals that we prepare. Just like in real Victorian times."

"Really?" I asked.

"Oh, you bet. Formal attire. Men in black tie, women in their finest." She smiled. "I'm sure you saw the clothes? And we'd talk, or anyway, Dan would, mostly. About the old days, in Victorian England. Mostly."

"He'd talk about them like he'd been there then?" I asked.

Huck considered that a moment. "Well, now that I think about it.... Not so much as if he'd been there, but he gave the *impression* that he had been. I'm not being very clear, am I?"

"Not sure," I said.

"Then I'm not. He never actually said, I don't think, that he'd like, talked to Emily Brontë, or Lord Byron, or anything that straight out. But," she said, earnestly, "he gave that impression, without saying it. He'd sort of refer to them, you know? Like they were old friends. But he never said he was actually there."

I looked at her quizzically.

"Okay, look, he'd say something like 'Like Byron used to say,' but he'd never say 'that's what he said to me.' See?"

"Okay."

"Now, in private, it was different. Well, with me, I know for sure. Once he told me about a conversation he'd had with a Prime Minister named Gladstone, and he said he'd known the Wyndam sisters."

"And they were?"

"Gorgeous women at the turn of the century, I think. Maybe in 1910 or so. High London society."

"And he's about thirty-five or so?" I just thought I'd better interject that.

"That's how old he appears," said Huck.

"Was Jessica at these dinners, then?" asked Hester, heading us back on track.

"They were *only* when Jessica was there," said Huck. "He and she were the Lord and Lady of the house, kind of, and we were their friends invited to dine." She sighed. "It was great, really great. We'd use the finest china, and light the real candles in the candelabras, and use the good goblets, and got to drink the old wines Jessica keeps in the basement." She looked wistful. "New Years is always the best."

"Does Jessica talk about the past?" I asked.

"Oh, sure. But not like Dan. Just asks him questions. Laughs at his answers sometimes. I don't know why she does, but she laughs."

I thought I might know, but decided not to say anything. Time to get back on track again. "What did you think when you first heard that Edie was dead?" I asked.

"That he'd killed her."

"Dan, you mean?"

"Yes."

"Deliberately?" from Hester.

"No, I thought he'd fucked up. He used to give us a bit of blood thinner, you know, to retard clotting with the little cuts." She held up her right hand, palm toward me. "Not with my 'special' cuts, though. No way. Neither of us was ever fucked up enough to try that shit, not those times." She shook her head. "Christ, I could have bled to death in no time."

We were all quiet for several seconds, as Hester and I brought our notes up to date.

"A moment ago," said Hester, "you said something about Melissa and believing Dan was a vampire, something like 'she does now,' or something close to that."

"Well, yeah," said Huck. "Sure. I mean, for one thing, we all know one of you shot him and it sure doesn't seem to have affected him. What else could we think?"

"What?" I asked.

"The young cop dude, you know. He shot him, and it didn't affect him at all."

"The younger officer didn't hit him," I said, rather embarrassed.

"Oh, sure. Yeah. You bet, but we looked for the holes, see, and there wasn't a mark in that doorway or in the little wall or anywhere, all right?" She looked disgusted. "We aren't stupid, you know."

It was the first sign of anger I'd seen in her, and it struck me that, what with time passing and all the talking about things being like a catharsis, her post-grief euphoria was wearing off.

"I don't think you're stupid, Huck. Not at all." That was certainly true, and I think she detected that. "He fired a warning shot," I said. "Two of 'em."

"Bullshit," she said. "Sorry, but I mean, even I know you aren't supposed to do that."

"True," I said. "True enough." I looked at Hester. "See? Even civilians know that." I turned back to Huck. "Well, Deputy Borman just didn't seem able to remember that, though. And he isn't around today, as you might have noticed. He got a one-day suspension for that little error."

She considered what I'd said, but didn't say a word.

"I'll prove it to you," I said. I picked up the phone, and dialed Dispatch, and pressed the speaker button. One of the new dispatchers, Gwen, answered.

"Yo ho! Donut shop!" They could tell it was on an intercom line. I hoped.

"Yeah, it's Houseman. Sally out there?"

"One sec..." she said, and then, obviously calling to the kitchen, "Sally, intercom!"

We waited a few seconds, with the constant crackling of the sixteen radio channels being picked up in the background lending an air of authenticity, if any were required. They almost never used the hold button on the intercom line.

"Yeah, whaddya want, Houseman!" That was Sally's voice, as she walked toward the phone. I could tell Huck recognized the voice. "You need the criminal history on this Peale dude?" This as she picked up the phone. "It just came back, give me a minute."

"No, no, I'll come out and get that," I said quickly. "No, hey, you're on speakerphone back here, and I want you to just say what happened to Borman, and why he's not here today."

There was a pregnant pause. "Uh, you sure you want me to do that?"

"I'm sure."

"Umm, well, okay. Well, as far as I know, Borman fired two warning shots, and you got all over his ass, and he got suspended today."

"And where did that happen?"

"Up at the Mansion, when the guy slashed his chest when he came out of that door."

I looked at Huck, who nodded, and gave me a "thumbs up."

"Thanks, Sally."

"Anytime I can help refresh your failing memory. If you're coming out here soon, we got fresh coffee."

"Cool. Thanks." I cut the connection. "There."

"Ah," said Huck. "Thank you. I'll tell the rest. They might not believe me, but I'll let 'em know. Thanks."

"No problem. Tell 'em not to spread that around, though. It's confidential information. Personnel records." It had been a toss-up, but it seemed to me the benefits outweighed the liabilities.

"Sure."

"I'm going to go out and get that coffee," I said. "You guys want some?" Two affirmative answers later, I was on my way to the kitchen.

While I was in the kitchen, I mulled over the young people who lived up at the Mansion. Huck, in particular. It was such a damned shame that bright people could lead such shitty lives, but there it was. We saw it all the time. Maybe their lives turned to crap because they *were* bright, bright enough to notice. They all seemed to have these perfectly reasonable expectations that just never got realized. They seemed to spend a lot of their lives trying to adjust to that. The upside was that they usually made it in spite of it all. The downside was that what emerged was so irrevocably affected, you'd never know what could have been. Well, not really all of them, I thought. Just enough to make it a really crummy thing.

As I listened to the coffee pot gurgling, I thought about Toby developing away from the comic relief role I'd unconsciously assigned him, and turning into a dedicated ferret with a head full of shit. At some point, we were going to have to get his attention.

And Borman. I don't know why, but the fact that his dumb mistake had inadvertently compounded the effort by Peale to be thought of as a "real" vampire made me angry all over again.

The pot gasped and wheezed, finished. I poured the cups, and searched the kitchen for a tray. Being unable to locate anything of the sort, I carefully placed the three steaming cups on the breadboard. It looked a little bare, so I put a half dozen little pink packets of nonsugar sweetener on it, and four or five napkins. An afterthought made me stop and pour a cup for Sally.

As I passed through Dispatch, I saw a stack of paperback books partially concealed by a monitor screen and a weather radio box. I peered at the titles. *Darkness on the Ice* by Lois Tilton, and both *Interview with the Vampire* and *The Vampire Lestat* by Anne Rice.

"Doing a little research?"

"Thanks for the coffee, Houseman," she said as she handed me the criminal history on Peale. "Research is everything. You should read these." She also told me that there were two people there to pick up Huck.

"Which two?"

"Melissa and Kevin," she said.

"Okay." I motioned toward her books. "Library?"

"You bet."

I stopped to read the criminal history on our vampire, before taking the coffee back to my office. It was interesting. First of all, he had apparently used an alias for the two offenses with which he had been charged. His real name was listed, too, along with his SSN and his FBI number. Convicted felon, twice, in two different states. Therefore, a first offender in each. Somebody hadn't done their homework and checked him out thoroughly in the second case.

I double-checked the secondaries, just to make sure. Yep. Same height, eye color, same finger print code. Just different names used upon arrest. Shifty, but not very thoughtful of him. A really dedicated criminal could maintain a false identity for a long time. Of course, most of them weren't delusional like he was, either.

The first case was from North Dakota. He'd been arrested for contributing to the delinquency of minors in 1989. That was all there was on the initial entry, but Sally had contacted the agency in North Dakota, and had obtained some details. This is what she handed me:

SUBJECT KNOWN AS F/N DANIEL L/N POOL CHARGED WITH ELEVEN COUNTS CONTRIBUTING TO DELINQUENCY OF MINOR BY SEXUAL MISCONDUCT. ENTERED PLEA AGREEMENT OF GUILTY TO ONE COUNT. ORIGINAL INVESTIGATION INDICATES SUBJECT POOL INDUCED JUVENILE FEMALES TO INFLICT WOUNDS UPON SELVES, AND SUBJECT POOL INGESTED BLOOD OF THOSE FEMALES. DUE TO WOUNDS BEING SELF INFLICTED NO CHARGE AVAILABLE. SEXUAL MISCONDUCT CHARGE AROSE FROM ORIGINAL INVESTIGATION.

POOL IDENTITY ESTABLISHED AS ALIAS. TRUE NAME SUSPECT: LN/ PEALE; FN/DANIEL; MN/GORDON DOB: 04/10/65.

The second entry was from Walworth County, Wisconsin, in 1993, and was remarkably similar, with two exceptions: He'd used the alias of Daniel Gordon, which was hardly a stroke of originality, and likewise used a false date of birth of 10/04/65; and he'd gotten a two-year suspended sentence this time. There was a teletype from the originating agency, which merely said that the original charge involved something they referred to as "consensual ingestion of small amounts of blood," and that he had pled guilty to one count of assault by injury to an unnamed minor. The guilty plea figured. If the state tries you, they tend to give you a bit of time in the slammer to make up for their trouble. If you plead guilty, and avoid them having to actually go to the expense of trying you, you usually get a reduced sentence as a reward. First offense, the sentence tends to get suspended. The thing's justified by the guilty party telling the judge just how sorry he really is for what he's done. Those who can maintain a straight face do best. Actual guilt, obviously, has little to do with it.

But there we had the blood involvement, again. I glanced up at Sally. I knew she'd read the sheets, even though they were officially supposed to restrict themselves to the headers. "So, what do you think?"

She lowered her coffee cup. "I think you ought to call Buffy," she said.

As I passed through the booking room, and back into the main office, I saw Kevin and Melissa sitting quietly on the old spindle-back chairs we had for "guests." Uncomfortable because the arms were too low and the backs too erect, they were rejects from the old County Home. All we could get with our budget. Cost our center a dollar each. We split for ten.

"Hi," I said. "If you two want some coffee"—and I sort of gestured with the old TV tray top we used for our "service"—"just go ask a dispatcher for some."

"No, thanks," said Melissa.

"So, how's Hanna?" I asked, mostly to be polite.

"She'll make it," said Kevin. "What's taking Huck so long?"

"Oh, you know how it is," I said, pausing for a moment before I left the room. "One thing leads to another, and all the forms we have these days, it's a wonder we get done at all." The "Aw shucks" civil servant routine isn't always convincing, but sometimes it helps.

I got to my office, and sat the coffee down, and handed Hester the criminal history data that Sally had given me. "Interesting," I said.

She took it, but didn't look at it right away. Instead, she said, "We've been discussing just where Dan Peale got himself to when he ran out the door."

"Ah. And?"

"If he made it to the bottom of the hill," said Huck, "he could probably get a ride. There's quite a lot of traffic on the highway."

Now, as a deputy for over twenty years in Nation County, I knew that wasn't altogether true. Except during leaf season, when people came from all over to drive through the area and ooh and ah over the trees, there was very little traffic on that road. And the tree colors at night just didn't attract tourists, believe it or not. But I agreed with her by nodding. She might want us to know he'd gotten down and to a ride, I thought, and just didn't want to come right out and say so. Maybe.

Time for the next step. "Okay, now how about Alicia and her boyfriend? What really happened there?"

"How do you mean?"

"Did Dan ask you to bring her to the Mansion? It's important."

She thought about it for a few seconds before she answered me. "Not really, no."

"Huck, if there's anything that can get somebody into trouble in a case like this," said Hester, "it's equivocation."

Huck sighed. "Look, I'm sure he saw her at the Mansion, but it wasn't the first time he'd seen her."

"Really?" Hester's eyebrows went up.

"No, he'd seen her at a couple of bars. They'd talked once, I think." She looked serious. Whether or not she was was up for grabs.

I described the suspect outside Alicia's window to her, fangs and all. "Would he have looked the same as he did behind her apartment the other night?"

She snorted. "Of course not. He was batting the other night."

"What?"

"Batting. When he gets all costumed up, and goes out and crawls all over buildings, he calls it 'batting.' You know. For when the movie vampires turn into bats." She looked at each of us. "They really don't, of course. Real vampires can't turn into bats."

Coming from somebody who professed to believe in vampires, the fact allegation that they couldn't turn into bats was a bit jarring.

"So you don't buy the whole vampire thing?" asked Hester.

"Not the fantastic stuff," said Huck.

"Back to the case," I said. "Did he know Randy Baumhagen?"

"I think he'd met him once," said Huck. "As far as I know."

"So," said Hester, "do you think he wanted to... what? Get it on? With Alicia?"

"He wanted to do it with just about every attractive woman he ever met, I think," said Huck.

"And you knew that when you asked her up?"

"Shit, yes," said Huck. "But, so did she."

Hester looked at the criminal history on Peale. The Illinois Peale, since we couldn't find an English version.

"Huck," she said, "it's illegal for me to share this with you, but this"—and she indicated the sheet I'd handed her—"really indicates that our Mr. Peale is a U.S. citizen."

Huck just shook her head. "Boy, I dunno. I mean, he's convincing."

"That kind of reminds me," I said, and took a drink of coffee. "Did any of you know that Dan Peale was still up on the third floor? When we were there, I mean?"

"Oh, sure. We all did." I got the impression that she took it for granted that we had, as well. People give us credit at the damndest times.

"Really? All of you?" That surprised me.

"Oh, yeah." She took a sip, too, using time the way I had. "Jessica and Tatiana, too, I assume. It's his pattern. After he does his thing, you know, with the sex and the blood, and the crystal meth, and all, he takes downers. Sleeps for at least twenty-four hours. It's a psych thing, I believe." She took another drink. "He goes for a good twenty-four hours, and then sleeps for twenty-four or more."

"He," I asked, incredulous, "has twenty-four-hour orgies?"

She nodded, with a little smile, again. "Oh, yeah."

"And his partner is with him the whole time?"

"Well," she said, demurely, "he usually has more than one. You know, an appetizer, and then a main course, sort of."

"Brother" was all I could say.

"Assuming Edie was the 'main course,'" said Hester, "who might the appetizer have been?"

I think we both thought we were talking to the "appetizer." Wrong again.

"Melissa, and I think maybe Hanna, too, this time. They both disappeared, off and on, and I didn't actually miss Edie for quite a while."

"Oh." Hester was beginning to sound as casual about this as Huck.

"And Melissa really looked beat when she turned up. Too much E, you know? Doubling up."

"Ecstasy?"

"That's right. That or crystal meth. And whatever else he brought. Or did." Huck shrugged. "And E always gives Hanna a migraine. Then she can't sleep for a week."

"Poor dear," said Hester.

"Yeah." Huck asked if we needed anything else tonight. "I'm a little tired. Been a day, like I said."

"You be all right up there?" I was concerned. I felt that Peale was gone by now, but if he was still up there and knew she had been talking to us, she was taking a real chance. In my estimation, anyway.

"Sure. No problem." She made the "thumbs up" sign again. It was a little strange, as I thought that had gone out thirty years ago. Well, it had with me. Like they say, everything old is new again.

We asked Kevin and Melissa to come back the next day. They said they would, after the funeral. We watched them leave from the outer office.

When they had gone, I looked at Hester. "You believe her?"

"What part?"

"Well, I think she's probably fairly close to the truth with her personal history. Not sure about some of the rest."

"You mean when she says she had sex with Dan, sex with Kevin, sounds like sex with Jessica, and was pimping for Dan Peale by bringing Alicia up to that big house? Yeah, I believe that part." Hester sat on the edge of the secretaries' desk. "Yes. I'd say all that's probably pretty accurate, but maybe just a bit exaggerated?"

"Well, the scars were real." I shrugged. "That's pretty compelling."

"I think we'd better watch pretty carefully what she says about Dan Peale," said Hester. "And reserve judgment. The best lie is ninety-nine percent true, like they say."

"Yeah," I said. "Chester, the Mighty Vampire Hunter, told me and Harry that the Renfield personality would have them covering up for their very own vampire. Lying for him."

"There's a lot she's not telling." Hester got up. "That's for sure. More coffee out there?"

"What do they see in this guy?" I asked, as we found our way to the kitchen.

"Similar to dope dealers," she said. "He's got something they need. It's a trade-off, at least until it goes way too far."

"Like protection or something?"

"Sure. That, and a sense of belonging. Of being somebody who means something. It isn't like he's going to abandon them."

"Oh. But he can kill 'em?"

"That's going to be the critical question," she said. "If he can convince them he was justified, or that it was a mistake..."

TWENTY-THREE

Monday, October 9, 2000
20:38

Hester and I went over our plan of attack. First, we needed to get a warrant issued for Daniel Peale. We now had a home address, and could teletype it to his home county. They should be able to pick him up, if he was home.

"Don't forget to add a 'Use Caution' to that warrant," said Hester. "He did try to gut Borman."

"Don't worry." It would have to be a warrant for assault only, at this point. We had sufficient evidence to bring him in on the Borman assault. We didn't have nearly enough to try to take him on murder. Not yet. But an assault on a police officer would get plenty of attention.

Then, we thought it behooved us to get to those house blueprints over in Lake Geneva. When we went over to interview Jessica, which we should do tomorrow, as well.

"If they get Peale in Illinois, it could take a while to get him up to Iowa, even if he waives extradition."

"Absolutely," said Hester. "Which he would be foolish to do." She paused. "You think we should go to the funeral?"

"Naw. We put in an appearance at the wake. Not necessary to go tomorrow."

"Good," said Hester. "I don't have anything appropriate in my little duty bag that I keep in the car. I don't think I'll have to go back home for three more days, as long as I don't have to get all dressed up for something. And as long as the State keeps paying my motel bill."

"This is one place you never have to get dressed up," I said. "Ever."

I got the warrant from a magistrate in Manchester, the County Seat of adjoining Delaware County, who was the one on night duty in our district. A fifty-mile drive, each way. I got home at midnight.

Sue had left a casserole in the refrigerator, with a note on the door that directed me to it. There was another note on the microwave, warning me to keep the dish covered so it wouldn't spatter.

After I ate, I got upstairs and found a note on the bathroom mirror. "Don't forget that the fourteenth is the birthday party for Betsy." A cousin. I would have, and probably would again, anyway. We were to be hosting the family for the afternoon and evening, since it was my day off. Fourteen guests, and our daughter, Jane, was coming home from Michigan for the event.

I hated the way we had to communicate with notes so much. I mean I know that some couples write to each other. But they're the ones who live apart, for God's sake.

I wrote on the bottom of the note that I'd be there no matter what. I hoped I was right. Then I took my flashlight, and, holding my hand over the lens and letting just a little light shine between my fingers, I crept into the bedroom, and turned down the blanket.

"It's okay," came a sleepy voice. "I couldn't sleep. How'd the day go?"

"Fine," I said. "No problems."

I went out like the proverbial light.

The phone rang, and stopped after the second ring. I rolled over and looked at the clock. 07:48. I was the only one in bed, and Sue left for school at eight. She had probably gotten the call downstairs. I turned back over.

Sue said my name, from the bedroom door. "Carl?"

"Yeah," I said.

"It's for you. The office."

"Okay," I mumbled. "Thanks." I rolled back over, and reached out for the phone by the bed. "Yeah?"

"You better come out right away," said Gwen, who should have been gone.

"Why are you still at work?" I asked.

"Bad wreck down by Freeman's Grove about zero two hundred," she said. "Just getting ready to go. But you have to come out right away, and get up to the Freiberg Funeral Home."

"What's up?" I swung my legs over the edge of the bed.

"I don't know. Really. But the Freiberg officer, Byng, says we need the investigator there right away."

"Can you give me a guess?" I asked.

"All I know is that we got a call about ten minutes ago from the funeral home, and they requested an officer. He got there, and I thought it was just some traffic arrangement thing, you know, for the funeral today. And I think he did, too. And then Byng called on the phone, and said not to say anything over the radio, and not to tell Lamar."

It all came out in a rush, and she just about lost me. "Right," I said. "But no idea why?"

"No. And he said that he'd be very busy, and not to call him until you get there."

Unusual. Very unusual.

I was in the car and en route to Freiberg by 07:59. Not bad, considering. There had been some very cold coffee standing in the pot, left over from yesterday morning. I'd slurped some from a cup, and winced. But it was coffee.

It was a school day, so I kept it under seventy all the way up, but I did turn on my red lights. Didn't encounter a single school bus. Figured.

I went out of the car on the radio at 08:18, at the Freiberg Funeral Home.

The first person I met was Mrs. Marteen, the director's wife, who was very pale and fluttering around like some sort of demented butterfly. All she said was "This way, this way," as she ushered me into the back.

The funeral director and Byng were standing back by the vault where they would keep a body when it wasn't being viewed. The door was pretty big, in order to permit the easy passage of the coffins.

"What happened?" It's the best question.

"It's awful," said the director. "Terrible. Just terrible."

Byng said, "Broke into the vault, here, Carl, and I found a place out back where it looks like they might have come in through an unlocked window. No breaks, though."

"Okay. What's missing?" I had an incredible feeling of dread that somebody had taken Edie's body.

"Nothing as far as we can tell," he said. "But you better see this."

We entered the well-lit, cool vault, and I could see that Edie's coffin was opened. I came around the right side, and looked down at her.

"Aw, shit," I said.

"Yeah. Me, too."

There was a crude wooden stake protruding from the center of her chest.

TWENTY-FOUR

Tuesday, October 10, 2000
08:35

"Where's your phone?" I asked the director.

He led me back toward the main part of the building. "What's wrong with this world today?" he asked.

"Lots," I said.

"Don't let anybody touch anything," I said to Byng. "After I make a call, I'm going to get my camera, and then take a bunch of photos. Stay around." The last thing I wanted was to have an esthetically offended funeral director pull the stake out. As I dialed, it occurred to me that we had about three or four hours before the funeral.

"Sheriff's Department," said Sally.

"It's me, Houseman. Get Hester up here, and don't let Lamar know anything about my being here until I can talk to him personally. Call Doc Z., tell him we're going to have a question. Then get Dr. Peters, the forensics man, on the phone and ask if he can call me up here. Tell him it's very urgent."

"Right. What's going on?"

"Not over the phone," I said. Then it came to me that mothers, even estranged ones, might want to pay a visit on the deceased before the funeral. "Hang on a second." I put my hand over the receiver and raised my voice so the funeral director or his wife could hear, wherever they had chosen to be to give me privacy on the phone. "Mr. Marteen? Could you come here a sec?" He appeared almost instantly. He hadn't been too far, probably within earshot. "Can you tell me if any relatives will be here much before the funeral starts?"

"Many times they are. I don't know about this one."

"And what time is the funeral?"

"Eleven. And the luncheon is at St. Elmer's, as well." Habit.

"Thanks." I talked back into the phone. "Look, you better have Lamar give me a call up here right away."

"Okay."

"We gotta move really fast on this one," I said. "Later."

I hung the phone up. "We might have to delay the funeral a bit," I said to Mr. Marteen. "Maybe not. Will you come here and see if you think we can close the lid with that damned thing still in her?"

"How will I explain that?"

It was a fair question. "Just tell them it's at the request of the family," I said. "After all, everybody got a chance to see her yesterday at the wake."

"It's the family I was referring to," he said dryly.

"You mean her mother?"

"Yes. How on earth can I tell her that she can't see her daughter one last time?"

I didn't really think that was going to be a problem, but you never know what a relative will do.

"You have a blanket? A nice one?"

"Yes."

"Can't you tell her that it's part of the process, you know, to sort of cover her up? Just expose the face for the good-bye?" I thought it might work. The head of the stake only protruded about three inches, and if you were to wrinkle the blanket sufficiently . . .

He thought about that. "We do have to tell her. We really do," he said finally.

He was right. Now I was going to have to tell Lamar and lay this additional task on his shoulders.

I looked at Marteen. "Let me make a call. Sheriff Ridgeway will handle Edie's mother for us."

I really hated to make that call. Lamar, bless him, said he'd get to his sister's house right away.

"What they do to her, Carl?" His voice was tight with anger.

I told him. Sort of. "They slipped something into the coffin," I said. "No point in going into the details. It's just that there's been some discoloration and stuff, and it's best to have the lid closed. If your sister has to see her, Mr. Marteen here will just explain that they always cover them up to the chin with a special blanket or cloth." It was true as far as it went.

Mr. Marteen and I went to Edie's coffin, and very gently let the lid close. Just by gravity. "We have to close it carefully," I said. "We can't use any pressure or anything, or it will change things just a bit for whoever comes for the lab work."

He looked questioningly at me.

"Court, Mr. Marteen. You'll have to testify to this in court. That we didn't use any pressure to close the lid."

The next fifteen minutes were pretty busy. First I had to photograph everything. I was very relieved the lid would close easily, and we were going to have to have a closed-casket ceremony. Better than none, I thought. I had Mr. Marteen remain there throughout, as an independent witness. Not a time to take a chance with the evidence.

I did photos inside first. It was backward procedure, but it was done that way to get things around the casket finished up and set back in place as soon as possible. I'd be able to take my own sweet time looking at the exterior evidence.

Just as I was heading for the back door, Hester came in the front.

"What's so urgent?"

I took her to the back room, and warned her. "Somebody's mutilated Edie's corpse," I said.

"Oh, no . . ."

"Yeah. A stake in her chest." I said it as matter-of-factly as I could.

"You have to be kidding me. Jesus H. Christ," she said softly. "What in hell is going on here?"

I raised the newly closed casket lid, and she looked in. We stared for a few seconds, neither of us really sure what to say next.

"You call Dr. Zimmer?" she asked, in a toneless voice.

"Yes. Told the office to tell him it was very urgent."

"Who do you think? Chester? Peale?"

"Don't know. Chester'd be the logical choice. Being the mighty hunter and all, this should be the thing he does, shouldn't it?" I was far from sure, but he seemed like the reasonable suspect.

"It could be," she said. "But, why would somebody do this, Carl?" She looked at me for the first time since I'd opened the coffin lid. "There's no such thing as a vampire, and . . . Anyway, there's no indication whatsoever that Edie ever even *pretended* she was one."

"I don't know. But I will." And I was sure that I would. A murder investigation, with its associated procedures, was rare in Nation County, and I was relatively unfamiliar with it. Burglary investigation, on the other hand, was my thing.

We hadn't been outside for more than five minutes, when I had the following information securely fixed in my notebook:

A. Entry had been gained through the unlocked window, as described to me by Officer Byng.

B. Unknown to Byng, who'd done a cursory check outside, the screen had been removed from the high window, and *that* had not been unlocked. The aluminum-framed screen was around the north side of the building, in some bushes. It had been bent, pried, and the screening material itself had been torn. All of that would have been unnecessary, if the suspect(s) had simply pried up near the wire latch.

C. There were traces of blood on the screen frame, and on some of the strands of torn wire.

D. The suspect(s) had approached the rear door, which had been locked, and had left some small pry marks near the lock, but right over the key mechanism. Not in the right place, they'd produced no result, and entry had not been gained.

E. There were three identifiable footprints in the dirt under the window where they'd gained entry. Two left shoe, one right shoe, of identical pattern.

F. There were shallow trench marks about a quarter inch wide and deep, and about three feet long, in the ground under the window. They indicated that either a box or a crate had been placed under the window to permit the suspect(s) to climb high enough to effect entry.

G. There was a heavy-duty, blue plastic milk crate across the blacktopped alley, that proved to have similar dirt on the top edges. As would be expected if it had been inverted for use as a step.

All this was very positive, and I was pleased. The icing on the cake, however, was provided by one Rosalind

O'Banion, a sixty-eight-year-old white female, who lived across the street from the funeral home, and who had shuffled over to watch the excitement. She was wearing a blue and white checked bathrobe, with a raincoat over it, and a gray stocking cap on her head.

"What's going on, Bingo?" she said, addressing Byng.

"Never mind, Rosy." He was pretty short, I thought. I didn't think that she'd come all the way across the street, dressed like that, just to stare. Her house offered a fine view, and she could have sat down with her coffee and watched from there in comfort.

"We've had a little incident here, ma'am," I said. Like I say, burglaries are my thing, sort of, and I knew from much experience that witnesses were worth their weight in gold. Rosy might have a bit of potential. "Can you tell me anything about it?"

"No," said Rosy.

Well, so much for that.

"If you do remember anything, or hear anything, would you let us know?" Not quite a brush-off, and it left the door open.

Rosy looked at me closely, and I figured that since I wasn't in uniform, it really hadn't sunk in that I was a law enforcement officer. "Aren't you the cop who busted Quentin Pascoe a while back?"

The worst sexual abuse case I'd ever worked. "Yep, that was me."

"The son of a bitch," she said, "is my brother-in-law." She thought for a moment, and then said, "Well, it probably don't mean shit, but..." Music to my ears.

Rosy was the cleaning lady for one of the local taverns, and had just been leaving her house last night to clean the place when she'd seen somebody in the alley. He'd been coming toward her, from the funeral home direction, and just stopped cold when he saw her. He'd apparently stood stock-still, and didn't utter a sound. She walked about fifteen feet from him, following her usual path to the tavern, and he still hadn't moved a muscle, nor said a word.

"I didn't speak nothin' either," she said. "Just walked by him like he wasn't there."

"Did you recognize him?"

"I think so. I can't put his name on my tongue, but you know him, too. The short one."

I'd need a bit more than that. "Uh . . ."

"The short one, the one from up at the Mansion. Oh, you know. . . ."

"Male or female, Rosy?"

She snorted. "He's a male, I think," she said disparagingly. "Comes into the tavern once in a while, I think for no good. You know the one, with the thing in his nose," she said, and pointed to the bridge of her own nose. "Right here."

I looked at Hester, who was grinning widely.

"Kid named Toby?" I asked.

"Yeah, sure. Toby. Toby, uh, Chalk or something, oh, it'll come to me . . ."

"Gottschalk?"

"No, that's not right. Is it? Maybe it is," she said, reflecting. "Maybe so."

"But you know him to live up at the big house on the bluff, south of here, right?" I had to make sure, but there was no doubt in my mind who she meant.

"Hangs about with that Huck girl, and the other, smaller one, a lot. Him."

"Did you see anything else?" interjected Byng, trying to be helpful.

"You're the one with the shiny badge, Bingo," she said. "How much help you need?"

"Thanks, Rosy. Thanks a whole lot," I said. "Big help, but now, don't tell anybody you talked to us, okay?"

"Quiet as a mouse," she said.

"Promise?" I smiled.

"On a stack of Bibles," she answered.

I figured that ought to buy us about ten minutes. But I was happy.

But Toby, for God's sake. I would have bet heavily on William Chester. Well, maybe Toby was just the lookout for somebody. Sure.

Hester and I rode up to the Mansion together, leaving the funeral home just as one of the area TV vans pulled up to get set to cover the funeral. Close.

I used her cell phone to call Lamar. I told him what had happened, sort of. He sounded angry and sad, but I think it helped when I told him we were on our way to bag a suspect.

"Let me know when you get him in custody," he said.

"You got it." I handed the cell phone back to Hester. "He wants us to let him know when we've got Toby."

"My pleasure," said Hester. "Hey, go slow through here. I want to see if there's any sign of the old lift track from the top of the hill to the landing."

I slowed, just past the silica mine, and we looked as closely as possible at the cliff faces and the ravines between them. There wasn't much to see, except a possible segment of a pathway up on the side of the bluff, just barely discernible among the trees. It seemed to disappear about fifty feet up the slope, among some boulders and old fallen timber.

"We should wait for winter," I said. When all the leaves have fallen, and the first light snow comes, tracks in the hills stand out like white lines on a dark field.

"If we haven't found what we're looking for before the first snowfall, Houseman," said Hester, "we're in real trouble."

"Yeah." I looked back, over my shoulder, toward the

possible path. "I sure as hell wouldn't want to try that in the dark," I said.

"Me, either. You could fall a good fifty feet onto those boulders. Especially if you were in a hurry."

It was food for thought, though. There had been a clear way down there once, according to Old Knockle. There could be, still.

Hester used her cell phone to call Harry, over in Conception County, as I drove. She told him about the staking, and asked where the body of the late Randy Baumhagen was being kept. It was apparently in Harry's jurisdiction, because she cautioned him to keep an eye out on a funeral home.

Calling Harry had completely slipped my mind. That sort of thing bothers me, because it means that I'm not getting enough time between events to process information correctly.

"I'm about a hundred percent certain that he's up here," I said, as we turned off the paving and onto the gravel that led to the Mansion. "He's pretty predictable."

"Oh, yeah," she said. "Where else can he go? Just remember how predictable he is, when he runs into the woods on us again."

"Good point." I turned onto the long drive, heading up the hill. I slowed way down, so that the occupants of the Mansion wouldn't be alerted by the roar and rush of the car. "I just hope he's got the right tread pattern on his shoes, and that he's got a cut somewhere we can see," I said, remembering the blood on the screen. Please, God. Please.

It's always amazed me how thieves and burglars tend to go home. I've never had one take off for parts unknown to me, at least not one who lived in Nation County. Itinerants didn't count, nor did the traveling pros. I was pretty certain we'd find Toby at home.

When we pulled up, Huck and Melissa were standing over a bonfire of burning leaves a little distance from the house. From the absence of the numerous piles Melissa'd raked when we'd been there before, it looked like they were just finishing up the yard work.

We got out of the car, and I waved. They didn't wave back, but Huck started over toward us, pulling off her gloves and stuffing them in the pockets of her hooded gray sweatshirt.

"Surprised to see you two," she said.

"Surprised to be here," I answered. "Where's Toby?"

"Toby? Uh, inside, I think. He was in the kitchen a minute ago. Eating."

"Thanks," said Hester. "Want me to give you a second?"

"Yep," I said. "About five, then go." I headed at a quick walk around the right side of the house, toward the back door at the kitchen, where Toby had exited before. Huck looked confused, and started to follow me. Hester went straight for the front door.

As I passed Melissa, she said, "What are you doing?"

A reasonable question, considering. I held my finger to my lips. "Shhh, you should see in a second or two," I said. "Just both of you stay back." I continued, stooping so I wouldn't be seen from the interior as I was passing the windows on the south side of the house, and reached back under my jacket and pulled out my gun.

I noticed that Huck stopped at that, and that Melissa moved closer to her.

I reached the back door, just as I heard Hester's muffled voice say, "Toby, you're under arrest!"

The back door flew open, I raised my gun up at arm's length, and greeted the emerging Toby with "Freeze!"

He stopped so fast, he slipped on about the third step, lost his balance and fell over backward, grabbed for the rail, missed that, and slid down toward me like a little log in a chute. It all happened in the blink of an eye, and he was as shocked as anybody I've ever seen. He looked up at me, open mouthed, and tried to speak, but only managed to make a wheezing sound, while looking cross-eyed into the muzzle of my pistol.

Hester appeared at the top of the steps, also gun in hand.

"You were right," she said. "Predictable." She nodded toward him. "Check him, I think he has a knife on his hip, and then check out the hands," she said.

I reached down, fumbled for a second, and pulled a folding Case knife from the sheath on his left side. I put it in my pocket, and looked at his hands. Band-Aids on three fingers of his right hand. Well, well. They were multicolored and had some sort of printing on them. I looked closer. "Buzz Lightyear?" I said. "Cool. What'd you cut your fingers on, Toby?"

Silence.

I glanced at his feet. Tennis shoes. Good so far. "Hold up your foot," I said. He looked at me strangely, but did. The same pattern that I'd seen in the alley.

"Get up to your knees," I said, "turn around so that you face the steps, and put your hands over your head."

He did, still not speaking.

I put my gun in its holster, and pulled my handcuffs out of my back pocket. I took his left hand by the wrist, snapping the handcuff on, and pulled it down and to his rear. I grabbed his other hand, and brought it close enough to the other to slip a cuff on that one, too. I put one hand on his arm, and pulled him to his feet.

"You're under arrest, like she said," I told him.

He spoke for the first time. "For what?"

The universal answer to my statement. "Burglary," I said.

He then inserted his foot into his mouth. "I didn't steal anything," he said.

I turned him around. "You have the right to remain silent...."

"It must have been the old hag," he said, swallowing his foot with that one. His attorney would probably call that a "statement against interest." But old Toby apparently felt compelled to speak, no matter what. That's a fine trait in a suspect.

We took Toby directly to my car, past the astonished Huck and Melissa, and put him in the backseat.

"Watch your head, Toby," I said, and shut the door. Hester motioned toward the porch. The four remaining residents were all standing on the porch, looking down on us.

"And then," said Hester, sotto voce, "there were four." She motioned me up toward the front of the car, and well out of Toby's possible hearing. "I don't know how to ask this," she said, "so I might as well come right to the point. Are you sure we had a burglary? I was thinking about that when I confronted Toby in the kitchen just now. Doesn't the code say you have to unlawfully enter a premises, with 'the intent to commit a felony, theft, or assault'? For a burglary...."

"Hmm." She was right in her quote, of course. It was felony, theft, or assault. The question being, was mutilating a corpse a felony? "Well, we may have just made a very strong trespassing arrest," I said. "Very strong."

"I mean," she said, "sticking a stake in a corpse damned well should be a felony, but I don't know if it is."

"It may not even be illegal," I said. "It may never have been *considered* in Iowa before this." I don't mind being near the leading edge, but I dearly hate breaking new ground. But, realistically, how many times could it have come up in Iowa before today? I knew it was illegal to exhume, but poor Edie wasn't even buried yet.

"This could be another very long day," I said.

"Where are you taking him?" came a loud voice from the porch. It may have been Melissa, but by the time I looked, I couldn't tell.

"Jail," I said, as loudly. Just to be polite.

"Tell him," said Kevin, "that we'll call his attorney." Hardly necessary, at that point. Veiled threat?

"Will do," I called back, got into the car, buckled up while Hester leaned back and buckled Toby in, and we were off.

I picked up the mike. "Comm, Three."

"Three, go."

"PBX One, advise him we have a suspect in custody, and are ten-seventy-six the jail." I'd told Lamar I'd let him know right away.

"Ten-four, Three. He's called twice, and will have your assistant go with the seventy-nine to the location."

Now, that might have sounded kind of cryptic to the normal person, but anybody with any savvy now knew that a coroner or medical examiner was going to a scene, that the boss had called twice, and that my assistant was being called out. I had to admit, though, that even I was thrown by the last bit. I didn't have an assistant.

"Uhh, Comm, Three?"

"Three?"

"Ah, who's my assistant this week?" As soon as I said it, I knew she had meant Borman.

"Eight."

Borman, all right. Well, we'd see if this examination of a mutilated corpse would get his act on track.

"Ten-four, Comm."

Toby was quiet for about the first quarter mile, and I was starting to get worried. As it turned out, I shouldn't have been concerned. His tendency to talk overcame all caution.

"It had to be done," he said.

"Toby," said Hester, "let's not discuss it. You've been advised of your rights, and we'd feel a lot better if you waited until you had an attorney present."

That was partially true. Sure, we'd like Toby to rattle on, but we had the old problem that, even if he said he waived his rights to the attorney, we could lose a suppression hearing later. If that happened, everything he said, and everything we'd found out based on that, could be ruled inadmissible. It happened just often enough to make us very leery about questions without attorneys there. I mean, we knew we'd be right, but that sometimes did very little good in court. There, it came down to the briefing and arguing abilities of two attorneys. We would have nothing at all to say about that. This was, well, safer, I guess.

It was also pretty damned prudent, because the more I searched my memory, the more convinced I became that there was no statute on the Iowa books about mutilating corpses.

Toby, thwarted in his first attempt to enlighten us, switched to philosophy.

"It doesn't make any difference, anyway," he said. He fidgeted.

I glanced at Hester, who was half turned in the front seat, to keep an eye on Toby since we had no cage in an unmarked car, gave an almost imperceptible shake of her head. Keep quiet, Carl.

I did, and so did she. That bothered Toby, who began to tap his feet against the back of her seat.

"Well, it doesn't, does it? Make any difference. I can't make any difference. You can't make any difference." He couldn't quit.

Hester and I, being in the process of making a difference in Toby's life, said nothing.

"Oh, fuck you two."

I grinned. I just couldn't help it. The tapping of his feet got more intense.

"What's so funny, cop?" He did try. He sort of had to, I guess.

Hester said, pointedly to me, "Well, most of the leaves are off the trees, now, aren't they."

"Yep," I answered. "Sure are. Ought to slow the tourist trade a little."

"Ought to slow the tourist trade," said Toby, mockingly.

"Especially," said Hester, "if it rains again tomorrow like they say it will."

"Are you fuckers stupid or what?" Toby was getting a bit angry, which is not what we wanted. Without a cage, we'd have to stop and restrain him if he started thrashing about in the rear, and he could get hurt. So could we, but it was a lot less likely.

"Nope," I said. "Not stupid, Toby, just not particularly interested. That's all."

"Just not particularly interested," came the mocking reply. "I staked the bitch, and you tell me you're not interested? Bullshit you're not interested!"

I glanced at Hester. "Just irrepressible, isn't he?" But I was also beginning to think he was a little high.

She smiled. She held out her personal tape recorder, down low in the seat, where Toby couldn't see it.

"We said we'd prefer not to hear about that, Toby," said Hester, "until your attorney can be present."

"Attorneys," proclaimed Toby, "don't know shit." His voice was lowering, though. He just wanted to talk, and didn't care to whom. The foot tapping ceased.

"Most don't," I agreed, grinning in the knowledge that his attorney would likely hear this tape, "but you might get lucky and get a smart one."

He seemed to think that over for several seconds.

"I doubt it." He sounded a little sullen. "Hey, I'm not mad at you guys," said Toby. "Really."

"We know that, Toby," I said. "Never thought you were." Big mood and attitude swing there. Toby was on something. No doubt.

"I been under a lot of pressure," he said.

"Things do have a way of piling up on somebody," said Hester.

"You 'got that shit right," said Toby. "What do you do, if somebody who's gotta be obeyed tells you to do something, right? What do you do?" His voice was becoming agitated again. "I'll tell what you do," he said. There was a pause, and then he said, in a more moderate tone, "You fuckin' do it, because you fuckin' better do it, you know?"

"Depends on who it is," I said, "but we all have to get in line once in a while."

"When it's Dan Peale, you do," he said.

I was glad we'd just gotten onto a paved road, otherwise I might have gone in the ditch. You don't get a gift like that every day.

TWENTY-FIVE

Tuesday, October 10, 2000
11:55

The first thing I'd done when we got to the jail was start the call to the county attorney. Now that we had Toby in our clutches, and in a talkative state, I wanted to keep him as long as I could.

The first conversation with our county attorney had been very brief.

"I'm sorry, he's with a client now," said his secretary.

"Tell him, Darlene, that this is really important. Really. I need to talk with him in five minutes or less. Something's happened that he's gotta know about."

In about ten minutes, he called back.

"What's so important, Carl?"

"We need some fast research," I said. "I've got to know what to charge somebody with who broke into a funeral home, and drove a stake through the chest of a corpse."

There was a pause. "You're kidding?"

"Nope. I've got the dude in custody, but I gotta have a good charge, and quick."

"You've gotta be kidding?"

"No, Mike, I'm not."

"What's wrong with burglary? Just plain burglary, Carl."

I reached behind me, and pulled one of the volumes of the 1999 Code of Iowa off the shelf. "Got your code handy?" I asked. I was going to have to work with him on this, and I really resented the time.

"Sure."

"Okay, under 713.1 . . . the burglary statute . . . got it?"

"Yes."

I read it to him. The pertinent part was "Any person, having the intent to commit a felony, assault or theft therein . . ."

"So?" he said.

"Well, he didn't steal anything, and since you can't assault the dead, he has to have intended to commit a felony, right?"

"Yes. Sure."

"Well, is it a felony to mutilate a corpse? We gotta know, Mike."

"I'm sure it is," he said, and I could hear pages flipping in the background.

"Here it is," he said. "Chapter 709.18. Abuse of a corpse. Right here."

I flipped my pages. It said, "A person commits abuse of a human corpse if the person knowingly and intentionally engages in a sex act, as defined in section 702.17, with a human corpse. Abuse of a human corpse is a class D felony."

We were both silent, as we read it. "It wasn't exactly a sex act, Mike."

Naturally, he had us both turn to 702.17, which defined sex acts. They all included the word "genitalia." No go, and I told him so.

I could tell he was getting worried, too. Just about everything else regarding dead human bodies had to do with licensing funeral directors, medical examiners, and the paperwork required when one came into possession of a corpse. It was too bad Edie hadn't been buried, because if she had, and she'd been exhumed by the suspect, it would have been an aggravated misdemeanor. But, of course, she wasn't in the ground yet.

"Wait, Carl. . . . Just a second. . . ."

"Mike, the only statute that covers it is the trespass section."

"Wait, let's check 716, criminal mischief. . . ."

We did. Criminal mischief required damage to "tangible property."

"I don't think a corpse is 'tangible property,' I'm afraid, Carl. I'll look, though."

I had to agree with that. "Yeah, when was the last time you saw a price tag on a corpse?" I flipped the page. "Yep. Right. So, look at 716, trespass. That fits."

It did, too. Under 716.7.2(a). Very specific. "Entering upon or in property without the express permission of the owner, lessee, or person in lawful possession with the intent to commit a public offense, to use, remove therefrom, alter, damage, harass, or place thereon or therein anything animate or inanimate . . ."

That covered it. Edie was definitely "inanimate," all right. And she'd been both "altered" and "damaged." By something that had been "placed" there by hammering it into her chest. Unfortunately, trespass was a simple misdemeanor. That meant a hundred-dollar fine, maximum. Burglary charges required a felony.

That's when Mike, bless him, finally earned his keep. Sort of.

"Wait a minute, Carl, wait a minute. . . . look under the 'hate crime' provision, down in 716.8. See, it says that if there's the intent to commit a hate crime, the penalty goes up to a serious misdemeanor."

Wow. A whole five-hundred-dollar fine. Still two

steps away from a felony, but we'd made some progress, at least.

"Hate crime?"

"Well, won't the relatives be offended, on, well religious grounds, Carl?"

I gotta admit that would never have occurred to me. I would have just been very, very angry, religion aside.

"So, what do I hold him on, then?"

"Uh, well, a serious misdemeanor, I guess," he said, "at least for now."

At least for now. What did he think, that Toby was going to commit some more serious crime while he was in jail? A serious misdemeanor would keep him just long enough to do the paperwork, if we were lucky.

"It's gonna have to do," I said. And if the bond were typically reduced to ten percent of the fine, he was going to walk on a fifty-dollar deposit. Great.

I got back to Hester, who was baby-sitting Toby in my office. No real point in beginning the process that would book him into jail, at least not if he was still talking, and there wasn't a really good reason to distract him with a lot of jail-related questions.

"How we comin' for an attorney for him?" I asked.

"Attorney Junkel called," said Hester. "He's on his way down. Wanted to know what he was being charged with."

"And?"

"I told him the charges were still being determined." She looked at Toby, who was listening closely. "He told Toby not to talk about the case with us until he got here."

Expected, as any good attorney would say that. Toby, unfortunately, simply had to talk, and about anything that came into his head, I guess. Talk, talk, talk. And bouncing his feet. Still handcuffed, he looked pretty disheveled, because his hair was falling down over one eye, and he couldn't reach out and push it back. Consequently, he kept tossing his head, to clear his field of vision. I was thinking in terms of crystal meth or ecstasy. I didn't want to ask him, though, because it might lead to a charge, which his attorney would use to discount what he'd said.

"Nothing can be done, anyway," said Toby.

When you deal with someone who is wired like that, you talk to them. If you don't at least provide some input from an outside source, they get angry, and sometimes violent. It's not difficult to talk with them, though, because they will chat about virtually anything you toss their way.

"I'm not so certain about that," I said. "Frequently..."

I'd started him off on another tangent, and he interrupted.

"A lot you know. There's this physics thing called the Uncertainty Principle, you know, and it says that nobody can know anything for certain. Ever. Nope, they can't, and it's been scientifically proven, too."

My, he was wired. "You mean Heisenberg's Uncertainty Principle," I asked, offhandedly as I was wondering what to do when Attorney Junkel arrived.

"Ooooh, you can read," he said.

"I think Uncle Werner was referring to subatomic particles that can be influenced by the impact of a photon," I said. "Not whether or not your bank account balanced."

"Uncle? He was your uncle?" There was wonder in his voice. It was apparently easier for him to believe I was related to the famous physicist than for him to believe I had read anything concerning the man. Helped along, no doubt, by the fact he was stoned.

"Figure of speech, Toby," I said. "Just a figure of speech." I kept a straight face, but it wasn't easy.

"My bank account never balances," he pronounced with great dignity, "because I don't have one." He began to giggle. "But I had one once, and I couldn't keep it balanced on the end of my nose to save my ass!" He broke himself up with that one.

While our captive entertained himself, I told Hester about my conversation with the county attorney.

"I figured as much," she said. "Shit."

"Oooh, lady," came from Toby. "The 'S' word."

"Go balance your checkbook, Toby," she said. That got him laughing quietly to himself, and he left us alone for the moment.

"Do we want the county attorney here for Junkel? On the off chance that he might let us interview Toby in his presence?"

She shook her head. "Not at this point."

Toby started to sing in a thin voice, using what he evidently thought was an English accent.

"D'ye ken Dan Peale with his teeth so white?
He sleeps in the day and comes out at night,
His unearthly powers give the mortals a fright
Till he goes back to his coffin in the mor-ning."

Hester and I looked at each other. He sang it again, in a quavering voice, keeping time with his foot.

"D'ye ken Dan Peale with his teeth so white?
He sleeps in the day and comes out at night,
His unearthly powers give the mortals a fright
Till he goes back to his coffin in the mor-ning."

He stopped, and looked at us. "He's gonna kill me, 'cause I failed him twice, and you don't get a third chance. Not from old Dan Peale." His eyes darted about the room. "In the crypt, he told me to kill her, and I couldn't. He told me to keep her dead, and I couldn't do it right. He's going to kill me now, 'cause I failed him." He spoke in a calm, steady voice. "Plonk, plonk, plonk," he said. Just like that first night in the woods.

"He was born in 1604 in London fucking England, and he never, never dies."

It was creepy.

I glanced at Hester, and mouthed "Crypt?"

She nodded.

"It's all right, Toby. Don't worry," said Hester. "Wait till your attorney gets here. Quietly." Her tape was obviously still running.

"Not my attorney. Their attorney," he said, suddenly getting petulant on us. "He'll save me, all right, but he'll just be saving me for them." He looked beseechingly at Hester. "Don't let 'em kill me, lady. Please?"

"Now you're putting me on," I said. "Just wait for Mr. Junkel."

"Don't I wish I was."

"Yeah. Hey, why'd you run on us the other night? Just curious, no charge or anything." I really was interested in why, and there wasn't anything that an attorney could glom onto with that question.

He tittered. "Well, I forgot to lock the fuckin' door, didn't I?"

"Yeah, you're just not fast enough," I said. "But why'd you run?"

He positively giggled. "Toby wins," he got out. "Yes!"

I tried another tack. "And who's this 'they' you keep referring to?" I tried to keep it matter-of-fact, but there was a tinge of anticipation in my voice, I'm afraid. It was a justifiable question, though, even in the light of *Miranda*. Our knowing who was going to "kill" Toby was in his own interest.

He regarded me for a moment, suddenly quite calm. Sober, in a way.

"Vampires all over the world," he said. "That's who 'they' are."

He was lying again.

"I mean the 'they' you were just talking about," I said. "The ones represented by Junkel." And we all knew who at least one of those clients would be. I really expected him to say "Jessica Hunley." Of course, that would have been a truthful statement, and I should have known better.

"Corporate America," he said, looking me right in the eye.

"Can't help you unless you play it straight," I said. Hoping against hope that he'd tell.

He suddenly cocked his head, squinted, and then began to breathe more rapidly. The dope again.

"You're the one," he said, to me. "You're the reason. I heard you say that Edie was telling on us. You said so. So I had to make sure she stayed dead."

I was taken aback for a second, both by the accusation and the sudden mood swing, until I remembered that I *had* said something about Edie, and speaking to us. Holy shit. I'd meant at the autopsy.

Before I could say anything, he said, "I fucked that up, too. You're supposed to stake 'em through the heart, then cut off their head, then burn 'em. That's what you gotta do, and I..." Tears, now. Big ones. "I couldn't do that." He got blubbery. "I luh, luh, loved Edie!"

While he cried, Hester looked questioningly at me.

"I said something about Edie's dead body giving us information at autopsy, the other day, and I remember the look on his face." I spoke very softly. "Well, at least I do now, for sure. He looked kind of shocked. Now I know why, I guess." I looked at Toby, who was pretty self-involved at the moment. "Where do you suppose the 'crypt' is? The basement?"

"That'd be my guess," she half whispered back.

"But there was no blood evidence down there...."

"He said he couldn't kill her there," said Hester, staring at Toby. "Probably wouldn't be, then...."

Well, sure, Carl. Pay attention. "Ah," I said, tapping the side of my head with my finger. "Thank you."

"He called and told me I'd be really strong," came from Toby. We both looked at him. "He said I'd have his strength. I did, too, boy. I did. I hit that stake once, and it went right into her chest." The tears had stopped, but his nose was running. He grinned, an evil grin if there ever was one. "Slicker 'n shit. One powerful hit, was all. He was so fuckin' right." Then a worried frown came over him. "But I couldn't take her head off. I just got... weak." His face screwed up, tears started again, and he went back to referring to himself in the third person. "Toby's a failure. But he tries!"

Hester pushed a piece of scratch paper over to me, with one word written on it. "Committal?" I nodded. It looked like we'd have to.

"The first time we killed her, she knew it, and she asked me for help," he said, and this time the crying that he did was nearly hysterical. He lurched to his feet, and came right at Hester. She started to step to the side, and I started for him, and he tripped on the chair leg, and went facedown on the carpet with a resounding thud. He just laid there and cried. "Help!" he wailed, into the greenish gray nap.

"The first time we killed her" I mouthed to Hester. She was wide-eyed, and nodded.

"Where were you, you and Edie, the first time you killed her?" I really hated to ask, but we just had to know where she'd been killed.

He stopped crying instantly, and turned his head so he could see me. "No fuckin' way, dude. No way. That's between me and her and Dan."

Well, it had been worth the try, I thought. Probably couldn't have used it anyway, at least not against him.

I picked up the phone and dialed Dispatch, while Hester knelt down by his head. "This is Houseman. We need an ambulance back here, to transfer one subject to the Maitland Hospital."

"Is it ten-thirty-three?"

"No, but ASAP would be real nice." Crap. Once there, the diagnosis would probably be of a psychotic episode, or something. The committal process to the

Mental Health Institute at Independence would take about two hours. Then one of us would either have to haul him the fifty miles to the mental ward, or one of us would have to go with him in the ambulance. The Board of Supervisors would crap, because, since he was in custody, Nation County would have to pay the bill. And, since he was in custody, we might have to either hire a cop to watch him down there, or send one of ours to stay. Those damned complications, as they say, complicate things. But it needed to be done. Not that I was all that altruistic, or anything. If we didn't commit at this point, and we did have a murder suspect on our hands, we could well lose the case. We were going to need excellent medical testimony as to the fact that Toby was totally tweaked on either meth or ecstasy, or some combination thereof, and not insane. We really needed not insane.

Hester and I sat him back up in his chair. Physically, he seemed to be just fine. Hester got a wet paper towel and wiped his face, clearing away the tears, mucus, and spittle and that seemed to help. It at least made him easier to look at. I figured the ambulance would take about fifteen minutes.

And, of course, Attorney Junkel picked that moment to make an entrance.

"What's going on here?" asked a strident, courtroom voice. I didn't even have to turn around to know it was Junkel.

"Hi."

"What have you done to my client?"

"Very little, actually." I shrugged. "Basically, we arrested him," I explained.

"How are you, son?" he asked.

"Toby is shitty," said Toby. "And Toby thanks you for asking."

Junkel looked at me. "Just what is going on here?"

It took about all I could muster not to answer him in third person. What I said was, "We arrested Toby for breaking in to the Freiberg Funeral Home, and driving a stake into the chest of the corpse of Edie Younger."

You just don't get to see an attorney look like that every day. His eyes widened, and his jaw dropped perceptibly. Seeing his startled look, I had an inspiration.

"It's either a simple misdemeanor, or, if you consider it a hate crime, it becomes a serious misdemeanor. The statutory bond for the most serious one is fifty dollars. Cash."

"Can he post?" asked Junkel.

I played my ace. "Nope. Looks like he's ours."

It worked. Just to spite me, Junkel reached into his back pocket, pulled out his billfold, and removed a fifty-dollar bill. Why not? He'd probably received a call from Jessica Hunley, he was on retainer, and the bill would now include a fifty-dollar expense.

"The hell he is," he said. "He's now in the care of his attorney!"

I looked down at the money, then up at Junkel. "I suppose you'll want a receipt?" I tried to sound disappointed.

He glared at me. "Of course I will."

I thought for about two seconds about a possible aiding and abetting in a murder case as another charge for Toby. But to pop him on his statements, while in his current state, would just be asking for trouble. We didn't have any good evidence against him yet, and moving too soon would tip our hand. I rejected the notion.

"And you might as well also help him with his committal to the Mental Health Institute. We've started that. You might not have noticed, but your client is pretty well pharmaceutically enhanced," I said.

Eventually, the mental health referee came up, pretty much took one look at Toby, and told Junkel that, "Your client's having a bad trip," and offered to sign Toby into the MHI for detoxification and counseling. Translated, that was roughly a three-day involuntary commitment. I was very pleased with detox.

"Unless, of course, your client wished to commit himself," said the referee. I could tell he was thinking about the paperwork. "If that's the case, all this would be unnecessary."

Junkel leaped at the offer, so Toby obligingly agreed to commit himself. Cheap trip, as he could check out any time he wanted to, he would be guaranteed to be back out in three days, and his attorney was going to have to figure out how to haul him to the mental health facility at Independence. But at least he wasn't a drain on our meager resources.

Besides, with what we actually had on him, it would have been three and out, anyway.

_____

About two hours after we had arrived at the office, Toby was on his way. As we helped pack him into Junkel's car, he giggled, and began to say "Plonk, plonk," faster and faster.

"What's he saying?" asked Junkel. "Isn't plonk a term for cheap wine?"

"I dunno," I said. "Maybe he's thirsty." Actually, plonk, in this instance, is a usenet term, and it's the sound that a novice internet user makes when he hits the bottom of the kill file. To be "kill filed" means that his correspondents have told their computers to automatically ignore anything from him. The meaning here was that Toby was, if not already dead, considering himself as good as. I felt no compunction to enlighten Junkel. Let him ask his own kids.

Toby hadn't been out the door five minutes, when Dispatch told me that Lamar was on the phone. He was calling from the church hall, where the after-funeral luncheon was winding up.

"Hi, boss."

"Marteen told me the details," he said slowly, evenly. "All of 'em."

"Shit, Lamar, I really didn't want you to have to deal with that." I was about ready to kill the funeral director, too, but didn't say so.

"I want whoever did it, Carl. I want him bad."

A good moment, at last. "Oh, we already got him. He's charged, and on his way to MHI." I thought for a second. I figured I better tell him. "We think the same suspect was there when she was killed, Lamar. He's shaping up as an accomplice. We only have his verbal statement to that effect, and he was wasted when he said it. He's telling the truth, but we have absolutely no hard evidence. I think we should have some pretty soon."

After a pause, Lamar asked, "Who is it?"

"Toby Gottschalk. There's more, but it'll have to wait."

"Fine. So long as you got him."

"What I have to find out now is where she was killed. But we're working on that."

TWENTY-SIX

Hester and I had a fast chat.

"Toby admitted to conspiracy to commit murder," she said. "If I heard him correctly."

"Yeah," I answered. "I think you did. Not any evidence but his statement, yet, though." It was not nearly enough, even if he'd been completely rational and had provided it in writing.

"True. But it opens the doors wider and wider."

"Damn, Hester, we really gotta find out where Edie was killed. There has to be evidence all over the place, wherever it is."

"We also have to find Peale. Any ideas?"

"I'd like to talk to Jessica Hunley about him," I said.

"Me, too. You think Toby was on meth? Or ecstasy?"

"I'd say both of them, plus a little home grown psychosis. Too bad, he's sort of a bright guy."

"When he talked to Peale, and from what he just told us I think we can safely assume it was by telephone, he really must have been convinced. He even thought he was stronger," she said.

"Yeah." It obviously hadn't occurred to Toby that, since the autopsy, Edie's internal organs weren't all in the same place, or in the same condition, that they had been when she was alive. Not to mention that the chest had already been opened, to enable her heart and lungs to be removed for examination. It was no wonder the stake had gone in so easily. He probably could have just leaned on it, and it would have penetrated into what had once been her mediastinum, and gone all the way to the spinal column.

"You know," I said, "he mentioned something about striking the stake. We didn't find anything. I wonder what he used, and where he put it?" Evidence.

"If he was as wired then as he is now," said Hester, "he probably used his forehead."

I checked my "to do" box at the dispatch counter. There were three notes in it, from the dispatcher who had gotten off duty at 09:00. The first said she'd received a phone call from the DCI crime lab. The blood in the white body bag we'd found in the trash had been human, as expected, and the lab had confirmed the blood type with our pathologist, Dr. Peters. It was the same as Edie's. Type B negative. Not a lot, but one more little piece of the puzzle. We'd have to wait quite a while for DNA matching.

The second note was hand written on a teletype page. It was confirmation from the London Metropolitan Police, and indicated that there was no such person as Daniel Peale in the London Directory. The third said that Dr. Peters had called, and wanted to talk to me as soon as I came in.

I called, and his secretary said he was on his way to

Davenport to do an autopsy, and patched me through to his cell phone.

"Peters, here."

"Doc, it's Deputy Houseman, up in Nation County."

"Carl! I called earlier."

"Yeah, we got a little busy with the case. Did you know that somebody snuck into the funeral home and drove a stake through Edie's chest?"

There was a long pause, and I thought something had gone wrong with the phone.

"You've absolutely got to be kidding me," he said, at last.

"No, 'fraid not. Our local ME took a look at it this morning. So did I."

"My God. Who did it?"

"Toby. You remember? The squirrelly one. And we've pretty well established that he was probably there when she was killed, too."

Another silence. Then, "Right. Well, then, you might like to know this when you talk with him." And he went on to explain what he'd done.

He had, as a routine precaution, examined each section, piece and fragment of the tissues from the wound in Edie's neck under magnification, primarily to make certain that the edges of the pieces were consistent with the use of a sharp edge, and not inflicted in a contrary manner. For court purposes. But, while looking at the three main segments of her right jugular vein, he'd come across a puncture mark. It was small, with a cut running right above it. But a puncture mark, nonetheless.

"Really?" What else to say?

"Remarkably like the puncture you'd expect to find from, say, a syringe. Or an IV stick."

"Really?"

"And, I've found an amount of a substance called warfarin in the blood samples. It prevents clotting; you can find it in Coumadin. Not naturally present in the body, of course. It has to be administered."

"Really?"

"You know how I hate to speculate," he said. "I don't want you going off on the wrong track because I've misled you."

"You bet."

"But I'm virtually certain that the massive wound in her neck was inflicted post mortem."

I was quiet.

"And that the wound was inflicted to cover up the needle mark," he said. "There doesn't seem to be a corresponding mark in the skin. We're not completely finished with the examination yet, but I'd be willing to bet that the cut was made directly on the external puncture, to cover it up."

Wow.

"With the warfarin, the puncture . . . She could bleed to death very easily. Not really quickly, but fast enough." He paused again, and I heard him mutter something about "idiots," that sounded traffic related.

"Where was I?" he asked, and then answered his own question. "Oh yes. Do you remember when I said that the cut in the trachea bothered me at the autopsy, that there was no significant amount of aspirated blood?" he said. "If the trachea had been cut while she was alive, she would have aspirated blood."

"Okay."

"So, just another item on the report, but all this says she died, then her throat was cut post mortem, and the minimal stains on the floor in various places indicate that she then was moved into the tub post mortem." There were more road noises, and then he said, "She bled to death. There just isn't any other evidence of any injury or trauma other than the puncture wound in the jugular. No blood chemistry consistent with asphyxiation, for example. But massive blood loss prior to death is indicated, and there's no other evidence of any hemorrhaging other than via that puncture. There were abnormally constricted vasoconstrictors in the surface vessels, the kidneys, and the GI tract. The vessels were shutting down due to loss of blood volume. There was a remarkable lack of fluid in the interstitial spaces. There was an elevated amount of epinephrine and norepinephrine in the tissue samples. All consistent with a reducing blood volume. She had to lose at least forty percent of her blood volume, more likely fifty percent. Judging from what we found, I'd say at least that much, but some probably post mortem. I'm not in any doubt about that."

"Right, then."

"Carl?"

"Yeah?"

"Carl, with the use of the IV stick, that's the only point where the circulatory system was breached, you know. So, it very likely took her a while to die, and she was conscious almost to the end."

"Okay . . ."

"When people bleed to death, they become feisty after a bit, agitated. They tend to get aggressive on you. You might not be looking for conspicuous blood spurts after all, but I'll bet there was some sort of thrashing about going on, at a later stage."

"How later?"

"I expect that she passed through the agitated stages a good forty-five minutes before she died. She would just have been sleepy after that. Subdued state, going to a shocky one. You know."

That I did. Accident victims will do that, for example. But *forty-five minutes?*

"Doc, you said forty-five minutes, is that right?"

"That's right. It took her some time, I think."

"Okay. So, maybe not any indentations, from ligatures, at least."

"Right. Oh, and Carl?"

"Yeah?"

"She'd maybe tend to get whiny, you know? Like some drunks. Mumbling, too, maybe. If you need anything like that to confirm an account. From a suspect."

"Thanks. I really appreciate this."

"Just get whoever it was, Carl."

"Yeah. We will."

Afterward, I briefed Hester on the conversation.

"So, now we know at least one more piece of the thing," she said.

"Yep. Jesus, Hester. Forty-five minutes, at least. I get this image of her knowing what's going on, at least at some point. That she was going to die that night." I took a deep breath.

"I wonder how long it really took," she said. "For her to die, I mean."

"I got the impression of an hour or so," I said. "At least." I shrugged. "Gets us right back to 'where' doesn't it? Where could you have that level of isolation and privacy for a good hour?"

We stood in the kitchen, and drank our coffee.

"We gotta talk to Jessica Hunley," said Hester, running a little cold water in her cup at the sink. The coffee was too hot and too old. "We just have to do that." She took a sip and poured the rest of the cup into the sink. "Think you'd be able to come along?"

That was a good question. First, our budget was a bit thin. Second, we were short of help due to the damned flu. Third, there was the awkward complication of Hester and me not being able to share a room.

"Let me check with Lamar," I said.

"Don't go paying for it out of your own pocket," she said. "I'm serious."

"Okay." I sat at the table. "I won't."

"Remember when Toby said 'When we killed her the first time.' That one gave me the willies, Carl, and I'm not kidding."

"Me, too. And she asked for help." I shook my head.

"The little shit was there, all right. She asked for help. She had to know, then, didn't she? That she was going to die."

Hester nodded her head. "Yeah."

"Makes you wonder just who else was there, doesn't it?"

"Of those we know, Hanna, Melissa, and Kevin come to mind." Hester grabbed a paper towel, and wiped up a small coffee spill on the table, from the previous occupant. Busywork.

I hated to ask, but, "How about Huck? Think she was there?"

Hester shook her head. "At the murder scene? No. But she knows who was, I'd bet my life on it."

I called Lamar, and got him thinking about my trip to Lake Geneva. I could tell on the phone he'd approve it, but it would take him a little while.

I called Harry over in Conception County. I wanted to have him connect me with the local cops in Lake Geneva, but he went one better. He said he'd just come along, since he thought we were pursuing the same suspect. Great news.

Hester and I decided against calling Jessica Hunley to make an appointment. We both agreed the element of surprise, or at least unexpectedness, was going to be the key when we came calling on her. We'd just have Harry contact the locals and make sure she was in town.

On the other hand, we wanted to be expected, if not downright anticipated, at the Mansion.

We left instructions with Dispatch that we would give them a "ten-twenty-one" over the radio, at which point they would telephone the Mansion. We told them exactly what to say when they called to tell the group we were coming.

"Just handle it all as code sixty-one traffic," I said. "Everything to an absolute minimum."

About thirty minutes later, we'd driven all the way up the Mansion lane, until we could just see the door of the house over the crest of the hill. We stopped. It placed us about a hundred yards out, with just the edge of the car roof and about two thirds of the windshield visible to anyone looking our way from the house.

I picked up the mike. "Comm, Three..."

"Three?"

"Ten-twenty-one." She knew what I meant.

"Ten-four. Stand by One..."

A few moments later, after having informed whoever answered that Hester and I would be there in a while to bring them up to date on the situation with Toby, she came back on the radio.

"Three, ten-sixty-nine, they said 'Fine.' " A ten-sixty-nine is the code for message received.

"Ten-four."

It was that simple. Then we waited; to see if anybody did anything unusual, like try to leave. Although we weren't able to see the rear of the house, the relative lack of success of people leaving via the back door should have been having some effect. Well, with the mere mortals, anyway.

We waited two minutes, by the dash clock. Nothing.

"They're still pretty confident, aren't they?" Hester shifted in her seat.

"They sure seem to be."

"Well, let's go see what we can do about that."

TWENTY-SEVEN

Tuesday, October 10, 2000
15:17

We drove ahead, and as we got out of the car, Kevin came to the door. Excellent.

"What do you want?"

Direct, and to the point. I was encouraged.

"We want to tell you about Toby, where he is, and what's happening with him."

"Can't he just call us himself?"

"Not just yet," I said. By that time Hester and I had ascended the steps, and we were standing just outside the front door. "May we come in?"

He hesitated. Even better. Then, "Sure. Why not." He stepped back, and held the door for us.

We were met by Huck, who was just coming down the stairs.

"Hello, again," she said.

I could see Melissa in the kitchen, with her back to us, doing something at the counter. She turned as she heard us in the parlor, wiped her hands on a towel, and moved to join us. She didn't look particularly happy to see us.

"Can we get you some coffee, or anything?" asked Huck.

"Sure." I almost never refuse.

Melissa and Huck passed each other.

"Hi, Melissa. How's it going today?"

She regarded me with the sort of look you'd expect a girl to give her parents, when she knew she'd pissed them off, and was going to be defensive about it.

"Fine."

We were all still standing. Permitted in the house, but not welcomed. We get that a lot, and it's pretty understandable. It's also pretty uncomfortable.

"Mind if we sit down?" With the offer of coffee, it was reasonable.

"Go ahead," she said.

There was a woman singing, obviously a recording, coming from the music room. It sounded kind of old, and not in English. Vaguely familiar, but I couldn't place it.

"Is that French she's singing?" Just killing time until Huck got back with the coffee.

Melissa rolled her eyes. "It's Edith Piaf."

"Oh, sure." I remembered. "Boy, I haven't heard her for a really long time."

Silence.

"Iowa City, in the dorm. About '64 or so." I smiled. "Long time."

Huck returned with the coffee, in time to hear most of the conversation. She gave me a pretty genuine, if weak, smile. "Black for both of you, right?" From last night.

"Yep."

"So, you're here to tell us all about Toby?" Kevin asked, sarcastic as ever.

"Well, as much as we can," said Hester.

I began, "You all know we arrested Toby this morning."

Silence, interrupted by footsteps on the main stair. Hanna came around the corner. "Oh!"

Melissa explained why we were there. Hanna stood in the doorway.

"Do you know why he was arrested?" I asked.

"You said it was trespassing," said Melissa. "That's about all we know, except that you pointed guns at him, and scared him nearly to death. That really wasn't necessary."

"Well," I said, "Toby broke into the funeral home last night, and drove a stake through Edie's chest."

That hit most of them pretty hard. It was meant to.

Hanna said something along the lines of "Oh my God, what did he do that for," and promptly sat on a small bench just inside the door. Huck just looked stunned, Melissa sat abruptly on the couch, saying to Huck that that explained the closed coffin at the funeral.

Kevin, on the other hand, didn't have any visible reaction at all.

"Why are you accusing Toby of that?" asked Melissa. "He couldn't any more do such a thing."

I held up my hand. "We have witnesses. He was seen. He had cuts on his fingers from the broken glass. The soles of his shoes matched the footprints outside the broken window. And," I finished up, "he told us so. Without prompting."

"I just can't believe it," Melissa said, with the tone of someone who simply didn't want to. "That's so, so, gross. Disgusting."

"Why can't they leave her in peace?" asked Hanna, much more to the point.

"Did you know this last night?" asked Huck. "When we talked?"

I shook my head, and Hester said, "It hadn't happened yet."

"Anyway," I said, "we'd like to talk to each of you for a few minutes at a time, if that's all right."

"About what?" asked Kevin.

"The case in general," I said.

Kevin said, calmly, "I think I'll just leave, now, if nobody minds."

"You might want to stay," I said. "We've got some interesting stuff."

"Really?" He said it with that same cynical tone he always seemed to use, but he stayed. The hook was being scrutinized by our fish.

"Yep. I think so. Like I just said, we busted Toby, and now you all know what for. When we got him, he was also very wired," I said, "and as a direct consequence, he's en route to the Mental Health Institute at Independence, for detox."

I swear every one of them winced.

"I feel for him," said Huck. "Believe me, it doesn't get easier as you get older."

Melissa and Hanna both nodded. Kevin just stood there, being as much of a nonparticipant as he could.

"Not for detox for me," Hanna said. "I went in for being 'rebellious' and 'uncontrollable.' Well, according to my parents."

"We were there at the same time," explained Melissa. "Up on four. Where the crazy kids go."

Four was the floor where those who needed close attention were kept. It was interesting to find they were bound by another common experience.

Melissa spoke in a soothing voice. "Take your Thorazine, dear, like a good girl, and mommy will like you better."

"But, I've found happiness in depression." That came from Hanna, doing a passable little girl impression, and both Huck and Melissa nodded.

Huck chuckled. "But Doctor, if I'm manic-depressive, how come I'm never manic anymore?"

"Well, at least in detox," said Melissa, "he'll be back here in three days. Seventy-two and out, the detox shuffle."

An intergroup conversation was starting, off subject, and I thought Melissa was deliberately orchestrating it.

"I hate to interrupt," I said, "but could we get back on track?"

"If you can show us the track to get on," said Melissa, "sure."

It was time for the punch line, before we lost their curiosity.

"Okay. How about this? Toby was there when Dan killed Edie," I said.

I took a sip of coffee, just to appear totally in charge, and the clunk when I put the cup back down seemed to resound throughout the house.

Melissa broke the silence. "That can't be right."

"Why not?" interjected Hester.

"Well, he just couldn't. He followed Edie around like a little puppy," said Melissa.

"That's right," said Hanna. "*They* weren't in love, but I think he was."

"It was an accident, anyway," said Kevin, with a tone of dismissal. "Nobody meant to really kill her."

Every eye in the room was on him.

"Well, you know," he said, talking to Melissa and Huck more than us, "it was just Dan and the pheromone thing. He messed up, that's all." He looked around, and spread his hands, palms up. "I don't know what all the fuss is about, it was just an accident."

It was working.

"How do you know that?" Kevin and I locked gazes again. "How do you know?" I asked again. Quietly. Always quietly.

"Toby told me."

"He did? When?"

He shrugged. "That morning."

"What," asked Hester, "did he say?"

"He said, 'Well, it was a mistake.' That's what he said."

"Want to explain that a little more?" asked Hester.

"Look, lady," he said, "all I know is this. About three-thirty that morning, Toby came into my room and woke me up and said that Edie was having a little problem. He wanted me to help get her to her room."

"And?"

"And I told him to fuck off, it was a workday and I had another hour to sleep. So he went away."

"Did he say what was wrong with her?" I asked.

"No. He just said, 'There's been an accident. Dan really fucked up this time.' That's what I remember. I was asleep, like I said."

"Did he say where she was?"

"No, he didn't say where she was. Like I said, he was in a hurry and I was pissed off. We didn't discuss the thing, he just woke me up."

"What did he look like when he came into your room?" asked Hester. "Was there anything unusual about him?"

"How would I know? It was dark, and all he had was a flashlight."

"So," she asked, "he just went away?"

"Look, I remember he was all whiny, like a dorky little kid. But he left, and I went back to sleep."

"When did you find out she was dead?" I asked.

"When they called me and Huck at work," he said.

"So," asked Hester, "when did Toby tell you about the 'mistake' that was made?"

"When we got back," he said.

"Not on the phone?" I asked.

"He just talked to me," interrupted Huck. "I told Kevin she was dead." She looked squarely at him. "You never told me anything about Toby coming to you that night."

"That's because you don't matter," he said simply.

Huck flinched.

"Who does matter, in this?" asked Hester, quickly. This was no time for an argument between Huck and Kevin.

Kevin smiled, enigmatically. "Depends."

"Well right now," I said evenly, "it better be us." I was getting really irritated with his attitude. "So tell me what Toby told you."

It worked. Better than I'd hoped.

"All he said was that Dan and him and Edie were together, and Dan wanted to do that 'secondhand' experience thing he kept talking about, and he had Toby and Edie get it on, and then Edie got all wild on them, and things just went all ugly from there."

Well, at least it was fairly succinct.

"And, where did he say they were when this was going on?"

He sighed, all exasperated and put out. "I *told* you, Toby didn't tell me."

He was, of course, lying. He was an easy tell, too.

After that, it was pretty much a communal effort to inform us about what Dan Peale considered a good time.

Because Dan Peale apparently believed that he would be able to experience emotions "secondhand" if he ingested the blood of another, at a time when that other person was experiencing a strong emotion, he had tried his theory out first with pleasure being the target. He said it worked, and was able to "experience the afterglow" of a woman's orgasm with Edie. Given the fact that he was probably doing some meth or ecstasy at the time, and so was she, go figure.

Anyway, things progressed, as they always seem to, toward more and more extreme events. It dawned on him at some point that blood coming directly from the brain would contain the most undiluted pheromones or endorphins, or something. He obtained some needles, and as far as they knew, did his first jugular stick in June 2000.

"That was me," said Hanna. "I was pretty high, and it still hurt like hell, and it was the scariest thing I ever did. I never let him do that again. Ever."

"Why did you let him do it in the first place?" asked Hester.

Hanna gave it about one second's worth of thought. "Because he scares me to death," she answered. I think the irony escaped her.

As it turned out, it wasn't just the pleasures life offered that Dan Peale wanted to experience.

"The next step," murmured Melissa, "was fear. Well, he called it 'terror,' and I suppose it was." She looked up. "That was me. Back in August." She shook her head. "Terror isn't the word. You really can't move, you know. I mean, with that thing stuck in your neck. Hell, he tied my hands, but he really didn't need to. 'If you move, you could kill yourself,' he said. No joke." She shuddered, and rubbed the right side of her neck with two fingers. "He told me that it made such a small hole, there was no problem. Then, after he got it in, he said he'd lied. The prick stuck it in there, and starts telling me that, if I moved, I'd bleed to death. That the hole was bigger than he'd said. Then he'd, like, make sudden moves, you know? Clap his hands. Yell. Just to startle me, scare me. Shit." She seemed to get more of a grip on herself. "But I made it, didn't I? He didn't use too big a needle, after all. He said he was sorry. Afterward. I didn't know whether to hate him for scaring me or for lying to me. But he didn't really injure me," she added quickly.

I was dumbfounded, truly, that he could get them to do that. But this wasn't the time to go there.

"See?" said Kevin. "That's probably what happened to Edie. Like I said, an accident."

"But you don't know?" Hester was starting to press him.

"Well..."

"So you don't, then." She said it with finality.

"Don't jump to conclusions, lady." Kevin was getting insulting with the "lady" business.

"I'm not the one jumping," said Hester. "So Toby only *told* you that's what happened? Right?"

Right, but with a twist. It seems that Toby had told Kevin that he, Edie, and Dan Peale were involved in a threesome, and that both he and Edie had been surprised when the blood thing had been brought up. They weren't expecting more than just some heavy sex, apparently.

"So," I asked, "he didn't always get into the blood?"

"No," said Huck.

"Not all that much," said Melissa. "Just sometimes. Sometimes you could tell when it was going to be, sometimes you couldn't."

"Edie got a little reluctant," said Kevin. "So Dan had Toby hold her."

"Wait a second," I said. "If Toby was in love with Edie, why would he do that?"

There was a long enough pause that I began to think I had really missed something obvious. Huck finally spoke.

"He'd help Dan," she said, "because the only time Edie would let him get into heavy duty snogging with her was when Dan was there, too. Edie did it for Dan, and without Dan, Toby would never have had a chance with her."

It took me a second to digest that.

"Right."

"See," said Kevin, "Toby wouldn't have helped kill her, though. Like I keep trying to tell you, it was an accident."

It was left to Huck to play the last card.

"No, it wasn't. It was not an accident." Huck put her chin in her hands, and regarded me for a beat. "I know for a fact that the times with Hanna and Melissa were 'test flights,' like he called them." She stopped my question by saying, "Dan. Dan called them that. He told me what he really wanted, and he told me that I'd have to die if I told anybody else."

She folded her arms across her chest, defiantly. She took a deep breath, and then said very rapidly, "He told me that he wanted to experience death secondhand. But that to do it right, the donor would have to know they were going to die, and he'd probably have to kill them."

TWENTY-EIGHT

"Brilliant," said Kevin. "Just brilliant, Huck. Do you really have a death wish?"

That got me involved, from a slightly different angle.

"You got someplace safe to go?" I asked Huck.

She shrugged. "Oh, I think. But I'll probably just stay here. I don't think Dan's coming back."

I raised both eyebrows, as meaningfully as I could. "You sure?"

"I'll let you know. But thanks, anyway. For asking."

"Your call."

She just nodded.

Here we were, about to begin mining a mother lode of information, and we were looking at the clock, wondering when we could head for Lake Geneva to interview Jessica Hunley. Hester and I talked quickly, and then I went to the phone in the hall, and called the office and had Borman head up. I told them to send Sally, too, since she was a reserve. Both of them knew the witnesses we were interviewing, and both could do a credible job of follow-up.

When I got off the phone, Hester used her cell phone to call her boss, and get another agent assigned and started up to meet with us. It was going to aggravate him no end, because they were short, but she'd get one, even if it meant overtime.

We were going to be getting a late start, but talking to Jessica Hunley was too important to let go for another day or two.

We continued the interviews, to keep the information flowing. I began to suspect that, although they'd cover for Dan, his absence was loosening the bond.

At one point, Melissa asked a probing question that I fielded as well as I could.

"Why don't you go talk to Jessica?" she asked. She looked pleased with herself for asking, and that tripped a warning switch.

"Jessica," I said, "is out of our jurisdiction right now." Technically true. I said it in a brush-off tone. It made it more believable.

"Oh. Oh, yeah. She is, isn't she?"

"Yep. Now, like I was saying. . . ."

I made a mental note that our replacements couldn't know where we were going. Just so they couldn't spill the beans.

Borman and Sally arrived fairly shortly after I'd called. I briefed them on what we'd accomplished. Sally was a little freaked.

"No shit? He killed her slow, so he could drink her blood, and live her death? Jesus, *Dark Shadows,* all over."

Sally liked soap operas, too.

"Yep. That's what he did."

"Christ," said Borman. "That's one evil dude."

"Yeah," I said, "he's bad all right. So, anyway, what you are going to be doing is obtaining thorough statements, and taking notes. There's another DCI agent headed in, and whoever they send will be helping with the follow-up here, just like you are."

"So," said Borman, "what are you guys going to be doing while we do this?"

"We have a lead we're going to follow up. Has to be done right away." True.

"Need to know?" Completely insincere, Borman was developing a way of asking questions that assured he wasn't going to get a complete answer.

"Yeah. Need to know only." I changed the subject. "I want you two to emphasize the possibility that Peale might return here. I don't want these people endangered in any way. It's their choice," I explained, "but if you can convince them to be in a safer location, try to do that. Especially Huck."

"Where?"

"If I knew that, Sally, I'd tell you." I handed her some of my notes. "Maybe parents? Relatives, friends...just somewhere that they can rely on somebody calling if Peale shows up."

"I'll try," she said. "I can transmit fear," she said, her face crinkling in a smile. "Believe me."

We were out of the Mansion at 20:20.

"Okay," said Hester. "It's about eight-thirty. Get me back to my motel, I'll get my car, meet you at your house at, oh, what? Nine-fifteen?"

"I'll try, but it's going to be closer to nine-thirty. What you think, one night? Two at the most?"

"Two at the very most."

"Okay," I said. "Then we pick up Harry, and we're off." We would each take our separate cars. That was a given, as our bosses could suddenly request our presence, and we'd have to leave at once. In this case, two of us wouldn't want to be pulled out of Lake Geneva just because the other had to leave. It was most likely that the one called would be Hester, and I didn't want to end up stranded a couple of hundred miles south of Nation County, killing time while she went to some unrelated murder scene. It was getting late, and the gas stations in Nation County would be closing around ten. If she needed gas, I was sort of gently reminding her where she was.

"I'll get some before I pick you up."

"Okay, and if you can't, for some reason, I can get you to the county pumps."

"I'd prefer real gas," she said. "If I can get somebody to accept my state card."

I dropped Hester off at her motel, and headed home. Sue said, "Welcome home! And before ten, too!"

I kissed her, and broke the news.

"Lake Geneva?"

"Yeah, but you don't know that. Harry and Hester and I are going over to do interviews, and nobody can know that."

"Okay. I guess."

"Lamar knows, but nobody else. It's just for a day or two, at the most."

I kept talking to her as I sat at our computer, and looked up accommodations in Lake Geneva. Several were just too pricey, especially those on the lake, itself. I checked maps and addresses, looking for something inexpensive.

"This is going on our credit card, isn't it?"

"I'm afraid so." I looked up from the screen. "You know the county."

"We will get reimbursed?"

"Oh, sure. Within six months."

She sighed. "You want help packing?"

"Well, I'm trying to remember where the small overnight bag is...." I settled on a motel that had no stars at all in its rating, in Fontana. I checked my map. On Lake Geneva, the western end. Maybe three to four miles from the town of Lake Geneva, itself. Good enough. It not only had no rating stars, it had no internet capability, either. I had to make a long distance call, and just give my card info over the phone. The clerk was pretty disinterested. With a room rate of thirty-four dollars a night, I suppose interest was a bit too much to ask.

I went upstairs, and Sue had my bag out, and already laid out underwear, socks, and sweatpants for me to lounge in.

"Hester sees you in these, I'll sleep better for knowing she fled laughing," she said. But it did bother her a bit.

"There's no reason to worry."

"I know that. But I just...well, it's a little uncomfortable. You know?"

I squeezed her shoulders. "Yeah, but don't let it be. Strictly professional." She looked up, and I kissed her. "Besides," I said, "Harry's rooming with me."

"Now I'm really worried," she said. "Go get your shaving gear, while I pick out a couple of shirts."

I made a quick call to Lamar, and told him that we were leaving.

"Okay, Carl. I already called the office. Nobody will call you, on the phone or the radio. You're officially on a stakeout in a confidential location."

"Thanks."

"Don't even check out with Dispatch on the radio, and just keep track of your mileage and meals."

"Okay, Pop. I'll call you when I get back, if not before, if we find out anything. Sue's got the phone number of my motel, and the Walworth County Sheriff's Department in Elkhorn, Wisconsin, will know where we are all the time. Got a pencil handy?"

"Yeah."

"Okay, their ORI is WI0650000, in case you want to teletype them for any reason." ORI is an abbreviation for Origin, and is the teletype address of any particular law enforcement agency. The numbers are usually carried over into the call sign of the particular department, and in this case, the radio call number of their sheriff would probably be 65-1. All their county cars would begin with sixty-five.

"Okay, they're sixty-five with the zeroes. Okay. Good. Let me know right away...about anything I should know about."

"Don't worry, Lamar. How's your sister taking things?"

"Just like I thought she would," he said, disgustedly. "Now she wants to sue the funeral home."

Fifteen minutes and a flurry of packing later, Hester knocked on the back door.

"Hester, nice to see you," said Sue. "Come on in."

"Sorry to have to borrow your husband for a day or two," said Hester, "but I'm afraid it's necessary."

"Just watch what he eats," said Sue. "Or, as long as you can stand it, anyway. I don't envy you going with both Carl and Harry together."

"It's scary, isn't it?" said Hester. "I'll submit a written report on Carl's diet."

"You be careful, too," said Sue. "All of you, be careful."

I hugged her. "Be back before you know it," I said.

Hester's car was running in the driveway. As she got in, she said, "Harry's waiting for us just across the river."

"Okay," I answered. "When we get where we're headed, I have reservations for me and Harry at a motel in Fontana."

"Fine. I'm in a place called the Geneva Inn. In Lake Geneva, on the other side of the lake."

"Okay!" I hoped she had a nice place.

I got in, buckled up, checked everything to make sure it was either working or turned off, and backed out of the garage. I could see Sue, waving, from the back door. I honked my horn, and waved back.

We three took our separate cars on Highway 18 to Madison, then I 90 SE to Janesville, where we stopped for a bite to eat. It was 23:40. We only had about another hour to go.

We pulled in to a McDonald's, which seemed to be the only place open, although they were mopping the floors as we entered. We got the stuff to go, and ate in my car, Harry in front with me, and Hester in back. As Hester said, "It's not so noticeable if we spill in yours."

We'd all been thinking as we drove, and we used this chance to plan a bit.

"What do you hear about your missing girl, Harry?" asked Hester.

"Haven't really heard shit," he replied, munching a Big Mac. He swallowed. "It's strange. She just went into the ladies john, and disappeared. Took her car, as far as we can tell, and just left."

"Foul play?" I asked. That was a formal designation in "Attempt To Locate" bulletins for missing persons. "Foul Play Feared."

"Beats the crap out of me," said Harry. "But we put in, just in case."

By categorizing the case as a "Foul Play Feared," it opened up the nationwide system about twelve hours earlier than a normal missing persons report, and was flagged for immediate attention.

"Not one fuckin' sign of a struggle," said Harry. " 'Scuse me, Hester. Just a bunch of worried friends." He wiped his mouth with a napkin. "At least I ain't had nobody drive a stake in any corpses this week."

"That," I said, searching for my fries in the bag, "was one of the weirdest things I've ever seen."

"Me, too," said Hester. "It was just plain spooky."

"Mmmph," said Harry.

"I've been thinking about our little group at the

Mansion," said Hester, holding open the other sack for me to get my two Big Macs.

"Yeah?" I lifted both burgers out in their cardboard containers, and placed them carefully on the dash. "Nonconformists, aren't they?"

"Dedicated," said Hester, handing me my napkin.

"I kinda like most of 'em," I said, opening the first burger box. "Boy, I'm hungry."

"I do, too," she said. She started rustling around in the sack, looking for the fries she'd ordered. "I'm going to tell you guys something, and you keep it to yourselves, okay?"

"Yeah, sure." I took a bite of my burger.

"You betcha, Hester," said Harry, earnestly.

"Okay, I think this might help us figure them out. That's the only reason I'm telling you this."

She paused so long, I'd swallowed and taken a second bite before she began again.

"When I graduated from Iowa State," she said, "I thought I had it all. Or thought I was going to get it, anyway. I don't want to be immodest, or anything, but everybody I knew sort of assumed I was on my way to the top. My parents. My professors. My roommates. Even me. You know?" She paused again.

"Sure. I know," I prompted. To give some idea of how little of our background information we'd ever exchanged, I hadn't known until now that Hester had gone to Iowa State.

"My plan was, I was going to be a famous chemist, was going to marry some guy who was, oh, maybe an equally famous architect or something. Live in New York. Paint landscapes in my spare time." She took a sip of her Diet Coke. "You know the sort of thing?"

"Yep," said Harry.

"Well," she went on, "just two days after graduation, Dad had a stroke. I missed about a year and a half in the job market, because I stayed home with Mom, and helped take care of him. No problem. Hell, for what they'd done for me, it was hardly a drop in the bucket."

"Sure." I took another bite of burger.

"My sister graduated a year behind me. She didn't stay home. Hey, I told her not to. No point in both of us being there." She took another sip. "Okay, and then, when Dad died, then, there wasn't quite enough life insurance to even pay off the house mortgage. All borrowed against to help us in school, and to take one family trip. What was left was eaten up by the noncovered medical expenses. So much for teaching." She produced a sad excuse for a smile. "He was a teacher. Math. I didn't tell you that."

I took a drink from my Coke cup. "Doesn't pay too much," I said. "Sue's been a teacher for almost twenty years now, and makes about what I do."

"I dated a teacher once," said Harry.

"My Mom taught chemistry. Same deal." She shrugged. "More to life than money. Except, all of a sudden, my installments on my college loan came due. I got my first job with an ag chemical company. Not doing chemistry, you understand. No, I was part of a team that went all over Iowa and Nebraska, trying to tell farmers not to put too much of our products on the soil." She took a long swig from her Diet Coke, and started rummaging around in the sack. "Had to tell 'em that, in small doses, what we sold was just fine. In larger doses, it was poison."

"Must have been really fun." Harry took a rattling pull on his milkshake.

"Oh, yeah. And, it paid less than teaching, let me tell you. And I finally figured out that since I was a young woman, they wanted me on the 'Responsible Usage Team' so the farmers could look at my legs while I talked." She half giggled. "Really. I was sort of an agri-cheesecake girl."

I couldn't help grinning at the image. "With your attitude?"

"I couldn't bite people, we had a script," she said.

"Anyway, I could see I wasn't going to get out of that job until my legs went. And I *liked* chemistry. And the real chemists made pretty good money. Well, better, anyway. I had to keep living with Mom, because I couldn't pay off the loans, and help her with the bills, and pay rent at the same time. Mom knew I hated that job, but she kept telling me that it was the responsible thing to do, so I did it. I hated myself for it, though."

She turned on the overhead light. "I can't find all my fries. . . ."

"How long did you stay?"

"Three years, Carl. I'd send resumes out all the time, but the longer you've been out of school. . . . Anyway, the only decent offer I got was from this place in California, and the money just didn't work out. It did after the first couple of years, or it would have. But I just couldn't get away. And all that time, Mom was entertaining suspicions that I was failing. That I wasn't really trying, you know?"

"Yeah," said Harry. "I had a wife used to feel that way about me."

"She wondered why I didn't get married. She asked me once. I said I didn't want to. It really surprised me, that she'd ask. Like she didn't know that if I got married, I'd leave and she wouldn't be able to make ends meet. A job close to home, that paid okay, was going to be the only way out, for me, anyway. So I heard about the criminalistics lab in Des Moines. I applied, and got an interview, and it wasn't too far from our house. I got the job. Better pay, and I started to make headway on my student loans." She pulled three or four fries from the bag. "Found some," she said brightly.

I watched her bite the ends off the little bundle of fries. "And then?"

"What bothered me was that my sister, she'd gone ahead. Like I told her to, I admit it. She got hired as a geologist with a big oil company, met an engineer, married him, they moved to Scotland to work the North Sea Oil,

she even sent me and Mom tickets so we could visit."
She shook her head slowly. "We went, all right. Mom
just went ape over their house, the fact that it was in
Scotland, that they were friends with important people.
Hell, there was even an honest-to-God still-life painter
living next door." She'd turned toward me, and now
leaned back against her door. "My sister was living my
ideal damned existence. My little sister had achieved my
ideal life, while I stayed home and all I had accomplished was, I had disappointed Mom."

Ouch.

"That'd be tough," said Harry. "Really tough."

Hester took a deep breath, and let it out slowly. "I
mean, you know, good for her, and all that. But, anyway,
I was really depressed. I honest to God hoped for a plane
crash on the way back from Scotland. I really did. I'll tell
ya, guys, I would have run to just about anywhere, just
to get out of that. But, there just wasn't any place to go.
No Mansion, with free rent and people like me."

It was silent for a few seconds. I took another bite of
my first burger. It was starting to cool.

"So, the reason for sharing all that garbage with
you," said Hester, straightening up, "is that those girls
up there, especially Huck and Melissa and poor dead
Edie...life was just not cooperating with them. And
they were just looking for a place to run. Hell, probably
even Toby and Kevin, for that matter."

"Yeah." Harry had fished out an apple turnover,
and was unwrapping it.

"They're really all victims. Victims of some rich
woman who can afford to provide a phony hiding place
for them. And this Peale bastard. Oh, yeah, Mr. Peale.
Her pet vampire. But Jessica, she's acquiring them,
they're just being kept like a bunch of livestock. Peale
killed Edie, and with Toby's help. That's a given. But
Jessica Hunley's the one who made the whole thing possible. And that really pisses me off."

I simply said, "Okay." It got sort of quiet again.

"Look," she said suddenly, "I'm saying that, if they'd had some more time for things to sort themselves out, none of 'em would be in this mess in the first place. Jessica just recruited at the right time."

"Okay."

"Don't humor me, Houseman." She rummaged some more. "Did you take the salt?"

"Nope. I found some pepper, though." I held up the little packet. "See?" I remember thinking that her fries had to be cold by now.

"Well there's a bunch of ketchup packs, but unless I squeeze 'em into my hand..." She looked up from her search. "Do you see what I mean, though?"

"I think so. She found some people at an unstable time in their lives?"

"Part of it. It's not just that when all the expectations you've had for yourself don't come true, it's when everybody who is important to you had them for you...." She stopped abruptly. "Shit happens, Houseman. But not at the same time or the same way for everybody. So, when it happens to you early on, you just watch others pass by, with no shit sticking to them at all. And you feel betrayed."

"I can see that," said Harry. "Shit really does happen. Boy, I know that."

"And you sometimes do things to cover up the disappointment." Hester sounded tired. "Things you normally wouldn't do, even a while later, but once you start it's almost impossible to stop, because you think you've found your..."

"Place?" I tried to help.

She sighed. "No, no. Guys are so dense. No, it's much more than that. It's like, you've found your accomplishment. You have to settle for a little less, but you've found it."

"Oh. I see."

Hester shook her head. "Oh, Houseman, eat your hamburger."

"I do get it, though," I said, leaning forward so the special sauce wouldn't drip on my shirt.

She sighed. "Okay. So, anyway. We agreed that we go right to our motels, and start fresh in the morning?" She was still burrowing through the sack, looking for the rest of her cold fries.

"Mmmph." I love Big Macs, but they're kind of hard to talk through.

"Here they are!" She fished a bunch of them out, along with a wad of napkins. They'd apparently spilled from the cardboard container, and gotten in with the pile of condiments, napkins, and salt that the employee had swept into the bag. "Okay, then, you want to start with . . . ?"

I swallowed, and used one of the napkins to wipe some sauce off my chin. "I think with the Walworth County Sheriff's Department would be good, don't you?"

"Mmmm." This time she was the one with the mouthful of fries.

"Got it covered," said Harry. "Already talked to them. We got the run of the county as long as nobody fucks . . . oops . . . screws up."

"Okay, then," I said, "wherever we can find Jessica. We drop in, agreed?"

"Sure." Hester took a long pull on her Diet Coke straw. "What time?"

I thought about it. "Nine-thirty? Ten?"

She looked at her watch. "Let's go for nine-thirty. We aren't going to get squared away tonight until one or so." She was already tidying up, folding her paper napkin, and getting ready to go. I quickly took a large bite of my second Big Mac. It was cold by now, too.

"You know how to get to Fontana?" asked Harry. "Hester should be taking fifty to Lake Geneva, but we should take sixty-seven south to Williams Bay, and then back westerly to Fontana."

I swallowed again. "Oh, sure. No problem."

"What I was trying to say, you two," said Hester, suddenly, "is that gathering victims at such a hard time in their lives is more despicable than recruiting people who want to get into this vampire stuff."

"Sure." Harry agreed. I guessed I did, too.

About thirty minutes later, Harry and I correctly turned south on sixty-seven, and watched Hester disappear down highway fifty. I wondered if her mother knew Hester had worked dope cases.

Six minutes later we were in Fontana.

The room wasn't too bad. Two queen-size beds. Shower. Sink. Toilet. Chair. TV. Even a place to hang hangers. It was cold, and the heating mechanism was integral with the air-conditioning. I turned it on, and had instant tobacco smell. Turned it off, opened a window, and tried to set the little digital alarm clock that came with the room.

Finally, Harry said, "If you'd put your fuckin' glasses on, Houseman, so you could read the dials, we could get another half hour of sleep."

I got it set, but then picked up the phone and left a wake-up call for 08:30.

"What you do," said Harry, "is why I divorced my ex-wife."

I blew him a kiss. "Good night, Harry."

TWENTY-NINE

Wednesday, October 11, 2000
09:12

I was awakened by the phone. I glanced at the clock.
09:12. I groggily wondered why the wake-up call was so
late. "Yeah."

It was Hester. "You guys like to come over here for
brunch?"

"Jesus, Hester. They didn't call, and the alarm didn't
go off...."

"I'm waking you up?"

I told her she was. She, as it turned out, had taken
her morning five-mile run, cleaned up, and had been
wondering what was taking us so long to call her.

"Brunch?" I asked.

"What about brunch?" came from Harry in the next
bed.

"You guys gotta come over here to eat," said Hester.
"Really. You gotta see this."

That sounded really good to me. "Give us twenty

minutes," I said. I showered first, while Harry contacted a Walworth County detective named Jim Hawkins, and told him that we were going to have a bite at the Geneva Inn. He said he'd try to meet us within an hour.

I drove, while Harry navigated. All the way through a spot called Linton, on a county road, and then north on Highway 120. The real estate got progressively more upscale as we went. We turned left into a kind of obscure drive, and into the parking lot of a very beautiful hotel. Hester, it appeared, had scored big.

My favorite DCI agent met us in the lobby. It was beautifully done in light wood, natural lighting, with uniformed help who exuded confidence and capability. We continued on into the split-level dining room that had huge windows on three sides, with a fantastic view of Lake Geneva.

We sat at a table with real linen. Heavy silver. Quiet atmosphere. Elegant. Refined. Nice.

"Sleep well?" I asked Hester. She looked absolutely refreshed.

"Wonderful room," she said. "Wet bar, Jacuzzi, balcony overlooking the lake...."

"We," said Harry, "are in the Bates Motel."

"Poor dears," said Hester.

A pretty, perky, and efficient waitress, in her twenties, offered us the breakfast buffet. We partook, as Old Knockle would have said. I never wanted to leave.

Over a great cup of coffee, we gazed out the windows at the huge homes on the lakefront. I thought I could make out a sliver of a rounded dome in the far distance, across the lake and in thick trees. As the waitress asked us if we needed more coffee, I pointed to the dome. "Is that Yerkes Observatory, do you know?"

"Yes, it is."

"Wow," I said. "We gotta try to get there."

"What's there?" asked Harry.

"Enormous telescope, the biggest refractor in the world," I said. "I'd really like to see that."

"They have tours," said the waitress, smiling.

"Excellent." I shifted my gaze to the left a bit. "And that big gray building over there? That wouldn't be the courthouse, would it?"

The waitress giggled. She gestured to the enormous, pinkish gray building. "That one?"

"Yeah . . ."

"That's the Hunley place," she said.

It was a four-story building, although there didn't seem to be any windows on the fourth floor. It was absolutely huge. It made the Mansion in Nation County look like an outbuilding. Composed of a large central four-story block, with arched glass, flanked by two equally large sections with square windows, and flanked again by two wings with vast windows. I never would have thought it to be anything but a government office building or library.

"Whoa." I was impressed. "That's not a public park, then?"

"No, that's the lawn. About three hundred yards of lakefront lawn. And it runs back to the highway at least that far. With a big stone wall, and a huge iron gate. You won't be able to miss it when you go by."

"I'm impressed," said Hester. "What does Mr. Hunley do, to be able to afford a four-story home like that?"

"It's Mrs. Bridgett Hunley," said our waitress. "She's a widow. I don't think she does anything, really. My brother works for their landscaper. Full-time job, mowing that lawn and taking care of the grounds. All summer and into the fall. I'm not kidding. Every day but Sunday. Eight hours a day. Three of them working."

As she left our table, we exchanged glances. "Holy shit," said Harry, in as close to a sotto voce as he was capable of assuming, "maintenance on that sucker must cost close to a hundred thousand a year."

"God bless waitresses," said Hester. "Carl, why don't you leave a nice tip?"

_____

About halfway through the second coffee, a thin, balding man dressed in slacks and a sweater came toward our table. Harry stood, and greeted him. "Guys," he said, "this is Jimmy Hawkins, the best detective in this end of the state." He introduced us.

After the waitress brought Hawkins a cup of coffee, Harry gave him the ten-cent brief, including both murders, some details, the window peeking incident, and the disappearance of Alicia.

Hawkins listened very intently. "Glad those aren't my cases," he said, when Harry had finished. "I just wish they weren't connected to my town. So, what can I do for you?"

"We need a little background," said Hester.

"On Jessica Hunley, for instance," I said.

Hawkins told us a lot. Jessica was something of a fixture in the community, and a welcome one. She did lots of charity work, arts oriented, and spent a lot of time working on community projects that furthered music and dance. She was well known, and highly regarded. There was nothing, as far as he knew, that had ever indicated she might have any criminal involvement of any sort.

"Besides," he said, "her Aunt Bridgett Hunley would have a fit if she thought Jessica was into anything that might damage the family reputation."

Bridgett Hunley was a "mega-millionaire," according to Hawkins. He looked very serious, and said, "I mean 'mega,' too. Really one of the wealthiest women going."

Jessica lived with her Aunt Bridgett. We sort of knew that already. "I understand she might have taken ill recently," I said.

"I hadn't heard that, but I'll check," he said. "She's always struck me as being healthy as a horse."

"And that," I said, indicating the four-story building across the lake, "is her house?"

"Yeah, it is. Good size, isn't it? There are about a hundred places with about that much property, or more, around here," said Hawkins. "But that's the biggest house. Well, the biggest stone house, I should say. Lots of the upper crust from Chicago, years ago, discovered Lake Geneva. People like Wrigley, and Marshall Field, and people like that. Large money. They built summer homes here."

"That's not a summer home?"

"Not today. But it was in the twenties." He sipped his coffee. "Today, I think Bridgett and Jessica own four or five places, in fact. But this is the main place."

"How did they make their money, do you know?" asked Hester.

"Meat packing and railroads, I think. And one of their ancestors married into lumber, as well." He held his cup up in a "toast" gesture. "Here's to diversification."

"It's going to be a little intimidating just going to the door for an interview," I said.

"You can probably find Jessica at her studio during the day," he said. "That's right at the end of the lake, here, in Lake Geneva. Got a map?"

I was disappointed, I have to admit. I'd had hopes of getting inside the estate.

Hawkins smiled. "Unless you'd care to wait until this evening." My disappointment must have showed.

"No, that's okay. Some things are just best left to the imagination." But I felt pretty certain that the residents of the Mansion in Nation County had been guests at the Hunley estate, at the invitation of Jessica. No wonder they were impressed. Just being ushered in there must have been an event.

———————————

Hawkins led us to Jessica's dance studio, on Geneva Street, just about downtown Lake Geneva. We all parked, and got out, except for Hawkins. He stayed in his car, with the engine running. He pointed to a door between two stores. "The dark red one, there. The studio is upstairs. Only thing up there."

"Thanks."

"You want company? If you do, I could make the time."

I shook my head. "No, that's okay. We can piss her off all by ourselves."

"Well, feel free to keep in touch. You need anything, just let me know."

We squared ourselves, and walked across the street to the dark red door.

"You all set?" I asked.

"You bet," said Harry. "You two take the lead, and let me just listen in for a bit, okay?"

"Fine with me," said Hester.

"Well, then . . ." I said.

There was a small, brass plaque on the door that said, "Hunley Studios." The buildings looked pretty old, and I was expecting kind of a dingy, narrow stair in a dingy, narrow staircase. Hardly.

The blond wooden stairs were nearly brand new, nicely varnished, and the pale yellow stairwell was both wider and more brightly painted than I'd expected. The stairs didn't even creak. The stairwell was lined with dance posters, most of them featuring either Jessica Hunley or "The Hunley Dance Repertoire Company." At the top, we found a large, oak framed, glazed door, again with the sign "Hunley Studios." As we entered, I noted the time at 11:39.

The music was loud, but pleasant. I recognized it instantly, a thing by Ahmed Jamal and his group, called "Poinciana." We were in a small waiting room, for want of another word, with three new wooden chairs, and a bulletin board. On it, there were several notes, and a "rehearsal schedule" that indicated today, October 11, was for "rep rehearsal, J & T, 9–5." I pointed it out to Hester.

"They rehearse for eight hours?"

"Sure," she said. "Repertory. That's a series of their performance dances, you repeat those all the time so they stay fresh in your head."

One more reason to be glad Hester was along.

The divider between the waiting room and the studio was only waist-high, and the door was on a swinging hinge. On the other side, I could see a nice hardwood floor, flanked on the right by a line of floor to ceiling windows, and on the left by a long mirror. No bar in front, unlike in the movies I'd seen, which were as close as I'd ever been to a rehearsal. At the far end was a set of lockers, and a table with a large boom box.

There were two dancers working on the floor, in black tights, leg warmers, and sweatshirts. Their feet were bare. They were both facing away from us, but the one with the iridescent hair could only be Tatiana. I guessed the other to be Jessica, and when they both turned in unison, I saw I was right.

I don't know what they thought when they saw us standing there, but they never missed a beat. Now that they were facing us, I could hear Jessica counting cadence, sort of.

"Down and up and down and up," she said, as they went down on the floor, rose, went down and rose again. Very gracefully, with flowing movements. "And turn two three, ten two three, and point and twist and point, and turn . . ." and with that, they had their backs to us again.

I turned to Hester. "Wow." Not only graceful, it looked a lot like hard work. Not the way they did it, but the way I knew I'd have to do it. Hester just smiled, and watched them as they moved away from us.

Harry nudged me in the ribs. "You get to investigate *them?* I wanna work in Iowa."

The music stopped, and so did the dancers. They sort of stood, talking for a second, and then Tatiana walked over to the boom box, and opened a tape case. Jessica came over to us.

"My two favorite officers," she said. "And are you an officer, too?" she asked Harry, with a pleasant voice.

"Detective Harry Ullman," he said. "I'm a Wisconsin deputy sheriff."

"What brings you all to Lake Geneva?" She stood in a completely relaxed pose, and I noted that her breathing was entirely normal. If I'd been moving the way she had, I'd still have been breathing hard.

"Business, I'm afraid," I said. In the background, Tatiana closed the boom box, and started walking over toward us.

"Oh, I'm sorry to hear that," said Jessica. "Should we hold up our hands?"

"Only if you do it to the music," I said.

"Actually," said Hester, "we need to talk to both of you for a short while."

Tatiana had joined us by then, and I stuck out my hand. "Hello, again."

We shook hands, and she said, "Taking a break?"

"Working," said Hester.

Jessica looked at her watch. "Unfortunately, we are, too. We have a lot to do today," she said. "But we'll be taking a break to eat in about half an hour."

"Fine," said Hester. "We'll wait."

With that, both Jessica and Tatiana turned, and walked all the way to the end of the floor, and turned on the boom box. I recognized "Body Language" by Queen.

"Great music," I said to Hester.

"They've got a half hour to think," she said. "Get ready to work."

I watched the two dancers as they faced in opposite directions, and did precisely the same moves as they maneuvered apart. Hands and feet in slightly different positions, due mainly to the difference in their heights, they clapped in perfect unison, as they moved to the music.

"I could watch this for hours," I said.

"Me, too," said Harry. "Hours and hours."

"That's good," said Hester. "You'll probably have to."

"Hey," I said. "My pleasure."

"You know, Houseman," she said, deadpan, "it's probably a good thing you're over the hill. Otherwise, you could be influenced by this."

"My age is my consolation." I leaned up against the wall, rapt.

"Again," said Jessica. Tatiana walked quickly over to the boom box, and started the music again.

Exactly the same moves, repeated flawlessly. Well, that's the way it looked to me, anyway. Jessica had Tatiana stop the music.

"How about like this, starting with the first 'sexy body,' and then two, three..." intoned Jessica, and shifted from side to side, with her hands on her hips.

They did that four or five times, with Jessica counting it. Satisfied, they started the music up again.

My favorite part was where they were back to back, then moved about thirty feet apart, but in the same plane. They moved sideways across the floor, coming together again, and snapping their fingers to the music. When they were directly opposite each other, they each put their arms at shoulder height, and clapped each other's hands while they were back to back. Precisely in time to the music, and at the precise instant when the musicians clapped. I was astonished. I couldn't do that even if I were facing my partner, and never if it involved moving my feet at the same time.

Hester apparently noticed my fascination. "It's in the counting, Houseman."

"Bullshit," I whispered. "It's supernatural."

"I can't help thinking," said Harry, "that they... Oh, never mind."

"You two aren't thinking about the case," said Hester.

They went through "Body Language" five times. Then Jessica got out a mat, and signaled to us.

"We just have to rehearse this one bit, then we'll eat."

"Fine, go ahead," said Hester.

With the music off, Jessica clapped her hands in time, and Tatiana spun, and went over onto the mat, slapping her cheek into the plastic surface, with her weight on her raised right arm and her left wrist, which was under her hip. At the same time, her left leg went straight up, foot pointed directly at the ceiling, and her right leg came up with her right foot on her left knee, forming a tripod. Damndest thing. She froze in that position for a full five seconds, then collapsed with a heartfelt complaint.

"Oh, man!"

"Again," said Jessica.

Tatiana stood, and as Jessica clapped time, spun into the floor, assuming the same position and holding it for five seconds.

Relaxing again, she said, "Aw, boy, that hurts."

"Now the other side," said Jessica.

"Aw, geeze," said Tatiana, but with complete good nature. You could tell she would do almost anything to excel, and to please Jessica. "You know that isn't my best side."

As Jessica clapped, Tatiana reversed, and did it going the other way. Perfectly, as far as I could tell.

"Ow," said Tatiana.

Once more, and then both of them walked over to us.

I was thinking lunch. Like, in food. Instead, Jessica motioned us through the divider, and to the three chairs. As we three cops sat, she and Tatiana just sort of flowed into a sitting position on the floor, near a black gym bag. Jessica opened a door under the counter, and removed two bottles of water, some crackers, a small brick of white cheese, and some grapes.

"Would you care for some?"

"No, thanks," said Hester. "We just had brunch."

"Oh?" asked Jessica, handing Tatiana a water bottle. "Where?"

"The Geneva Inn," said Hester.

"Oh, very nice," said Jessica. "That's where you're staying?"

"I am," said Hester sweetly. She gave them the name of our motel. "Do you know the place? These two are staying there."

"Wow," said Tatiana. "Who'd you piss off?"

"It's a long story," I said. "But it's worth it, just being here. I don't think I've heard Jamal playing 'Poinciana' in fifteen years."

"I'm impressed," said Jessica, in a warm tone. "So, what can we do for you?"

"Well," said Hester, "we have a few questions. Some things have come to light, and we need to see what you can tell us about them. Clarification, really."

"Do I need my attorney?" asked Jessica.

"You're not a suspect," I said.

"Why don't you just tell me what you want to know, and I'll decide whether or not I need an attorney with me," said Jessica.

Reasonable. Not quite the way I'd hoped, but it was a good chance to get her mind moving in a direction we wanted.

"Fair," I said. "And Tatiana? What about you?"

I really think she was both surprised and flattered that I'd asked.

"I'll just listen, if this is for both of us."

"Good," said Hester. "I think it might be."

Jessica reached into the gym bag and pulled out a Swiss Army knife, which she opened and used to slice the cheese for both of them. "Go ahead," she said.

I leaned back in my chair, and pushed my legs out in front of me, trying to look relaxed. I pulled a little notepad from my pocket. They're really handy. You can pretend to be writing, to buy yourself some time. I also put on my reading glasses. They're handy tools, since they can emphasize questions, when you look over the top of the frames at your witness. "Well, to begin with, we know that it was Dan Peale upstairs, who ran on us."

"Ah." That was all Jessica said.

"And, we know he killed Edie."

"For certain?" asked Jessica. Very calm.

"It looks like it. The evidence is compelling." I wanted to draw her out on that point.

"Mind if I ask what kind of evidence?"

"Nope. Mostly testimonial, supported by some physical evidence, and some observations."

"Really? Whose?"

"Whose observations?" I love a good game.

"No. Testimony, if I can ask."

"Toby's."

First point to me, as her eyes widened. "Really? Where would he hear that?"

"He didn't," I said. "He was there when Dan killed her."

Tatiana reacted that time, while Jessica just stared at me.

I shrugged. "I was surprised, too, to tell the truth."

"When did he tell you that?"

"When we arrested him," I said.

It got pretty quiet for a few seconds.

"I'm just not sure what to tell you at this point," I said. "Let me explain the sequence of events, here."

I started off with the pursuit of Peale the night Borman was attacked, and while Jessica and company were still at the Mansion. As I talked, she interrupted once, to tell me that their muscles would be getting stiff, and did I mind if they sort of stretched them while I talked. No, as a matter of fact, I didn't. I think that was a mistake, though.

When I interview somebody, I watch for cues they send my way, to tell if they're being truthful, or are becoming nervous, or seem to be inventing things. Gamblers call them "tells," and that's a fine term for it. I listen to their voice. I watch their eyes. And I check the body language. If I'm really attentive, I can tell a lot about an answer regardless of the verbal content. But when Jessica, and then Tatiana a few minutes later, started to stretch and contort, the normal tells were taken right out of the picture. When they'd hold an awkward position, for instance, they would send spurious signals. Sometimes, when they'd answer, I couldn't see their eyes. Their exertions would strain and contort their voices, just a little, and made it very hard to judge expression. I was stuck with relying solely on content.

When I got to the part where Toby had stuck a stake in Edie's chest, though, both dancers seemed shaken.

"That's horrible," said Jessica.

"It's sick," said Tatiana, "is what it is."

I continued, and when I got to the part about Toby telling us about his holding Edie, despite knowing Dan was killing her, Tatiana stopped her stretching, and just stared at us with a horrified expression.

"But, it was likely that it was an accident, wasn't it?" asked Jessica.

"No. Not at all." I leafed through my notepad, pretending to search for what I was about to say. I was not going to give them Huck's name under any circumstance. "Dan Peale wanted to experience death," I said, and then tried to make it appear as if I was reading from my notes, "ah, here we go, 'secondhand.' " I looked back at Jessica. "To do that, it looks like he not only had to bleed Edie to death, he had to make her fully aware she was going to die."

"Oh," said Jessica, "No. I simply don't believe that. Not for a minute."

I did note that Tatiana was silent.

Hester came in from her position of observer for the first time. "All the physical evidence, and all the testimonial evidence, are in complete agreement with that fact," she said. "Trust me."

"I believe you think you're right," said Jessica. "I know you're being honest with me. But if you're relying on the testimony of that Toby, after he mutilated Edie's body . . ."

"Oh, no. No, we're not," I said.

"What?"

"Hell, Toby didn't decide to go after the body with a stake," I said. I had her.

"But you just told us . . ."

I was paying special attention to Tatiana, who was absolutely hanging on our every word. I spoke slowly, for best effect. "Dan told Toby to do it."

"Impossible!" Jessica was quite convincing at that point. It was the strongest vibe I got from her during the interview.

"Not in the age of cell phones," said Hester, with a smile.

We let that sink in for a minute.

"Can I have a turn?" asked Harry.

I know Harry Ullman pretty well, and I trust him implicitly. If he wanted in at this precise point, I knew it was a good idea.

"Sure, Harry," I said.

"When was the last time this Dan went mountain climbing?" he asked. "I mean, the last time you have knowledge of."

Jessica looked startled. Too bad, because it gave Tatiana a slender opening.

"Last August, wasn't it?" she asked Jessica.

I could see Jessica's mind racing. She didn't know why Harry had asked, and the sudden change of direction had thrown her off.

"Possibly," she said. It was the only answer under the circumstances. She was fast. She was also cool. She looked directly at Harry. "Why do you ask?"

"Just a second," he said. "I have another question first. Would that be okay, and then you can see where I'm goin' with this?" He grinned apologetically. When Harry gets humble, I know he's on to something. "I can't think of any other way to say it."

"All right."

"Do either of you know of a gal named Alicia? Works on the gaming boat at Freiberg?"

Jessica and Tatiana exchanged glances. Tatiana shrugged. "No," said Jessica. She sounded believable on that point.

"Well, this Dan dude knew her, and he went and did his mountain climbing thing with the ropes and stuff behind her second-floor apartment. Asked her to let him in, I'm told. She told him no."

"That's bizarre," said Jessica.

"It gets worse," said Harry. "This Alicia had a boyfriend named Randy Baumhagen. Ever hear of him?"

Both dancers shook their heads.

"Well, Randy Baumhagen got invited in by Alicia, where Dan didn't," said Harry, "and it looks like that pissed Dan off. Dan snuck up behind him one night, and whacked him in the head with a blunt instrument." He watched the disbelief on both women's faces. "No shit, ladies, that's what he did. Know what else he did that night?"

He got two blank looks.

"He used some pliers on Randy Baumhagen, after he was dead. He tore a hole in his neck. Sort of a signature, we think."

"That's absurd," said Jessica. "It's absolutely..."

Harry used an old ploy. He looked at Hester. "You agree with me?" he asked.

"Yes I do," she said.

"You, Carl?" he asked.

"You bet. All the evidence leads there."

With that, Harry had established that three of the five people in the room were in agreement. It's surprising how well that can work.

"Why are you telling us this?" Jessica looked at each of us in turn.

"Because," I said, "we think you can tell us where Dan Peale is."

It got very quiet in that room. Neither Hester, nor Harry nor I were about to say anything at that point. We wanted Jessica to come across with some information herself, and we wanted to see what it was going to be.

"If you can't find him"—and she looked quizzically at us—"then what makes you think I can tell you?"

"To begin with, our information indicates," I said, "that you know more about him than anybody connected with the Mansion. We've been told about your, uh, relationship with Dan Peale."

"Long-term relationship," said Hester. "You know we were on the third floor. Believe me, we didn't miss a thing."

Jessica said, "All right." Just like that. Tatiana let her cheeks puff out, and let out a long breath. She'd apparently been holding it in.

Jessica took a quick drink from her water bottle. "He and I have been lovers for years. I admit it freely, although not publicly. You do understand? He's involved in another relationship, and I would not want to embarrass him."

"Sure." I tried to sound encouraging.

"You must know he's into a bit of blood tasting. Not often, but we both consider it to be an intimacy enhancing act. I would like to keep that private. Many people don't understand that sort of thing." With that, she graced us with a smile. "Especially my Aunt Bridgett." She shrugged. "But all that aside, I have only contacted him at his office. I presume he is not there?"

"You presume right," I said. Office?

"That doesn't surprise me," she said.

"Why not?" asked Hester.

"Well, the night he escaped," she said. "You knew who he was as soon as the shots were fired. We could hear your officers calling him by name, on the loudspeakers."

You know when, in cartoons, the little lightbulb comes on over the character's head? Epiphany city.

"They did his name over the PA systems in the cars, now that you mention it," I said. "I heard it myself. We were calling him by name, all right. But at that time, we were spelling it P-E-E-L. Not P-E-A-L-E. We had no idea who he was, then, or where he lived."

"Oh?"

"That's right," said Hester. "But if he could hear, then he must have thought we had him dead to rights, and that he couldn't go home."

"Certainly," said Jessica. "How very silly of you."

Shit, in a word. We'd prevented his running to the only place we were going to know where to look. His home. Silly wasn't the word for it.

"So," said Hester, "you don't know where he is?"

"No," said Jessica.

I got mixed signals on that one. Her head was turned more to Hester, so I didn't get a good look at her eyes. Her body was kind of levered up on one hip, and she had her hand on her ankle, pulling toward the center of her back, stretching her quad muscles. No signals or tells from the body language, that was for certain. But her voice was just a tiny bit too high. Strain from lying, or from stretching? I thought from lying.

Tatiana was just sitting with her legs straight out in front of her, pulling a perfect "L." I looked at her squarely.

"What about you?"

"Me?" She sounded a bit surprised.

"Yes. Do you know where he is?"

"No. Why would I?" She answered as she bent forward, pressing her rib cage to the tops of her thighs. She stretched and extended her neck, so that we didn't break eye contact. A difficult read. But the nonchalant "question with a question" told me that she, too, was lying to me. It also told me she wasn't as adept at lying as Jessica. She was the weak link, all right.

I smiled at her. Flies and honey. "Now, I suppose a

really good cop would say something like"—and I lowered my voice—"I dunno, 'Why would you?' Right?"

"Maybe," she said, with a hint of a smile.

"Well, speaking as one of the cops who unintentionally misled our suspect into eluding us, I think I better ask something else instead."

"Good idea," she said, straightening back up into a seated position.

"So," I said, "who would *you* ask if you had to find out where he was?"

It worked. Her eyes shifted to Jessica for an instant, and then back to me. I don't think she was aware she'd done it, even after it had happened. Jessica was looking directly at me, and I was pretty certain she hadn't noticed it, either.

"I can't think of anyone."

"Okay." I made a totally bogus check mark on my little notepad.

Jessica made a large point of pulling a watch out of the bag, and checking the time. "We really have to be getting back to work," she said. "I can't think of anything I know about this that I haven't told you."

"One more question," said Hester. "Why does Dan Peale pretend to be from London?"

Jessica handled that one on the fly. "It's an affectation. A charming one. We just play that he is."

"Ah. But it's made clear that it's an affectation, then?"

"Yes, of course."

"But there are a lot of people at the Mansion convinced he's from England," persisted Hester.

"And," said Jessica, "if they choose to believe it ... What's the harm? Some people are more naive than others." She replaced some of their luncheon items in the cupboard under the counter.

"I'm just making sure in my own mind," said Hester, "that it isn't a case of the two of you acting together to conceal his real identity."

Again, Jessica seemed to be unconcerned. "Well, of

course we are. I certainly wouldn't want one of them trying to contact him."

She was really good.

She straightened up. "All this is being treated with the strictest confidence, isn't it?"

"Absolutely," I said.

"Won't tell a soul who doesn't need to know," said Harry.

"I thought as much," she replied. "But I'm sure you understand that this little ruse we played to avoid, oh, complications, was just that and nothing more. That's all."

"Sure," I said. Right. I was thinking how tough this woman would be in front of a jury. I thought I'd give her something to think about. "Before we go, could you tell us how to get to the historical society building?"

"Yes." She told us.

"Thanks," I said. Being so damned self-possessed, she hadn't asked. Because of that, I had to tell her why we were looking for it. "I understand they have blueprints of the old Givens place, from way back. We'd just like to see 'em." That certainly took the bite out of it.

"They're fascinating," she said. "I hope you enjoy them."

"And we'll be needing to see you once more," said Hester. "This evening?"

"For?"

"I really hate being melodramatic," said Hester, "but I can't tell you that until then."

Hester had salvaged my objective.

"Perhaps after supper?" Jessica shrugged. "We have some guests coming late this afternoon. I'd rather not disturb them. It will be brief?"

"I hope so. Where can we call you?"

Jessica gave Hester the number of Bridgett Hunley's private line. "After seven," she said. "I'll answer."

After we got back downstairs, and out onto the sidewalk, I nudged Hester. "Why the hell did you have to tell her this evening?"

"I don't know." She quickened her pace. "But I'm not going to let the woman off the hook that easy. She's lying, and we all know it. She knows where that SOB is, Houseman, and she's gonna tell me if I have to strangle her."

"Attagirl," said Harry.

"That'd be a sight," I said. "But I think we might have a good lever in her Aunt Bridgett. It strikes me that Jessica would do just about anything to keep this sort of involvement from her."

We still had a card up our sleeves. We hadn't mentioned anything about vampires.

We walked to the historical society building, and I noted us in at 12:39. In five minutes, we were looking at the blueprint and history of the Mansion.

In 1903, a vertical shaft had been completed between the silica mine and the top of the hill where the Givens Mansion was located. He owned that mine, and much to my surprise, the tunnel system in 1900 already extended more than a mile and a half along the Mississippi. All they apparently had to do was drop the shaft through about thirty feet of limestone before they got to the silica sand. Piece of cake. We were looking at both plan and elevation diagrams, and it appeared that shaft was vertical, with a simple elevator box, and the machinery at the bottom.

According to the illustration, the previous tramcar and track that had run down the hill, and that Old Knockle had described to me, had been abandoned. The shaft replaced it. Complete with a small building that looked suspiciously like a shed, which was labeled "upper terminus" on the blueprint. The "lower terminus" was in the mine itself.

The "upper terminus" was precisely located on the blueprint. It was 112 feet south southeast of the rear door of the Mansion. In the drawing, it was a simple shed kind of structure, with a steeply angled, one-sided roof.

"I'll be damned," I said. "The upper portion has to be one of the old foundations, right there with the ones that the German Kommune group built before the Civil War."

"That would be those," said Hester, pointing to a series of dotted lines arranged in rectangles that salted the area.

"Yeah. Right about in this area here," I said, pointing with my pen to an area northeast of the Mansion, "is about where we found Toby that night."

"If that shaft's still functional..."

"Yeah. That's where Peale went after he got past Borman. Damn." I indicated where Toby had been found. "When Sally and I were headed over here, looking for Toby, something ran past us. Coming from the direction of the 'upper terminus,' back toward the house from us. I'll bet it was Toby that ran by us. I'll bet it was."

"Why?"

"Beats me, but I bet that little shit was over by the elevator shaft, or goin' in that direction."

I looked at the plans on the table. "I wonder how much farther the mine got, before they closed it down. I know it was still functional in the sixties."

"Regardless," said Hester, "Peale could easily have made it to that elevator, if he knew where it was. Right down to the highway, a good half hour before he could have made it any other way. Hitchhiked, or the train tracks, or the landing about what, a half mile south?" She pushed her chair back. "Everything but an airport."

"Or the mine," said Harry. "You don't suppose he could still be in the mine, do you?"

We exchanged glances.

"I think our budget can stand a photocopy of this plan," I said. "Let me get one from the lady over there...."

"I'd better," she said. "You'll have to stand the initial cost. My department pays me back faster than yours."

"Well, okay. Twist my arm. While you do that, though, let me use your cell phone," I said. "I want to call the office and see if we can get somebody up to the Mansion and check on things. And then get hold of somebody who can get us into the mine."

"I gotta make a call, too," said Harry.

The first part was a snap, as Borman was to be sent up right away, to check the status of the Mansion's residents. The second part was a bit more complicated. The mine was officially closed, as I was already aware, and ownership was with a corporation in New Mexico. That I hadn't known. We knew who the Nation County man was who oversaw the place, but he wouldn't give permission for us to enter the mine on his own. It was going to take a call from our county attorney to their corporate headquarters to obtain permission. I told Dispatch to get Lamar to arrange that.

When I was finished with my call, Harry said he had some information for us as well.

"You know that hot-lookin' Tatiana Ostransky gal? Jessica Hunley's dance partner?"

"No," I said, "I hadn't noticed."

"Uh huh. Anyhow, I just checked with Hawkins about her. Turns out that her real name is Hutha Mann, she's from Milwaukee, and that she was in this area in 1993." He looked at us expectantly.

"And?" I asked.

"Peale was busted here back in ninety-three," he said. "Didn't you get our fuckin' reply to your inquiry?"

"Oh, yeah! Yeah, okay. Consensual blood ingestion, wasn't that it? And some involvement with a juvie, too."

"You got it. Want to guess who the fuckin' juvie was?"

"Hutha Mann," said Hester. "Hutha Mann, a/k/a Tatiana Ostransky, right?"

"You got it." He laughed.

"The plot thickens," I said. "So, what did he do to her?"

"Probably a statutory sex thing, I bet. The reporting officer says that she was not a complainant in the matter. She was seventeen at the time, so she could have legally consented, but this Peale dude provided her with booze, and since she was not able to consent to drinking, and she was intoxicated at the time she was discovered, he was in problems."

"Ouch." I grinned. "Bad choices, there."

"Yeah. He didn't get shit out of it, with the plea bargain and everything." Harry shrugged. "She had a fresh cut on her lip, but she claimed that was an accident."

"I'll just bet she did," said Hester.

"Now, here's the good part," said Harry. "The guy who was in charge of that bust retires next week, but he was in, and he said that Jessica Hunley was involved in the edges of the case. She wasn't at the cabin at the time they made the arrests, but the Hunleys' attorney came to the cop shop and made everybody's bail. And this Hutha Mann, a/k/a Tatiana, gave her address as a place that turned out to be Jessica Hunley's fuckin' dance studio."

"No shit?" I said. "So they go way back as a group, then."

"Apparently so," he said, looking very satisfied with himself.

We walked over for lunch at a great place called Popeyes. Multiple levels, it had a maritime décor and a great menu. Well, a cop would think so.

"It must be great," I said, "to work in a town that has restaurants like this."

There was a faint, multi-tone sound, and Hester pulled her cell phone from her pocket.

She answered it, and then held it out to me. "For you. Your office."

I took the phone. "Yeah?"

"Carl, Lamar. Nothin' major, but the attorney we got to talk to to get in the old mine won't be in until tomorrow sometime. Is this a problem?"

"No, I don't think so." I didn't think we'd be back there until then, anyway. "I'd appreciate it if you'd look for some sign, down at the highway level, where somebody might have gone over the fence, or something. Stack of crates? Rocks? We think there's a really good chance our buddy might have made it down there pretty fast that night."

"Borman and Knockle are already up there, and everything is okay, as far as they can tell. Most of the kids up there are at work, I guess." He paused. "I'll have 'em check the mine area. Do you want 'em wandering around up on the hill, looking for an entrance?"

I did not. No point giving the game away before we were ready.

"You do know that it runs for about three miles or better?" asked Lamar. "Inside the hill, mostly north and south, but it does go back in under the bluffs for a good five hundred feet, too?"

"Okay...."

"I just asked because, if you want to do a search or something, it could take a real long time. The chambers are big enough to be easy to search, you know, but they cover a lot of territory."

"I sure hope not," I said. "I hate caves."

He chuckled. "The troops been getting really curious why I'm telling 'em to do all this stuff. I ain't told where you are, and they're thinkin' that I'm on the case."

"Hey, we brought in the best."

"Uh, Carl, while I got you on the phone ... did you have some sort of confrontation with Borman about that warning shot business?"

"Not really," I said. "Why?"

"Well, he says you jumped in his shit in front of witnesses. Embarrassed him, or something. Gave him a lecture, I believe he said. Here in the office. You know anything about that?"

"Sure. He flagged me down on my way through Dispatch, and wanted to know why I told on him. Just like a little kid."

"Yeah. Well, Carl, he's filed a grievance with the union. Alleges harassment on your part. Wants you disciplined."

"Bullshit."

"Yeah, but that's what he says."

"Ask Sally," I said. "She was there. She was there for the whole thing."

"Okay," said Lamar. "But don't you talk with her about this. She's a witness, let the process take its course."

"I want that little moron off this case," I said.

"Can't do that, Carl. You know the rules, here. Just watch your step."

"Watch my step, hell," I said. "I'm gonna strangle the little shit."

"Right. Oh, before I forget, that Huck girl called for you guys a few minutes ago. Dispatch didn't tell me 'cause it went in your 'to do' box, but I was readin' the log."

Quite a gear change, as Lamar intended. "When did she call?"

"About an hour ago. No message, just said she needed to talk to you before you came back." He stopped, surprised. "Let me check that note. . . ."

"Back? How did she know we were gone?"

"Okay, Jesus, I didn't think. Yep, here it is. The note says '. . . before they come back . . .' You didn't tell her you were leavin'?"

"No. I didn't . . . just a sec." I covered the phone. "Hey, did you tell Huck we were leaving the area?"

"No," said Hester. "No, I didn't."

"Me, neither," said Harry, just to make me happy.

"She called for us, and left a message saying that she'd talk to us before we got back." I was getting concerned.

"Hey, Lamar? No, Hester didn't say anything, either." I pulled a pen from my pocket. "Give me the call-back number on the note, will you?"

He did. I knew it wasn't the Mansion, but it sounded familiar.

"You know what number that is?" If it was familiar to me, it would probably be familiar to Lamar, as well.

"Yeah, it's the main administrative number for the casino boat."

"I'll give her a call," I said.

I handed the phone back to Hester. "Gotta get one of those."

"The whole state would appreciate it," she said.

"Huck had to talk to either Jessica or Tatiana right after we left the dance studio," I said. "She called our office a few minutes ago. I think she's on the 06:00 to 14:00 shift, which means that she was at work when she called our office, and would have been when we left the studio, too."

"So they called her at work, then?" Hester and I were both figuring that a long-distance call from work was something Huck probably wouldn't be doing.

"Probably. I better call her."

Hester just handed me her phone.

The gaming boat hated to interrupt dealers, understandably, and told me to call back in fifteen minutes. That gave me time to gripe to Hester and Harry about Borman and his grievance.

Hester just shook her head. Harry related a similar incident between him and a rookie that ended with the rookie working in a discount store. "They just seem to hate constructive fuckin' criticism, these days, you know?"

"Yeah," I said, ruefully. "What my boy doesn't know is how restrained I was."

Our food arrived just as Hester's phone rang again. She answered, grinned, and handed it to me. "Lamar," she said.

"Yeah?"

"Your friend Huck just called back," said Lamar. "She gave this number, and said you're to call it right away."

I got my pen back out, and wrote it down. "Thanks."

"You bet. Let me know what's going on. . . ."

"Okay."

I broke the connection, and dialed the number he'd given me. Of course, since he hadn't had to use the area code, I hadn't copied it down. Being in a hurry, when I dialed, I left it out. There was the familiar oscillating tone.

"Area code," said Hester, her spoon between the soup bowl and her mouth. I noticed the spoon didn't even slow.

"Right." I redialed.

"Hello," said a muted voice. It was Huck, and she was half whispering.

"Houseman. You wanted me to call?"

"Yeah. That was fast. So, how you like Lake Geneva?" Still whispered.

"Great, so far."

"You get around. Look, Tat called, she had some stuff to tell me, and I told her she could trust you. She can, can't she?"

"Sure." Tat? It sounded like she knew Tatiana better than I had thought.

"Okay, look, she wants to meet you in about a half hour. Jessica's got stuff to do, and Tat wants to talk with somebody. She's getting scared," said Huck.

Well. "Okay, fine. Where at?"

There was a pause. "Before I tell you, you gotta know that Tat's in love with Jessica, all right? I mean, really in love with her."

I wasn't exactly thunderstruck, but I was surprised. "Oh?"

She sighed. "You gotta know that so what she says makes sense."

"Okay."

"She wants to meet you at the observatory. You know where that is?"

"Yep. If you mean the big one? The Yerkes Observatory." Oh, yeah.

"Yes. She'll be at the rear steps, I'll call her right now, gotta go, thanks, be good to her." Dial tone.

"So?" asked Hester.

"Jessica and Tatiana did call her," I said. "She wanted to make sure they were telling her the truth, for one thing."

"She wonders about that, too?" asked Harry.

"Huck says that Ostransky, Tatiana, wants to meet us at Yerkes Observatory."

Hester put down her soupspoon, got a map out of her purse, and said, "Looks like we take fifty west to sixty-seven, then sixty-seven south into Williams Bay. Follow it on West Geneva Street. Piece of cake."

THIRTY

Yerkes Observatory is run by the University of Chicago. It's an incredible building, sort of dumbbell shaped, with a long hall connecting two observation areas. The building itself is an architectural delight. Built in 1895, it's a golden sandstone, ornately carved, complete with gargoyles, griffons and other mythological critters, as well as astronomical and astrological signs, cherubs, and just about anything else that would lend a Victorian Gothic air to the place. The domes themselves are very ornate, with pillared arches running around the lower levels, and making them look a lot like the exterior of the Leaning Tower of Pisa. The whole place has a Jules Verne atmosphere, and you can almost see the famous astronomers Hale, Barnard, and Burnham out of the corner of your eye.

We all got into Hester's car, and followed the map. As we turned in the long drive, Hester got a good look at the place, and said, "Wow."

"Cool, no?" I gave her the basic details I'd gotten years back when I took the tour. "Some momentous stuff happened here, but in a quiet way."

"It is quiet," said Harry.

We parked right in front of the main entrance. There were only three or four cars there, and space for about twice that many.

The mirror image of the main entrance was on the other side of the building, so we walked on the lawn around the main dome, and approached the deserted rear of the building.

Sure enough, Tatiana was sitting on the stone steps, about fifty yards from us. She'd apparently pulled a pair of black slacks on over her dancing tights, and had on a pair of ankle-high, laced walking boots. She was in bright afternoon sunlight, and her hair shone like neon. She held her hand to her forehead to shade her eyes as we approached, and stood.

"Hi," I said.

"What can we do for you?" asked Hester.

Tatiana didn't appear at all nervous, just in a hurry.

"Okay, look, I don't have a lot of time, and there's a couple of things you should know about what's going on."

"You've got our complete attention," I said.

"Let's take a little walk," suggested Tatiana. We did, she and I walking together down a winding walk that crossed the big lawn, Hester and Harry following about a step behind. "Okay, first...well, you should know that we picked up Dan Peale on our way home, and gave him a ride."

"You and Jessica? When you left Freiberg?" Always make sure.

"Yes."

"Where did he spend the night?" asked Hester.

"Here," said Tatiana. "In Lake Geneva."

We stayed on the sidewalk, and meandered through a stand of trees.

"Wait just a second," I said. "Your attorney told us

that you two left early that morning. How could he have spent the night here, and then you gave him a ride?"

Tatiana snickered. "Early that morning? You might say that, I guess, and still be truthful. We left about ten after midnight."

Ah. Attorneys. Always the most deceptive when they tell the truth.

"And where did you pick Dan up?"

"Right at the mine entrance, where we knew he'd be," she said. "Just pulled over, and Jessica honked the horn. He came over the fence in a few minutes, and we were on our way."

"How did you know that?" I asked. "Where to find him, I mean?"

"Cell phones," said Tatiana, with eyebrows raised and an unspoken "duh" dangling from the end of the sentence.

Ah, again. I was going to have to buy one of those damned things, just so I wouldn't keep forgetting they existed.

"Where is he now?" I asked.

"I don't know. I think Jessica does, but I don't."

"When did you last see him?" Hester asked.

"About seven-thirty this morning," was the reply. "That's what I want to talk to you about. He's got one of Jessica's cars, and I'm afraid he's going to drag her down with him."

She wasn't about to break down or anything, but she did seem to be getting toward an edge.

"Why do you say that?"

"He wants her to stay with him forever," said Tatiana. "She's really mad at him right now, and that's good, but she let him have the car, and that's just because they spent last night together, and he's working on her emotions." She took a deep breath. "Jessica's such a wonderful person, and he's going to get her in trouble because she cares."

"How do you know she's mad at him?" I asked,

leaving out any reference to them spending the night together. Their sleeping together really didn't strike me as an anger reaction. That, plus an image of a caring Jessica Hunley was hard to achieve.

"Oh," said Tatiana, "you should have seen her when he got in the car down at the mine. She slapped him. Really. Three times, and called him an idiot and a fool." Her eyes widened as she spoke. "I've never seen her mad like that. She was just furious."

"And he didn't stop her?" asked Hester.

"He just sat there. Really. I was driving, and he got in the car, and there wasn't really room, and she just started slapping him, and he just sat there and let her."

"Really?" Hester didn't look convinced.

"Really, I'm telling you. You'd have to see her that way. I'm not kidding. He just got this stony look on his face, and never even said a word."

Interesting. She'd established Jessica as the dominant personality, without a doubt.

"Well, since she's already been harboring a felon," said Hester, "how much more damage can he do to her?"

"He wants to go to London," said Tatiana. "See?"

"No," I said, "I guess I don't. Why London?"

"You know. He says that's where he's from, originally. Anyway, to go all that distance, he needs more energy," said the dancer. "Lots of it."

"Yes?" She was losing me, and fast.

"We're afraid he has to kill again, to gain energy, before he can go on such a long trip."

"Wouldn't killing somebody like that just drain more energy?" I asked. Thinking to myself, *Jesus, what kind of nuts are these people?*

"You know what he is. Huck said she told you what he is."

"You mean a vampire?"

"Yes."

"Yeah," I said, "she and Toby and I guess everybody

at least thought that's what he might be, to varying degrees." I shrugged. "I don't think Huck believes that, really. Do you?"

"He is." She said it very simply, and very convincingly. "He's a vampire. He gets energy from drinking blood. I know that."

This was no time to bring up the subtle differences between actually being a vampire, and just being very delusional. She believed it, and that was going to have to do. The important thing was, if he really thought he was a vampire, there was a good chance he'd be tending to act as if he were. The downside was that if he was playing an elaborate game, he was only going into vampire mode to impress or frighten certain people. If that were the case, we were then dealing with somebody who was going to act normally outside their view. The latter scenario had my vote.

"So," said Harry, "where do you think he's headed?"

Tatiana was silent for a second, organizing her response. She was genuinely worried, no doubt about that. She glanced at her watch. "Okay. Okay, look, Toby contacted us on e-mail, and said that he had some stuff to tell Dan. We just said to send it to us, and we'd try to find Dan." She looked seriously at me. "Toby's not all that reliable, you know?"

"Yeah," I said. "We know." I made a mental note to obtain a search warrant for Toby's computer. I knew Harry was thinking the same about Jessica at this end.

"So Toby told us that Edie was talking to the cops. That'd be you, I suppose," she said, almost as an afterthought. "So Dan called him, and told him to stop Edie by . . . by putting the stake in her heart, and other stuff." Another deep breath. "So, you guys told us today that he really did that. Right?"

"Right. Or, at least, some of it. He did the stake thing," I said, "but he couldn't do the other stuff." She opened her mouth to talk, and I held up my hand. "Just so there's no misunderstanding, I really didn't say that Edie was actually talking to us. I indicated that her body could tell the pathologist things. Toby just put his own spin on it."

"Oh." She considered that, and I got the impression she didn't believe me. "Well, whatever. Anyway, Toby also said that Huck was talking to you, and that he thought Melissa was about ready to give up everything."

"Well," I said, "that's not been the case."

"He thinks it is," said Tatiana, "I can tell you that. Toby told him, and he's just furious."

"So?"

"I'm afraid that he's going to go back to the Mansion and hurt somebody."

"Why would he go back there? The cops know all about the Mansion," Hester said.

"Because they've been *cultivated* by him, just for that," said Tatiana. "They're his, well, his disciples, you know? And his livestock, kind of, at the same time."

"Look," I said, "why don't you come with us to some place where we can get all this down, and you can—"

"Jesus Christ, you guys! I gotta get back," she said. "If Jessica finds out I'm gone..." Her eyes darted to her watch, again. "Maybe later? Maybe tonight sometime? You do believe me, don't you? God, Huck said you were pretty real people."

"I believe you about everything that counts, that's for sure," I said. "I believe that Dan's pissed, and I believe Toby's an idiot. And I believe we better get some people to that house."

She started walking away very fast, almost skipping as she turned back to us. "I'll call you," she said. "Later," and she was gone.

We decided that we'd better get word to the people at the Mansion, just in case he was really headed back there. I sort of doubted it, frankly. Delusional doesn't necessarily equate with dumb.

I called the Nation County Sheriff's Department on Hester's phone. I asked Sally to get a message to Borman.

"Just a sec, I'll let you talk to him."

"What?" I didn't want to do that, not until I could reach him, anyway. But I had no choice.

"He's right in the back room," she said. "Writing his reports."

Borman came on the line a second later. "Hi."

"I thought you were up around the Mansion?"

"No, we went up there, and everything's fine. I thought I better come back down and get writing on these reports."

I could see why he'd want to do that, but I wasn't all too happy about it. I thought he was trying to avoid working overtime, as opposed to being efficient.

"Look, go back up and talk to them again, will you? We have indications that Peale was in Lake Geneva this morning, early. He left. He's driving one of Jessica Hunley's cars, but we don't know which one for sure. There's a good chance he may be on his way back to the Mansion. Tell them that. All of them." I really tried for a friendly voice. Well, a normal one, anyway. He didn't know that I was aware he'd filed a grievance, and he'd figure out Lamar had told me if I mentioned it.

"Oh, okay. Sure. So, like, you're over in Lake Geneva, then?"

Well, it was a good guess, and there really wasn't a reason to keep it secret anymore, since we'd already talked to Jessica.

"Yeah, we're in Lake Geneva. We got a few interviews to do yet, and should be on the way back tomorrow sometime."

"Oh. Rank has its privileges, huh?"

I couldn't tell from his voice whether he was kidding or being sarcastic. "It sure does. You might want to remember that." I took a breath, and lightened back up.

"Keep all this to yourself, though. Just you and Lamar. No point in the whole world knowing just yet."

"Okay, I'll get right on it. Nothing much going on here, at all." He sounded fairly earnest, and sincere.

"Okay. You might want to pick up some OT, and hang around up there this evening. Maybe a good idea to have a couple of reserves up there tonight, all right?"

"You got it."

"Give me back to Sally, will you?"

"Yo!" Sally always managed to sound cheerful.

"Yeah, hey, keep me posted on anything that comes up, okay?"

"Always, Houseman. Hey," she said, "I hear I'm a witness."

"Ah, yeah, I guess. But I'm not allowed to talk about that with you."

"Sure. I think it's a crock of shit, though. He's acting like a little brat."

"I have no official opinion," I said, smiling in spite of myself. "I can only say I agree with you completely."

"Gotcha."

"Anyway, I can be reached at Hester's cell phone yet today, and Lamar has my motel number for tonight. Lake Geneva."

"I guessed," she said.

"Not surprised. How long did it take you?"

"Just until Lamar called you from Dispatch." I could hear the smile in her voice.

"No secrets in Nation County," I said.

"You got it. Oh, hey..."

"Yeah?" I was just getting ready to break the connection.

"Did Lamar tell you he had the flu?"

"Lamar? No, not a word."

"He's pretty sick, I think. Be ready to get recalled, Houseman. We have Norris and Willy both out, too. You might have to come back here."

"Right." I broke the connection this time before she

could give me any more bad news. The department was now down to four effectives, counting me.

I told Hester and Harry. They thought they could get the job done without me, if it was necessary. Put it gently, though. Like Harry said, "We'll miss you at mealtime."

The next call was to Hawkins at the local sheriff's office, with Hester doing the calling. I felt I should let her use her own phone once in a while.

She told him that our man Peale had likely been in Lake Geneva until early this morning, and that he was en route to points unknown, in a car that was probably registered to Jessica Hunley. Made his day. Hawkins told her he'd put out an E-1/F-1 bulletin, immediately. That would send the data to all the Midwestern states, including Iowa, Wisconsin, Michigan, Minnesota, and Illinois. With the notation that the suspect was armed, dangerous, and wanted for questioning in a murder in Iowa.

"That ought to produce something," I said, when she told us.

"You'd think," said Harry.

"So, we have," she said, and looked at her watch, "about three hours to kill before we call Jessica. Mind if I check out a couple of these antique stores?"

By closing time at 5 P.M., Hester had acquired three brass candlesticks, and I had picked up a small cinnabar vase for Sue's collection. Harry, surprisingly, had shopped very intensely, but had no luck.

"Can't find good Royal Daulton anywhere, these days."

Apparently to cope with his disappointment, Harry also engaged one of the store owners in a conversation about the "big gray building." Bridgett Hunley's house, of course. Everybody seemed to know it as soon as we said it looked like a large government office building. The lady told Harry quite a bit of local lore about the Hunleys, replete with the veiled implication that all their money hadn't been acquired on the up and up, and ended with her assessment of Jessica.

"And she's going to inherit the whole thing," she said. "She seems nice, but there's something about her."

"Really," said Harry, "I think there's 'something about' everybody who has that much money, don't you?"

"Oh, yes. I've known her...well, known of her, since she was in high school. Always able to buy her way out of any sort of trouble."

"Those rich kids always seem to get into their share of trouble, don't they?" said Harry, sounding bemused. He was really good at that.

"Yes, they do. Can I interest you in something else?"

"No, Royal Daulton is my thing, honey."

"That's nice," she said. "That Jessica, she does seem to have problems with her protégés, though. For some reason."

"Oh, really?" said Harry, with more charm than I'd seen him display since his last murder trial. "Well, young people are a little different these days."

"They just don't last," said the clerk. "She has one now, with really horrible hair, who's been with her the longest of any of them. Must be all of three years. I don't give her much longer, and Jessica will be ready for a new one."

"Oh, I'm sure," said Harry.

"She really has bad luck with them. Some just leave, I guess, but one was drowned out there in the lake, and one was killed in a car crash just about four years ago."

"Really?"

"Oh, yes. One ran off with a local insurance man. Ruined his family. I truly think," she said, very seriously, "that it must be something with dancers."

"Oh," said Harry, confiding in her, "I do agree. Yes I do."

When we got in the car, Harry was smiling all over

himself. "I still got, it, don't I? Don't I? Am I fuckin' charmin' or what?"

"Uh-huh." I agreed. "Charm the birds from the trees."

Hester was shaking her head. "I don't care what anybody says, Harry, you can be almost human if you really, really try."

"You really think so? You ain't just being nice, Hester? Wasn't that great?" asked Harry, of either of us. "But, hey? Two deaders associated with Dirty Dan the Vampire Man? Nobody has to draw me a map of that one."

As if to punctuate, Hester's phone rang. Hawkins. They'd checked out Hunley's home and studio. The silver 2000 Mercedes Benz SUV was nowhere to be found. Not conclusive, of course, but if Peale was in one of her two cars, and they had the BMW accounted for. . . .

Hester thanked him, and then told him about Harry's conversation with the clerk. I couldn't hear what he said, but it took a few seconds. She said, "Right. Good. Thanks," and broke the connection. She took a deep breath, and let it out very slowly. "This damned case just keeps going, doesn't it?"

"Seems to."

"Well," she said, "I hope Hawkins didn't have anything planned for the next month or so."

"We gotta be careful," I said when she was done with her call to Hawkins. "It gives good old Jessica a really sinister cast, here. Maybe more sinister than she would ever deserve."

Hester gave a devilish smile. "Does, doesn't it?"

Our shopping spree over, we drove to Lake Geneva proper, parked, and went sight-seeing while looking for a place to have supper. On the way, we took a walk on the enclosed bricked dock and pier, called the "Rivera." The Rivera had a ballroom on the second floor, and who knew what on the third. Turrets, as well. A thoroughly fascinating place. We could see Bridgett Hunley's enormous home from there, kind of a complementary balance to the Rivera. There were several inboard motorboats moving about, as well as a couple of late sailing boats. Nice scenery, and it gave a little insight into the young Jessica. And just how easy it would be for somebody to "drown" in that huge lake.

We stopped and looked over the pier rail. You could see fish swimming along the sandy bottom about ten feet down. Thinking of a body down there, the calming effect you normally associate with swimming fish was somewhat reduced.

The sky was clear, the sound of the water was soothing, and there was even some color still in the trees. It was gorgeous. I savored the thought that this was the first real perk I'd had in twenty years on the job.

We grabbed supper at a little place called Speedos Harbor Side Café, across the street from the Rivera. From our table, we had a fine view of the lake. While we watched, a rescue boat came gliding smoothly to the dock we'd just left. Brought the subject of drowning to my mind again. The coincidence of a drowning and a car crash taking her partners out was a little too much to buy. Maybe one had been an authentic accident, but both?

Hester was apparently thinking the same thing. "Car crash, especially fatal, is a lot harder to fake than a drowning," she said.

"True."

"The word 'true,' all by itself," she said, "is absolutely no encouragement at all. Means you're humoring me."

"True."

Harry chuckled. "You're right, though, Hester. Odds are way against it."

Car crashes really are a lot harder to fake. One of the reasons is that there's just such an enormous amount of data regarding wrecks that had been compiled over the last fifty years. That, coupled with the intense interest of insurance companies and courts regarding claimed damages, has produced entire fields of study that are related to car crashes. Every fatality is thoroughly studied, measured, photographed, analyzed, and subjected to reconstructive procedures that virtually ensure any foul play will stand out like a red flag. A good traffic investigator can tell you precisely what happened. Precisely. And if there are any inconsistencies, you'll hear about it.

Murder via car wreck is easy to accomplish, don't get me wrong. It's just virtually impossible to make it look accidental. Physics is physics.

"I wonder, though," I said absently.

"What?" asked Harry, lowering his menu.

"Oh, I dunno. Just thinking. If you wanted to do somebody, it would be a lot easier to make a drowning look like an accident. Just for instance."

"True." That was from Hester.

I looked over at her. "You're right. No help at all."

"Hey. I told you." She looked out the window, toward the lake. "A little too much to drink, splash, gurgle. Nothing weird, just drowned."

"Well, yeah. Bad swimmer...better if a nonswimmer. And, most of the time, people are murdered for mundane reasons like rage, for instance, or jealousy. Things like that. By people they know." I looked expectantly at Hester.

"Jealousy is good," she said. "Would lead to a more cold-blooded approach than the heat of anger. Just for example, you know? More of the 'gee look at the neat fish...splash...oops' kind of thing." She pursed her lips. "Jessica ain't gettin' no younger, Pilgrim," she said, sounding quite remarkably like John Wayne.

"True."

That earned me a withering glance.

"Really, when you find somebody who seems to be just surrounded by, oh, certain events," she said, avoiding the word murder in deference to a passing waitress, "there's just every indication that they may have something to do with causing those events. Like, if the drowning victim was messing with our vampire." She half giggled. "Count boy-toy."

I didn't say "true." Harry did.

She drummed her fingers on the table. "Got to stop this speculation, Houseman. It's making it too easy to feel like there's some real evidence, here."

"Sure makes the time pass, though," I said.

She pulled her cell phone out and dialed.

"Can you get us copies of the investigations we just talked about? Both the car wreck and the drowning? Great. Great. Oh, and when did that drowning occur? Really? Well, that is interesting. Thanks."

She disconnected, looking very pleased. "The drowning was in the summer of ninety-seven," she said. "Hawkins thinks late July or early August."

The hamburgers were great.

It had been a satisfying day, altogether. And the tour of the interior of the Hunley place was coming up in less than an hour and a half. I was anticipating being impressed.

Hester got another phone call, and handed it to me. "I'm beginning to feel like your answering service, Houseman."

It was my office. They were down to two full-time deputies, because of that damned flu. Lamar had said that, if at all possible, I was to return to the county immediately. He had also said that with Hester and Harry in Lake Geneva, I should be able to do that. He was, of course, right.

I bid farewell to Hester, Harry, and Lake Geneva at 6:14 P.M., and headed back to Nation County. I hated to leave, but my two cohorts assured me that they would keep me posted on any developments. Damn. I think I was as disappointed to miss the visit to the Hunley estate as I was to miss the interview itself.

I drove right into rain, but it was an uneventful trip, until I was contacted by radio near Dodgeville. Our Mutual Aid frequency was the same as Wisconsin's WISPERN, which stood for Wisconsin Police Emergency Radio Network. They always have had better acronyms. Anyway, I was instructed to go directly to the sheriff's department in Dodgeville. There was a moment's confusion on the radio, because Dodgeville was the county seat of Iowa County, Wisconsin. They were calling me Iowa Car, which was a bit of a kick.

There was a deputy waiting for me. "We have a number for you to call," she said. "I guess it's pretty urgent." She ushered me into a private office.

My first thought was that something had happened to either Sue or our daughter, Jane. I needn't have worried. The number she handed me was for Hester's cell phone.

"Gorse," answered Hester.

"Houseman here. How was the big house?"

"Great, but later, right now you should know that they've located Jessica's silver 2000 Mercedes Benz SUV. It's been abandoned, in a place called Capron, Illinois."

"Where's that from Nation County?" I asked. I'd never heard of the place.

"Well, just a sec," she said, and I could hear paper rustling. Her map. "Okay, it's southwest of Lake Geneva, and northeast of Rockford. About thirty road miles from here."

"So, he's not headed toward Nation County?"

"Don't bet on it," she said. "The car was abandoned at a used car lot, and the owner is checking right now on whether or not he's missing a car. There's also a good chance he's headed home to Moline. Jessica apparently told him we were here, asking questions."

"Oh."

"There's absolutely no doubt that he had it. Jessica

told us that she'd 'left the keys in the car' and he took it."

"That's cute," I said. "Nice dodge."

"Shit, Houseman, her local attorney was there. She's hell on wheels, and she has just about every base in the world covered. She denies knowing how Peale got to Lake Geneva. We didn't reveal Tatiana to her, just asked how he'd gotten her car, and led into it." Hester sounded disgusted. "We got to her twice, though. I think she's finally getting really worried. And her aunt seemed to be a bit pissed off at her by the time we were done."

"Cool."

"Tell you what we'll do," she said. "You continue on, and if we get a make on a missing car from that lot in Capron, we'll have them tell you by radio. Just so you know as soon as possible."

"Right. Hey, Hester?"

"Yes?"

"If you do the brunch again tomorrow, could you bring me a doggy bag?"

I was about twenty miles east of the Mississippi and Nation County when Wisconsin State Radio contacted me again. They gave me a simple message. I was to be looking for a blue '96 Honda four-door. It had no plates, naturally, since it was stolen off a sales lot. The keys, according to the dispatcher, had been under the floor mat. No direction of travel was given, for the obvious reason that nobody knew one. I just had to assume he was headed our way.

I checked in with Dispatch in Nation County at 22:44 hours. The dispatcher, Norma, the new one, said I was to contact Borman via radio immediately. I did, and he asked me to meet him at the foot of the Mansion driveway.

The rain was steady as I got out of the car. Not hard, just one of those long, drawn-out rains that come in October, putting the last nail in summer's coffin, and giving us our first taste of the cold that was to come in the next few months. It was about forty degrees, or so, but felt much colder. I hurried across the soaked gravel road to Borman's squad car, carrying my green rubber raincoat. It's impossible to put the things on in a car, and by the time I would have gotten it on, I knew I'd already be in Borman's squad. I was startled when Sally just about knocked me over when she opened the front passenger door.

"You get in front, you'll never fit behind the cage," she said, and scurried past me to open the back door and squeeze in to the backseat. She left the back door open a crack, so she could get out without having somebody open it from the outside. There are no door handles on the inside of the back doors in a squad car. Makes it harder for prisoners to escape.

I dropped into the front passenger seat, knocking my left knee against the damned radio console, which was angled away for the driver, and encroached on the passenger's leg room. I shut the door.

"Shit weather," I said. "What's up?"

"What are we doing here?" asked Borman. "We can't see crap, nobody has come in or out for the last four hours, and I've been up since six this morning."

I was beginning to think the kid was taking a course in how to irritate a superior.

"Well, for starters, your friend 'Slasher' Peale left Lake Geneva shortly before I did. There's a good chance he's headed this way."

Silence.

"Then, there's the information we got that says he's really, really pissed at some of the folks in the house, up there." I shivered. "Got any coffee?"

He fished a thermos out of the space between the armrest and the steel safety plate of the plastic cage. "Here."

"Thanks. I've been up since seven, myself." I unscrewed the top, and Sally reached her hand through the sliding section of the cage, and handed me a Styrofoam cup out of the backseat. I poured the steaming coffee gingerly, sat the cup on the dash, and screwed the thermos cap back in place. "Who else we got available tonight?"

"Ten is the late car. He's on at midnight. That's it. Other than him, it's just me. And Sally."

"Damn," I said. "That means we stay here all night."

"What?"

"Yep. All night." I turned in the seat. "How about you, kid?" I asked Sally. "When you gotta be back at work?"

"Day off tomorrow," she said.

"Okay," I said, taking a sip of coffee from the cup. "Old coffee," I said. I sniffed. "What's that smell?"

"Smell?" asked Sally.

"Yeah, that weird smell."

"I don't smell anything," she said.

"You better tell him," said Borman. He was smiling. Sally took a deep breath. "It's garlic."

"What?"

"You know, like you put on bread. Garlic." She reached down to her utility belt, undid the little nylon pouch that we kept exam gloves in, and produced a small plastic bag with a small garlic medallion in it.

"You're kidding."

"Houseman, you can never be too safe," she said, replacing the bag. "Take it from me."

I sighed. "Okay, mother. Just keep it sealed up, okay?"

"You bet." She looked down, replacing the bag. "Want to see my crucifix?"

I laughed. "No. Honest to God . . ."

"No different than a ballistic vest," she said. "Insurance is insurance."

That reminded me of the matters at hand. "Now, can I ask you guys a question?" I looked at them both.

"Sure," said Borman.

"What are you doing down here?"

"Watching the place. Just like Lamar said."

I sighed, mostly for effect. "No. When you're all the way down here, all you can see is the road. You aren't supposed to be watching the road. You're supposed to be watching the house."

"We tried that," he said. "Kevin came out and told us to get out of the driveway. He's got that right, it's private property."

"The woods up there aren't private property, they belong to the state."

"But there's no road into the woods." He sounded exasperated.

"What kind of rain gear you got in here?" I asked.

"Hooded raincoat, like yours. Gortex overalls. Boots. But I'm not hiking up into those woods in the rain."

I made an effort to sound thoroughly disgusted. I think it worked. "No, you're not. Our suspect is probably in a blue '96 Honda four-door, no plates. I have no idea whether or not he's armed, so assume he is. Got that?"

"Yeah."

"Okay, I'm going to put my rain gear on, go into the woods, to where I can see the house. You stay down here, and keep alert. I'll call on my walkie if I see anything, and you do the same." I started to open the door.

"Wait," said Sally. "We've got the night-vision scope with us."

Our department had purchased some Russian Army surplus night vision gear in 1998. Right out of a commercial catalogue. It was inexpensive, and adequate, except the battery didn't last more than four hours. We had one battery, and it took a good four hours to recharge. The recharger, naturally, was in the office.

"I'll take it," I said. "How much time you got left on the battery?"

"A good three hours." Sally sounded apologetic. "We used 'em for a few minutes after we got here."

I would have done the same thing, but didn't say so. Instead, "I'll only use 'em when I think I need to."

"I really think we need two in the woods, and one down here," she said. "Much safer down here. Can I go?"

"You got rain gear?" She had guts.

"I'll make something work," she said. "Go get your stuff on."

I had a pair of waterproof winter boots in my trunk, along with my rain coveralls and a shelter half. Since it was impossible to dress in the car, by the time I got the stuff on I was wet all over.

I sloshed back over to Borman's car. Sally, being only about five feet tall, had been able to get most of his gear on while she sat in his car, so she was comparatively dry. She'd rolled up his coveralls, and looked totally lost in his hooded raincoat.

"How do I do my gun?" she asked.

"Keep it all under the coat, and when we get set up up there, unzip the bottom of the coat so you can reach the holster."

"Got it."

"You gonna be all right down here?" I asked Borman.

"Yes." He was the irritated one now.

"I dunno just how long we're going to be up there," I said, "but at least until three A.M. Don't go to sleep, and keep your car locked. You really don't want that bastard getting your car."

The odds on that were very slim, but I figured it'd help him stay awake.

Sally and I sat on the right side of the hood of Borman's car, as he crept up the drive with only his parking lights on. That way, we could be deposited without any sound of closing doors.

A minute later, she and I were standing in the cold

rain, watching the receding red glow of Borman's brake lights as he backed down the drive.

"Hope nobody sees that," said Sally.

"Not likely," I said. There were a lot of lights on in the house. Nobody looking our way from a lighted room would be able to see anything. "Let's go this way."

I led us to the left of the gate pillars, following the shoulder-high wall. As long as the house was lit, it was going to be easy to find the wall. Our landmark.

We went about twenty yards, to where the wall blended into the slope, and the line of trees became the demarcation between the Hunley property and the State of Iowa. It was easier to see than I had anticipated, because the house was so brightly lit. I ducked down and signaled Sally to follow me under a couple of big spruce trees. It was fairly dry under there, and it kept us out of the wind.

I knelt down, and opened the big plastic case that contained the night vision scope.

"This isn't so bad," she whispered.

"No, better than I thought." I fumbled a bit, got it by the big handle, and felt for the switch. I peered into the eyepiece, and was in a very brightly lit world of green hues. I swept the area, quickly. We were about fifty yards from the house, on the southwest corner. I could see pretty clearly to the opposite tree line behind the house, although the lights on the lower floor tended to overpower the scope. I looked to my right, back the way we had come. Clear. To my left, I could see about fifteen feet before the trees and undergrowth blocked the view. Behind us, it was even thicker. Good cover. I hit the zoom button, and everything got twice as big. Cool. That was a handy feature, but it was a two-edged sword. If you zoomed, your field of view was so small; you'd miss a lot of stuff. The secret was to use the zoom feature only when necessary.

I shut the night scope off, and put it back in the box, careful not to engage any latches that might make noise.

"Comfortable?" I asked.

"Yep."

"Good. Now let me tell you this . . ." and I explained the elevator shaft to the mine to her.

"You mean," she said, after I was done, "Peale could just pop up any time?"

"Yeah, sorta."

"Jesus Christ, Houseman."

"Don't get too worried. Just check around once in a while, that's all."

"Just where is this elevator shaft?"

"Well, now that's a good question." I grinned in the dark. "Somewhere to our right, I think, and a lot closer to the bluff."

"You think?" she hissed.

"It's in with some of the old Kommune foundations. Not sure just where."

"Jesus Christ."

"Don't know why you're worried," I said. "You've got the garlic." I got a discreet kick for that one.

For the next twenty-five minutes, nothing changed except the occasional occupant moving from room to room in the house. I found we could recognize them, sometimes, if they lingered in front of a window. I saw Huck, and Melissa, for sure. Otherwise, it was just cold and damp, with constant dripping as the rain filtered down through the trees.

Sally seemed to devote most of her time to looking toward our right.

Then lights started going off in the house. The parlor and dining room lights went first, then most of the lights in the kitchen. I could see Kevin at one point, very clearly, in the glazed main door. He just stood and stared out the door for a while, then disappeared from view.

"Sally?"

"What?"

"Use the night scope, and check the whole area for a

minute. Especially to the right. Make sure we aren't missing anything."

"Oooh. Okay."

After about a minute, she said, "Nothing."

We waited some more. Finally, she said, "Do you really think he might come here?"

"I don't want to take the chance that he will," I said.

Twenty minutes later, Sally spoke. "I thought I saw something."

"Where?"

"Over there."

That did me a lot of good. I could hear her fumbling for the night scope. "Just a sec..."

"Where?"

"Look toward the back door, then keep going to the right. About halfway to the tree line, I thought I saw something move...."

I looked. I saw nothing. Then I heard the click of the night scope being turned on.

"Jesus Christ!" I'd never heard somebody yell in a whisper before.

"What?"

"There's somebody out there!"

"Give me the scope."

"Just a minute..."

"Just give me the goddamned scope!" I hissed.

"Jeeez," she said, but handed it over, reluctantly. I was about to ask her where this somebody was, when I saw him. He was keeping low, and moving around the house from the back to the front, staying under the first floor windows, and apparently going to the front door.

"He looks like he's headed to the front door," I said.

I watched for a moment. The rain had let up a bit, but he was still difficult to make out. There was something about the way he walked that struck me as familiar.

"Call Borman," I whispered, "and alert him." Coming from the direction of the rear of the house, our intruder would have come up from the east, or bluff side.

Not from Borman's direction. I wanted Borman to be aware that he might have to move in a hurry.

Sally keyed the mike on her walkie-talkie, and said, "Eight? Eight?"

Either she'd had her receiver volume turned up earlier, or she'd bumped the dial when she took it out of the case. Either way, there was a loud scratching sound from her radio, and Borman clearly said "Eight..." in what I thought was a booming voice. I must have jumped a foot.

Sally was quick. Very. She had the volume back down before he finished with "... go ahead."

The man I was watching turned, and cocked his head. He might have heard the radio, but probably not clearly. He listened for a few seconds, and then turned back toward the house. But in that few seconds, I hit the zoom button, and I made him.

"Son of a bitch," I said.

"What, what?" said Sally. Over in her direction, I could hear Borman's voice, barely audible now, calling us.

"Answer him, tell him to stand by, we have movement."

She did.

"I made our man out there," I said.

"Peale?"

"William Chester."

THIRTY-ONE

Wednesday, October 11, 2000
23:30
_____

"The vampire hunter?" asked Sally.

"Yep." He was holding very still, as I looked. There was no doubt. I could see bulges on his back and down one side, that looked like that pack he'd had earlier, and something else I couldn't quite make out. But it was him, all right. I watched him move toward the porch, creep up the steps, and then crouch down using a pillar as cover, and peer into the house through the glazed doors. He froze there. After a minute, I handed the night scope to Sally.

"Look at the front porch, behind the right-hand pillar."

Without the benefit of the scope, the night was suddenly much darker.

"Oh, yeah. I see him." After a second, she said, "Carl, ya think, I mean, since he hunts vampires, you know..."

"That he's got one now?"

"Yeah. Like that."

"Naw. I think he's still looking." I tried to sound convincing, but I was thinking on another track altogether. I was hurriedly going back through all the evidence regarding Dan Peale. Could he and Chester be the same person? They were close to the same height, if the data on Peale was correct. They could be of an age. He'd appeared just as we were getting into Peale, and that had been a remarkable coincidence even at the time.

"What's he doing?" I whispered to Sally.

"Just squatting there," she said.

I picked up my own walkie-talkie, and called Borman, sotto voce.

"We have a man on the grounds," I said, "but I believe I recognize him. Whiskey Charlie."

"Ten-nine?" he crackled back.

"Initials Whiskey Charlie."

There was a pause, then, "Ah, ten-four. The expert, then?"

"Ten-four. That's the one. Heads up, he might know more than we do. Ah, and let's go code sixty-one on this...." No names, no locations.

"Ten-four."

I placed the walkie back in its carrier. "What's he doing, now?"

"Hasn't moved."

My mind was flying, trying to evaluate our situation. It occurred to me it was possible that if Chester wasn't Peale, he may have followed Peale to the house. If we approached, we would cause some sort of commotion, especially if we confronted him on the porch. If Peale were in the house, he could well take off.

But the actions of the people in the house, at least those we'd seen, seemed very normal.

Which left me with Peale not in the house, but meant

that Chester could be Peale and just be waiting for the residents to go to bed before he entered.

That didn't add up, really, either. I completed my little circle of reasoning.

"Bullshit," I said, "it's just Chester."

"I know it's just Chester," answered Sally, "and now he's moving," thereby relinquishing her right to the night scope.

"Give me the scope," I said.

She did, and I picked him up as he crossed the porch and kept going left, toward the far side of the house. He hesitated at the corner, then disappeared around the side of the house.

"Shit. He went around the other side."

What to do? Move, and possibly reveal our position? Stay put and never see where he went? One set of night-vision gear didn't help, although I probably wouldn't have split us up, regardless.

"Okay, Sally. We gotta go to our right. We'll go about a hundred feet, then head toward the house. Maybe fifty feet, to the big tree that's in the yard, there. We'll be out of the trees, so we lie down. Got that?"

"Yeah."

"Okay. We stay on the ground, and we look at the back side of the house, and this side, and I think we also get the front from there." I began moving. "Keep it quiet," I said, "and just hang on to my coat." I had the scope, and could see very clearly, indeed. Sally would be moving into darker ground without that benefit.

It took us about a long minute to cover the distance. I glanced at the house through the scope, and saw that we could see the back and the near side. Just the edge of the front porch. That would have to do.

"We're at the tree. It's on your right."

"I can see it when we're this close," she said.

I looked up, without the night scope. The tree loomed large, and distinctly. I cleared my throat quietly. "Okay. Well, then..."

With that, we both lay down in the wet grass, in the rain, and waited.

I handed the scope to Sally. "You watch, I'm going to try to contact the office from here."

"Right." She eagerly took the vision gear from me. As soon as she started looking, she said "Nothing." That at least let me know the equipment was still functioning.

I tried the office three times on the INFO channel, to no avail. Then I tried Borman on the OPS channel. Damn. We were now way over his radio horizon, and had even more trees between us. I'd probably have to stand up to get either one of them.

We lay there in complete silence for a good fifteen minutes, and I was beginning to believe that Chester, or whoever he really was, had either gotten into the house, or left altogether.

"You think Mr. Chester could be Dan Peale?" whispered Sally.

"Possible," I whispered back. But I'd had a little time to think about it. "Don't think so, though. I don't think the timing's right for some stuff." But I was tired, and I couldn't be absolutely sure that there *hadn't* been time for him to be in both Nation County and in Lake Geneva. "Not sure, though."

"How do we find out for sure?" she asked.

I hate whispered conversations. If we're supposed to be quiet, then, by God, shut up. In this case, however, it had a benefit. Because she'd asked the question, I stopped planning alternative approaches to reacquiring Chester, and realized that Borman was the only person on our side who'd actually ever seen Dan Peale. And I didn't think Borman had ever actually seen William Chester. How do we find out, indeed?

"We let Borman take a look at him," I said. "Now hush up."

I got a sharp little fist in the ribs for that.

We lay there in the rain for another five minutes, as I tried to persuade myself that patience was, indeed, a virtue. We'd already moved once. Twice might be pushing our luck too far. I was a little concerned, though, because the area where I thought that elevator shaft into the mine was located was now more behind us than to our right. All I needed was for Peale to emerge from the ground at our rear.

"You might use the scope," I whispered, "and check behind us once in a while."

I could almost hear her mental relays click into place. "Shit," she whispered. "Shit, shit, shit..." as she rolled over, and raised her head to see behind us.

After a second, I made out, "Clear." There was a rubbery rustling as she rolled back onto her stomach, to see ahead again.

It was relatively quiet for almost a minute, with only the heavy dripping of the tree to listen to. Then, Sally made a subdued noise that sounded like a cross between a balloon with a slow leak, and a frog with sinus trouble. As she did, I caught a faint movement at the far end of the Mansion. It had to be Chester, coming around to the rear.

"Give me the scope," I hissed. Reluctantly, she did. I pressed it to my eye, and sure enough, there was William Chester in all his green glory. As he crept under the rear kitchen window, the interior lights suddenly came on, and framed him in a brilliant rectangle. He ducked back, and I blinked, because of the "bloom" of the night scope as it failed to adjust instantly to the light.

I lost sight of him. At first, I thought he'd stepped back around the corner, but as I made a precautionary sweep of the area, I caught a glimpse of him moving to our right, toward the bluff and the trees. Toward the same area where Old Knockle had spotted him and the illegal car on the day of Edie's wake. Of course. He must have parked down there again, and was on his way back to the road.

I stood, to get a better view of him as he faded into the wet woods, and said to Sally in a normal tone of voice, "Call Borman. Have him go to the face of the cliff, down at the highway. He's heading for the highway!" I hated to move Borman, but we needed him to get a look at Chester, to make sure he wasn't Peale. We also needed him to make sure that Chester didn't get away in a car.

I started off toward the bluff, a good distance behind Chester, but I knew where he was headed. I could hear Sally behind me, telling Borman to get moving.

Running while holding a night scope to your eye is about impossible. There's no compensation for the bouncing you do as you move, and everything is just a blur. I put the scope at my side, and kept moving, but slower, since I couldn't see much in the natural light, and I didn't want to run smack into a tree. The damned night scope had degraded my night vision for a few minutes.

"Where are we going?" asked Sally.

"He went into the woods just ahead of us here," I said. "It'll take him a few minutes to get down a ravine that's just ahead here somewhere." I put the scope back to my eye, and looked around. I thought I could see the upper reaches of the ravine just to our right.

"Tell Borman to shut his headlights off before he gets to the highway. We don't want our boy seeing him coming."

Sally was a good dispatcher. She repeated exactly what I'd said into her mike. While she did, it occurred to me to try the little infrared searchlight that was a part of the scope. It only had a range of about twenty-five yards, but it made everything within that distance much clearer through the scope. It also drained the battery about four times as fast.

The beauty of the IR searchlight is that people can't

see it without a night scope of their own. Wily, those Russians.

Sally had a hand on my raincoat as I slowly threaded my way into the ravine. The rocks, which had been slippery the other day, were like greased marble now. It was very slow going.

"I can't see shit," said Sally.

"Good thing," I said. "Stop here."

She did. "What for?"

"He's got to be down the ravine from us," I said. "Let me watch for a few seconds. I think I should be able to pick up movement." I must have watched for a good fifteen seconds, which seemed like forever. Nothing. No sound, no sign of Chester.

"See him?"

"Nope. Nothing."

"Can I," asked Sally, "take a peek at where we're going? It'd help."

Good idea. As we were transferring possession of the night scope, there was a rattling among the rocks somewhere below us. We fumbled the scope, and I heard it hit what sounded like a wet branch, and then a sharp click as it struck a rock.

"Shit."

"Sorry, I'm sorry," said Sally.

"You got a flashlight?" I asked, disgusted with myself.

"Yeah, a Mini-Mag, in here somewhere...." And I heard the sound of her raincoat being unzipped and pulled about as she tried to find a path to her utility belt.

"Not your fault," I said, waiting for her to hand me the light. I wasn't going to move, because my only orientation for finding the night scope was the knowledge that it was just about straight down from my feet.

I saw the glow of her little flashlight still inside her raincoat. She must have hit the switch. She was about to cast light all over the place as she brought it out.

"No! Turn it off!" I whispered as loudly as I could.

She tried, she really did. I think she reached her other hand inside the twisted raincoat to try to turn the light off without fumbling it, too. In doing so, she lost her balance, and disappeared with a thud and a bump and a rush of raincoat against branches.

It was thunderously quiet.

"Shit, Houseman" came a faint voice. "I fell."

"You okay?"

"No."

I slowly bent my knees, hanging on to a branch. I had no idea whether I was on a large rock, or just a small one, and I sure as hell didn't think I'd help Sally if I came crashing down on her.

"What's wrong?"

"My butt hurts," she said.

"You still got that flashlight?"

"Yeah."

"Go ahead and turn it on," I said. "We gotta get you up."

The light came on right beneath me. She had fallen about four feet.

"Anything else hurt?" I asked.

"Just my butt," she said. She slowly got to her feet, which brought her head to about the level of my knees. "Everything else seems fine."

Although the rock I was standing on was pretty big, I was about three inches from the edge. I took about a half step back, and said, "As long as you're down there, see if you can find the scope."

She shone the light downward, and said, "Got it." She reached down and handed it up to me.

I laid it on my rock, and reached down with my left hand. "Grab hold, and I'll get you up here. Turn off the light before I pull, okay?"

She did. I counted three, heaved, and up she came.

I peered through the night scope as soon as she was stable on the rocks. It still worked. One thing about Red

Army gear, it's known for being rugged. I panned down the ravine. Nothing.

"See anything?"

"Nope. Even if he didn't hear us, he's long gone." I decided a little more noise didn't really matter. "See if you can reach Borman," I said. "See what he's got down at the bottom of this ravine."

She did. He reported that all he could see was what he thought was a car. I guessed he still had his lights off. At least he was getting better at following instructions.

"Tell him we're on the way down, and we think the suspect is ahead of us."

She did, and we began moving down the ravine again. It took us about five or six minutes, but we made it to the bottom.

With my night scope, I could see the car Borman meant, along with Borman and his car about fifty yards up the road, off on the shoulder. There was no sign of our intrepid Mr. Chester. I looked back up the ravine, and over the parts of the bluff below the trees. Nothing.

"Tell Borman to come on over," I said. I was disgusted with myself, and with the way things had turned out.

We checked on the car. A rental out of Jollietville, Wisconsin. No wants, no reports of any activity concerning it. Just a bland car.

We looked into the car from the outside, but there was nothing in the interior except a receipt on the passenger seat. I could see the header of the rental company on the pink paper. No name. The doors were locked. Lack of clutter was to be expected from a rental. None of us could read the information on the sheet through the rain-spattered window because the drops reflected our flashlight beams. In a moment of inspiration, I lifted the night scope to my eye, and hit the zoom button. No reflections, and the paper became twice as big. "William Chester," I said. "Rented yesterday, at one-fifteen P.M."

When such a simple thing as thinking to use the

night scope makes you feel better, you know you're having a bad night. The fact that it was a rental though, and not stolen, confirmed in my mind that Chester definitely was not our vampire.

"Where the hell'd he get to?" asked Sally.

A very good question. My first thought was that he'd just climbed out of the ravine when I dropped the night scope, and had gone deep into the trees. Either that, or he knew about that private cable car arrangement.

In my experience, the most exotic explanation is just about invariably wrong. "Probably back over into the trees," I said. Even with a night scope, there was no way that one or two of us would be able to track him down in the trees, the underbrush and the rain.

I looked at Borman. "Not one of our better nights," I said. "How about giving Sally and me a ride back up to the Mansion? That's probably where he's headed."

"Sure. You think he's really Peale?"

It was somehow reassuring that it had occurred to Borman, too. "Not now. This car isn't something snatched off the lot, it's a rental."

"Oh."

"But be damned careful. Somebody else could be doing some hunting tonight, too."

"Right." He sounded just a little unsure. Good. At least he'd keep his doors locked.

"Okay," I said, "after you drop us off this time, come back down around here, and set up someplace where you can watch this car. If he sees us leave, I think he might try to leave."

"Could he try to get back to the Mansion on us?" I liked that. It was the first time Borman had used "us," and it made me think he might be coming around.

"I dunno," I said. "He's a persistent bastard, but he's gotta give up sometime."

We piled in Borman's car, and off we went. We'd find out.

When we got to the top of the drive, and we were

getting out of the car, I turned on the night scope to check the front of the house. The thing flickered, and went dead.

"Shit," I said. I tapped it a few times. Nothing. I tapped it a bit harder with the heel of my hand. Nothing. I removed the battery, wiped it with my hand, and reinserted it, making sure it wasn't shorting out due to the rain. No luck.

"What's wrong with it?" asked Sally.

"Battery seems dead. Nothing works."

"Great."

"Well," I said, "that just means we stay here near the front. I don't want to go making a lot of noise stomping through the brush."

Borman rolled his car quietly back down the hill, and Sally and I trudged the last few yards to the edge of the gate and the wall. We found a relatively dry spot where a pine branch hung over the wall, and hunkered down there.

"Did you bring the case for the night scope?"

Damn. Of course I hadn't. I'd left it at our first surveillance point.

"We'll find it at first light," I said. "Ought to be about six-thirty or so, up here on the bluffs." I looked at my watch. It was 01:19. "About five hours from now."

We watched the front of the house in turns, after about 01:45. One of us would doze a bit under the trees, in a crouch with our back against the tree trunk, while the other watched. We agreed on thirty-minute shifts. Sally stood first watch.

Sally was the one watching at about 04:40 when we heard the noise. I wasn't dozing at the time, and joined her at the wall before she even tried to get me.

We both listened. Nothing. Just the patter of raindrops, and the heavier dripping from the eaves of the house, striking the porch roof.

"What was it?"

"It sounded to me," said Sally, "like somebody hitting something. Thumping sound, like wood on wood. Two, maybe three times."

"I only heard one," I said. "Loud, but soft, you know?"

"Yep."

"Loud footsteps, maybe?"

"I don't think so," she said. "Maybe like somebody throwing a snowball at the side of the house."

Obviously there was no snow. But she'd described the sound perfectly.

We waited. Any more dozing was out of the question. I really missed that night scope.

About ten minutes later, I could have sworn I heard a muffled male voice, angry. It sounded like it came from inside the Mansion.

"You hear that?"

"Yeah," I said. "Shhh."

It was quiet again, but not for as long.

Even in the dark, we could see the front door fly open as a figure ran down the porch steps, slipped, fell flat in the driveway, rolled, got up, and came running toward us as fast as it could go. The sound of bare feet slapping onto the drive was audible even at our distance, and got louder as the figure approached.

Sally and I didn't utter a word. We just both started moving quickly to our left, to intercept whoever it was.

We beat whoever it was to the gate by about two seconds.

"Stop!" I said it loud enough to be clearly heard. The figure didn't even slow down.

I didn't have time to think, I just stepped out, lowered my right shoulder, and got bowled over by the impact. But I hung on, and rolled on top.

Sally shined her flashlight on us, just in time for me to see Toby's mouth open as he took a deep breath and screamed right in my face.

I was startled, but clamped a hand over his mouth, and said, loudly, "It's just cops!"

He went silent, but I kept my hand in place. His eyes were darting, and I could feel his chest heaving under me. I shifted, to let him breathe, and he started to try to get up.

"Stay put!"

He was looking right at me, but I don't think he had the slightest idea who I was.

"Get ten-seventy-eight," I said to Sally. If we ever needed help, it was going to be now. Whatever had scared Toby out of that house. . . .

His first words, at least those that were understandable, were "Oh, fuck, oh shit."

"Toby, what are you doing here?"

I got a frightened, blank look. Sally stopped talking on her portable long enough to say, "He signed himself out."

Of course. Voluntary commitment meant that he could sign out of the treatment center whenever he wanted to.

"Listen up!" I said to him. "Get a grip!"

"He's here!"

"Who?"

"Dan, you dumb fuck! He's here, I gotta go . . ." And with that he began to struggle to get away from me.

"Settle down, damn it!" I needed him to at least stop struggling.

It was then that he brought his fist up and smacked me on the left side of my head. I think it was a reaction, nothing more, but I responded by hitting him squarely in the face. I felt his head thud back down into the drive, and saw his eyes cross. But he stopped struggling.

"Ow," he said groggily. He had one of those instant nosebleeds, that looked much worse than it was, because the rain was keeping his face wet. "That hurt."

No time for an apology, although I was aware of a

surprised look from Sally. I was just glad I hadn't hit the
stud between his eyes.

"Tell me what's happening in there!"

"Don't fuckin' hit me again," he said.

"Talk!"

"Dan's back, man. He's in there, and he's really, really pissed. I told you fuckers, he's not gonna like this
shit. I told you!"

"Who all's in there with him?"

"What?"

I grabbed him by the collar, becoming aware for the
first time that he was clad in flannel pajamas. "Get your
shit together," I said. "Tell me who else is in that house
with Dan." I said it slowly, and fairly quietly.

He snuffled some blood in his nose, grimaced, and
said, "Me. Me, and Kevin, and Huck and Melissa."

"What about Hanna?"

"I dunno," he mumbled, sniffed, and then sneezed,
covering both of us with a fine spatter of blood droplets.
"Excuse me." He wiped his nose with the back of his
hand.

I had a dilemma. We had to get into the house, and
fast. I didn't want to take a chance and leave Sally out
here with Toby, in case Dan got by me and came out this
way. Yet, I didn't want to have to drag Toby into the
house with us, either. I couldn't cut him loose, and have
him wandering about, because he wasn't in any condition to be left on his own.

I stood him up. "We're going into the house. Come
on." I started guiding him toward the Mansion, and he
actually took two or three steps before it dawned on
him.

"No way!" He started to twist, and I was afraid he'd
tear his pajamas and break free.

In a moment of inspiration, I grabbed both his arms,
and got right back in his face. "I think Dan's out here."

His eyes widened.

I was lying, but what the hell. It was his turn to be deceived.

I must have been very convincing, because Sally reached for her gun, and started to look behind her.

The three of us hustled across the drive, and up the porch steps. Toby was looking behind us all the way. Good. Sally had her service weapon out, and I pulled mine, as well.

"What did the office say?"

"Borman's on his way up now," she said. There wasn't a hint of a quaver in her voice. Dispatch training.

"And?"

"They're rounding up everybody they can get," she said.

Just as we reached the door, I heard an engine roaring up the drive. Borman. We paused on the porch, as he came steaming up the drive, through the gate, and slid to a halt just a few feet from the bottom of the steps. He jumped out, and came running up the steps.

"Whaddya got?" he asked, breathing heavily.

We told him, in about five seconds.

"Now," I ended, "you shove Toby here in your car, lock the doors and make sure the cage is tight. Then follow us in."

He didn't even ask a question. That was the way it was supposed to work.

Sally and I entered the house.

As we passed through the main doors, the patter of the rain was filtered out, and the sudden quiet was remarkable. I hadn't realized how much the sound of the rain had pervaded our world outside.

We stood still, the sound of the water dripping from our rain gear making the only noise in the whole, huge house. It was completely dark, and very warm in contrast with the outside temperature.

"Use your Mini-Mag," I said, "and see if you can find the lights."

A moment later, the overhead light in the entryway came on.

We looked around. Nothing appeared disturbed. I holstered my gun for a second, slipped out of my raincoat and let it drop to the floor. I pulled my gun again. "Take off your coat," I said softly. "It'll be quieter."

I heard her removing it. Silence again. Then, a little bump of a sound, from the direction of the inglenook under the stairs. I glanced at Sally. She nodded that she'd heard it, too. The two of us moved very slowly toward the foot of the stairs, and into the darkness again.

Sally shined her light into the inglenook. Curled up under the wooden bench seat was a body clad in a flannel nightgown. Hanna.

"Hanna," I said. "You all right?"

She simply stared.

"Hanna?" said Sally.

"Go away," Hanna hissed.

"Where's everybody else? Come on, Hanna, tell me," I said evenly.

At that point, there was a noticeable suction in the air as the main doors opened and Borman came in. Hanna curled up tightly, and covered her eyes with her forearm.

"Leave me alone. Go away."

"Hanna, look at me. Tell me where everybody is."

She did look at me, but she didn't speak. Then her gaze shifted up, toward the staircase. I didn't know whether she was looking for an escape path, or hoping to see someone start down the stairs.

"Just tell me where everybody is," I said quietly. "That's all you have to do."

"I don't know," she said, in a faint, shaky voice. "Maybe you better go upstairs."

"Why upstairs?" I hoped.

"I'm not going up there," she said. "But I think you better go upstairs."

"Upstairs?" I asked. "Who all's upstairs?"

"I think Melissa and Huck are up there," said Hanna. "Please don't talk to me. You'll make him mad at me."

"What's going on up there?" I asked.

"He's angry with them," she said, very calmly and simply. "I heard it."

"Where's Kevin?" asked Sally.

"He left," said Hanna. "Please, please don't talk to me anymore."

"There will be some more police coming," I said. "Don't be afraid of them. Officer Borman here will take you to his car. You'll be safe there."

Before he could protest, Sally and I were already on the bottom steps. I was leaving him with his car, because I thought he could more ably hold his own against Dan Peale, if he showed up to get at the two in the car. Sally was good, but I thought she'd be better off with either Borman or me. And I wasn't too keen about going upstairs alone, to tell the truth.

I reached out and flipped the switch at the bottom of the stair, and the chandelier above the landing came on. We headed up the stairs.

At the top, I looked down the hall. Everything seemed perfectly fine, except for one jarring note. There were wood splinters on the hall carpet, near the door across from Edie's room.

"Whose room is that?" Sally whispered.

"Edie's on the right, Melissa on the left, I think," I said. I saw the switch plate, and turned on the hall light.

"Oh boy."

"Let me go first," I said.

"No problem."

"Keep alert."

"Oh, yeah."

Except for the sounds of our muffled steps on the carpet, it was absolutely quiet. A very bad sign.

I glanced in Edie's opened door as we got to it. It seemed empty. I stuck my head in. All looked to be as we had left it the last time we were here. Except for some purplish flowers on the bed.

"It's clear," I said, as I pulled back into the hall.

We crossed diagonally to Melissa's shattered door. It had obviously been hit very hard.

"You stay here in the hall. He could be anywhere. Don't come in unless I tell you to."

"Okay," said Sally.

I looked more closely at Melissa's door as I entered her room. It had been struck repeatedly with considerable force, probably kicked. There were two places where something had penetrated completely, and the removal of whatever it was had pulled fragments out into the hall. Probably the kicker's foot.

I reached around the door frame, found the light switch, and turned it on.

The door was off its hinges at the bottom, and I pushed it back with my shoulder as I crossed the threshold. The first thing I saw was the overturned chair. The low bookshelf under the window was also overturned, the books spilled out onto the rug. The curtains had been pulled down, the dangling rod bent but still in the bracket. The window was opened about three inches. I moved my eyes to the right, and saw that the mattress was half off the bed frame, and the sheet and blankets were on the floor. There was a broken bed lamp near the head of the bed, and a framed picture all askew on the wall beside it. In the plaster wall was a large dent, at about my eye level. Another, a little lower, with what looked to be blood in the center. I followed the logical line downward, and there was a pool of blood on the floor, at the corner of the bed. And a foot with a bloody, white cotton sock on it just visible as it protruded from the space between the bed and the wall.

I was over there in two steps. I peered down into the narrow space, and saw a crumpled body in a pair of pink polka-dotted cotton pajama bottoms and a blue T-shirt. The body was on its left side, facing the wall, and the knees were drawn up toward the chest, and the right arm was bent over the head, the elbow covering the face, in a familiar protective posture. The left arm wasn't visible. There was quite a bit of blood, mostly dried.

The purplish red hair told me it was Melissa.

I put my gun in my holster, and leaned gingerly on the bed, reached down, and felt for a carotid pulse. She flinched, startling me, and filling me with relief at the same time.

"Melissa," I said, "it's me, Houseman. We're here. It's going to be all right."

There was a slight movement, and her left hand moved, just a bit. She made a weak "thumbs up" sign.

"Sally!"

I unclipped my walkie-talkie from my belt, and called Dispatch, as Sally entered the room, and hurried over.

"Comm, Three, ten-thirty-three."

Because we'd prerequested help, the dispatch center was unusually alert.

"Three, go," came snapping back.

"Comm, we're at the Mansion, we have a civilian down, multiple injuries, need a ten-fifty-two. This is ten-thirty-three."

It never hurts to repeat the 10-33.

"Ten-four, Three."

I shoved the walkie-talkie in my back pocket, and watched as Sally lay on the bed, reached down, and took Melissa's pulse. We couldn't move her, in case there was a spinal or severe internal injury, until we got help and some equipment.

"I can't see my watch," said Sally. To read her watch and take Melissa's pulse, she had to have both arms down into the small space that contained the victim. It was too dark in that crack to see the hands. "Tell me to 'go' and 'stop' when fifteen seconds are up."

I looked at my watch. When the second hand reached the numeral six, I said "Go!" I watched it sweep through fifteen seconds. "Stop!"

"Okay, when the fifty-two goes ten-eight," said Sally, "tell Comm to relay we have rapid, shallow breathing, weak pulse of ninety-five."

I did. "Comm, Three, when the ambulance starts to roll, tell 'em victim has rapid, shallow breathing, weak pulse of ninety-five." They had me repeat it, and I complied.

I didn't want to leave Melissa, but we didn't know what else we had going on. I checked her bathroom, found nobody, and came back into the bedroom. I took a second to study the scene more closely, and tapped Sally on the shoulder.

She looked up from Melissa. "Yeah?"

"Looks like the door was kicked in fast. While she was sleeping. Looks like she tried to escape out the window and he got in too fast. See?"

Sally looked around. "Yeah."

"And he slammed her head into the wall," I said, indicating the dents. "Twice, at least." I didn't say it, but it looked as if he'd shoved the back of her head into the wall the first time, and the face into it the second, as there didn't seem to have been much blood on the back of her head. "How's she doing?"

"No heavy bleeding I can see," Sally said. "You might take a look out in the hall. Just past this door. I noticed it while I was waiting. A heck of a dent in the wall, across the hall," she said. She bent back over the small space containing Melissa.

I went to the door and looked. The dent was very similar to the head impressions on Melissa's wall. I stepped back into the bedroom.

"That doesn't add up," I said.

"How are you doing?" said Sally to Melissa. I heard a response, but couldn't make it out. Sally looked up, and said, "She says fine." She mouthed the word "shock."

I nodded. "Ask her where Huck is, if you can . . ." and pulled my walkie-talkie out again. "Comm, Three?"

"Three?"

"Yeah, how we comin' with the ten-fifty-two?"

"Ambulance is ten-eight, ten-seventy-six your location. ETA less than five."

"Ten-four." At least, when the ambulance got to us, we could move Melissa. I was about to ask if we had anybody close to escort them, when I heard a squeak of tires outside. I looked out the window, and saw the Freiberg PD car in the drive. Byng. He'd be able to help the ambulance crew.

It took the ambulance another three minutes to make it up the drive, but it seemed like an hour. I contacted them on my walkie-talkie, and told them we were in the house, and not to come in unescorted. As I looked out the window, I could see two white sheriff's cars, and a black state patrol car around the drive.

I tapped Sally on the shoulder again.

"Yeah?"

"I'm gonna look for the rest of 'em. Our boy has to be here somewhere. He's probably high on meth or ecstasy, or both. Draw your weapon. If Peale comes into the room, if you think you have time, tell him to stop."

She nodded.

"If you don't think you have time, shoot the fucker. Shoot until your gun is empty. You understand?"

"Yeah, but . . ."

"Just do it. You gotta protect her, too," I said, motioning toward Melissa.

My trip down the hall was a little tense. I entered each room in turn, and found nobody home. No evidence of a struggle. Nothing. That left the third floor.

I hustled back down the hall to Sally.

"Sally? It's me!" I said that very deliberately before I stuck my head in the door.

"Okay," she said. As I looked in, I saw that she had both hands on her pistol. Good.

"I'm going upstairs. Nothing on this floor but us folks."

She nodded. "Melissa says that Huck tried to help her. She doesn't know where she is."

I hate going up a stair when I believe there's somebody at the top who wants to kill me. I really, really hate that. But if Huck was alive, odds were that she was up there, too.

I figured I might as well go up in a hurry. I had my gun in my right hand, and tried the door with my left. It opened easily. A bad sign. It should have been locked, I thought, unless Dan Peale had gone up with a key.

I took two deep breaths, and then just ran up the damned stair.

The upper floor turned out to be just as empty as it was the day we searched it. I double checked, even under the bed and in the little slot between the refrigerator and the wall. Empty. So was the back stair leading down to the kitchen. And that door turned out to be locked.

I went back to check Sally and Melissa, and found a real crowd.

An ambulance crew of two women and one man were there, just getting started. We moved the bed away from Melissa while the smaller of the women EMTs wedged herself into the widening space, and began taking vitals. The only sound in the room was the puffing of the blood pressure collar.

"Nobody on three," I said to Sally. "Back door's locked."

"Where . . . ?"

"I don't know," I said.

"Okay," said an EMT, "cervical collar."

She was handed one, and she pushed the bed away from the wall another foot. In a few seconds, she looked up, and said, "Backboard."

We shoved the bed back about five feet; they slipped a backboard against Melissa, tightened the straps, and gently rolled her over onto her back.

She looked like hell, with her left eye swollen out almost as far as her nose, and her left ear had a vertical tear in it that split the upper portion in half. That could have been from her head hitting the wall. That hard, she had to have at least a concussion. There was a lot of blood clotted on her face, her nose looked broken, and her lower lip was split. She opened her right eye, and said something. Sally leaned in, to try to hear over the rasp of opening Velcro and the tearing of bandage packs.

"What?"

Melissa said something again. Sally answered her with, "We will, don't worry, we will." Melissa spoke again, and I heard the words "Huck," and "stop."

Sally stood, and turned to me. "She says that we gotta help Huck. She thinks he took her with him."

"Did she say Dan or Dan Peale?"

"Just a sec," said Sally, and leaned over Melissa once more. They were just putting an O_2 mask on her, and just the glimpses of her split lip moving as she tried to talk made me wince. They had a small problem with moving the blood matted hair from her cheeks and mouth on the left, finally using alcohol wipes to get it loose before securing the transparent mask over her face.

Sally straightened up. "Yep. Dan. It's him, for sure."

"I'll bet he thinks he killed her," I said. "And I'll bet he gave Huck the same treatment, outside in the hall."

"I agree," said Sally.

We were both moving into the hallway as we talked.

In the hall, we met up with Borman, Byng, and the state trooper, who were just getting to the top of the stairs.

"He's hurt one of the girls pretty damned bad," I said, "and he went after another one. We think"—and I pointed to the dent in the wall—"that's from her head. He kicked in this door. I already checked up on third. Empty."

"You guys need help?" croaked a voice coming up the stairs.

Lamar. He sounded like he had strep throat.

"What're you doing here?" I asked. "You're sick."

"Right," he scratched. "Don't worry about me. Maybe you should see this first," he said. "They told me to stop at the office for this." It was almost painful to hear him. He handed me a piece of the ubiquitous dispatch notepaper; used computer sheets with the perfs still attached.

I read the note. Hester had phoned our office, about 12:20 A.M. Told I was busy, she left a brief message.

"Hester says to tell you that subject Tat tells her subj DP is mad +++. He thinks subjs at Mansion have been making up lies re him and telling them to her and you. Hester says subj Tat tells that subj Huck has been snitched off. You should call her ASAP in am."

Written in at the bottom was Hester's cell phone number. I put it in my pocket.

"Okay. Watch out for him," I said. "I don't know if he's armed this time, but he's sure as hell violent. Hester says he's mad at the people here in the house, and we know he snorts and probably mainlines crystal meth and ecstasy, and he thinks he's immortal. Really," I added, seeing the look on some of the faces.

"You got anybody but one victim?" said Lamar, scratchy but loud, from the bottom of the stair behind us.

"Not yet, but let's go over it again, just to be sure," I said.

Where the hell was Huck? The basement?

No. The basement had been checked by the time we got back to the main floor.

"God, Houseman," said Sally, "Huck's as good as dead."

"Not necessarily," I said. "He could have killed her right here, but he didn't. Why take her somewhere else? To keep her alive awhile." I didn't want to think of why.

As far as I could see, the only other route off the cliff, other than stomping down through the woods and the ravine, would be to go down that old elevator shaft we'd found out about.

I explained to Lamar and the rest about the possibility of an elevator shaft down into the mine. I also explained that we didn't know exactly where the shaft was. As I did so, I remembered a conversation I'd had.

"But I know who does," I said, with a smile. "Our man, Toby."

As we exited the Mansion, I was surprised to see it was much lighter. Sunrise on a rainy day can sneak up on you.

Toby and Hanna were still in the back of Borman's car, being guarded by a state trooper. Excellent.

As I opened the back door of the idling squad, and motioned him out, Toby said, "Are you gonna beat me again?"

Coming from somebody with a little dried blood on his face, and a clot in one nostril, it sounded worse than it was.

"Probably not," I said. I shrugged at the trooper. "He hit me first." Lame. I knew that when I said it. The trooper didn't say a word.

I helped Toby out of the backseat, and stood him up. "Two things. Was Peale in the house when you came out, or had he been there and gone? And I gotta know where that damned elevator shaft is, and I gotta know now."

"What elev—"

I really got in his face. Well, to within three or four inches, I think. It probably looked like I was going to bite him.

"Dan Peale wants to kill you," I said, "as soon as he's done with Huck. Got that?"

He blinked, but didn't say anything.

"I think the only way he ain't gonna kill you is if we find him first. Think I'm right?"

"Yeah. Yeah, I do."

"Wonderful. Now, was he in the house, or did you hide and just get up the guts to run when you knew he was gone?"

He kind of hung his head.

"That's what I thought. Do you know how long it was that you hid, before you knew he had left?"

"Maybe ten minutes."

"Don't fuck with me, Toby!"

"Half an hour!" he said instantly. "Half an hour. For sure."

"Did he have Huck with him?"

"It sounded like it," he said softly.

"What do you mean?"

"Something bumped on the stairs. He was dragging something, I think."

I took a deep breath. Hell, he probably couldn't have stopped Peale anyway. But Huck had tried to help Melissa. He should have tried. I was sick of him, but I needed him. "Let's go to the elevator shaft. Now."

We did. A whole bunch of us, in fact. Toby, Sally, Lamar, Byng, two troopers, and me. We walked right past the tree that Sally and I had gone to when we tried to close in on Chester, and a little way into the woods, ending up less than a hundred feet from the head of the ravine we'd negotiated only a couple of hours ago. We stopped, and Toby pointed to an old foundation that was cluttered with dead leaves and some decaying branches.

"There. That's it."

"That?"

"Yeah. The door's in the wall on this side."

I moved around the foundation. Sure enough, standing on the bluff side of the rock-lined excavation, I could make out an old, wooden door frame, with a half dozen vertical slats and an angled crosspiece forming a door. The wood had faded to gray, and the edges were rotting, but it was a functional door, nonetheless.

I looked at Sally. She and I had just missed it last night.

"How do you get in?" I asked, as I gingerly lowered myself into the wet leaves on the floor.

"Move the rock at the bottom of the door," he said, from above me.

I looked. There was a scraped path discernible in the leaves. There was a large, limestone block that looked as if it made that track, but it was several feet from the door.

"You mean this one?" I asked, as I bent over and pointed to it.

Toby took two or three steps forward, toward the edge of the foundation, so he could see me and where I was pointing. He stared for a moment. "Oooh, man..." he said, drawing it out. "Oh boy. It's been opened. ... He's down in the crypt, sure as hell." He spun around and would have left then and there, but one of the troopers just reached out one arm and stopped him in his tracks.

I pulled my gun, and with my other hand gingerly reached out and opened the door.

What it revealed was pretty damned unimpressive, at least at first glance. A dark recess, about seven or eight feet into the hillside, one that would be high enough for me to stand in, if I bent a bit. Maybe six feet, or just a bit less. Just an old, wooden floor, with a hole in the middle that was about six feet square. That was it, as far as I could see, and it was quite a disappointment.

"There's nothing here," I said.

"It's at the bottom," said Toby.

"What's at the bottom of what?"

"The car. The car's at the bottom of the shaft, just look down the shaft. . . ."

I looked up at the assembled faces. "Anybody happen to have a flashlight?"

The second trooper handed one down. I stooped a bit, leaned over the black square, and shined the light downward.

Instant vertigo. The shaft descended what had to be at least eighty or ninety feet. As I lurched back I caught a glimpse of two things. A vertical, rusty track with shiny edges; and a big, rusty wheel with what looked to be a very large bicycle chain running in a channel.

"What you got?" croaked Lamar.

"Just a second," I said. "I hate heights."

"In a hole?" asked Sally.

"It's a high damned hole," I replied, irritated. "Just give me a minute." I took a deep breath, and got down on my stomach, and crawled forward, toward the edge of the shaft. As I did, I heard Sally wondering aloud how you could have a high hole.

Being so solidly supported, I could look down. Sure enough. The wheel, chain, and rails were part of the elevating mechanism. As I looked all the way down, I thought I could see something at the bottom. Probably the car Toby referred to. I also noted that the chain seemed to be oiled. I backed out.

"It goes way down, there's rails and a chain, and I think I can see some sort of car or box thing at the bottom."

"That's it," said Toby.

"Can we climb down there?" asked Lamar.

"No," I said emphatically. "No way." I simply

wasn't about to try a climbing descent to the bottom of that shaft. Not at any price.

"Use the box," suggested Toby.

"What box?"

"Inside the door, to the left."

I looked in again. Sure enough, in the corner was a dark gray electrical box, labeled "Square D," with a lever on its right.

"How does it work?"

"Just pull the lever up or down ... whatever way it ain't now," advised Toby. "It'll bring the car up for you."

The problem with simple solutions is that they sometimes hide complex problems just under the surface. That was the case here. First, I wasn't sure that I wanted to alert Dan Peale that we were coming after him. If he heard the elevator, and if Huck was still alive, that could easily cause him to kill her. Second, I had no idea what we would find at the bottom, so I didn't know how many of us should be going.

We stationed Borman and Byng at the top of the shaft, as the rest of us backed off and questioned Toby.

We were in a hurry, but we really needed the basic layout of what Toby called "the crypt."

He said the elevator shaft went to a section of the sand mine that had been closed off for years. There were five big chambers, and Dan had appropriated two of them.

"They're both on your right as you get off," said Toby.

"Dan got any guns down there?" asked Lamar.

"Guns? No way. He doesn't *need* guns. You'll see."

"Knives, though?" I asked.

"Yeah. He's got knives."

I wanted to ask why the knives if he didn't need guns, but didn't. Time was short.

"How do you see down there?" I asked.

"Turn on the lights," he said.

"What?"

"Yeah. I mean, nobody uses the mine, but it still has power. For inspections, I guess. We just tapped into the wires in the main part of the mine. That's all."

Well, sure. "And that's what powers the elevator?"

"Yeah."

"How loud is it?" asked Lamar.

Toby looked bewildered. "I don't know...compared to what?"

"Can Dan hear it coming down, Toby?" I asked, as patiently as I could.

"Oh! Oh, I think so. Yeah, unless he's in the far chamber, and then if he has the music on, probably not...."

"Music?"

"Yeah. Dan plays the music really loud when he gets into a mood. Hey," he said. "He's got all the comforts of home. You're gonna be surprised at what's all down there. It's beautiful!"

"I expect I will," I said. Then I tossed him a tough one. "Is that where Edie was killed? Is it the crypt?"

He went pale. I think he'd been getting into the whole pursuit thing, and had lost his sense of the real situation.

"Is it?" asked Lamar.

Toby nodded, but didn't speak. That was probably just as well.

"Well," I said, "let's get going."

Lamar called one of the troopers back at the house, and had him collect flashlights from the assembled cop cars, and bring as many as he could. They were all rechargeable, and good for at least three hours each.

Lamar took me aside. "You sure he's down there?"

"Nope. But Huck's gone, and didn't have to be if he wanted to off her on the spot. Okay ... and she's not anywhere in the house. So that would either leave here, or he's got her to some transportation, and they took off.

They didn't go by us last night at the gate. Nobody did. So the egress point to the house is here. The elevator's at the bottom, but that doesn't mean much. They seem to be able to get out the main entrance, too."

"Okay." He really sounded horrible.

"I think he got into the mine last night, or at least yesterday sometime. We were trying to track his progress with stolen car reports, but they could have lagged a couple of hours or more."

Lamar nodded. "Two hours, easy." It was almost funny, the way he tried not to talk, and lost.

"Last night, Mr. William Chester made an appearance. Up in here." I pointed to the general area, and then to the ravine. "Came up that ravine where we spotted him Monday. His car was parked down at the bottom. We followed him, not too far from this place, and Sally and I went down the ravine, and we sent Borman around the bottom. We lost him."

Lamar looked surprised.

"Yeah. Well, anyway, while we were chasing the goddamned vampire hunter, the vampire was paying a visit to the house. Far as I can tell."

Lamar shook his head. "Too bad," he managed to get out.

"No shit. I dunno, though. The silver lining might be that I don't think Dan Peale knew we were up here last night. I think he might think he's gotten away with something. That he has some time to play with." I looked at him squarely. "But, no. No, I don't know if he's down there. But I think he is."

We decided that Byng, Borman, Sally, and I would go down, two at a time, via the shaft. Another group headed by Lamar would try to enter at the main mine entrance, about a mile south of the shaft, at the bottom of the bluff. We'd have two troopers at the house, and two troopers at the upper end of the elevator shaft to the mine.

"Hey, Lamar?"

"Yeah?" He barely got it out. He really should have been home in bed.

"If you run across that idiot William Chester, super vampire hunter, see if you can arrest his ass for something, will ya?" I meant it. "Anything. Just keep him the hell out of our way."

"Sure, Carl."

"And, if somebody can get ahold of Hester or Harry, get 'em headed back here, too. If we get our boy, they're both gonna want to talk to him ASAP."

As we waited for the night scope, I thought about what we'd been told earlier about Dan wanting to "experience" Edie's death secondhand. The more I thought about that, the more I thought I knew why he'd taken Huck out of the house. He needed the time to "experience" her terror, by ingesting her blood while he... Jesus. It made the hair on the back of my neck stand up.

The briefing at the top of the shaft was short and sweet.

"Okay, listen up," I said. "We won't have any radio contact down there. Don't even try. There also might be blasting caps and stuff in the mine, and radio transmissions can set them off. Got that?"

Sally, Byng, and Borman nodded.

"We're in a real hurry, here. I think she's being kept alive for a little while, but I can't say for sure. If we find her, don't move her unless you have to. She might have an IV stick in her neck, or something, and she could bleed to death if it pulls out. Understood?"

It was.

"This son of a bitch is about as delusional as you can get, and might really believe he's a vampire, and that he's immortal. He's very likely high on meth, or ecstasy or some sort of combination of the stuff. That means fast and strong. Don't count on stopping him just by sticking a gun in his face. Be prepared to shoot." I took a breath. "Ready?"

Byng and I went first. The next pair was to be Sally and Borman.

THIRTY-TWO

We pulled the lever on the electrical box, and the mechanism immediately started to rumble and grind. Not too loud, though. Great.

The cab took about a minute to crawl its way to the top, and when I saw it I wasn't so damned sure it was a good idea to get into the rickety thing. It was old, rusty, riveted iron bands holding old, rotting wood together. Top, sides, and floor. No door. To give you some idea about the cramped quarters, once we were jammed in, Byng was able to easily reach out and reverse the lever on the junction box. That started us rumbling and grinding toward the bottom of the shaft. There was no light in the thing, either. That was just as well, as we were going to have to dark-adapt as quickly as we could. But I could almost feel damp limestone running by about six inches from my face. I guess you just don't appreciate elevator doors until you don't have them.

It was noticeably cold when we ground to a halt at the bottom of the shaft. Cold, but not as damp as I'd expected. That was a plus.

But it damned sure was dark.

There was a faint glimmer of yellowish light, though, off to the right. One point for Toby.

Byng put his hand over his flashlight, and just opened a small crack between his fingers to let a thin beam play over the wall nearest us. His hand glowed red over the lens. Spooky. He found a companion junction box, and pulled the lever down. The elevator car started its labored climb back to the top.

We moved toward the faint yellow light. The surface underfoot was silica sand, packed down into a pretty smooth surface by lots and lots of traffic. Silica sand is about as fine as table salt, or finer. It packs well, and doesn't impede movement the way beach sand would. It's quiet to walk on, too.

We'd gone about thirty feet, slowly, when the motor stopped, the elevator having reached the top. It was the first opportunity we'd had to actually listen for any sounds in the mine, and the faint strains of some music reached us.

"Music," said Byng.

"Umm," I said. "From where?" We couldn't really tell. "Close one eye," I said to him. "I'm turning on a flashlight."

I followed my own advice, which would enable me to have one eye that had begun to adapt to the dark while I used the other one to follow the beam around our area.

It helped get our bearings, and it also gave us some sense of the size of the place.

We were standing in a chamber about thirty feet high, by about sixty feet square. There was an enormous pillar just to our left, that seemed the same size as our chamber. Past it, my light reflected off the far wall of an adjacent chamber and pillar. That was about 180 feet, and it appeared to just keep going on and on, although the light was damned faint that far off.

Ahead of us was a similar arrangement, and to our right, the pillar-chamber sequence seemed to continue for as far as the beam would reach.

"Big place," I said, quietly.

"Goes for several miles," whispered Byng, "north and south. Only about three chambers deep, though. Maybe four, I hear. In places."

We were in an older part, for sure. The walls and ceiling were covered with little troughs and gouges, made by hand-wielded picks.

I put my hand over the light, letting a small beam escape. I found that, while I could see fairly well out of the eye I'd closed, the red-yellow afterglow in the other eye was very bothersome. Not such a good idea, after all. The darkness was just too complete.

It was still very quiet, and I was beginning to wonder if the elevator had broken, leaving Borman and Sally stuck on top. Even as I was wondering about it, the electric motor started up.

"Sally and Borman," said Byng.

The four of us assembled, and I came up with a plan. I decided to move toward the light, and see what we found.

"Quite a plan," whispered Byng, his amusement evident in his voice.

"This isn't exactly D-Day," I said.

"What's that smell?" whispered Byng.

"What smell?" I really didn't smell anything out of the ordinary at all.

"Reminds me of an Italian restaurant," said Byng.

"Ah," I said softly. "That's Sally."

"What?"

"I've got some fuckin' garlic," she hissed. "All right?"

Byng cleared his throat. "Yeah. Sure."

We moved toward the light, and the symphonic music got increasingly louder as we went. The lighted chamber turned out to be at right angles to the right of the one directly ahead of us. Maybe I just hadn't understood what Toby meant.

We crept along one of the enormous pillars, attempting to stay in the dark as long as we could. We paused, squatting or kneeling down, at the entrance to the lighted chamber.

Two overhead fluorescent units, of the type you'd find in a home workshop, suspended about twenty feet off the floor, lighted that entire chamber. The light was dim, but not as bad as it could have been, given the vast area they were lighting. It was certainly good enough to let us see the furnishings.

Along the walls were large, predominantly reddish, Oriental-style carpets, hanging from lengths of iron pipe that were wired into rings about fifteen feet off the floor. The hangings were around all three sides of the chamber that were visible to us, and it looked to me as if they were hung across the entrances to other chambers on all three sides.

The floor was covered with new wooden planking that peaked out from under more carpeting that covered most of the floor area of the chamber. The ceiling was formed from transparent plastic drop cloth that was suspended from the iron pipe that supported the wall hangings.

"Lot of carpet, there," said Sally.

There certainly was. Lots of planking, too.

On the floor were several overstuffed chairs, in two clusters, between which was set a long dining table complete with chairs and a large china cabinet that stood against a wall. The chamber was divided by an enormous breakfront, a good thirty feet long and about eight feet high. Hanging carpets at each end made it an effective wall, splitting the chamber in two.

"That's where that went," murmured Byng.

"What?"

"That long thing. That was in that hotel, the Larabee, that was torn down about ten years ago."

Ah. Sure. It had been behind the hotel bar, loaded with liquor bottles and glasses. I'd seen it at more than one fight call.

"That sure as hell didn't come down that little elevator," said Borman.

Good point. That implied fairly easy access to the main entrance.

"I thought Toby said it was beautiful," said Byng.

"Well," I whispered, "it was dark, and he was probably stoned."

The main point, though, was that there was nobody home. At least, not in this half of the chamber. The music was louder in here, as well. Almost too loud.

"Where is he?" asked Sally, underscoring the point.

"Best bet," I said, very quietly, "is the other half of the chamber."

It looked as though there were two logical paths to whatever lay behind that looming old breakfront, one around each end.

"Two around the left, two the right," I said. "Be fast, but don't make any noise."

"Be vewy, vewy quiet," said Sally. "We are hunting wampires."

We all smiled at that. It helped.

Byng and I went right, Sally and Borman left. We crossed the chamber by moving as close as possible to the walls, skirting the furnishings in the middle. Byng and I reached our end of the breakfront first.

Gun in hand, I took a deep breath, gently moved the edge of the hanging carpet aside, and stepped through.

THIRTY-THREE

Thursday, October 12, 2000
05:46

Inside, there were three separate rooms, of a sort. Tall, maybe six and a half foot, walls with openings in the middle. Cubicles, right out of an office supply catalogue. These were a dark, uneven red. I stepped closer to the nearest one. It looked to me as though it had been sloppily spray-painted. I heard Byng come through behind me.

The rooms seemed to be raised on old wooden cargo pallets.

It was much quieter in this area, the music being muted by the intervening carpets.

I heard a click to my left, and looked toward the sound. Borman and Sally were just rounding their end of the breakfront. They apparently had heard it, too, as all four of us froze for a moment.

There was a hollow metallic sound, barely audible above the music. Like somebody striking two large pots together.

"Please don't," said a quavering, contralto voice. "I didn't tell anybody, please don't, please." It wasn't a scream, or a yell for help. It was in an eerily normal, almost conversational tone of a woman speaking to someone in the same room. It was Huck.

I heard a deeper, male voice that seemed to reply, but couldn't quite make out the words. But he laughed. Nothing demonic or anything of the sort. That would have been easier to take, I think. This laugh was kind of quiet, polite almost. He was amused.

We all started to move at once. It was impossible to tell which of the three rooms the sound had come from, so each pair took the one closest. We had him trapped, I was sure.

Byng and I won. I stepped into the room on my right, and saw a workbench with wide, sheepskin straps that were restraining a supine Huck, and a man clad only in running shorts standing near her.

I pointed my gun at his back, and said, "Freeze."

Things just sort of stopped at that point. In that instant, I took in the fact that there was a transparent length of surgical tubing leading from the side of Huck's neck into a stainless steel basin on the floor; that there was a forceps clamping the tubing off; that his hand was on the forceps; that the tubing was secured to her neck with a tape wrap.

He froze, exactly what I'd told him to do. Looking at his back, I could see his shoulder muscles twitching. I remember thinking that he had great definition.

I moved to my left, toward Huck's head, keeping my gun pointed at him. I felt Byng come in behind me.

"Cover him from there, Byng," I said. "He moves, shoot him."

"Yep," said Byng, sounding very matter-of-fact.

"Your bullets," said Dan Peale, with an excellent upper class English accent, "cannot harm me."

There was something very disconcerting about the

way he said that. Calm, informative, with absolutely no doubt in his mind. He didn't turn.

"Step slowly back away from her," I said. "Don't make any sudden moves. We don't want to put that theory to the test, do we? . . ."

He was obedient. As he began to step back, slowly, he very deliberately squeezed the forceps, and then released it. Blood flowed instantly from Huck's neck, down the tube, and into the basin. Before I could stop him, he continued his motion by raising his left hand, and almost casually flipping the forceps over the back wall of the cubicle. Then he completed his step back from her.

Huck started to make gasping sounds, and strained at her straps. Dan Peale made a series of hissing noises, sucking air deep into his lungs, and forcing it out. Ventilating. He turned his head, farther than would have seemed normal, and I saw his face for the first time.

Dan Peale had a longish face, with pronounced musculature at the jaws. Dark hair and dark brown eyes. No facial hair except the eyebrows. And fangs, nearly an inch long, made more prominent by a wide, predatory grin. Even knowing that they were prostheses, they were startling. There was a smear of blood on his lips and chin.

I'd never seen him before in my life, but I felt I knew him.

"Put your hands behind your back," I said. "Now!" I had to get to that tube. . . .

"Bleeding. . . ." came from Huck.

Dan Peale grimaced and hissed again.

I reached down without taking my eyes from Peale, and got my left hand on the tube. I fumbled and felt the warm liquid running over my hand. Now the tube was slick, and I couldn't get a grip on it without looking down. I glanced at it for an instant, got a purchase, and squeezed it as hard as I could between my thumb and forefinger. It greatly reduced the flow, if not cutting it off completely.

"Cuff him," I said to Byng.

Dan Peale had a fine sense of timing. Byng, out of his view, had glanced down at his holster, as he put his gun away so he'd have both hands free for using the cuffs. I had relaxed just a tad, having succeeded in nearly stopping the blood pouring from the tube in Huck's neck. And Dan Peale just lifted his knees, dropped way down, straightened abruptly, leaped up onto Huck's table, and jumped over the back wall of the cubicle. One, smooth motion, and he was gone.

I got off one shot, and thought I might have hit him.

I dimly heard a "Hey!" from outside. Borman. I had been nearly deafened by the sound of the shot.

Byng, taking the best action he could, jumped back through the door, and took off around the back of the little room. I saw Sally and Borman going by, and I hollered "Sally!"

I looked down at Huck. "We'll get you out now," I said.

She was gulping shuddering breaths, trying to hold still. Her eyes were wide, and I don't think she understood a word I said.

Sally came in behind me. "Holy shit," she said. It was like I was hearing underwater, with the addition of a monotonous squeal. That shot had been really loud.

"You want to kink this tube, and squeeze it for a minute? Don't let go, and don't try to remove the needle from her neck."

"Right." She reached out, hesitated. "Gloves?"

"Later. Unless you got a cut on your hand. I'm going to try to find a clamp or something, and we can start getting her out of here."

"Right."

As Sally took over the job of closing off the tube, I released the restraints from Huck's wrists and ankles. She was wearing faded green sweatpants, and her feet were bare. They looked very pale and cold.

She had on a thin, dark blue T-shirt. She was shivering, a combination of the cold air and blood loss. The only thing I could find was a large roll of paper toweling. I unrolled strips about as long as she was, and placed several layers over her.

"Do you feel strong enough to walk?" I asked her.

"Nuh, nuh, no."

Great. Well, I wouldn't have, either. I had no idea how much blood she'd lost, but I suspected it had been quite a bit. The basin at my feet was just about full.

"We'll get him," I said. "You're going to be fine."

"Yeah," she said, weakly, and her head bumped softly back against the bench. "Sure."

Borman stuck his head in the cubicle. "Where'd he go?"

"I don't know," I said. "Did you see a forceps laying on the ground outside here?"

He looked down.

"Out that way," I said, pointing to where he'd come from.

"No." He was already starting off toward the other cubicles.

I left Huck and Sally, and worked my way into the yard wide area behind the cubicle where Dan Peale had pitched the forceps. I shone my flashlight on the ground, and sure enough, there they were. My relief was a palpable thing. I holstered my gun, and bent down to pick them up. As I did, my light moved, I became aware of a fine trickle of sand sparkling its way down onto the floor about six feet ahead of me, alongside the bare wall of the chamber. I picked up the forceps, bracing myself for a blow to my back. Nothing. I straightened up, and held the forceps up, over the cubicle wall.

"Sally, here you go," I said.

A moment later, I felt her take the forceps from me. The primary mission was accomplished.

I drew my gun, and took one more step away from the falling sand. Then I turned, abruptly, and shined my flashlight straight up into the darkness above the level of the fluorescent lights.

There he was. About twenty feet up, in the clear area between the pillar and the drop-cloth ceiling support, clinging to God knows what with his hands and feet.

"Hey, Dan!" I hollered.

He looked down. Those damned fangs glistened, pressing into his lower lip. He was gripping tightly with both hands, with one foot parallel to the pillar's face and braced against a small bump in the surface. The other foot was nearly perpendicular, with the toes wedged into a crack. I could see a dark spot on his lower left side, toward his back. There was a trickle of blood running down from there into his shorts. It looked like I'd hit him.

"You need any help gettin' down?" I yelled, unable to resist.

Two things happened at once. Byng and Borman came flying around the far end of the cubicles, looked up, and Byng said, "Damn!"

At the same time, Dan Peale just pushed himself away from the wall. For the life of me, I thought he hung up there, suspended in space, for an instant. I think in that moment, we were both wondering if he could really fly. Then he plummeted twenty feet to the sandy floor. I guess he was prepared to fly, because he did absolutely nothing to break his fall, or roll with it. He hit feet first, arms outstretched to his sides, with a jarring thump that seemed to send a visible ripple upward from his ankles to his neck. His legs went all weird between the ankle and hip, and he collapsed onto the floor of the mine.

I sent Borman up the elevator to get help. Byng and I tended to Dan Peale. Along with a gunshot wound in his back, he had a compound fracture of his lower right leg, an obviously broken or very badly sprained left ankle, and I feared some internal injuries as well. He was silent, never uttering a word of pain or complaint. Meth combined with ecstasy, they tell me, will do that sometimes. I met his gaze a couple of times as we put toweling over his fracture. He never blinked. I really think he would have tried to escape by crawling, if we hadn't both been there.

We kept clear of his teeth.

Borman returned, with a paramedic, who was being followed by two more. He told me that Lamar and the others had finally gotten in the main mine entrance, and should be up our way very soon. They could easily drive an ambulance up to us, as soon as they figured out which chamber we were in.

I left them, and went back to Huck. She was asleep, and Sally was just standing there, staring at her and adjusting a trauma blanket to try to keep the younger woman warm.

"She's wiped out," she said.

"Yeah. Who wouldn't be? The last ten or fifteen years have been long ones for her."

"Peale alive?"

"Yeah," I said, "but pretty well busted up."

"Did you hit him with that shot?"

"No doubt."

"Attaboy," she said.

There was a commotion in the outer chamber, followed by Lamar and our reinforcements arriving. They'd brought an ambulance with them.

"Sorry we're late," said Lamar, after hearing my verbal report. He looked around the area where Huck was lying, and saw the tubing and the basin and the straps and everything.

"Is this where Edie . . . ?" He couldn't finish.

"Yeah. I believe so."

"Aw, hell," he said with his sore throat. "It's cold here. Damn. Edie hated the cold." He turned away, and went back through the hanging carpet.

"I've never seen him like that before," said Sally.

"Yeah."

She looked around. "This really is a lonely place."

Harry and Hester showed up just as we were taking Dan Peale out to the ambulance. Harry, in particular, was very disappointed to have missed the excitement. Hester told me that she and Harry thought Tatiana had snitched Huck off.

"I believe," she said, "that she wanted to make sure Dan did something terrible. So he'd get out of Jessica's life, permanently."

Considering that we thought Jessica had damned near invented Dan Peale, and would probably create another one, it had been a waste of time.

After countless examinations and three separate hearings, Dan Peale was eventually declared insane, and placed in a secure mental health facility. God only knows what he'll do there. He is scheduled to stand trial in Wisconsin, for the murder of Randy Baumhagen, but is currently fighting extradition on the grounds that he's been already declared legally insane. What really bothers me is that, since he wasn't tried, we haven't been able to get a determination on exactly what happened with Edie. Hester and I talked about that at some length, and what we came up with was this:

Dan and Toby had Edie in that "crypt" of his. Dan seems to have planned to bleed Edie for a while in advance, and while he intended to bring Edie very close to death, we couldn't prove he intended for her to die. That would have been enough for second-degree murder, though, and we were fairly certain he would have been convicted. That left us with the question as to just what happened after she died. We found that out at Toby's trial.

Toby said that Dan didn't want people snooping

around, doing a search for a missing woman. He was afraid they might stumble across the elevator, or just go looking for her in the mine. He decided to make it look like a suicide, to prevent a search. Dan was the one who made the cut in Edie's neck, to cover the needle entry point. Toby insisted it was post mortem.

Then they had to carry her back to the Mansion, and put her in the tub. They'd used the elevator, and that explained the wood stain on the body bag. They carried her to the house, and had to set the body down while Toby was sent to get Kevin. Since they didn't want to be seen, Dan had unlocked the back stair door to the third floor, and they'd placed her in the stairwell. That fit nicely with that bloodstain.

While Toby was up with Kevin, Huck had awakened, and was moving about. Toby thought she was taking a shower. He hustled down to Dan, and they took Edie right up the main staircase, so they didn't have to pass Huck's room. The stain on the carpet came from setting her down, just as we figured. Our only mistake on the direction was in thinking the stain at the bottom of the back stair meant that they'd brought her down from the third floor.

The weird part was, Toby was the only one who actually did any prison time for the whole thing. He got five years for helping Dan kill Edie. When he'd told us that he hadn't been able to kill her in the so-called crypt, he'd told the truth. But he'd held on to her while Dan did it. But, I mean, is that ironic or what? Here he was, the only one nuts enough to really believe the officially insane Dan Peale was a vampire, and he was the one judged sane enough to stand trial. "The fool? or the fool who follows him?" I think it goes.

Hanna and Melissa continued rooming together, around the general area. Huck, after a brief stay in the hospital, moved to Dubuque, and got a job dealing on the gaming boat down there. She came back to testify at Dan's hearing, but seemed distant to us.

Kevin turned up in Freiberg. He'd split as soon as he became aware that Dan was back in the house. The county attorney said we didn't have much on him, and subpoenaed him as a hostile witness in one of Dan's hearings.

Jessica and Tatiana both testified that Dan had flagged them down, and taken them hostage at gunpoint, and forced them to take him back to Lake Geneva. They got away with it. Hester, Harry, and I approached the prosecutor's office, with a request to prosecute Jessica as the principal orchestrator of the entire business. They told us that they'd never be able to convince a jury of that, especially in the light of the defense team she could afford to retain.

I'll never forget what the head prosecutor said. "You guys just have to learn to be realistic about these things." Right. While working a vampire case?

Jessica is still doing her thing, as far as we can tell. Hawkins keeps in touch.

We found William Chester's pack in the woods well north of the elevator shaft. It contained a stake, garlic, a crucifix, and a mallet. We didn't have any idea where he'd gone for several weeks, and were beginning to wonder if Dan Peale had killed him and dragged him into a dark area of the mine. Then Harry got a call from the cops in Lake Geneva, wanting to know if he'd ever heard of the man. They'd popped him in a stalking case. Apparently, he was taking an interest in Jessica Hunley. When questioned, he'd actually used Harry as a reference. That was a hoot. Personally, I think he caught a glimpse of Dan Peale that rainy night on the bluff. I think the reality of Peale finally dawned on him, and he just couldn't handle it. I think he simply ran away.

The Mansion is still there, although Jessica sold it soon after Dan was committed. I understand it's about to become a resort, since it's so close to the gaming boat and the Mississippi. I don't think Sue and I'll be staying there. I never did get inside the Hunley estate in Lake Geneva.

Oh, yeah. Borman. He lost his action against me. He tried to say that I'd done the same thing that he had done—fired a warning shot. One that just happened to hit Peale by accident. Right.

Borman left the department after that, and signed on with a university security service on the West Coast. That was too bad, in my opinion. I still thought he had a lot of potential.

GLOSSARY

AG: Attorney general, either state or federal.

COMM: Police radio call sign of the communications center in Nation County.

DCI: Division of Criminal Investigation, a division of the Iowa Department of Public Safety.

DEA: Drug Enforcement Administration, an agency of the U.S. Government.

DNE: Division of Narcotics Enforcement, an agency of the State of Iowa and an offshoot of DCI.

DNR: Department of Natural Resources, an agency of the State of Iowa.

FBI: Federal Bureau of Investigation, a bureau of the U.S. Department of Justice.

ISP: Iowa State Patrol, the uniformed division of the Department of Public Safety.

ME: Medical examiner.

SA: Special agent, either of the Iowa DCI or the FBI.

SAC: Special agent in charge, either of the DCI or the
   FBI.
SO: Sheriff's office.

SOME NOTES ON CODES IN GENERAL

In law enforcement communications, codes are used
both as a shorthand method of communication and as a
way of concealing information from the prying ears who
listen in on police radio transmissions. The Ten Codes,
listed below, are our basic shorthand for radio use.

   Other codes are used to fill in the gaps or to cover unusual situations that arose after the Ten Codes were
established. One example would be the use of "code
blue" to indicate that the subject of concern in deceased.
This has become so well known that it's really no longer
very useful, and has often been replaced with other codes.

   Many departments developed a code system that
would use a common number and give it another meaning known only to the officers and dispatchers. Code
sixty-one is a good example. Briefly, it started with the old
10-61, which meant "Personnel in area." Being a super-
fluous number, it slowly changed over the years to mean
"Unauthorized personnel in area," and eventually came
to indicate "Be aware that this conversation is not secure
because an unauthorized person is listening." That particular definition proved to be pretty useful, and is used in
that context today. It then developed, by replacing the
"10" with "code," into "Be very circumspect in all your
transmissions, as we don't want any casual listeners to
garner information from your radio traffic." Strangely,
code sixty-one came into general usage about the time the
general public began obtaining police scanners.

SOME USEFUL TEN CODES

The so-called Ten Codes were developed in the very
early days of police radio communications. Range was

very short, and most of the vehicles that carried the expensive equipment for two-way communication were owned by states or large cities. The codes, as used in Iowa, were meant to cover the situations commonly encountered by the Iowa Highway Patrol. The IHP in those days was very likely the only outfit that operated in rural Iowa which could afford radios. Many times, the early equipment was so unreliable that the first part of a transmission would be lost due to equipment vagaries. Long transmissions merely meant that the chances of a message becoming garbled were just that much better. The Ten Codes enabled the reduction of the length of the transmissions, and their clarity was improved by assigning simple numbers to the most common messages. Therefore, the "10" was used to alert the listener that a message number was to follow. This system has remained in use, and seems likely to do so for the foreseeable future.

10–2   Good signal, now usually used to mean simply "good."

10–4   Acknowledged, frequently used to indicate agreement.

10–5   Relay.

10–6   Busy (as in doing cop work), often used as a "do not disturb" sign on the radio.

10–7   Temporarily out of service (as in lunch).

10–8   Back in service (as in done with lunch).

10–9   Repeat.

10–10   Fight.

10–13   Weather and road conditions.

10–16   Domestic case.

10–20   Location.

10–21   Telephone, as in "Ten-twenty-one the office."

10–22   Disregard.

10–23   Arrived at scene.

10–24   Assignment completed.

10–25 Report in person to meet, usually used simply as "meet."

10–27 Operator's license information.

10–28 Vehicle registration information.

10–29 Check records for stolen; modern usage also means "warrant" or "wanted."

10–32 Suspect with gun, also used in reference to knives and other devices.

10–33 Emergency.

10–46 Disabled vehicle.

10–50 Motor vehicle crash.

10–51 Wrecker.

10–52 Ambulance.

10–55 DWI.

10–56 Intoxicated pedestrian.

10–61 Personnel in area, frequently used to indicate that a civilian can hear the radio.

10–70 Fire.

10–76 En route.

10–78 Need assistance.

10–79 Notify medical examiner, also used to indicate a deceased subject.

10–80 High-speed pursuit.

10–96 Mentally disturbed subject.

As an example, if you as an officer were to suddenly encounter an armed suspect, shots were fired, you needed help, and thought somebody had been injured, you might transmit: "Ten-thirty-three, ten-thirty-two, need ten-seventy-eight, and get me a ten-fifty-two—this is ten-thirty-three!" (Note the use of 10-33 twice, which officers tend to do when emphasizing dire straits.) An excellent dispatcher will get the whole picture, and may merely try to discover your position by saying, "Ten-four, ten-twenty?" As with any system, the clarity and usefulness depend entirely on the quality of the personnel involved. An excited officer may be merely garbled, and the transmissions result in a "Ten-nine?" An inattentive dispatcher may "tune in" halfway through the message and receive incomplete data. This, too, can lead to additional risk and hazard.

This is, by the way, one example of why the retention of your top-notch people is so important.

Donald Harstad is the author of *Eleven Days, Known Dead,* and *The Big Thaw*. A former deputy sheriff and twenty-six-year veteran of the Clayton County Sheriff's Department, he lives in Elkader, Iowa.

If you enjoyed Donald Harstad's *Code 61*, you won't want to miss any of his exciting police thrillers starring Carl Houseman.

Look for the latest, *The Heartland Experiment,* coming soon in hardcover from Doubleday.

And turn the page for an exciting preview....

THE
HEARTLAND·
EXPERIMENT

By

Donald Harstad

ONE

NOW

Slugs came ripping through the old boards of the barn, showering us with dust and debris. I got even lower than I had been before, pressing my face against the old, dusty limestone foundation. I could see George hunkering down against the thick support beam he'd found, and I heard Hester, who was off to my right in the gloom, say "Shit." At first, I thought it was just a comment, but then she kept talking.

"Shit, oh shit, shit, shit..."

I turned, and saw that she'd rolled away from her vantage point near the rotted boards, and was half sitting with her back against the foundation wall.

"What? You okay?"

"My face," she said. She held the right side of her face with one hand, while she struggled to re-holster her sidearm with the other, and I saw blood oozing between her fingers. "Shit, shit..."

George and I both got over to her as fast as we could crawl. "Let me see . . ."

She reluctantly moved her hand from the right side of her face, and I saw some blood and torn flesh. Not too much. It was hard to see in the shadows. I unsnapped my windbreaker, and daubed her face as gently as I could with the fleecy lining. It was all I had.

"Ahhh!" and she pushed my hand away.

"Sorry, sorry, just a sec, just let me look . . ." I said.

"Don't press . . ."

"Yeah. Yeah," I said, as I fumbled in my shirt pocket for my reading glasses, and then looked more closely. Sticking out of her right cheek was a half-inch stub of an old, rusty square nail, flattened but about half as big around as a pencil, embedded back toward the corner of her jaw. "I see it . . . it's a nail. Part of one. There's a chunk of nail stuck in your cheek," I said.

"Don't touch it!"

"No, no . . ."

"I can feel it," she said, after a second, "with my tongue." As she spoke, a rivulet of blood dripped over her lower lip, and onto her sleeve. "It's gonna hurt," she said, and shivered, violently. "It's inside my mouth. Oh, shit."

"It doesn't seem to be bleeding very much," I told her. "But spit, don't swallow it . . ."

"I just had a first-aid class," came Sally's voice from over behind the rusty milking stanchions. "Somebody get over here, and let me come take a look."

George reached out and patted Hester on the arm. "It'll be all right," he said. "Okay," he told Sally. "Be right there. I'll get my stuff."

Hester nodded, but said nothing as George crawled away.

"It's not a bullet," I said. She was shivering pretty hard, and I wanted to reassure her. "It's just a piece of old nail, must have been hit by a slug. It's not life-threatening, okay? It's not a bullet. There's no damage other than a little hole." It had occurred to me that she might be worried about disfigurement. And it really wasn't a very big hole.

She nodded. "It'll hurt," she said, with a quaver in her voice. "Hit my teeth. Numb now...but it'll hurt...oh boy." She didn't look at any of us, just stared at the floor, concentrating and breathing slowly and deeply.

If she was right about her teeth, it really was going to hurt like hell.

Sally came scuttling over on all fours. "Hi, Hester. Let me see what I can do here, okay? You're gonna be all right..."

"Sure," said Hester. Her words were less distinct. Swelling inside her mouth?

Sally briefly examined the wound. "We need some sort of compress," she said. "Just to protect it, if we can. Some water to irrigate it, maybe? Later, later, we better let the doc remove it, okay?"

As soon as I heard "irrigate," I reached into my pocket and pulled out one of my bottles of water and handed it to Sally. As far as I knew, all our first-aid equipment was kept in our cars, and they were effectively out of reach. I thought for a second. "My tee shirt? It's clean today..."

"It'll have to do," said Sally. She, too, reached out and patted Hester on the shoulder. "You're gonna have the world's biggest compress," she said.

Hester made a muffled noise, and I think she wanted to sound like she was laughing. I took off my jacket and started pulling my sweater over my head.

"It starting to hurt yet?" asked Sally.

Hester shook her head, gingerly. "Mumm." She tried again, making a real effort to be distinct. "Numb." It was swelling, all right.

"Here, put your sweater back on," said George, and I heard the distinctive sound of Velcro ripping open. "This stuff is part of my kit." He tossed over a blue nylon bag, with a red cross in a white square stitched on the front.

"All right!" said Sally, and opened it up. There were several individual packets inside, each labeled for a different medical problem. "Fracture. Burns. Drowning...Ah, Wounds and Bleeding..." Inside the packet there was a large compress, gauze, disinfectant ointment, and a scissors. "Shit, this is great..."

"I'll get an ambulance coming," I said. For all the good it would do. There was no way we could get Hester to it until we got lots of backup. I keyed the mike on my walkie-talkie. "Comm, Three...10-33."

Of course it was 10-33. This had been an emergency since the first shot was fired. But I had to say something to convey the extra urgency, and there's no code for "more urgent than before."

"Three, go ahead."

"Okay, we have an officer down now. Get me a 10-52 down here at the old Dodd place. Fast...but tell 'em to hold until we clear 'em in."

"10-4, Three. Copy officer down?" She repeated it that way so everybody who was listening knew what we had, without her having to inform them separately.

"10-4, need as much 10-78 as you can get, and the ambulance. We are still pinned down. Repeating, still pinned down. How close is backup?"

"10-4 the 10-52," she replied, and I could imagine her hitting the page button for the Maitland ambulance service. *"And...uh...backup is en route."*

I was glad she acknowledged the ambulance request, but just telling me that the backup units were on the way, without giving me their current location, meant that it was going to take a while. There was obviously a problem with backup. It was so damned typical of the complex kind of plan that we were working under. I was angry, but there was nothing Dispatch could do about it. I was just sorry she hadn't been able to give me an estimate, though. That was bad.

"10-4. Look, tell the responding units that we are still taking automatic weapons fire, from two or three locations. Repeat that, will you. Auto weapons fire from multiple locations."

"*10-4, Three.*" She repeated the message, and as she did so she sounded about ready to cry. Being completely powerless in a tense situation will make you sound that way. "*Can you be more specific regarding the location of the automatic weapons fire?*"

"I'm giving you the best I've got," I said, as calmly as possible. "They were already here." The calm was mostly for Hester's benefit. The last thing she needed to hear was me getting all worried. "Just make sure you don't send the EMS people in until we clear them."

"*10-4, Three. One says to keep them there until backup gets to you.*"

Well, that wasn't going to be too hard. It was them keeping us pinned down, not vice versa.

"I think we can do that, Comm," I said.

"The dumb one's coming back out," said George.

The "dumb one" referred to one of the group who was shooting at us, off and on. This particular idiot wore a New York Yankees baseball cap and a gray sweatshirt. He'd step out of the old machine shed, half crouched, point his AK-47 either at our barn or the old chicken coop, and just blow out about thirty rounds in a couple of seconds. The first time he'd done it, George had said, "Look at that dumb son of a bitch!" It stuck. So far, shooting from the hip the way he was, he'd not come close to even hitting the barn, let alone anybody inside. It wasn't for lack of trying, though. I thought it was pretty obvious he was trying to draw fire, and that was the other reason for "dumb one." There was something about the jumpy way he did it that told me that this wasn't really his idea. The comfort was, it let us know they weren't sure exactly where we were.

"Back in a minute, Hester," I said. I crawled toward my vantage point, and pointed my AK-15 through the hole between the old foundation and the rotting boards of the barn wall. The elevated, black front sight just cleared the hole, but I had him dead to rights almost instantly. He was only about fifty yards away, and the upper two-thirds of him was in plain view. He'd be hard to miss. I squinted as I aimed at the white NY on his blue cap.

"Whadda ya think? Take him out?" I asked George. So far, we hadn't returned fire since the first exchange about ten minutes back. We hadn't because they had pretty much been shooting the upper floor of the barn, and into the loft, and were down in the stone foundations. They were far enough off-target, we'd been reluctant to reveal our actual position by shooting back. They had a lot more firepower than we did. But now Hester had been hurt. They were getting closer.

"Not yet, I think," said George. "Wait and see what he does."

The dumb one started waving his assault rifle in the air, screaming something at us.

"Gotta be stoned," I said. "Gotta be."

"Any idea what he's saying?" asked George.

"No," I said. "Don't even know what fucking language. But I don't think he's trying to surrender."

The dumb one took the hint, I guess. He lowered the assault rifle to hip level, and pointed it right at us.

"Down!" yelled George.

My name is Carl Houseman, and I'm a Deputy Sheriff in Nation County, Iowa. I'm also the Department's Senior Investigator, which is a title that probably has about as much to do with my being fifty-five as it does with my investigative abilities. It's also a title that can get me involved in some really neat stuff, even in a rural county with only 20,000 residents. That's why I like it.

I was about halfway through my usual noon-to-eight shift. Hester Gorse, my favorite Iowa DCI agent, and I had just finished interviewing Clyde and Dirk Osterhaus, brothers, antiques burglars, and new jail inmates, regarding seventeen residential burglaries that had been committed in Nation County over the last two months. The interviews had been conducted in the presence of their respective attorneys, who were both in their late twenties. The brothers, both also under thirty, had thrown us a curve when they'd readily confessed to only fourteen of the break-ins. Why just those fourteen, when we all knew they'd done the whole seventeen? Some sort of strategy? A bargaining chip? It beat both Hester and me.

Anyway, the attorneys had left and the brothers were back in the jail cells, arguing with the other prisoners over whether or not they were all going to watch *Antiques Road Show* at 7:00 P.M. We only had one TV in the cell block. I was pretty sure the Osterhaus boys were going to win. Research comes first.

Hester and I were in Dispatch, having a leisurely cup of coffee. We were talking to the duty Dispatcher, Sally Wells, about whether she should take her niece to see *Harry Potter* or *Lord of the Rings* when she got off duty. The phone rang, and our conversation stopped.

Sally answered with a simple "Nation County Sheriff's Department...," which told me it wasn't a 911 call. They answer those with "911, what's your emergency." I relaxed a bit, and had just brought my coffee cup to my lips when Sally reached over and snapped on the speaker phone.

"*...best get the Sheriff down here...there's this dead man in the road just down from our mailbox...*" came crackling from the speaker.

"And your name and location, please?"

"*I'm Jacob, Jacob Heinman,*" replied the brittle voice. "*Me and my brother live down here in Frog Hollow...you know, just over from the Welsh place about a mile.*"

"I'll be paging the ambulance now," replied Sally, very calmly, "but keep talking because I can hear you at the same time."

"*We don't think he needs a ambulance, ma'am,*" said Jacob, politely, "*I saw 'em shoot him just about right smack in front of me. We went back up there. He's still laying there just like they left him. He's awful dead, we're pretty sure."*

I suspect, even in departments where they have two or three hundred homicides a year, the adrenaline still flows with a call like that. In our case, with maybe one or two a year, the rush is remarkable. Hester and I headed out the door.

As we left, I said, "On the way. Backup, please."

Sally waved absently. She knew her job, and would have everything she could drum up out to help as soon as possible. You just like to remind even the best Dispatchers, in case something slips their mind.

The Heinman brothers were known throughout the area as the "Heinman boys." Confirmed bachelors, neither of the so-called boys was a day under eighty, and you couldn't excite either of them if you set his foot on fire. Or, apparently, if you shot somebody right in front of him. As I got in my unmarked patrol car, started the engine, and strapped on the seat belt, I could hear Sally telling a State Trooper whose call numbers I missed that she was looking the directions up in her plat book. Frog Hollow was an old place-name for a very remote stretch of road about two miles long that wound down through a deep, mile-long valley where there were just two farms. I don't think anybody except the rural mail carrier and the milk truck went there in the daytime, and just kids parking and drinking beer ended up there at night. Sally probably had a general idea where it was, but considering there were more than 2,000 farms in Nation County, this would be no time to guess and end up giving the Trooper bad directions. Hester, behind me in her own unmarked car, couldn't possibly know where we were going and was going to have to follow me to the scene. Her call sign was I-388, so I waited until the radio traffic between Sally and the Trooper paused, and picked up my mike.

"Three and I-388 are 10-76," I said. That meant we were heading to the scene, and was meant as much for the case record as anything else. You always need times. "Which Trooper you sending?"

"216 is south of you, I'm working on the directions..." There was no stress in her voice, but I could tell she was really concentrating. *"Be aware I've confirmed there at least two suspects. Repeating, at least two suspects."*

Two for sure. That always meant, to my mildly paranoid mind, that we were talking a *minimum* of two. Okay. Well, there was Hester, me, and 216. Fair odds, as 216 was a new State Trooper sergeant named Gary Beckman, who'd transferred into our area about six months ago. He was about forty, and really knew his stuff.

"I'll direct him," I said so she could forget the directions for him and concentrate on getting an ambulance and our Sheriff notified. "216 from Nation County Three, what's your 10-20?" I needed to know Gary's location before I could give him directions. I also needed to find out where he was because we were both going to be in a hurry, and it would be extremely embarrassing if we were to find ourselves trying to occupy the same piece of roadway at the same time.

"I'm four south of Maitland on Highway 14, Three." I could hear the roar of his engine over his siren noise. He was moving right along. Hester and I pulled out onto the main highway and headed south. The Trooper was four miles closer than we were. There was no way I'd be able to have him just follow me and skip the directions over the radio.

"10-4, 216. We're just leaving Maitland now. Okay, uh, if you turn right at the big dairy farm with the three blue silos, take the next right, and, uh, continue on down a long, winding road into the valley. That's the right road, and the farm you're going to is the second one."

"10-4, Three." His siren was making a racket in the background. My siren was making a racket under my hood. Hester's siren was making a racket behind me. I

reached down and turned the volume way up on my radio.

"Okay, and the, uh, subject is right in the roadway, so..." The last thing I wanted was for a car to run over the victim. "And Comm confirms two suspects."

"Understood."

I hoped so. After 216 and I shut up, I heard Sally talking to our Sheriff, Lamar Ridgeway, whose call sign was Nation County One. From listening to their radio traffic, I could tell Lamar was a good ten miles north of me. Since he drove the Department's four-wheel-drive pickup, he wasn't going to be able to make more than eighty or so. Which begged a question...

I called Sally. "Comm, Three?"

"Three, go."

"Subject say whether or not the bad guys were still there?"

"Negative, not there. Repeating, the caller says the suspects have fled the immediate scene. He thinks they went southbound from near his residence, but he didn't get a vehicle description...just heard it leave, as it apparently was around the curve from his place, and out of his line of sight."

Great. "Give what you got to Battenberg PD..." The town of Battenberg was about five miles south of the Heinman boys' farm, and their officer could at least say who came into town from the north. Assuming that the suspects continued that way.

"He's already on the phone." Sally sounded a bit irritated. I wisely decided to stop interfering and let her do her job.

It had taken us about three minutes to cover the four miles to the cluster of three blue silos, and I braked hard to slow enough to make the right turn onto the gravel. I anticipated because I knew the road. Hester, who didn't, just about ended up in my trunk.

"Could we use our turn signals?" came crackling over the radio.

"10-4, I-388," I said to her. "Sorry 'bout that."

We were having a pretty mild winter so far, and there was no snow at all on the roadway. Just loose gravel. Almost as bad as ice and snow, if you oversped it. Without snow cover, though, there was much better traction. There was also a lot of dust from 216. Another reason I was unhappy he was ahead of me. Hester, behind both of us, had to back off quite a distance just to be able to see.

At that point, I heard *"216 is 10-23"* come calmly over the radio as the sergeant told Comm that he had arrived at the scene. After a beat, he said, *"The scene is secure."*

That meant that there was no suspect at the scene who was not in custody. Good to know, as it tended to affect how you got out of your car. Hester and I both shut down the sirens as soon as he said that.

I almost missed the next right due to the dust. It was just over the crest of a hill, and judging from the deep parallel furrows in the gravel, 216 had almost missed it, too. I was in an increasingly thick dust cloud for almost a minute, and when it tapered off suddenly I knew I was at the point where 216 had slowed. Seconds later, I rounded a downhill curve and saw the Trooper's car about fifty yards ahead, parked in the center of the roadway, top lights flashing. Excellent choice, as he was completely protecting the scene. Nobody could get by him on an eighteen-foot road with a bluff on one side and a deep ditch on the other. I stopped near the right-hand ditch, and waited until I saw Hester in my rearview mirror.

"You go on up," I said on the radio, "I'll make sure nobody hits us," and then carefully backed up around the curve until I was sure somebody cresting the hill could see the flashing lights in my rear window before they got into the curve. This was no time to get run over by an ambulance. Or the Sheriff. "Comm, Three and

I-388 are 10-23." I hung up the mike, grabbed my walkie-talkie, and opened my car door.

Sally's acknowledging "*10-4, Three*" just about blew me out of the car. I'd forgotten about cranking up the volume in order to hear over the sirens. I took a second to turn it way down, and then got out of the car, locked it up, and headed toward the scene. You always leave the engine running in the winter so radio traffic doesn't run down your battery. It's also a good idea to have at least three sets of keys.

The Heinman farm sat well below road level, about fifty yards to my left. On my right, a steeply sloped, heavily wooded hill rose maybe a hundred feet above the roadbed. The farm lane came uphill toward the mailbox at a slant, with bare-limbed maple trees between it and the road. As an added measure, between the road and those trees was an old woven wire fence, covered with thick, entangled brush and weeds. Done, I was sure, to keep the larger debris from the roadway out of the Heinman property. There was a Ford tractor from the 50s quietly decomposing within ten feet of the galvanized mailbox that was perched on top of a wooden fencepost. That old tractor had been there the very first time I'd seen the farm, nearly twenty-five years ago. By now it and its rotting tires had become part of the landscape.

I saw Hester and 216 talking to the two elderly Heinman brothers. They were near the mailbox, looking toward the area ahead of his patrol car. As I approached, a body came slowly into my view in front of 216's car. It was lying kind of on its left side, parallel with the direction of the road, with its feet pointing away and downhill from me. I started making mental notes as I walked. Faded blue plaid flannel shirt, blue jeans, one black tennis shoe ... and hands bound behind its back with yellow plastic binders. Damn. We called them Flex Cuffs, and used them when we ran out of handcuffs. They were like the bindings for electrical wiring. Once they were on, they had to be cut off. What we had here was an execution.

Two more steps, and I saw the head. More accurately, I saw the remains of the head. You often hear the phrase "blow their head off," but it's rare to actually see it.

Hester and 216 joined me at the body.

"Hi, Carl," said Trooper 216.

"Gary. Glad you could come."

"Notice the hands?"

"Right away," I said. "One shoe. And the head ... or what used to be the head." From what I could see, the head from about the ears on up was gone. Although nearly all the bones of the cranium seemed gone, lots of skin was left, and had sort of flapped around back into the cavity. One ear, still attached to the neck by a flap of flesh, seemed to be perfectly intact. Seeing things like that has always had kind of a sense of unreality about it.

"Uh, yeah," said Gary. "Used to be is right. I think I'm parked over the top of some, uh, debris, from the head and stuff. I didn't even see it until I was just about stopped."

"Okay." His car was about fifteen feet from the top of the body's head, and still running. That was fine. We could have him move his car back when the crime lab got there.

Hester spoke to him. "Doesn't leak oil, does it?"

He looked offended. "No."

"Just checking." She smiled. "Wouldn't want oil all over the ... debris. Just make sure your defroster or air conditioner's off. It's a lot easier if we don't get condensed moisture on the stuff."

"Right. Uh, you two better talk to the two old boys over there. Very interesting stuff."

"Just a few seconds more," I said. "Tell 'em we'll be right there."

Hester and I just stood and looked at the scene. You only get one chance to see it in a relatively undisturbed state, and I've learned to take in as much of it as I can when I have the chance. An ambience sort of thing, you might say. You try to see, smell, and hear as much as you can. Sometimes it helps, sometimes it doesn't. But if you don't do it, you always seem to regret it later in the case.

A sound was the first thing that struck me. The Heinman brothers had some galvanized-steel hog feeders near the roadway. Looking like huge metal mushrooms, they had spring-loaded covers on them, and every time a hog wanted to eat, all he had to do was press his snout into the mechanism and open it. When he was done, out came the snout, and that spring-loaded lid slammed down with a loud clank. Usually two or three clanks, in fact. One, a beat, and then two very close together. All the time we were at the crime scene, those hog feeders made a constant racket in the background.

Bodies look smaller dead than they do when they're alive. This one was no exception, and it wasn't just the fact that he was half a head shorter, so to speak. Even with the legs straightened out, he'd probably only be about five three or five four. It was sobering to see this wreck of a corpse, and think that he'd been alive and well only a few minutes before. I looked around for his other shoe, but didn't see it.

"Sure looks dead," I said.

"You must be a detective," said Hester.